HUNTER'S CROSSING

Sarah Wagner

2

This world, the magical realm, and the demon-filled Netherworld.

Creatures that lurk in shadow are coming into the light.

THREE WORLDS, ONE SAVIOR

Hunter Leilani Scott hasn't been on the job long, but she knows an uptick in monster attacks can't mean anything good for humanity. The powers responsible for protecting the borders can't—or won't—put a stop to it. In fact, the only person willing to believe her is sorcerer Blake Pratt. Distrustful of anyone or anything not entirely human, and certain the handsome magic-user knows more than he's telling her, Lei senses they'll have to act as one as she crosses into realms where human life is forbidden. She and Blake will risk everything—their lives, their souls, and their newfound love—to fight an army of demons to stop an apocalypse.

Hunter's Crossing

Sarah Wagner

www.BOROUGHSPUBLISHINGGROUP.com

PUBLISHER'S NOTE: This is a work of fiction. Names, characters, places and incidents either are the product of the author's imagination or are used fictitiously. Any resemblance to actual events, locales, business establishments or persons, living or dead, is coincidental. Boroughs Publishing Group does not have any control over and does not assume responsibility for author or third-party websites, blogs or critiques or their content.

Hunter's Crossing
Copyright © 2015 Sarah Wagner

ISBN 978-1-942886-31-0

To my husband, Rob, who puts up with me.

ACKNOWLEDGMENTS

Thank you to my children for more or less behaving during the creation and through the edits of this book and without whom life would be far more boring. I must also thank my father for believing in me and being my favorite beta reader. A very special thanks goes to JR and Amanda Hagy for finding all the little flaws and helping me buff them out. I must certainly thank Boroughs Publishing for believing in me and in this book. And last, but certainly not least, an enormous thank you to Jenni Hendriks for being so awesome an editor and making the process so easy.

CONTENTS

Hunter's Crossing

Chapter One

"This can't be where the fairies come to play." Leilani Scott shook her head and stared at the bar on the outskirts of a little town in the Pennsylvania hills. The bar, like much of the small town she'd just driven through, needed a coat of paint, some nails, and a new roof. Two of the letters in its sign had burnt out, proclaiming it the "verlo k" instead of the Overlook. What the bar overlooked beyond a stand of old pines, Lei couldn't figure out.

Drumming her long fingers on the steering wheel, she glanced at the parking lot—trucks splashed with mud and spotted with rust showing the wear of hard labor parked amid a half-dozen old-school motorcycles built from parts scrounged from the local junkyard. Her old gray Land Rover fit right in with its layer of road grime and worn tires.

She checked Willy's notes one more time. The bar didn't look like the sort of place where a powerful fairy, rumored to be related to the queen, would hang out, let alone own. Willy kept meticulous notes and had never steered her wrong before. If Willy said she'd find Melli tending bar at the Overlook, she would. Not that Lei had any better leads to run with anyway.

Lei shoved Willy's worn book back into the glove compartment and pulled her long black hair into a ponytail. She double-checked her weapons. Even if she wasn't expecting trouble, she'd learned very early in her career not to go anywhere unarmed. Ever. She carried two guns, a Beretta in a shoulder holster and a small derringer in her pocket. The derringer held two silver bullets. Other pockets in her leather jacket contained slightly more unusual weaponry: a vial of salt and garlic immersed in pure olive oil that she'd blessed herself, a switchblade with protective runes carved along the blade's edges, an iron rod about the length and width of a pencil, and last, a small but effective stake whittled from a section of old oak.

Lei took a deep breath and swallowed her nerves. If she wanted this fairy to talk, she needed to be Leilani the Mighty Hunter, not Leilani the nervous wreck. She pulled down the visor and smiled. To anyone looking in, it might seem like she was checking the make-up she didn't wear. The two pictures of her and her parents were the only things she'd taken with her from her old life. They reminded her why her job mattered. Why she was Leilani the Mighty.

Her parents gave her pieces of themselves, in her heart, mind and body, and it kept them close. Her Hawaiian mother's hair, eyes, and cheekbones. Her Heinz 57 father's jaw and narrow nose. Her temper and his courage. So far, the combination served Leilani well enough. It kept her breathing anyway. She closed her eyes and held her family close in her heart. Eight years gone and she missed them still, always.

Her boots crunched on the gravel of the parking lot as she crossed to the weathered, pockmarked steel door. The shadows of the evening gathered there, offering both respite and warning. Lei felt the first tingles of fairy magic along her skin and smiled. Unlike elf magic that brought humidity and density to the air, fairy magic was more subtle, as if the air carried a charge, just enough to make the hair on her arms stand up and wave. Once again, Willy led her to the right place.

***

Blake pulled the shadows closer to him, reinforcing the spell that kept him from being seen when he saw Leilani walk through the door. He smiled and felt a bolstering hope rise inside him. His mother may have gotten the day wrong but she got the place right. No seer could be right about everything. Leilani was much smarter than he'd hoped, certainly more so than his mother believed, but she had blinders on when it came to humans who had no talents. Leilani stood on the edge of putting the mystery together without his help and that didn't bode well. For things to work out the way he wanted, he needed to be the one to explain it—the one to answer all the questions she was asking. Soon, when the time was right, he would do exactly that. Until then, he'd just watch her. Fortunately, he rather enjoyed the view.

***

Lei paused for a moment just inside the door to get a feel for the place. The inside of the Overlook was much nicer than the outside. Deep booths upholstered in navy blue vinyl lined one wall. Thick wooden tables with matching chairs ringed the worn, empty dance floor. An old-fashioned jukebox in the corner pumped out Bon Jovi. People gathered around the two pool tables, the dartboard, and the bar.

It was more than Lei expected, not just the earthbound hangout for a fairy, but a watering hole for all sorts of otherworlders. She spotted several groups of them: fairies, elves, and more, as she walked toward the bar. She felt eyes on her, watching, but no one seemed to be interested in her beyond the fact that she was a stranger in a small town and maybe open to a little fun. Neither model thin nor bunny built, Lei knew she wasn't any man's ideal, but she was cute enough for a flirt and ride, at least for the Appalachian farm boys and coal miners looking for some company.

She spotted the bartender and smiled. Melli's glamour was very good, unless you knew what to look for. The slight sheen on her chocolate caramel skin looked like sweat, but Lei knew better. It wasn't that warm in the bar. All the fae created that dew, but Lei imagined Melli smelled of pine, fir, or cedar and not the flower gardens she'd met in the past. Melli was a different sort of fae, a warrior fae and possibly royalty.

Perched on a worn stool at the end of the long bar, Lei waited and watched. Melli smiled and nodded at her as she finished pouring a beer and handed it, and three others like it, over to a young woman with a large tray and a tiny skirt.

"What can I get for you?" The fairy's melodic voice held just a hint of suspicion.

"Guinness if you have it." Lei dug into her pocket for a five and a very special token.

"Aye, a girl after me own heart." Melli winked at her, emerald eyes trying to assess the stranger in her bar, even as her faked accent felt mocking.

Lei put the money and small gold coin on the bar. Melli's eyes went very wide for a moment before narrowing to really inspect Lei.

"Where did you get this?" The pleasant music in her voice disappeared, replaced by a low, angry snarl.

"Willy gave it to me, said if I was ever out this way, I should look you up, Melli." The tiny lie rolled right off her tongue without hesitation.

Melli laughed, throwing her head back, letting her long red and black curls shake with it. "So you'd be the hunter that has everyone all in a tizzy then. Leilani something."

"Scott. Call me Lei." She reached out and tried to take back the coin, but Melli laid her cold hand down, gripping Lei so tight it hurt.

"I'll be deciding if you're worthy of that little bit of magic, if you don't mind. This drink is on me. After, stick to coffee or soda. We close in," she glanced up at the cuckoo clock on the wall, "three hours, give or take. I'll be talking to you then."

"Fair enough." Lei left the cash and the coin, taking her beer and settling in to an empty booth by one of the pool tables.

Lei knew Melli was watching her, understood the cunning fairy would likely test her somehow. Perhaps a test of patience or persistence. Or merely whether or not Lei would be willing or even able to overlook the various otherworlders who populated the bar. A young werewolf sat at a table near the door. Three fairies gathered together in a shadowed corner. And, if she wasn't completely mistaken, an honest to God rakshasa in the form of a devastatingly beautiful man stood at the end of the bar chatting up a middle aged woman and making her laugh. He made Lei twitchy and she fought her instincts a little. Lei knew some about the Hindu demons, but research never compared to face-to-face discussion.

Willy truly believed all those from the otherworld were abominations, even those willing to help. The hard and defined line Willy drew, and tried to impart to Lei, left no room for tolerance. Once she was on her own, Lei unlearned the line. Some of those *abominations* were better people than some humans she'd met and worked so hard to protect.

She looked over at the werewolf. He looked young, but the condition made it hard to pin down their ages. His eyebrows were a little too perfect, probably religiously trimmed, like his beard. His ears were scarred where someone had reshaped them. A thin gold wedding band winked on his finger. His eyes picked up the light a little too well, the occasional yellow reflection giving him away. He didn't look like he wanted to be in the bar at all, glancing from his soda to Lei with wary disdain. She found it interesting that he chose something non-alcoholic. He seemed to know what she was and that sent a ripple of unease through her.

Some hunters held the same hard-line position Willy lived by, and the otherworlders ran the moment they spotted a hunter or a Justice. Not that Lei hadn't walked that line for a few years herself, especially after the attack that had pushed her headfirst into the business.

The Justices and hunters weren't so different, except that one of the two got a paycheck. Just because the Order had been around almost as long as human history, the Justices believed they were the only ones with the know how to protect the humans from the not so human. Most hunters thought the Justices were arrogant bastards more concerned with killing the monsters than protecting civilians.

Lei wondered just how much Melli knew about her and why she felt so cornered. So many otherworlders gathered in such a little town felt like a trap waiting to spring. Perhaps having a werewolf in the bar was calculated, but how had she known Lei would be there at all? Lei finished her beer and looked up at the clock with a heavy sigh. She'd barely killed half an hour, and she hadn't thought to bring a book with her.

Edging towards bored at the end of the first hour, Lei started watching one of the games of pool. Three young men, all blissfully human and entirely unaware of the kind of creatures they shared a bar with worked the table like they knew what they were doing. She appreciated their playful taunts, their wide farm boy grins, and the way their flesh filled out their jeans. All in all, they were just about her type: big men who looked like they really worked for a living.

She watched the blond one with the broad shoulders and arms that looked like they could bench three of her when she noticed a little flicker in the shadows gathered in one of the booths near the pool table. Without outright staring at the shadows, Lei watched it closely for a few moments, noticing how the depths of the shadows never seemed to change, regardless of how the light played there.

Annoyance flickered through her. It was bad enough Pratt continued to follow her, but if he really believed she was stupid enough not to notice him, it was the worst kind of dismissal. The man had been a thorn in her side from the moment they'd met, the first time he played knight-in-shining-armor and screwed up her case. She didn't need his help. She didn't trust him. It seemed every time she went digging for information, he showed up, ready to stop her from getting any answers. Not this time. If he messed with her this time, she'd put him down for good.

Lei sauntered back to the bar, letting her narrow hips sway provocatively. Melli poured her a Coke.

"How do you like my bar so far, hunter?" She laughed without malice.

"So far, so good. I think I'm going to see how your tables play, since I've got time." Lei shrugged. "You run a pretty calm joint here, but I suppose the night is young."

"Calm is relative." Melli's smile didn't reach her eyes.

Lei turned away from the bar and made her way toward the pool table where the three men played. She shed her leather and her shoulder holster together, folding the jacket carefully around the gun so she could still get at it if she needed to. Reaching up, Lei pulled her hair free of the fabric band. For some reason she hadn't yet figured out, men all seemed to have a thing for her long hair.

As she approached the table, the man with the arms smiled at her, showing his white, but crooked teeth as his eyes traveled the length of her cascading hair. "Looking for a little company tonight?"

"Just a game or two maybe, if you and your friends don't mind." She smiled at them all, wishing it were a different kind of night. A little fun would have been nice. Too bad the timing sucked.

"We don't mind a bit. I'm Steve." The man with the arms, Steve, didn't even glance at his friends for their opinions. "We'll play doubles. You and me against Stix and Donnie here."

The taller of the other young men racked the balls in preparation for a new game. Lei glanced around for a cue and smiled. She would have to pass right by the corner where Pratt had gathered his shadows up like bubbles in a bath. After collecting her cue, she passed him again, accidentally banging the cue into what were probably his ribs. She hoped it left a hell of a bruise on her wanna-be savior.

She played three games with the young men, watching the clock and trying not to lose, or win, too much. Lei almost felt bad about flirting as shamelessly as she did, knowing she wasn't going to be going home with any of them. Almost. Steve and his friends were enjoying themselves and, better, serving a purpose. Melli might be testing her, but she was testing Pratt. He seemed to pop up any time he thought she was in over her head, which was apparently all the damned time.

Having drunk nothing but Coke since her one lonely beer, she wasn't even edging towards tipsy, but Lei knew how to pretend. She pulled Steve of the amazing arms out on the deserted dance floor just as Whitesnake's *Here I Go Again* came on. She wanted Pratt to react enough for his little shadow magic to shimmer, and it did. But he must have realized she wasn't drunk as he stayed in the shadows. Obnoxious pain in her ass. What good was a knight who wouldn't come to the rescue when she actually wanted him to?

When the song ended, she led Steve back to his friends and gathered up her jacket, careful not to show her gun. "I think that's it for me tonight, boys. Thanks for letting me join you."

"The night doesn't have to be done just yet." Steve took a step toward her with a gleam in his eyes that made Lei sigh.

"Timing sucks, babe, let me tell you. Tonight's just not the right night. Maybe next time I pass this way my schedule won't be so snug." She stood on her tiptoes and brushed her lips over his cheek.

"You don't know what you're missing." He wrapped one arm around her waist and picked her up, planting a kiss on her that sent a singing shock all the way through to her toes.

She groaned as he put her back down. "I think I have some clue and boy do I wish the timing didn't suck."

Lei walked away with his number in her pocket and the desire to hurry back this way when she had a little time to herself. Hopefully, Steve wouldn't be snapped up before she got the chance. For a moment, Lei considered plopping herself down at Pratt's shadowy table, but she wasn't ready for him to know she knew he was there. She wanted him to come out of hiding himself. Mostly so she could be certain he wouldn't get in her way. But if he got in her way again, if he tried to kill Melli before they could talk, she might just have to kill him. She'd come to Melli as an absolute last resort.

A trip to the relatively clean bathroom and a soda later, closing time arrived. The bar didn't quite clear out. The werewolf, Pratt, and a waitress stayed behind with her and Melli. The waitress busied herself cleaning up while Melli sat down across from Lei with two long necked bottles and a pack of long, slim French cigarettes.

"I've heard about you, Ms. Scott. Those telling the stories said you might be different from other hunters, but I didn't believe it. A hunter trained by a Justice, I didn't see how it was possible for you to come out of that without a whole streak of hatred for us. I'm not sure what I believe just yet. Not completely." She lit a cigarette and sighed smoke.

"I don't blame you. It's not like the Justices have a good history of being any kind of fair." Lei smiled briefly. "Of course, I happen to think that's the Order's biggest problem. In all the little hunts, they miss the big picture. They don't see the scope of things or look to the future."

"And you do?" Melli spun the little gold coin in her fingers. "You believe you're that different from them?"

"My first months as a hunter, I was just as bad if not worse than the Justices. I wanted blood so bad I could taste it. I wanted revenge. I wanted everyone from the Otherworld to know what a mistake had been made when my family was slaughtered. I wanted them all to know how bad they fucked up when they didn't finish the job. I wanted them to know I was as badass as any one of them. I considered you all monsters then." Lei took a deep drink of her beer, forcing herself to step back from the flood of emotion that swamped her. "I did some horrible things to otherworlders, some of whom were probably just trying to live their lives. But, I came to understand my mistake. I've done my best to make up for it. I've saved a lot of innocent people, both humans and otherwise. You don't know me from anyone but you are powerful enough that Willy didn't consider you a target. I've got no one else to ask and I've come to you for help."

"Help? A great hunter coming to a 'dirty fairy' for help?" Melli allowed her glamour to drop for a moment, her gold wings fluttering against her dark skin, her green eyes growing larger and deeper, her pointy-toothed smile disbelieving and suspicious. In the blink of an eye, she looked human again. "Do you have any idea what that talisman you returned to me is?"

"I assumed it was a token, a reminder of a friendship made or a favor owed." Lei shrugged. "I never had the chance to ask Willy about it."

"She didn't get a chance to teach you much of anything, did she?"

"She taught me what she believed was most important. She taught me how to spot, fight, kill, and keep killed pretty much every kind of otherworlder there is." Lei took another sip of her beer. "The cancer had already taken root before she saved me. A little over a year after that, she died. Everything I've learned in the years since has been from her books or my own experience."

"When that Justice," the word dropped from her mouth like a curse, "took that coin, it was no promise or gift. It was a bribe. It's a protective charm to keep whoever possesses it beyond the ability of the otherworlders, maybe even the sorcerers, to track. I gave it to her to save my daughter. Willy didn't have friends or allies, she had people who owed her something. People who feared her."

"I can make no apologies for my mentor." Though she'd done so from nearly the moment Willy died.

Melli sat back and took another drag from her cigarette. "She apologized enough with you. She could have sent you to the Justices, taken you on as a true apprentice, but she didn't. Perhaps she saw something in you that showed her the truth."

"She couldn't have made it official. I was too old to be recruited and I wouldn't have passed their entrance exam. It doesn't really matter and she's not around to ask."

"I understand that. You've done a lot of good, Lei. Enough that it's been noticed."

"Look, I didn't come here to banter about my mentor or my own good deeds. I need your help. Someone as well connected as you must surely have some idea what's going on. Why some otherworlders are showing up in places they've never been, or coming back after they've been gone for decades or centuries."

"I don't know what's going on. I really don't. But you're not the only person who's come here asking that same question. I told them the same thing."

"I find it hard to believe you don't know. That the queen's *daughter* doesn't know what her own people are doing."

Melli leaned forward and snarled. "I make it a point *not* to discuss these kinds of things with my mother. I live here not there. Besides, if you wanted a connection to my mother, you should have hunted down my sister. I am not a part of her court nor will I ever be."

Lei swallowed her smile. She didn't want Melli to know that she hadn't been absolutely certain about her parentage until just that moment. "You don't want to know, do you? If you don't know the truth, you can't betray your own. I get that, I do. But, since you won't help me, I should be going. Looks like I have another fairy princess to find." Lei picked up her beer and drained it.

Melli stood as Lei did and walked her toward the door. "Can I ask you a question before you go?"

"You might not get an answer." Lei pulled on her holster, then her jacket.

"After what happened to you, after what that werewolf did to you and your parents, how can you even sit in the same room with one?"

Lei looked over at the young man who trembled at her glance. "First of all, he's not the one who slaughtered my family. That one died that same day, thanks to Willy. Second of all, he's scared to death of me but he's itching to run, not attack. The ring on his finger tells me he has something to lose, something to protect, but he's more interested in getting away than putting me down. He's taken great care in altering his appearance, to fit in with humans. I'll note that he's here, just in case something happens that brings me back this way, but he's no threat. In fact, I am left wondering what you are holding over his head to keep him here."

Melli stared at her for a long moment. "I'll help you as much as I can, Leilani Scott. I believe you are many things. Perhaps even what the Justices were first meant to be. Fair. Just. You aren't out to cut a swath through us, taking out the good with the bad. How you've come from Willy's guidance, I will never know."

"I'm only doing my best to do the job."

"I see that." Melli took Lei's hand and pressed the coin into it. "You'll need this and you'll need help. All the help you can get."

Lei shook her head. "I'm on my own, Melli. The Justices think I should be shot for letting so many otherworlders live. They wouldn't help me if I brought them the head of Vlad himself. And I've already asked a lot of the other hunters I know. We all work best alone. Goes with the job, really. If you work alone, you have no one to lose."

"The Justices and the hunters aren't the only ones out there."

"I don't trust the sorcerers. They might be human but the things they can do, aren't." Lei couldn't help it; her eyes darted towards Pratt and his shadows.

"What about the fairies? Sorry, no. Don't answer that. Look, start in Pittsburgh. There's something going on there for sure.

There's a nest of vampires there that's growing larger almost daily. The way I hear it, the local Justice turned his back while they took good humans and changed them into vampires."

Lei stared at Melli open mouthed. She'd had run-ins with the Justice in Pittsburgh before and no way would he let a vampire run his city. "Guess I'll have to take a look."

"Be well, young hunter."

"Thanks." Lei smiled and walked over to the young werewolf, leaning in close to him. "So long as I don't catch a hint of you killing innocent people, you have nothing to fear from me. Just keep your head down and, if you have pups, you teach them to do the same. That's all I ask of anyone." She walked out the door Melli held open for her.

She thought it best to put a few hours between herself and the Overlook. Between the fairies, the werewolf, and Pratt, she just didn't feel safe here. She figured Melli probably knew Pratt was there. She couldn't imagine the princess couldn't feel him or that the werewolf couldn't smell him. The idea that Melli was likely working with the man who kept messing with her job didn't sit well. If they were working together, they were hiding something and neither of them could be trusted.

***

Blake waited until the waitress and the werewolf left before releasing his shield of shadows. He leaned against the bar beside Melli. She looked up at him and shook her head. "You had the perfect opportunity to explain yourself tonight."

"She needs to trust me first. I've told you that before. I've tried to prove to her that I want to help but it never goes well."

"She's not what I was expecting, Blake." Melli calmly lit another cigarette. "You could have shown up here and talked to her, instead of hiding in your shadow and watching her flirt with another man all night."

"No. If she'd have seen me here tonight, she wouldn't have trusted you." Frustrated, Blake shoved his fingers through his long black hair.

"What does your mother have to say about all this?"

"It varies. Most days she does her best to persuade me to give up on her, that we'll find another way. But when I push, she tells me this is the best way, the most sure way of fighting back. She says Leilani will need help and if I'm the one to help her, I might be able to get her to trust me. But I've tried three times now! The woman is not only pissed at me, she thinks I'm stalking her!"

"Maybe you're going about it the wrong way. Maybe she isn't as helpless as your mother would have you believe. Maybe your mother is trying very hard to sabotage this path because she wants you to walk away from it." Melli laughed. "Can you get to Pittsburgh before she does?"

He nodded somberly. "I can. Can you arrange a meeting with the queen? Once she's on board—and I will get her there—Leilani will need to hear the rest."

"I'll try. I can't promise anything. You know that."

"Ounathir knows why she must help, why it all matters. She's the one who explained it to me, once upon a time." Blake stepped away from the bar and smiled at Melli. "I'll keep my end, see that you do the same or we'll all suffer for it."

Blake tipped an invisible hat to her and vanished into his shadows.

Chapter Two

Lei allowed herself an extra hour of sleep. She needed to be as rested as possible before walking into hostile territory. Not only were there likely to be vampires to deal with, there was definitely a resident Justice to contend with and he was no fan of hers. And probably Pratt too, since he just kept popping up everywhere she went.

With a fresh cup of coffee and a quick drive-thru hamburger, Lei drove the last hour into Pittsburgh with the radio blasting and the windows down. Football season painted the city black and gold. She wasn't much for sports herself, but Lei appreciated the sense of loyalty it inspired. Plus, it was kind of pretty, in a masculine way.

She pulled her Land Rover into the litter-spotted lot of a little motel not too far from where Lei figured the vampires would be centered. She'd studied a map of the city on her phone earlier, making great circles around the local colleges and marking their overlap. Colleges were heavy favorites of the vampires. The population had expanded from what it had once been. More than just young, virile men and women, but people from every age group, every heritage gathered there. No vampire would be questioned for being too old, too young, too pretty, or too weird.

"You will never find a more wretched hive of scum and villainy." Lei smiled to herself but it didn't quite make her feel better. It was a sad day indeed when a little Obi Wan couldn't lighten the mood.

She checked into the motel using a fake name and a not so legally acquired credit card. She wouldn't be going out until closer to dawn. The first night in a strange town was not the best night to hunt. If she didn't have some kind of feel for the area, she was too vulnerable. One good solid day of on the ground research was usually enough. If she were really lucky, she'd only have to contend with the vampires and not the Justice. Hell, it might be better if Cam was dead. Which Lei figured he might have to be to allow the vampires to colonize in his territory.

Lei double checked her weapons, the IDs in her wallet. For the time being, she was using an ID that made her a licensed private investigator with a concealed carry permit in West Virginia. The date on it was still new enough that she could probably pretend she didn't know all the rules about crossing state lines if she needed to. She hated to lie but, sometimes, that was the job.

Rather than obsess over her preparations, Lei got comfortable and pulled out a book to read. She had a few hours before it would be time to get to work. Even as dedicated as she was to her job, to her mission, Lei knew she deserved a little escape sometimes and what better way than within the very safe, very distant pages of a good mystery, especially one with a healthy dash of romance.

About an hour before dawn, Lei took to the streets, leaving her car in the motel lot. There was no need yet for the arsenal it held concealed in and under the seats and floor and she didn't want to risk getting lost in the city and chance a search. GPS wasn't always reliable and her sense of direction was much better on foot. She watched the waking city for signs of both the vampires and the Justice, hating the very nonspecific direction Melli had shoved her in and wondered, not for the first time, if the angry little fairy hadn't just pushed her head first into a trap.

Perhaps the little coin in her pocket wasn't what Melli said it was. Lei's own research on it had revealed nothing so she had no way to verify. Not much of the true fae lore made it to the states and Lei didn't have the time or inclination to trek over to Ireland or Scotland where she might have better luck.

The Boulevard of the Allies was quiet in a way that only 4 AM can manage. The partiers had all gone home, the students were yet to rise, and the early bird commuters had yet to reach the outer edge of the city. From the moment Lei stepped onto Forbes Avenue, she felt eyes on her. They were not Pratt's eyes, though she expected him to show up before too long. Lei walked with purpose, like she knew exactly where she was going, and did her best to ignore her watchers.

A police car rode past her slowly. The man in the driver's seat smiled at her, gave her too many teeth, a few of them too long and sharp to be human. It was a flagrant and obvious display made to drive home one point: the vampires knew she was in town and they wanted her to know that they weren't afraid of her. She smiled back at the cop, pulling the stake from her pocket, almost daring him to stop. Relief slipped through her blood when he kept on driving but she couldn't afford to let it show. She didn't want a fight yet, not until she knew the score.

The eyes in the darkness were still on her; she could feel them appraising her. The look had no power, no zap of magic, so it wasn't any otherworlder. No. The eyes belonged to humans—probably servants or associates of the local Justice. Which meant that Cam wasn't dead and she was likely going to be fighting whether she wanted to or not.

Lei walked, trying to act like she was unaware of the threats all around her. Three further blocks and she found Pratt in his shadows, waiting for her. She didn't acknowledge him but was actually glad to see him. Maybe this once, having a sorcerer for a stalker would be a good thing. Maybe this time he'd actually get to save her. It seemed like he was waiting for exactly that opportunity.

The city was full of signs of otherworlders. She'd already seen the vampires, but there were signs in the alleyways and the shadowed corners of werewolves, sprites, pixies, and trolls—graffiti written in languages most humans didn't know existed, circles of spotted fungi growing out of place in dank corners, small shiny treasures piled in tucked away crevices. She'd passed through Pittsburgh a time or two before and the signs had never been this evident, this open. Maybe something *was* wrong with Cam.

Near the Cathedral of Learning, three sleek, black Town Cars stopped on the side of the road. A large, muscular man stepped out of the middle car, the streetlight shining off his bald scalp. He opened the door for his master. The man who stepped out wore a beautifully tailored suit of black with the sword and scales insignia of the Justices tacked to his lapel. His brown hair was cut short but not shorn. A long, jagged scar shaped the plane of his patrician face, making him more fearsome than pretty.

"Get out of my city." Cam laid his hand on the hilt of his sword and took a step towards her. His voice was loud, deep, and tinged with a slight accent that Lei had never been able to place. "You aren't needed here."

"Funny, that's not what I'm hearing, Cam. I hear you've got a nest and I've seen that you have some other restless not-so-natives." She stood her ground as he approached her and hoped he couldn't see the slight tremble of nerves in her knees or the quickness of her pulse in her neck. "You never struck me as the lazy type."

"You hear that, do you? Did you get that from some abomination you let live? You think you can trust them but one day, they're going to kill you." He stepped closer, coming within inches of her face until she had to tilt her head back to look into his eyes. "You think you're so damned brave. Standing there like you aren't afraid of me, like you're better than me. You think you can come into my city and tell me how to run things? Is that what your mentor taught you?"

"I'm not here to tell you how to do anything, Cam." Lei tried to keep her anger out of her voice. He was pushing her buttons on purpose. He was damned good at reading people, at finding just the right note to bring out the recklessness that came with anger. "I'm just here to deal with the nest. They've got at least one in your very own police department already."

A flicker of something passed over his face in the dim yellow of the streetlight. "You aren't welcome here, Ms. Scott." He reached for her and she shifted slightly to the side so he would miss her but she didn't shimmy quite far enough or fast enough and Cam's arm grabbed her arm tight, spun her and pulled her tight to his chest. As she squirmed and tried to stomp on his instep, he reached a hand into her pocket and pulled out her vial of garlic oil. He bent his head low to her ear and whispered so softly she strained to hear him. "Listen carefully, Leilani. There are things we need to talk about. Follow the directions but stay hidden. Wait until I'm gone to read it."

Confusion spiked through Lei as she watched Cam lob her vial against the wall, shattering it needlessly.

When he spoke again, it was loud enough for whoever was sitting in his car to hear. "Remember, this is *my* city. I don't want you here and I'd suggest that you're gone before the sun sets. After that, you're fair game." Cam turned and returned to his car. His over-sized goons quickly followed suit.

"What the fuck was that?" she whispered to no one. Lei watched as Cam and his people drove away. She waited, fingers clasped around the folded paper he had slipped into her pocket when he took the vial. When the cars disappeared around the corner, Lei started walking again, waiting to see if her watchers would continue to follow her. Only Pratt stayed on her tail.

Knowing he was several strides behind her and couldn't see, Lei took the note out of her pocket and read it. She almost stopped in her tracks. Cam wanted a meeting. She wasn't about to meet him alone.

Lei was many things, stupid wasn't usually one of them but she was going to have to make an exception.

Ducking into the mouth of an alley, she waited for Pratt to slink by. When he did, Lei stepped back out onto the sidewalk. "You know, this is getting really irritating, Pratt. You think maybe it's time you tell me why you're following me around? I can't so much as play a game of pool without my extra shadow anymore."

The shadows fell away and Pratt had the decency to look at least a little ashamed of himself, his brown eyes staring at the ground as he shoved his shoulder-length black hair out of his face. He put his hands in the pockets of his leather jacket and shrugged, his broad shoulders falling a little further than they'd risen.

"I didn't think you'd noticed me in the bar." His eyes narrowed slightly. "You hit me with your cue on purpose, didn't you?"

Lei shrugged. "I'm pretty good at noticing things and you deserved a bruise. What is with the stalking, sorcerer?"

"That's not really a conversation for here. I know a place nearby that has pretty decent coffee, excellent pie, and a strict no otherworlders policy. If you're willing to hear me out."

"Lead the way, Pratt." Lei motioned for him to start walking.

"Please, call me Blake and I'll call you Lei. Though I think I prefer Leilani. It suits you better."

"Whatever. I answer to both." She followed him, always out of arm's reach and watching behind them. Too many strange things were afoot to let her guard down even for a moment. If she weren't in need of a little bit of trained back up, she wouldn't be talking to him at all.

They walked a few blocks to a 24/7 diner. Small runes decorated the doorway designed to keep anything out that was entering with malicious intent—otherworlders, sorcerers, and humans alike. Lei wondered if the owners were hunters or just got lucky with their shop. Lei checked the address on the note and shook her head. Of course Cam would pick a place like this too. It made things a little easier for her.

It was clean, the waitress friendly but not pushy even as she batted her long lashes at Pratt. Lei shook her head and sat down at one of the empty tables.

***

After Blake ordered for them, coffee and lemon meringue pie, he sat back, pressing himself into the overstuffed pleather cushion. He had wanted her to be what he expected her to be, but she kept surprising him. Nothing was going according to his mother's visions.

He wondered for a moment if the woman across from him was everything he and Ounathir thought she might be. And how she'd learned to read the shadows. Spotting that kind of magic was a talent very few possessed. Nothing she'd learned from Willy would prepare her for the days to come. Of course, he very much doubted that Willy had ever told the lovely Leilani anything more than shadows of the truth. The old bat probably poisoned her to sorcerers entirely.

Blake was a good judge of people. He had no gift of sight, not like his mother, but his instincts were good. Years of being on his own, protecting himself against otherworlders who wanted to make sure his powers couldn't be used against them had honed those instincts to a razor's edge. And yet, he doubted himself where Lei was concerned.

He knew he should be trying to take Lei to his mother, but he didn't want to know the woman's future, he wanted to know her. There were things even a seer couldn't see. Like a person's heart. Everything he'd seen said that maybe Melli and the werewolves were right, maybe Lei was the woman mentioned in the ancient fae scroll. Not that Lei would ever believe *him*. She'd have to see Ounathir for that.

Setting his coffee cup down, Blake leaned forward slightly, drawn to Lei. "Can I ask you about the night your family was attacked or is that off limits?"

Her black eyes narrowed. "It's not off limits, but it's not a story I share with just anyone and I don't know you."

"Fair enough." Blake nodded. "Let's fix that. You know I'm a sorcerer already and that I've been watching you for a while."

"No. You've been stalking me and fucking up my cases." She crossed her arms over her chest in annoyance.

"Anyway." He sidestepped that line of conversation. "My clan is centered mostly in the South, but I travel a lot. I'm sort of the black sheep of the family, we'll say."

They fell silent for a moment as the pretty blond delivered their pie. She smiled and giggled. Blake wasn't oblivious to her, but was largely ignoring her. He didn't want to ruin his one chance at this conversation.

Once the waitress left, Blake gave his complete attention to his pie for a moment. He felt Lei's eyes on him, probably trying to figure out his motives, his plan. She said all the right things, did all the right things. He'd watched her and discussed her for longer than she could possibly suspect. But she already thought he was a creepy stalker. He had to make her trust him. He had to be careful with her. It'd be a lot easier if his conscience would allow him to just put a spell on her and be done with explanations. Alas, he was trying really hard not to be a complete asshole for once.

"Look," Lei dropped her fork on her empty plate with a clatter, "If this conversation isn't going anywhere, I have things I really need to do."

"Wait. Give me another minute, please." Blake pushed his plate away and sat back. "I heard the questions you were asking the aswang in Detroit. I know you're on the verge of seeing what I have. Something is going on. Something big and no one seems to be paying attention but you and me."

"Maybe we'd both know a little more then if you'd let me question her. I had it under control."

"No you didn't. Even as you were speaking, she was drawing you away from her legs. She would have killed you to get them back, to put herself together again before dawn."

"You don't get it. I knew exactly what she was doing. She was more likely to answer my questions if she thought I wouldn't live to share her answers. I didn't need your help. I needed those answers and you just so happen to show up, *again*, and make sure I don't get them. I'm not stupid, Pratt. And I can handle myself better than you seem to think. Maybe I don't have the experience you do but I have been doing this for seven years, five of them on my own, and I'm still alive and kicking."

"You underestimate my opinion of you." Blake tapped his fingers on the table in irritation. "Whatever this is that's going on, we're going to have to work together not just to figure it out but to stop it. I'm trying to put together a team. Hunters, sorcerers, otherworlders… I'd like you to join us."

"You don't want me. You need someone with more experience. Someone whose ass you don't think needs saving all the time. Jim

Weston has been at this for almost thirty years; he's the kind of hunter you should be talking to. Compared to him, I'm just a babe learning to walk." She shook her head, anger flashing in her eyes. "I appreciate what you're looking to do, I might even think it's a good idea and I'm glad someone's paying attention, but I'm not the girl you're looking for. I don't work well with others."

"I like your style, Leilani. I like your integrity, your moxie." He laughed and looked into her eyes, measuring just how much to tell her. "My mother is a seer. Perhaps the most powerful one in this country. She's searched the futures, seen many different outcomes to our current situation and only one thing is certain. The world fairs better when I am sitting here right now talking you into joining me. Yes, you're going to be stubborn about it, wrongly think I find you lacking, and get all bitchy with me, but I've figured out that you're just like that. In the end, you'll agree to work with me, so why don't we just jump over all this bullshit and get to work."

"You are out of your mind." Lei pulled out a few dollars and set them on the table. "Willy warned me about your people more than once."

"The same Willy whose instruction you are going against all the time?"

"Just because some of her particular views were skewed doesn't mean she was wrong about everything. Besides, you and yours don't have Willy to thank for my opinions on sorcerers. You have all of these incredible abilities and you do nothing with them. Willy believed you were monsters, like the otherworlders. I don't. I think you're assholes. Your healers don't spend their time in human hospitals making a difference. Your people would rather bicker and war with each other than help the people around you, just because they aren't like you. Sorcerers only give a damn about their own."

"But you aren't willing to reserve judgment on me like you did Melli's werewolf friend? What's that say about you?" Damn, she was going to be a harder nut to crack than he thought.

"It says nothing more than that I'm cautious. I've learned that I have to be. Put yourself in my shoes for a moment. Would you immediately trust someone who's been following you, listening in on conversations, and only showing himself to help you out or fuck up your interrogations?"

"Damn it, if I was going to hurt you, you'd already be hurting."

"Depends on what you really want from me." Lei shrugged, the wariness still foremost in her eyes.

It pained him to admit that not only did she make an excellent point, but she was far more interesting than he'd wanted her to be. He'd wanted nothing more than friendly indifference. But something about her attitude, her strength, and her nature intrigued him as much, if not more, than her pretty face and trim figure. He looked forward to seeing her in a real fight.

"All I want from you is your skill. You're a good hunter, but you don't just go in guns blazing and kill everyone. You think things through, double check your facts. That's a rare thing in our line of work. I think you'd suit this team I'm putting together. Tell me what I can do to convince you."

"I'm not sure there's anything you can do, Pratt."

"Blake. My friends call me Blake."

"That's fine, Pratt. I haven't decided if I want to be your friend or not. Let me ask you something." She leaned forward and lowered her voice. "If you wanted to, could you whip up a little of your magic and make me agree to it?"

Blake sighed heavily, knowing he had to be truthful with her. "I could, yes. But I won't. If I wanted to, don't you think I already would have? There's too much riding on this to have anything less than your full heart behind it."

Lei narrowed her eyes at him and chewed on her lower lip as she thought. Complications weren't unusual in her line of work, but she'd never for a moment thought that anyone would *want* to work with her. She had her own way of doing things, what she believed was the right way. She'd learned a lot from Willy, but Willy hadn't been her only teacher. Her parents had eighteen years to raise her right and they'd succeeded in a lot of ways. Their only failing had been in not being prepared for a werewolf attack. And that was a failing shared by better than 99% of the population, so it was hard to fault them for that.

"Here's the thing, Pratt, I have a meeting this morning that I don't much want to go to alone."

"A meeting? With whom?"

"The local Justice. Cam is coming here to talk to me. Likely about the vampires."

Astonishment spread across his face, then realization. "When he took the vial, he left something behind. Damn but that's slick, and you covered well. I didn't see it. Do you think you're safe with him?"

"Not in a million years." Lei pursed her lips, trying to decide how much to tell him. "I don't know how much you actually know about the Justices. I know more than I ought to, more than they're comfortable with. Willy didn't leave out their secrets when she trained me and they know it. They know I'm just a set of vows and some formalities from being one of them, even if I didn't pass their tests or get chosen by some high and mighty council. Some of them don't like that much at all. Cam maybe most of all."

"Why?"

"Well, seeing as he actually asked the Order to have me killed at least once that I know of, I figure he doesn't much care for me."

"No, I mean why doesn't he like you?"

"It wasn't personal in the beginning. The Order thinks hunters beneath them, incapable of protecting anyone from otherworlders. They consider us more like security guards, we know what's going on but are powerless to really do anything about it. Like we're unarmed. The Order has a special dislike for me though, because of my training years." She shrugged. "Cam especially believes I'm a dangerous thorn because I have Willy's journals. There are a lot of things the Order doesn't want people to know. Their part in the Crusades for one, their participation in some of the bigger events of history for another."

"Like what?"

"Let's just say that the Order knows exactly what happened to the Roanoke colony."

"Wow. Okay. What do you want me to do?" He leaned forward slightly, eagerly. "I want you to trust me, Lei. I want you to come work with me. I'll do whatever you need me to do."

"I don't know what I want, what's best. I do know that I think it's dangerous for me to be at this meeting alone. Or, given the protections on this place, dangerous for me to be leaving this meeting alone."

"If Cam wants you dead, I have to agree with you. You tell me what you want me to do. I'll stay hidden or sit somewhere else. It's up to you. Everything is up to you."

Lei stood and moved to his side of the table, pushing him in closer to the wall as she sat down. "Don't hide. Let him see I'm not alone. Just don't talk, all right?"

Immediately, she regretted her decision. Blake was an imposing presence, seeming to fill the whole room though he might have occupied only a few cubic feet. He made her feel small. She hated feeling like the little girl everyone saw when they looked at her. She checked her watch and her stomach clenched. Cam would be walking through the door any minute. The last time they'd met, he tried to kill her. If she hadn't been fast enough and clever enough to get out of the warehouse and onto a crowded bus heading for the mall, she'd be dead now.

Chapter Three

Lei fidgeted beside Pratt, alternating between watching her watch and the door. "Seems he's running late."

"I'm not sure I should be here when he arrives. At least, not visibly."

"Nope. I want you exactly where you are. Cam needs to know that I may not be a Justice, but I am not without friends. So, for the moment, let's be that. Okay?"

Blake turned to look at her, his eyes glittering dangerously. "And what do I get in return for this bit of play-acting?"

Lei stared hard into his brown eyes. "If this meeting doesn't end up with one or both of us dead, I'll meet this team of yours and hear you out. I will honestly listen to everything you have to say. Is that enough?"

"Will you go with me to Wyoming? That's where we're gathered."

"So long as I drive myself so you can't strand me there, I will."

"Then it's more than enough, Leilani. You won't regret it, I swear." He took her hand in his and Lei felt even smaller beside him than before.

The door opened and a wiry figure in a worn, hooded jacket and stained jeans came in out of the morning foot traffic. It surprised Lei when he pushed back the hood and she saw it was Cam.

"What's he doing here?" Cam pointed at Blake, his eyes blazing with fury. "I asked you to meet me alone."

"Because last time went so well?" She kept watch over his hands, waiting for him to draw his gun or his sword. "I'd be a fool to meet you alone and we both know I'm not that."

"You're a fool to trust this bastard. He's a sorcerer! You can't trust anything you say or do or even think when they're around." Cam took a step back.

"I'm well aware of what sorcerers can do. You're the one forcing me to take that risk so you let that go." Lei did her best not to look like her pulse was racing and her adrenaline was pumping hard.

"I've promised not to use magic of any kind. I'm just here to make sure you don't hurt Leilani." Blake motioned to the waitress for more coffee. "Why don't we have a little breakfast? I just want to keep everything friendly. That's all."

Cam glared at them both for a moment before sitting down across from them. "If I feel you inside my head, I'll kill you where you sit."

"Understood."

"Have we got all the pleasantries out of the way?" Lei steepled her fingers under her chin. "Last time we met, you wanted me dead. Now you want my help?"

Cam closed his eyes for a moment, the muscles in his jaw clenching and unclenching. "I would give just about anything to be anywhere else right this second. The problem is, I have nowhere else to go. I'm backed into a corner and there's too much at stake." He laughed at his unintended pun and leaned back against the booth. "What I'm doing this morning could get me killed. Maybe it should, but I don't have a choice anymore. I received orders, actual orders from the Head Justices, to allow the vampire nest here to grow. I'm to leave them alone. Allow them to overtake my city. *My* city."

"Are they out of their minds?" Lei sat up a little straighter, felt as if she wanted to leap up and get to hunting right that moment. "If something isn't done about it now, their population will explode. You'll have a nightmare on your hands. One you won't be able to keep out of the public eye."

"You think I don't know that?" Cam slammed his fist on the table, making the silverware jump and clatter.

The waitress hurried over to check on them and take their breakfast orders. When she left again, Lei rolled her eyes. "We'll have to try and keep it down a little bit here. No sense in getting everyone else tied up in knots."

"Fine." Cam lowered his voice a little, but his fury still came through clearly. "The Heads have tied my hands. I can't just let the vampires turn everyone in my city, but I can't outright disobey an order either."

"Why not? If you know it's a shitty, bogus order, why can't you disobey? You, of all people, I think, would put getting the vampires out of your town before obedience."

Cam shook his head, his nostrils flaring. "My vows mean something to me. Maybe they don't to everyone, maybe they didn't to Willy, but the Order is all I have. I can't just disobey because I don't fully agree."

"Then why are you sitting here with me?" Lei shook her head. "Man up, Cam. Either follow orders or don't, but don't ask me to clean up your mess. You want me dead."

"I can't disobey. That doesn't mean I can't maybe not see someone like you come back into my town." His voice dropped to little more than a whisper. "Just because I can't take them out doesn't mean I'm not paying attention. There's been some talk, that maybe this nest is part of a plan by one of the old guard."

"That's ridiculous. The old vampires haven't been in this country in decades. Last I heard, they'd all gone to ground in Eastern Europe." Lei chewed a bit on that information. "If that is what you're hearing, that's all the more reason for you to tell your bosses to shove it and handle it yourself."

"You don't get it. If I do anything out of the bounds of my orders, I'm dead. Period. What good would that do anyone?"

"Why me? You've tried to have me executed more than once already. Why should I believe this isn't some elaborate scheme to take me out?"

"Look, you take out this nest for me and I'll leave you alone. I promise, I'll stop pushing for your execution. So long as you don't take this situation as an opening to set up shop here in my city." Cam looked away. "As for why I'm asking you, you're available and here. I'd have asked any hunter passing through, though I figure most of them wouldn't have the balls to meet with me, let alone consider the deal. It doesn't help that half of the hunters I know to call are dead."

"So you want me to risk my life taking out a nest and all I get from you is that you'll quit trying to have me killed? That you'll forget that one of your own trusted me enough to give me all of the Order's secrets without permission?" Lei stared at him, trying to comprehend his audacity.

"What do you want? You want money? I know you could use it."

Lei laughed and shook her head. "Nope. I want you to owe me. A favor I can collect another time. When *I* need help."

They quieted as the waitress brought them their breakfasts and, for a time, the only sounds among them were the clinks and clanks of silverware on cheap, durable china.

"You'll do it as a favor for a favor then?" Cam wiped his mouth with a napkin and looked her, seeming to calculate the risk to himself. "Why can't you just want money?"

"I don't need money nearly as much as I might need a favor from a Justice down the road. You can bet I'll collect on it too." Lei smiled at him. "Can't promise when though. Hell, you might really luck out and I'll die before I come to collect."

"Just don't die before you take out my problem." Cam's mouth twitched like maybe he wanted to smile.

"No problem." Lei pushed her plate away. "Here's what I'll do. I'm going to leave town for a few days, let your fangy friends see that you've run me out of town like a good pet. But I promise you, I'll be back for them. It won't be long."

Cam closed his eyes and nodded. "Fair enough." He dug into his pocket and put a twenty down on the table as he stood. "I'll be careful to keep my men busier than usual in the coming weeks. When you come into town, try and keep your head down. It'll be easier for me not to see you. If I don't see you, the Order won't ever have to know we had this conversation."

"I'll try." Lei promised as he headed for the door. Too many strange things were going on. Cam asking her for help was a little like a Hatfield asking a McCoy to help him with his fence.

"We should leave the city." Pratt took her hand in his. "Let's go introduce you to my people."

Lei took her hand back. "I want more information, Pratt. I need to know more about what I'm getting into before I go anywhere with you. I don't trust you."

"Fine. We'll go back to your motel, get some rest, and I'll tell you more. Then we'll go."

"Fine. Is there a way to get back there without being seen?" She peered out the diner's broad window into the morning rush hour traffic.

"Of course. You'll just have to trust me a little." He held up his finger and thumb a hair's breadth apart.

"Your shadow magic won't be enough. Too conspicuous in the daylight."

"I have more than a little 'shadow magic' up my sleeve, Leilani." Blake smiled. "Let's get moving. I promise you, I won't bite. Unless you ask nicely anyway."

"Ha. So funny." Lei rolled her eyes and stood. She stared for a moment at Blake's outstretched hand, turned her back on him, and walked to the door.

The moment they stepped out of the diner, Blake grabbed her hand and pulled her close to his side as he began chanting. It was a language that didn't sound like any she'd heard before. Not Latin like the protective incantations Willy had taught her. Not Greek like some of the more ancient exorcisms that she'd learned. Not any living language she knew of. It was, however, quite beautiful.

A faint line of white touched the horizon and a light blossomed around them. Blake pulled her tighter to him, using his free hand to tilt her face so he could look into her eyes. "Now we walk. We have plenty of time."

"What?" Lei struggled to pull away from him but he refused to let her go. For a moment, she was unaware of everything but how close Blake was to her. His lips pressed over hers, searing her. Lei responded, against her better judgment, against her own will. She didn't know this man, barely liked this man, but she found herself wanting to lean in, to deepen the kiss.

When he stepped back, Lei let her anger flare, at him and herself. The sound of her palm against his cheek was sweet and loud in her ears. She wiped her mouth with the back of her hand and glared at him. "Was that necessary?"

"Nope. But it certainly didn't hurt." He smiled at her.

"If we're going to be spending time together, there are going to be rules. First rule: no touching. Try something like that again, and I'll have to really hurt you." As much for his sake as hers.

He laughed.

"Go ahead and laugh. You won't be laughing if you touch me again." Lei looked around for a moment, trying to figure out what he had done, how they were supposed to get to the motel unseen. At first it seemed like nothing was different. Until she realized that nothing was moving. At all. "Pratt? What did you do?"

"I kind of opened a little bubble in time." He smiled and shrugged as if it was nothing. "Every second, a minute, every minute, an hour. And we've got about five hours to get back to your motel. Shall we get going? Maybe get a little sleep in before we hit the road."

"A bubble in time? So everything around us has just stopped for five minutes?"

"Nope. We're just moving faster than everything else. I can't stop time. I don't think that's possible. I can make bubbles in it. Not many people can, I gather. I've never met another, actually."

"Is this how you always seem to be ahead of me?" She eyed him with a new respect born of fear. If everyone could do what the sorcerers could do, there would be nothing but chaos. No one would know if their thoughts were their own, or if their actions had been manipulated by someone else. She took most people on a case by case basis but, she had to admit to herself that the sorcerers scared her more than the Order, more than most monsters. She wouldn't break the promise she'd made. She'd hear him out, learn more about him, and find his weakness, just in case she ever had to take him out.

"I don't use the time bubbles a lot. Only when it's necessary or expedient to do so. Like beating you to Pittsburgh. Like now. Realistically though, I'm probably about two years older than my age because of it. Five or six hours at a time, eventually it adds up."

Lei nodded. "That is pretty awesome, Pratt, I have to admit. All right, let's go."

They walked together along the busy but seemingly paused sidewalk. Lei was more than a little in awe. It was flat out amazing, what this man could do. How could she trust anyone with that kind of power?

The motel room was untouched. None of Lei's alarms were triggered. She checked everything twice before feeling a sense of calm run through her, but even that wasn't complete with Blake standing in her room.

Lei perched on the edge of the big king sized bed. "I guess I'm safe here. You can go on to your own little hidey hole and meet back here when time catches up again."

"I don't think so. I'd like to stick with you, make sure you don't skip out on our deal." He shrugged out of his jacket and laid it over the chair.

"I don't go back on my word, Pratt. But, fine. Just keep your distance, all right?" She moved her bag off the bed and laid her jacket over it. Lei unbuckled her holster and laid her gun on the nightstand before slipping out of her sweater. She lay down on the bed in her jeans and t-shirt and closed her eyes.

She listened as Blake shed his jacket and boots and lay down on the floor. She could have let him lie down on the bed where it was comfortable. It was big enough for two. But she didn't want to give him any ideas. She had a feeling things between them were going to be complicated enough as it was.

Sleep hadn't always come easy for her. It had taken years to train herself to sleep whenever the opportunity arose. Her body was tired enough not to argue with her and sweet, edgy emptiness washed over her as she dropped into sleep.

***

Lei woke when she heard Blake stirring. He'd been good and stayed on the floor. Slowly, she opened her eyes to watch him. She had to admit, he was pretty nice to look at. Tall and muscular, heavy through the arms, which she really liked. His face wasn't too bad either, with that five o'clock scruff accenting his strong jaw and very impish smile. But, that line of thought wasn't going to go anywhere. It couldn't.

She glanced at the clock by the TV and saw that time had indeed caught up to them and passed them by. It was almost noon. It'd been a very long time since she'd slept that long or that well.

"You taking a shower?" Lei asked, her voice still scraping over sleep's gravel.

"Headed that way now."

"Just don't use all the hot water."

"We could do our part for conservation and share the water." Blake grinned at her and wiggled his eyebrows.

"I said no touching." She glared at him.

"Kidding. Kidding." He held up his hands in defeat. "Well, kidding until you change your mind anyway."

Lei grabbed a pillow and chucked it at him. He was still laughing when he closed the bathroom door behind him.

She got up and stretched, working the kinks out of her shoulders while she made coffee in the little complimentary coffee pot. Lei dug through her bag for clothes, pulling out clean underwear, a bra, socks, black cargo pants, a heavy black tank top with steel mesh sandwiched between layers of black jersey. She checked her guns, her silver blade, the stake, and dug a vial of garlic oil out of her bag to replace the one Cam had destroyed. Everything was now in order.

Blake stepped out of the bathroom looking refreshed and smelling of the complimentary soaps left by the motel. He was still damp, wearing just his towel and a wide grin.

"Feeling better?" she asked.

"Much. Your turn. Don't worry, I promise to behave myself."

"You'd better." Lei scooped up her things and walked into the small bathroom, locking the door behind her. She took a quick shower, barely allowing herself a moment to enjoy the pounding heat. She dressed just as quickly and packed up her toiletries.

Blake watched her as she strapped on her holster. "Do you always go out prepared for battle?"

"Of course. Don't you?"

"I don't really have a choice, my weapons aren't exactly ones I can put down or take off." He lay back on the bed. "I guess I'm asking if you ever take a night off, just have time to yourself."

"I read a book all by myself just last night. And it was a fun one too! Light on plot, heavy on the smut with a dash of mystery thrown in. Perfect for clearing out the cobwebs in my brain."

"I wouldn't have pictured you for a bodice ripper reader."

Lei laughed. "It's about the only thing I do for myself just for fun."

"We all have to have something, I suppose. I watch old movies."

"You strike me as a Bond type." Lei packed up every trace of herself, shoving it all in her duffel bag.

"Most guys are. I'll pretty much watch anything. Except zombie movies. I don't do zombies." Blake took the duffel bag from her and led the way out to Lei's car. "I think we should just take your car for now. Mine's safe where it is."

"Fine. Let's just get out of this city. Odds are there are people already out looking for the both of us." She turned the car on and pulled out of the motel's lot. After some wrong turns, she finally pulled onto the highway and headed west.

"We want to get on I-80 here." Blake pointed to the exit.

"Where are we going?" Lei took the exit and merged onto the highway.

"Wyoming. It's about two day's drive from here. I'll let Drew know we're coming when we stop for the night. I think you'll like him. In some ways, you remind me a bit of him."

"Pardon me?"

Blake laughed. "Not in a bad way. You're both very stubborn, play things pretty close to the vest."

They drove through the night, stopping near dawn at a motel to grab a few hours of sleep. This time they requested and received separate beds, much to Lei's relief. Sure she was attracted to him, but the timing was wrong. Hell, everything was wrong about it. She knew nothing about him beyond the fact that he was a sorcerer and he wanted to work long term with her. She didn't see any relationship in her future so that put having a little fun with him on the very long list of Bad Ideas.

The next afternoon, they got up, grabbed a quick dinner at a little diner and hit the road. She let Blake share in the driving this time. No sense in not taking full advantage of their sudden partnership.

"Tell me about your family, Blake." Lei broke the silence that filled the car.

"Not much to tell, really. They're a large, messy, obnoxious bunch, but I love them. My mother is a seer. My dad, he's not. His gifts are mostly focused on plants really. He's a great farmer. He is the seventh son of a very powerful sorcerer. My parents' marriage was arranged specifically for the gift of the seventh son, my younger brother. He's not come fully into his own just yet, but he has more magic then he knows what to do with."

She shuddered. "Are arranged marriages common among the sorcerers?"

"Yep," he nodded. "Trying to focus certain gifts, eliminate others, it's a game of odds really, but it mostly works out. Many arrangements become more than that though, of course, some split up as soon as the desired child or children are achieved."

"Sounds awful if you ask me. I guess, for me, there's got to be love."

"Were your parents in love? Tell me about them."

"My parents were completely normal." Lei laughed. "They met when my dad was stationed in Hawaii. He was a Marine. My mom was young, beautiful, and in awe of him. They used to tell me it was love at first sight. I believe it. They were always very affectionate with each other and with me. When I was younger, I dreamed I'd find the same kind of love, the same kind of fire with a man of my own. Not likely now, but it was a pleasant dream."

Blake glanced at her with a frown. "Why is it not likely now? What's changed?"

"Are you kidding me? Everything has changed. What are the odds of meeting that one perfect-for-me man and having him not think I'm a lunatic? The odds of meeting someone in this line of work are nil. At least the odds of meeting someone worth sticking around for more than one night." She laughed, the hollow sound echoing in the car.

With a sigh, Blake turned back to the road.

"What? Women have needs too, you know. Men no longer have the market on flings cornered."

"You are a very unusual woman, Leilani."

"Thank you, Blake."

"I'm glad you've decided to consider me a friend now." He smiled.

"What?"

"You just called me Blake not Pratt."

"Oh. Well, shit. Yeah. I mean. Damn it." She glanced out the window. "At least I know your name."

"Guess I've got one up on some of those flings of yours then."

Lei laughed a little more truly. "I've spent more time alone with you than I have anyone since Willy died. That's why my rule is so important. If you really want to work with me, we can't afford to have any weirdness between us."

"I suppose I should look on the bright side. You've decided to give this working together thing a chance." He sounded pleasant enough, but Lei saw his fingers clench the steering wheel slightly.

"Let's change the subject, shall we? Tell me about this mentor of yours."

"His name is Drew Stanton." Blake's lips tightened into a thin line. "You're a very observant woman, Lei, so I'm going to fill you in on a few things. Mostly so you don't accidentally say something, okay?"

"Okay." She raised a questioning eyebrow.

"Drew isn't exactly just my mentor. I told you about my mother's gift. I'm not kidding when I tell you she's powerful. Maybe the most powerful seer in the country. Years ago, when my mother looked into the future, she saw that her husband's seventh son would be hunted. Always in danger. And there was no outcome she could see in which he wasn't murdered before his sixteenth birthday."

"How awful!"

"I agree. My mother made a choice to protect the child she'd entered into the marriage to have. She found a willing sorcerer whom she could trust, who had a very different kind of talent than my father, and gave to the world a decoy. My dad doesn't know, but maybe he suspects that I'm not really a Pratt. My family and most of the rest of the world believe that I am the seventh son of a seventh son. I'm not. That distinction belongs to my younger brother. Just please, no remarks about how much Drew and I look alike. Especially if you meet my family. It's going to be difficult, but I'd like to tell them myself."

"Why do you need to tell them at all?"

"Because I'm supposed to be getting married in two months. It was arranged before my wife-to-be was even two years old. But the arrangement was based entirely on my being the seventh son of a seventh son descended…you get the idea. I'm going to have to tell them it isn't me they bargained for."

"Why? I've seen a little of what you can do, what's the likelihood they'd even notice?"

"It doesn't matter if they'd notice, Lei. From what you said yourself, I thought you'd understand. I don't want to marry her. She's a nice enough girl, don't get me wrong, but I guess I want that bond, that love, too. My parents have grown to like each other, and I guess that's important, but that's not want I want."

"How long have you known?"

"Just about my whole life, I guess." He shrugged and Lei saw the sadness that shadowed his features. "I've got enough of my mother in me to understand why it had to be done."

"How many times have you almost been killed because of what people believe you are?"

"Too many to count."

"Why? Who would want you dead because of some stupid seventh son bullshit?"

"First, it's not bullshit. Second, most of those in the know think I'm dangerous. Maybe they're right, but not for the reason they think. Other sorcerers, otherworlders, even Justices once upon a long time ago, they all tried to take me out. But we had to get Marcus to adulthood. His gifts are no threat to anyone. My mother is very reluctant to tell her baby the truth. I think she thinks he'll think less of her."

"What? I don't understand." Lei shook her head. She'd always been raised to value the truth above all else. Even when, maybe especially when, it was hardest to say.

"I know. Look, my brother is a gifted healer, maybe the best there has ever been, but he has no talent for pain or death. He is a remarkable young man, but if he had been born before me, he wouldn't have survived long enough for anyone to know that he is no threat. I, on the other hand, am a threat, but I can take care of myself."

"Sounds like you've had to." Lei reached over and put her hand on his arm, feeling a strange mix of anger and sorrow for him. "I give you my word, I won't say anything to anyone."

"Thank you."

"Does it bother you to be so used?"

"It used to. Not so much anymore. I get it. The world needs more people like Marcus and less like me. There are too many skilled at death."

Her heart broke a little at the resignation in his voice. "It must be more difficult to be born into this life than to be shoved into it. Knowing you were designed that way."

"Nah." Blake shook his head. "I've always known the truth of things, never had a time when I didn't. You, you had a baptism of fire."

"Maybe, but at least I got to have a childhood full of happy memories I can hold on to."

"Just because my family has always been at war doesn't mean I don't have happy memories. Life is what you make of it, not what you are handed."

For a time, silence spread between them. Lei stewed a bit, angry with people she'd never met for being so cold and callous toward their own child. But he didn't want her anger. Or anything else she was willing to give. "Want to trade off for a while?"

"Nah. I'm good. I like driving. Need to stop for coffee before too much longer though. I'd like to be in Wyoming today if we can manage it."

Lei nodded and watched the exit signs for anything that might have a decent cup of coffee and not the swill they'd gotten so far. What she wouldn't give to find a little artsy boutique coffee shop like the one she'd frequented in high school. They always had excellent coffee there. Sometimes, she thought she missed the coffee shop more than anything other than her parents from her former life.

After fueling up the car, and themselves, they headed back on down the road, choosing music over conversation for a while. Lei had a lot to think about. She hadn't actually decided whether or not to work with Blake. She didn't honestly think she could trust him. But, he was a better man than she wanted to give him credit for.

There were upsides and downsides to working with anyone. It wouldn't work with Blake. Their methods weren't compatible and he had the idiotic notion that she needed him to protect her. She would not work with him on anything less than equal footing. And they couldn't cross the line he joked around with so easily. Sex was all well and good when you never had to see the man again. She'd be spending much too much time with Blake for any kind of intimacy to develop. If they crossed the line, would he be willing to let her do her job? Would she be able to think clearly if something horrible happened to him?

As the road slid by, Lei fought sleep. The light, half sleep that came with boredom always brought things she didn't want to remember, things she never wanted to see again. The night her parents were slaughtered and her eyes were opened to the truth of the world came calling frequently in that state. Too tired to fend off the fear, too awake not to see the bloody mess the werewolf had made of her parents in order to clear the way to claim her. Her first solo hunt often followed. Alone in the dark, facing down a mean old banshee determined to rid her town of children. She'd nearly lost her own head trying to protect a little boy. In the end, she'd gotten rid of the banshee, but she failed to save the child. No memory was so vile as that of the broken child sinking down into the murk of a Louisiana swamp.

"Hey," Blake's voice pulled her out her troubled sleep, "are you all right?"

"Fine." She rubbed her eyes, embarrassed by the damp on her cheeks. "Sorry."

"No apologizing for being human, okay?" He smiled at her and patted her hand. "Can I ask what you were dreaming about?"

"People I couldn't save. Can't ever save, not even in my dreams. I'm always too late for them." She took a deep breath, pulling herself together. "I don't know why I'm telling you any of this."

"Probably because you've been on your own with no one to talk to, really talk to, since Willy died. I may not have liked the woman, but she was what you had. She knew what you were facing each time you left the house. She understood things no one else would have. It's no shame to suddenly unburden yourself when you find yourself traveling with someone else who gets it."

"Whatever. We haven't known each other long enough for me to be blubbering like this. You've got far bigger problems than little old me." She rubbed the last of the sleep from her eyes and stared out the window.

"Oh yeah? Like what?"

"Like an arranged marriage you don't want." Lei pushed the conversation back onto him.

"Nope. Nice try, Lei. Doesn't work that way." He laughed brightly. "I'm fine with my station in life. But, since you don't want to talk about you, I've run out of things to say about me, and we still have a few hours to go, we might as well find something else to talk about. Why not start with what's going on?"

"It doesn't make sense. Creatures are showing up in places they shouldn't be. Aswangs have always contained themselves to the

Philippines before, but there's no doubt that I dealt with one in Detroit. Then there's the vampires. One of the higher up Justices is working with them, otherwise, Cam wouldn't have been told to leave them be. I think they're making deals with monsters."

"Why? What's the point?"

"Why does anyone do anything? Money, power, control." She looked off into the dark and wondered for a moment how many would die as they turned their backs on Pittsburgh.

"The vampires don't have any power. Not really."

"Don't they? How hard would it really be for them to take over a city? Think about it. It wouldn't be that hard if they were smart. Their only real issue would be doing it without drawing attention to themselves from the media, from hunters. They'd have to be very careful. Take people in high or useful places first. Politicians, cops, society types." She thought of the cop who'd bared his teeth to her.

"But why now? They could have done that before I guess. Why all of a sudden? Why does it come when we're fighting a flood of things that have no reason to be here?"

"How should I know? Maybe the vampires are tired of being fodder for Hollywood. Maybe they think, rightly so, that the populace has been desensitized enough that either they won't believe the truth even when they see it or they'll be so thrilled that their favorite movies actually have some foundation that all those fans will fall all over themselves to be turned. It's a crazy-ass world we live in."

"Twenty years ago it wouldn't have been possible."

"And let's hope it's not really possible now. This may be a crazy ass world but it's mine and it's beautiful and I'm not going to let them have it. We still have our freedom, our own will. Neither of those things will continue if vampires are running the show. If the Justices are going to stand aside and let it happen, then I have to pick up the slack."

"You really plan to go back to Pittsburgh?"

"As soon as it's safe to. That nest has to go. I need to question the leader if I want to find out what's really going on. It won't be pretty. I doubt very much that he'll talk without some kind of persuasion."

"When we go back to Pittsburgh, I promise to let you question them, but I won't let it get out of hand. We have more than just vampires to deal with and they're crafty bastards."

They stopped talking for a while. Lei mulled over the fact that Blake seemed very persistent in attaching them together—we this and we that. And stubbornly, purposely ignoring the fact that she was asserting her desire to remain solo.

Even before she had her eyes opened to the truth, she'd never worked well with others. She didn't like handing over control. Not in high school, not in life, and certainly not when her own life was on the line.

So what the hell was she doing in a car with Blake going to meet his team?

Chapter Four

Blake pulled the car off the highway, towards a little town nestled in the northeastern corner of Wyoming. In the early light of sunrise, the fog crept in thick, like something out of an old horror movie, lingering on the road so the car's tires swirled it around as they drove through it. Pretty country, but not a place Lei was comfortable in. She'd been raised in the suburbs and learned to hunt in cities. Large tracts of wooded acreage gave her the spooks. Even the property Willy left her in Texas, as big as it was, was mostly flat and open. Not much chance of anyone sneaking in close, even in the darkest hour of the night.

After another forty minutes, Blake pulled off the two-lane highway onto a dirt road, negotiating the slight snow pack with ease. The house at the end of the road wasn't much to look at. Just a rundown old farmhouse, but Lei saw how Blake looked at the place. For him, it was home.

Before the car came to a stop, a tall man in a black parka stepped out onto the porch, a shotgun in his hand. "Let me get out first and talk to him, okay? Just sit tight."

"You didn't let your people know you were bringing a stranger?" Lei stared at him and shook her head. "Good way to get us killed."

Blake rolled his eyes and got out of the car. The man on the porch smiled for a moment. In the light of the headlights, Lei noted how much the two men looked alike. They shared a similar body type, facial structure, and coloring. The lines on his face and the gray in his hair marked the man in the parka as the older of the two. She doubted Blake's father was really as blind as Blake seemed to think. Lei thought the man must have been very young when Blake was born and wondered if that had something to do with why Blake's mom had chosen him for the donor—a young man with no desire for a family yet.

Lei squirmed in her seat. She was trying not to judge Blake's mother, but it wasn't working. She chose to have a sacrificial child, one who could handle the threats, take them away from the brother, the important one. It had to suck to know you were born specifically so people could try to kill you instead of your kid brother. How Blake didn't see it as a betrayal she didn't know.

The two men seemed happy enough to see each other, but the older one kept looking in her direction and gesturing with his gun. Lei wanted to know what they were saying, what Blake was telling him about her, but she didn't want to get out of her car so long as that shotgun was pointed in her general direction.

Suddenly, Blake turned and walked back to the car, coming around to her side and opening the door. "We'll be safe here. Get your bag and come on in."

Lei grabbed her duffel and exited the car, trying to keep her nerves at bay. The shotgun wasn't aimed at her, but he still had it in his arms.

"So, you're the hunter Blake's been talking about." The man looked her up and down, his lips pressed together in a thin, disapproving line.

"I suppose I must be. I'm Leilani Scott." She slung her bag over her shoulder so she could hold out her hand for a proper introduction. "Most people just call me Lei."

He took her hand and held it a moment too long. "I'm Drew. Let's get inside. I'm sure you're both exhausted."

"It was a long drive. Thank you." She followed him into his house, trying to tamp down the little ember of panic flaring to life in her gut.

The inside of the house was pretty close to Lei's expectations of a warrior sorcerer's home. Old books littered every surface. Artifacts, scrolls, ancient bones, labeled jars of weird liquids, everywhere she glanced, a tool or weapon sat. It smelled of coffee, polish, and steel, touched with a bit of soap and linseed oil.

"Why don't you put your things away and freshen up for breakfast, or dinner, food." He motioned to a long hallway off to her left. "Bathroom is at the end of the hall. The guest room is the last door on the right. Blake will be right across the hall from you."

"Thanks." Lei bowed her head slightly and walked down the hall and into the room he'd assigned for her, shutting the door tight behind her.

***

The moment Lei closed the door to her room, Drew motioned for Blake to follow him back out onto the porch. Blake took a deep breath and followed, closing the door quietly behind him. The man's face was, as always, unreadable.

"What the hell do you think you're doing?" Drew kept his voice low, but Blake could hear the anger as clearly as if he'd yelled.

"We talked about this before. I wasn't blowing smoke when I talked about the team. Hell, I've already convinced Melli. I thought I had you on board, too. You didn't have any trouble with my plan when I explained it. You seemed to think it was a pretty good idea if I recall correctly."

"I assumed you'd bring a hunter with some real experience, one who isn't afraid of her own shadow! How long as she been at this? A year?" He flailed his arm in the general direction of Lei.

Blake laughed. "Longer than you think. If you give her a chance, I think you'll like her. You'll see. She's got nerve and spunk. Now, are you pissed because she's young or because she's pretty?"

"Pretty only matters if that's why you picked her out of all the hunters in this country." Drew scowled and stared out into the woods.

"You know me better than that. Besides, she has a 'no touching' rule that she doesn't seem likely to break." Blake shrugged, more annoyed with the "no touching" than he cared to admit. "Talk to her. Give her a chance. She's more than the sum of her age. Besides, I think there might be something more to her."

"What do you mean?" Suspicion returned to Drew's face, deepening the lines around his eyes.

"For years, you pushed me to study everything I could. You told me I had to know as much about the otherworlders' history as our own. Hell, you dropped me off in their homeland like it was summer camp so Ounathir could teach me. So I could learn about the otherworlders. And I did. I studied them, their history, their culture. Have you ever read the Danann scrolls?" Blake leaned against the rough-hewn railing.

"It's been a long time since I studied fae lore, but I'm pretty sure those are mostly debunked prophecies written down before the splitting of the worlds."

"That's right. Not everyone believes they are nonsense. There are some people who believe Lei may be part of one of the Danann scrolls. It matches up with a lot of current events. It may have been

why her family was attacked in the first place. And maybe why
Willy took her on as a student but kept her away from the Justices."

"You give that woman too much credit, Blake. She was cruel
and vindictive."

"Maybe, but she was a smart one. Look, even if Lei isn't what
some think she is, she's still in danger because of it."

Drew crossed his arms over his chest. "That's very convenient
for you. And your sudden need to ride around with a pretty girl has
nothing to do with your upcoming wedding?"

"Are you serious?" Blake shook his head. "I'm not getting
married. Marcus is, he just doesn't know it yet."

"You can't do that. Your mother won't let you."

"I'm not a child. Maybe Mom and Dad will have some
problems for a while, but I am not her puppet. I can't do it anymore.
Marcus can take care of himself now. And I bet that little scared girl,
Whitney, she'll be so relieved it isn't me, she'll do cartwheels."
Blake shoved his fingers through his long hair. "She's terrified of me.
If her parents gave a shit about anything more than marrying her into
a powerful family, they'd have already backed out. She begged them
to."

"You didn't tell me that." Drew took a step toward him but
Blake stepped away.

"Yeah, because I'm going to shout from the roof tops that I
scare little girls."

"She's not a little girl."

"Bull. I'm thirty, she's about to turn eighteen. She's just a kid.
Besides, they bargained for the seventh son. I'm not one. I'm a first
born."

"And have more power in your little finger than Marcus could
ever dream of."

"Not really. His gifts are different, that's all. He lacks the
capacity to kill, that doesn't mean he's powerless. Besides, none of
this has anything to do with Lei."

"Really?" Drew arched an eyebrow and stared hard at him.
"And what does your mother have to say about it?"

"She's the one who told me to find her, to watch her. She said
I'd have the opportunity to save her and gain her trust. And she was
right." He didn't tell Drew that his mother had warned him away
from developing any personal connection to the woman.

Drew made a sort of noncommittal sound and walked back toward the door.

***

Lei listened carefully at her door. She couldn't quite hear the discussion they were having on the porch, but she knew it pertained to her. When she heard the door open and shut, she darted away from the door and began digging through her bag as if she were looking for something.

The knock on her door didn't surprise her. That Drew stood there and not Blake, did. "Come in." She stepped aside to let him in. As he stepped past her into the small space, Lei took a step back from him. Drew was almost as imposing as his son. He was as tall and as solid. His eyes had seen much more than his student, but it was tempered with something else—a wisdom and maybe a kindness Lei was unaccustomed to. She wasn't afraid of him and that surprised her too.

"I wanted to speak with you for a minute, if I could."

Lei nodded. The way he looked at her made her uneasy. Like he was trying to take her measure and finding her more than lacking.

"I'm not sure how much Blake has told you about the situation…." Drew shifted from foot to foot.

"If this is about his parentage, I've promised to be quiet. Though, given how much he favors you, the odds are good that Blake's dad already knows."

"I doubt it. Maybe he should, but he's blind when it comes to Blake. And to his wife."

"It's this whole seventh son crap, right?" Lei sat on the edge of the bed mostly just to have something to do.

"Yes, and it's not crap. Henry doesn't see the truth because he doesn't want to. He longed for a warrior son, even though his own lineage made that unlikely. Blake's kind of magic doesn't come down healer lines. It'd be kind of missing the point for a healer to wield such power, if you think about it." Drew shrugged as if to say 'what can you do?'

"Look, I really don't care about all this. It has no bearing on me whatsoever. Besides, I'm not good at all of these interpersonal politics. I don't really work well with others." Lei tried to keep her nerves from showing but she didn't think it was working.

"I suppose that comes with the territory. We so often work alone. I have come to appreciate this idea of Blake's though. Imagine how much more efficient we could be working together towards the same end."

"The question remains though, will that end always be the same? Would you be willing to put down a rogue sorcerer? That's like asking a werewolf to kill his own kind. My experience tells me that won't happen. How can you trust a team that has limits like that?"

"I see your point and it's a valid one. One I've made myself where Melli and you are concerned."

"Me?" She stared at him, flabbergasted.

"Can you honestly tell me you'd be willing to take on a Justice after you were trained by one?" His gaze pinned her but she didn't squirm.

"You don't know much about me then. I have no love for the Order. Most of them would prefer I died quickly and with all their secrets unspoken. I'm not a Justice. The Order meant a lot to Willy, but not to me. She had her reasons for not petitioning the Heads of the Order where I was concerned, and not just because they would have forbid her to train me. Something is rotten there and who else is going to keep it from spreading?"

"You believe you can stop it?"

"Maybe. If I can bring proof of it to the Heads of the Order, if I can make them listen. If they aren't a part of it, then I think I can."

"How do you plan to get this proof?"

"I plan to interrogate the leader of the vampire nest in Pittsburgh. He's been given a pass by the Order. If he doesn't know which Justice is organizing it, he knows someone who does." She shrugged as if the solution was an easy one.

"Do you plan to torture the vampire?" He crossed his arms over his chest but his eyes were thoughtful, not hard.

"I plan to use whatever methods I must to get the information I need to save hundreds if not thousands of lives. In my position, I believe you'd do the same. Unless I've completely misjudged you."

"You haven't." He smiled at last, and Lei felt almost as if she'd won his approval. "I see now why Blake is so insistent we bring you onto the team. You are an interesting woman."

"Don't get any ideas. We're working together, nothing more."

"You say that now." Drew shook his head, still smiling.

"Look, I'm not saying Blake isn't nice to look at or even pleasant when he's not being an asshole. But, the fact remains, there are more important things. I have my own goals in this mess."

"All right then. I won't say anything more about it."

She waited for him to move toward the door but he remained quite still. "That's not the only reason you've come to talk to me, is it?"

"No. You're very astute. I do have another reason for being here. I have my misgivings about you. Whether or not you can fend for yourself."

Lei stood up, spread her feet into a fighting stance. "I've been on my own for a few years now. I'm not defenseless. I'm not some little wallflower or someone anyone needs to worry about. Yes, I have a lot to learn still, I won't deny that. I'm fortunate enough to have had some very good teachers in my life and I'm willing to learn from anyone who has something to teach me. That doesn't mean I can't hold my own in a tight spot."

"Please, I'm not trying to offend you." Drew sat down on the edge of the bed. "There may be more to you yet than you know. Perhaps you are more special than you think."

"Drew, I'm just a girl trying to keep other people safe."

"Haven't you ever wondered how you picked up everything so easily? Why it's hard for people, even those with magic, to hide from you?"

"It's not my fault your little apprentice does shoddy work with shadow spells." She rolled her eyes. Was nobody observant anymore?

"He's the best there is at that, Lei. Better even than me and yet, you saw him. Or felt him."

"I'm nothing more and nothing less than me. Just a girl trying to do some good in the world." She shook her head. "If you believe there's more to it than that, you're going to be disappointed."

"I'm not sure I believe that. I'm not sure you really do either."

Lei looked down at him, the challenge in her eyes. "If not for that stupid werewolf, I'd be living a blissfully ignorant life right now."

"You could have walked away then. No way Willy forced you to be her student. In fact, I imagine you actually had to fight her pretty hard to get her to agree."

Lei wondered if Drew had met Willy at some point. He talked about her like he'd known her. "I did. How could I go back to living my life knowing there were things like that werewolf in the world? I had no one—he slaughtered my parents! I didn't know then how to tell them from everyone else. I was afraid of everything, everyone, even people I'd known for years. Can you imagine living like that and trying to be normal again?"

"No. I suppose not. But, you're sure you have no magic? None at all?" Drew pursed his lips.

"I'm observant. I've had to be. Fear made me learn to be. You have tells. All the monsters do. Willy taught me some of them. I've learned others. You can't blame me for going out and learning all I could."

"You really believe sorcerers are monsters?"

"Well, not exactly, but you aren't exactly normal either." Lei felt a little bad using the M word for them, but she couldn't exactly call them human. "You're human, at least genetically, but you're more than that too. The things you people can do, I'd be a fool not to be wary where you lot are concerned. I've never seen a sorcerer do anything purely to help someone else. If I could do half the things you can, I'd be curing cancer not sitting around twiddling my thumbs."

"All right." He raised his hands in defeat. "If you've got no magic, no mojo, I can't teach you to use it. It's just one less tool in our armory. That's why I was hoping."

"I don't think you're telling the whole truth, Drew, but whatever you're looking for, I'm sorry I'm not it."

"What do you mean?"

"I think Blake thought I was someone I'm not when he started getting in my way. If you tell me what you're looking for, maybe I can help you find it. Just because I'm not her, doesn't mean I can't help you find her."

"I'll keep that in mind." Drew stood to leave but turned back as he opened the door. "Now that we've got that all settled, come on and let me feed you. Melli will be here sometime this evening. Then we can get to work."

Chapter Five

Distant voices pulled Lei from her troubled sleep. She strained to
hear them. Blake and Drew's voices mixed together, tumbled over
each other. The third voice was female and harder to hear. Drew had
said Melli was coming. It was probably her. They were arguing, but
she couldn't pick out any words. It didn't sound violent and no one
seemed to be trying to kill anyone else, so Lei didn't rush.

As she stretched and dressed, she glanced out the window. The
setting sun cast deep purple shadows in the forest around Drew's
house. She hadn't slept particularly well, but she hadn't expected to.
She didn't know Drew or Blake well enough to trust them, not
completely.

When Lei opened her door, all the talking stopped. She smirked
and walked in the direction of the kitchen. Blake and Melli sat at the
table, Drew stood at the counter pouring a cup of coffee. "I'll assume,
since you all quieted awfully fast, whatever disagreement you were
having had something to do with me."

"Of course." Melli smiled, her green eyes flashing in the
fluorescent light.

"Did you sleep okay?" Drew asked as he handed her the cup.

"No worse than usual." Lei breathed in the scent of coffee and
slid into a chair across from Blake and Melli. "So, what's got
everyone all upset this beautiful evening?"

Melli smiled and ran a chocolate caramel hand over her red and
black hair. "I have a meeting scheduled for you tonight and Drew
here doesn't like the idea."

"Don't put words in my mouth, Melli. I said she wasn't
prepared. There's a difference." Drew dropped his frame into a
sturdy chair at the head of the table. "She was trained by a Justice.
She doesn't know the first thing of the hidden lands, what to expect,
how to behave."

"She's a smart girl, Drew. She can learn on the way." Melli
tapped her long, gold painted fingernails on the table impatiently.
"Queen Ounathir doesn't just agree to meet people, especially not
humans."

"First of all, sitting right here. I can hear you." Lei leaned over
the table, resting her arms on its cool surface. "While I am capable

of learning quickly, I like to be prepared. The real question is why is your queen agreeing to see me at all? That she is tells me she actually wants to. So basically, she'll see me whenever *I'm* ready. Not that I want to piss off the Queen of the Fairies, but don't overestimate your or her importance to me."

Blake laughed and Lei kicked at him under the table. "Sorry. It's not my fault you make me laugh. Unfortunately, they're both right. You need to go tonight, but you need to know what you're getting into."

"How do we even get there?" Lei asked.

"Well, fortunately, darling Drew—"

"Knock it off, Melli." Drew growled a warning.

"Fine." She stuck her little pink tongue out at him. "Fortunately, he had the foresight to build near an entrance. Where two ley lines cross, those from the hidden lands can make an opening to the Gray Road."

"The Gray Road?"

"It's sort of an in between place and it's not a nice one. There is a great war in the hidden lands. It is worse on the Road." Melli looked into Lei's eyes. "It is an ugly, lawless place. A bridge between my world and yours. Your weapons won't work there—no guns, only blades. Your technology can't exist there. It will crumble to dust. That is the law."

"Wonderful." Lei put down her coffee and rubbed her eyes. "I'll go. I'll meet your queen. And when the meeting is done, we're going to sit down and lay everything out. Then, and only then, will I decide if I'm willing to be a part of this team. I'm not promising anyone anything. I have no allegiance to any of you at the moment. Am I understood?"

"You will like my queen, Leilani Scott, and I believe she will like you." Melli leaned back in her chair and smiled at Drew. "Are you going to argue with her too?"

"No. But I *will* be going with her. You didn't quite make the danger as clear to her as you should and I won't let her walk unprotected on the Gray Road."

"You aren't invited to the meeting." Melli glanced at Blake. "Either of you."

"Now, just you wait a minute." Blake stood up and began to pace. "By law, any guest of the queen is afforded a guard of her own choosing."

Melli sighed. "I was going to fulfill that duty out of respect to my Queen. It's been a long time since you were welcome in our house, Blake."

"You are an agent of the queen, her freaking daughter! You have a bias!" Blake slapped his hand on the table. "That is unacceptable. Lei will have a guard of her own choosing, not yours. The other of us will stay behind on the Gray Road, keep an eye on things." Blake looked to Lei. "The choice is yours, Leilani."

She looked back and forth between father and son. "Who would you pick, Blake?"

"I'd like to say myself, but Drew knows more of the history, the laws. Knows more about their customs and tactics. You'd be better served with him as your guard as he can also be your adviser. Besides, as Melli pointed out, I'm no longer welcome at Ounathir's court." Blake stepped away from the table. "I'll go get the armor ready."

"Armor?"

Drew nodded. "Our armor is just for show but only because we don't have any real armor on hand. The Gray Road isn't a safe place for anyone, but humans are especially unwelcome and likely to be killed on sight. We will go disguised as elves and fairies. This isn't our first trip. I'm hoping you trust us enough to protect you."

Lei raised an eyebrow. "It's not about trust. I'm pretty sure I can protect myself. But that doesn't mean I won't accept advice."

"Fair enough." Drew nodded.

"All right, if I can't take my guns, what can I take?" Lei chewed on her bottom lip a moment.

"Blades. But you will likely have to give them up to meet with the queen. No way are they going to let you meet with her armed."

"Right. Okay. Give me a few minutes and I'll be ready to go." Lei drained her coffee cup and took it to the sink.

"Wear something light, breathable, and with good coverage. Even fake armor chafes a bit." Melli scrunched up her nose in distaste.

"I think I can manage." Lei went back to her room and dug through her duffel. She pulled out black leggings and a deep purple long sleeved shirt. It wasn't perfect, but she could wear it underneath armor without it being too bulky or bunching up. She sat down on the bed and took her hair out of its ponytail and began to braid it tightly. When she was finished, she shoved her feet into her combat boots, laced them up, and walked back into the kitchen.

Blake and Drew were busy strapping large metal plates on their chests and Melli watched with great interest. "Don't worry, they aren't at all heavy."

"How come?" Lei walked over to the pile and lifted one up. It weighed very little.

"It's plastic made to look like metal."

She inspected a piece closer. "Is it plated? It looks awfully good."

"That's the point." Blake smiled and started helping her put it on.

"I feel like I'm going to a damned Renaissance faire," Lei muttered as Blake pulled a woolen cap down over her ears, leaving her long braid trailing down her back. "This is ridiculous."

"You won't feel that way long. Have you ever used a sword?" Blake cinched a heavy belt around her middle, complete with a scabbard that fell to her knees. "You probably won't need it, but it's better to have it."

"I'll tell you what, if this is all some elaborate prank or whatever, I'm going to whack you upside the head with this sword." She took the blade he handed her and inspected it. "This seems a little short to me."

"You're too short for most swords. That's a short sword, a coustille-type sword. It'll be fine, just remember, it's not a toy. It is functional and sharp."

Lei rolled her eyes and placed the sword in the scabbard. Apparently, learning how to actually use a sword wasn't high on the agenda.

"One last touch and then we'll be ready." Melli flung a long gray cloak over Lei's shoulders and pulled the hood up over the cap. "If you keep your head down and don't say much of anything to anyone, maybe no one will notice you're human."

"So long as we don't run into any werewolves, we might be okay." Drew appraised Lei and nodded.

"What about you? Don't you need to hide this way?" Lei asked.

"Not really." Drew smiled as he and Blake both began to transform before her eyes.

"I guess a good glamour goes both ways then. Shit. All right. I'll behave. I promise." She realized for them to go so far to disguise themselves, they weren't just trying to make her nervous with all their talk of danger. The sorcerers could be anyone they wanted, if they wanted. If they gave a damn about what regular human world around them, that ability could be dangerous. Lei could do an exorcism, even a few protection incantations but to have that kind of power at her fingertips, she couldn't even imagine it.

Drew and Blake smiled at her from within their magicked disguises. Really, it was the wings Lei envied, even if they were just illusions. Great sweeping wings. Drew's were ebony black and very plain. Blake's wings were more elaborate, more spectacular—deep burgundy, like a moth's wings, with eye-like spots in the corners. Their ears were longer, angled to a rounded point. Their skin looked damp and smelled of earth.

"I smell wrong. Any good nose will know, even one that doesn't belong to a werewolf." Lei shook her head. "I can smell the three of you two houses over. They'll be able to smell me, or rather, notice the lack of scent, the same way."

"I told you she was smart." Blake grinned broadly and took five sachets and a bottle out of the cabinet. Dodging her hands as they tried to fend him off, Blake tucked the sachets under her clothes near the major scent points. One nestled in the center part of her bra, one tucked under each arm, one dropped down her pants, and one up under the helmet. He spread the oil from the bottle on every bit of exposed skin Lei had.

The smell of pine and fir overwhelmed her. She couldn't get away from it. "Oh my God, how do you turn off a nose? I think I'm going to be sick."

"Once we're moving, you won't notice it too much." Blake promised. "We'll take Drew's Jeep out to the cross point and then it'll be up to Melli to open the door."

"I have friends waiting on the other side." She looked at Drew and Blake with apology. "It's a long way to the Queen's palace. We'll need to ride."

"Damn. I hate those beasts." Drew shuddered and walked out the door.

Lei looked to Blake for explanation and got none. Melli didn't look willing to help explain either. Lei rolled her eyes and followed everyone out of the house, pulling the door shut behind her. She felt the fool's part even if she didn't look it. Which she did.

The ride in Drew's Jeep only took fifteen minutes over a worn path through the woods behind the house. Lei watched the shadows, watched the sky for any sign of a set up but found nothing. Scolding herself, Lei bowed her head. She wanted to find something wrong. She wanted a reason to dislike or distrust Blake. If she found something wrong with him, something to hate, keeping her distance would be easier. She couldn't let him get to her. "No touching" wasn't really her rule, "No getting close" was. Willy was the last person she'd let get close and she'd floundered for a long time when her mentor finally died.

Drew stopped the Jeep in a small clearing and got out. Lei looked around but there was nothing there. The trail continued farther, but since everyone else was getting out of the car, Lei did the same, her hand wrapped tightly around the hilt of her short sword. Not knowing how to use it properly wouldn't stop her from trying if she needed to.

Melli took a few steps and dropped her glamour, unfurling her great golden wings and letting them flutter. She began to sing. The song had no language, only sound. It didn't even seem that there was melody, just random notes, but the air stilled, the forest quieted, the whole world seemed to stop and wait.

The gate came from nowhere. It didn't grow or shimmer into existence. In the time it took Lei to blink, it just appeared—an opening into a shadowy gray wood. No one spoke. Melli stepped through it without hesitation, leading the way. Blake took Lei's hand and together they walked into the shadows of the tall, slender gray trees. Drew stayed right behind them, constantly looking over his shoulder. They walked a few short feet through the trees to a wide road of gray stone. Lei understood why they called it the Gray Road. Everything was a shade of gray—the trees, the ground, the road itself, even the sky above them. Lei felt as if all the color of the world was dying around her, inside her. If she stayed too long in this place, she would lose everything that made her human.

The moment the four of them stepped out onto the road, Lei wanted to turn around and go home. For the first time since she'd made her choice, since she'd become a hunter, she wished she'd at least tried to forget—to be a normal human. The road was beyond unforgiving, it pulled the best of her away, shredding it and leaving it in tatters.

Blake pulled four bright red ribbons from his pocket and handed two to Drew. They tied them on the trees immediately flanking the path they'd come in on.

Lei whipped around to face what she thought might be the east, hand on the hilt of her sword, when she heard the fast clip-clopping of horses approaching. Four figures approached, their long cloaks exactly like the one Lei wore. With them were creatures—horrible, gray beasts with long faces and dead, gray eyes.

"What the hell are those things?" She whispered to Blake as Melli stepped forward to talk to the figures.

"Those are the beasts of the Gray Road. They were horses once, trapped here when the bridge was first built," Drew answered instead. "This place is harsh. It drains life away until all that is left are shadows, shades of gray that can't die. No other beast will set foot in this place and nothing mechanical can survive it. They won't hurt you."

She stared at the beasts with their too long, too sharp teeth, their flat eyes, their too thin bodies, and didn't believe him.

"But they aren't friendly either," Blake added. "Can you ride?"

"Never saw a need to really since, you know, cars." She shuddered, trying to and failing to keep a grip on her fear as Melli swung up onto the back of one of the not-living beasts with ease.

"You'll have to ride with me then." Blake took her hand and pulled her toward one of the beasts. "We need to hurry. If we stand too long in one place, we're likely to get attacked."

"By what?" Could there be anything on the road worse than the beasts?

He pulled himself into the saddle and bent down to pull Lei up. "Anyone who thinks they can take a group of seven fairies and an elf."

"An elf?" Lei searched the group gathered around Melli, but all of them had wings. "Oh. You mean me."

"I could glamour you, as well, but that requires touching." Blake arched a brow and grinned.

Shaking her head, Lei situated herself behind Blake, between his carefully outspread wings, wrapping her arms tight around his waist as they began to move. The beasts moved quickly, covering ground almost as fast as a car might have. Impossibly fast for an animal that was once a horse.

Along the road, signs of life and death broke the monotony. A tavern, lit from within, but whose light didn't give warmth to the gray around them. What little comfort was gained by the tavern was lost in the wake of sporadic remnants of battles—heads of elves, vampires and fairies on pikes, the desiccated corpses of trolls, ogres, and werewolves. Some of the bodies wore clothes similar to those of Lei and her company.

Lei took in everything they passed, hoping to keep a series of landmarks in her mind but finding very little. "Why are all the buildings taverns, and why are they only on the one side?"

"They're places to rest and permanent entrances into the hidden world. Each one has a guard at the door to keep the fighting out. Those taverns are the only neutral ground in the hidden lands. Everywhere else, it's war. Technically, we aren't in the hidden lands yet. This road is the bridge between our world and theirs. There will never be any sort of building on the other side of the road, on the human side of the boundary. At least not in our lifetimes. Humans could never deal with it."

At least an hour went by as they raced along the Gray Road, passing other travelers not fortunate enough to have the not-dead horses, clustered together and well armored. The occurrence of death lessened some before they reached their stopping point, a smallish hut of broad gray stones with a sign above it's door proclaiming it the Sidhe. The riders all dismounted, tying the beasts to trees a short distance from the door, leaving behind two of the four fairies to watch them.

"You stay put, Blake." Melli put herself between Lei and Blake once they were on the ground. "I mean it. None of your shadow tricks. You won't be doing Lei any favors and I can't help you if they think you're a threat. So, promise me."

"Damn it, Melli! You can't expect me to just let her go with so little protection." Blake's voice sliced through the dead air.

Drew held up his hand to silence him. "You need to trust me. I won't let anything happen to her."

"All of you shut up." Lei stepped past Melli and approached Blake, laying her hand on his chest. Through the replica chain mail she felt his heart thunder beneath her palm, a strong rhythm that comforted her too much. "I'll be fine. I am *not* some helpless little girl. If you thought I was, you would never have wanted to work with me. Am I right?"

"Well, yes, but—"

"No. Enough. Let's just get this over with. You stay with them," she motioned to the riders by the beasts, "and keep out of trouble. The faster we go, the faster we can get back and go home where the air isn't so damned stale."

"Fine. Just listen to me." Blake pulled her close and whispered in her ear, "Remember, Ounathir is Melli's mother. They're a lot alike. Until you've proven your worth to her, you can't trust her. She's devious. Be careful, try not to piss her off too bad, but don't let her walk all over you."

"I'll see you soon." She took a deep breath, his scent, under the cloying pine, filled her head and gave her a rush. Lei followed Melli into the tavern with Drew at her side. She hoped Blake actually kept his promise and stayed with the riders.

The inside of the Sidhe was much different than the outside. Life existed here in a way it did not just beyond the door. The air was different, fresher, and color blossomed again. People sat at the bar, at tables. No glamours were used here; all types of otherworlders filled the place in their full glory, alternately hairy or smooth, with wings and without, beautiful and uglier than mud.

Melli walked with authoritative purpose through the place without so much as a glance behind her to make sure Lei and Drew were with her. They nearly had to run to keep up. Only when she reached the door on the opposite side of the tavern did she pause. "Now you will see where I come from, Ms. Scott." With a smile and a flourishing bow, she flung the door open and escorted them into the hidden lands.

Lei felt a sense of wonder run through her that she hadn't felt in a very long time, maybe not since she was a little kid on Christmas morning. Everything was bright, rich, and alive with color. Huge trees reached their great green branches toward each other with long trailing vines of wisteria and Spanish moss. Pixies flitted among the flowers like giant busy bees, their translucent wings reflecting and refracting the sun's light into a million tiny rainbows that lighted on leaves and the stone path beneath them.

A white carriage drawn by a matched pair of ponies, their coats velvet gray and dappled with white, as if snow had fallen on them and didn't melt drew near. They whinnied as Melli approached them and calmed when she laid her hand on one's back. "Come on, we're running late."

Lei allowed Drew to help her up into the carriage, feeling very bulky compared to the carriage's delicate and ornate carving, accented with gilt. "What kind of horse is that?"

"Their closest relative in your world are the Eriskay ponies." Melli beamed with pride. "We were afraid you were going let them die off a while back but you have made strides in keeping old, forgotten promises. Even if you have no recollection of them."

"What do you mean?"

"When the lands of Earth were divided, deals were made, promises, that you humans would be worthy stewards of the lands you were given. In some ways you have, in most ways, you have not. But there is no human that remembers the time before those promises. Your history is reduced to nothing more than fairy tales and whimsy." Melli sighed. "It doesn't matter. Not really. Not anymore."

"Why?" Lei leaned forward to hear her better over the echoing sound of racing hooves on stone. "What's changed?"

"Everything. Nothing. You cannot see it from these windows, but the hidden lands are at war. We have been at war with each other for so long. We are killing each other off all by ourselves with no help from you so, perhaps you were indeed the better stewards after all."

"You'll want to see this, Lei." Drew tapped her shoulder and gestured out the narrow window.

The palace was not what Lei expected—neither a cold, stone hulking mass nor a whimsical tree city in the sky but something of a marriage between them. Rooted beside a towering waterfall that must have been three hundred feet high, the palace was both stone and tree. Two large, living oaks stood as columns beside the open gate, watchtowers perched in their branches, great tree houses manned by armed fairies, their long bows drawn at their approach. The walls were rough stone in some places, boulders or great trees in others. Tactically unsound perhaps, what with the threat of fire, but one of the most beautiful structures Lei had ever seen.

"This is Queen Ounathir's summer palace, not her war palace, obviously. She left the battle to meet you."

Lei watched as a great many male fairies situated themselves around the carriage. She didn't like feeling so isolated, so vulnerable. But she wasn't helpless. Lei smiled as Drew helped her down out of the carriage.

Melli led them up a wide, white stone staircase and into a tunnel bored through a huge tree. On the other side of the tunnel was a great courtyard surrounded by living trees, sunlight creeping down through the wide, lush canopy. In the middle of the courtyard, a large stone table sat arranged for tea.

Six fairies stood before them, all of them wearing armor and long steel blades. One stepped forward and spoke quietly to Melli who nodded and shrugged.

"If you wish to meet with the queen, you must sit at the table unarmed."

Lei had expected as much, and prepared for it. Slowly, she removed the sword Drew had hung on her hip and handed it to Melli, along with a short bladed dagger from her boot, a longer knife from its sheath around her forearm, and a bottle of salt water with iron filings from around her neck.

"I hadn't realized you were so well armed." Melli narrowed her eyes slightly as if appraising Lei. "You are a continual surprise, aren't you?"

"I try." Lei smoothed her long braid and stepped aside as Drew similarly relieved himself of his own small arsenal of old-fashioned weaponry.

When the fairies were satisfied, they allowed them to pass through to the table. Lei removed her cap and tucked it under her thigh. Drew positioned himself behind her, putting both hands on her shoulders and Melli claimed the chair to her left. The fairies positioned themselves in a half-moon behind them.

From the opposite side of the courtyard, through a tunnel similar to the one Lei and the others had come through, a small army of guards led a woman of such beauty that it defied words. The woman glowed as the moon, as if gathering and reflecting the light of the sun. Her skin was dark and smooth like polished obsidian, flecked with gold and silver. She wore a simple white gown that flowed around her as she moved. Her great wings were a rich blue, edged with black and freckled with white dust. Her black hair was coiled around her head in a thousand tiny braids, looped and wound around her head, dotted with delicate gemstones.

"Welcome, Leilani Scott, to my summer home. I am Ounathir and I have been looking forward to seeing you for myself. I have heard so much about you. It isn't often a human catches my attention, you know." Her voice filled the courtyard but was quiet, as if a whisper carried on a breeze. "Please, be seated. We have much to discuss."

"Thank you, Your Majesty." Lei bowed slightly and sat down, watching as the queen situated herself and her wings on and around a low, backless seat. Not for the first time, Lei wished she paid more attention to her father's advice on dealing with powerful people. He'd done it in the military and tried to help her as she dealt with a certain megalomaniac teacher. "I'm not exactly sure why we're here, but thank you for having me. Your summer home is the most magnificent thing I've ever seen."

"That's only because you haven't seen my war palace." She smiled as one of her men poured steaming tea into delicate cups.

Lei thought about declining, but it would be rude. She could pretend to drink it and save herself the trouble. She wasn't about to actually ingest anything the queen handed her. If Ounathir was anything like Melli, there would be tests during this meeting and Lei didn't figure they'd have anything to do with werewolves.

"Have you ever heard of the Scrolls of Danann?" She motioned to a guard who brought forth a long wooden box. Ounathir opened it and removed a bit of paper. "The scrolls themselves are ancient and are not taken from the great library so we must make do with the translations I have brought with me. You see, the scrolls come from the time before the dividing of the Earth. They were written by an ancient race no longer among us. That is what we are meant to believe at any rate. They have predicted, with great accuracy, many of your wars, our wars, your discoveries, and our inventions. The Scrolls of Danann are trusted by all races among us."

"Except the humans." Lei reminded her.

"Of course, but only because there is none among you who remembers that time. Besides, you have your own prophets, do you not?" Her green eyes flashed with fire, like an opal.

"Not like that. We humans have pretty well debunked or dismissed those ancient prophets."

"Nostradamus then, is he not a trusted prophet?" Ounathir pressed.

"His words can be twisted to fit nearly anything a person has a mind to make them fit. It's natural to want explanations for things too horrible or too wonderful to really take in. We want to believe someone before us saw these things, so we make ourselves believe."

"You don't believe in future seeing then?" The queen laughed. "I imagine you have not told young Blake about this, nor have you met his mother."

"I prefer to believe that my future is of my own making, not designed. Were my life designed, I'd be forced to hate the power or being who designed it." Lei picked up her cup and pretended to sip it. It smelled good enough, like flowers and honey. "I don't trust anyone's vision, when it comes right down to it. In my experience, when someone is given clear directions, they do their best to find the shortcuts anyway."

"Perhaps you should read this one before you dig your hole any deeper." Ounathir sent her man around the table to present Lei with the scrap of paper.

When daughters of Earth fly to the stars and fall again home,
The path of humanity will fork.
Ancient things lost will be found once more,
Offering their guidance for the future.
Earth's blood will run on her face, her tears flood,
Her breath bringing great destruction and death.
The outerworld will turn to the East with great arrows of fire,
Steel birds falling dead.
The hidden worlds will tremble before great war,
The good shall flee in the face of the pale son.
The netherworld will stir,
Pushing on their prison walls to feel the breath of life once more.
Where the sea offers a lush jewel with eight fingers,
The Raven daughter will shed her cowl,
When day is as night complete

And the moon swallows the sun whole for the span of a song.
The Raven, born again in blood,
Will walk in peace among all the worlds, divides crossed.
If the Raven is free, all people shall rejoice in triumph and
brotherhood,
If shackles the Raven wears, all will fall to darkness
Until rivers run red and all hearts mourn.

Lei tried to digest the information on the paper for a moment before looking up at Ounathir. "And you think what? That I'm this Raven? Are you all lunatics?"

"If you really look at it, it is all very clear." Melli stood and pointed to the first line on the page. "'When daughters of Earth fly and fall.' Women went up into space the year you were born. 'Earth's blood will run,' is about the volcanic eruptions, 'tears flood' is pretty self-explanatory, there were many floods in 1991. The 'birds falling dead'—many lives were lost in plane crashes, including some very powerful and good men. Our world was at the precipice of war then, a young elf, a 'pale son,' believed he could unite the races through force and many of our people fled into your world. He is still trying to accomplish what he set out to do. You were born in Hawaii, an island nation made up of eight islands, during a total solar eclipse. You were awakened to the existence of the hidden worlds through violence, a rebirth in blood. All the signs point to you."

"All the signs could point to anyone. There is nothing there that couldn't have happened in the decade before my birth or the decades after. You believe it because you want to." Lei shook her head, her braid catching on the edge of the plated plastic on her back. "The real question is why do you want to believe so badly?"

"What you don't understand, dear Leilani," Ounathir stood, her wings fluttering furiously, "is that I don't care if *you* believe any of it is true at all, and it doesn't matter how I really feel about any of it."

From the canopy above them, a single fairy with black wings and black clothes dropped down onto the table, sword drawn. Even as Lei reacted, she could see that none of Ounathir's guards moved, Ounathir herself stood still and very much unafraid. But she couldn't take the chance. Lei grabbed her braid and bent it, revealing the long iron spike within its center. She leapt onto the table, knocking her chair back.

His blade cut into her useless armor, biting into the plastic with a dull "thunk." She stepped back, aware the queen had stepped back from the table now and two guards had come up to hold Drew back, though he struggled with them. For just a moment, she was doubly grateful Blake hadn't come with her. Test or no, he didn't trust her to be able to handle herself and would likely have gotten them both killed for his trouble. Lei might have stepped back, turned her back on Ounathir's test, if the attacker's blade hadn't sliced the flesh just above her left elbow.

With a scream of pain and anger, Lei charged him. They fell together from the table in a tangle of limbs. Her right leg bent oddly as she rolled with the fairy, trying to avoid his blind swings. She was too close to him for the sword to do much damage and with a pang of regret, she drove the iron spike into the soft flesh of his right shoulder. He seized, dropping his sword and clawing at the spike, begging for help. At least, she assumed that was what the sounds spewing from his mouth meant. She did not speak fairy.

Lei pulled herself to standing using the table. "You'll be fine in a few days, with the right care." She yanked her spike out of him and wiped it on her cloak.

Guards swarmed over her, holding her, making her drop her spike.

"You came to this meeting armed?" The queen's voice rang like thunder through the trees.

"Had it been a real attack, I would have saved us all. Tell me, Your Majesty, what would your people do if you were killed during a meeting with a human?" Lei strained against the steel grip of the fairies who held her. "Would they not seek out revenge, pour into our world en masse to right the greatest wrong? You tested me, and right or wrong, I've taken the test. I don't really give a rat's ass if I pass or fail. In fact, you are very lucky I didn't choose Blake for my adviser. You can't disarm him the way you can me. A fairy who doesn't deserve to die would be dead right now and his blood would be on your hands."

Ounathir said nothing for a moment, her eyes hard and cold as she stared at Lei who did not flinch. "Blake Pratt is not welcome in my home. Release them both."

Lei pulled free and limped back to the table, holding her wounded arm against her side. Drew stepped toward her but she waved him off. Regardless of her injuries, she would not appear weak in front of the queen. She would bleed until Ounathir offered assistance. It was the kind of effort a woman like her would appreciate.

"You see, you have proven yourself already. You are wise beyond your young years. You understand the way of war as surely as any daughter of the Raven must."

"This is bullshit, pardon my language. For every part of the *prophecy* you say points to me, it could point to any number of women in any number of years. I won't be used by you. You almost made me kill someone already, I won't let you do it again."

"It doesn't matter. I know all I need to know. Like I said, I don't care if you believe, it doesn't really matter if I believe, deep down in my soul. All that matters is that I can convince the other leaders of the races of the hidden lands to believe it is even possible. If they will believe, we can come together and stop this ridiculous war." She smiled.

Lei shuddered. For all her beauty, the queen was a viper just waiting to strike. "There are always those who don't want peace. Whether they believe or not, it's not a guarantee of anything."

"My people deserve to be free of this war. My daughter and my granddaughter need to come home to me. I will make sure it is all I need." Ounathir smiled again but Lei did not see beauty there this time. This time she was magnificent, fierce, and terrible. Lei believed that queen could well make a shaky belief enough to end a thousand wars.

Chapter Six

Queen Ounathir gestured toward her people as she sat back down. "Please, see to Ms. Scott's injuries."

Lei looked down at her arm, the wicked slice through her purple shirt and the blood seeping through it. It hurt, but she didn't trust the fairy. "I'm sure my own people can deal with it just fine."

"Please. You are bleeding all over my table, a wound you received during my evaluation of you. My people will not harm you or your adviser. I swear it." Her wide, green eyes appraised Lei. "You could almost be the Raven daughter, Leilani. It won't take much to convince the other leaders. And so full of surprises. Tell me, do you have any other spikes tucked into that marvelous hair of yours?"

"There's no sense in lying now, is there? Yes. I do."

"When we meet again, I must ask that you wear your hair loose." A stern warning crept into her otherwise sweet and pleasant voice.

"I figured it was a one time thing." Lei smiled and shrugged her shoulders. It was a trick she'd used before and would again but it worked best with the element of surprise. "If there is a next time we meet, I hope you don't feel the need to leave me unarmed. I'm no threat to you here."

Ounathir shook her head. "I don't believe that's true at all. But, we'll see. Perhaps I'll feel differently then. Now, just so you are fully aware, I intend to plead my case to the other leaders, regardless if you or I believe in the scrolls. They will likely want to meet you."

"No. I won't be used for political gain." Lei stood. "With all due respect, that *prophecy* you showed me is incomplete at best. There was no substance, no meat to it. I think you left a great deal out. Something you don't want either me or the other leaders to see."

"I was told you were very smart." Ounathir beamed at Melli. "I'm very pleased that neither your intelligence nor your bravery were understated to me. You could be a little less mouthy, but you're young yet. And yes, you are right. There is more to that particular section of the scroll, but it is not important for the moment."

"Which is exactly why you'll never convince me that you believe any of it or that I should. If you had any kind of faith in it,

you'd be touting the whole thing and not just this tiny little piece."
Lei inhaled sharply and sat back down as the fairy medic at her side
slathered her wound with some kind of antiseptic that stank of
camphor and tea tree oil.

"I only want what's best for my people." Ounathir stood, her
broad wings trembling. "We have been at war long enough—all of
us. Our people are killing each other for nothing. Our children are
growing up having no idea what it is to live without fear, without
wondering when one of their loved ones will die in battle. That's no
life. That certainly isn't the life we had in mind for our people when
we divided the world. If there is even a sliver of a chance that your
very existence can possibly put an end to it, even for only a day, it is
worth it."

"You keep saying there's a war here. I haven't seen it. All
you've shown me is beauty and tranquility. I've never seen a war
that looked quite so serene." Lei watched as the fairy wrapped her
arm in clean linen before moving on to her leg.

Ounathir stared at her and looked toward the sky a moment.
"You're right. You haven't seen the signs of war here. Should the
battle reach this place, I'll be dead and none of this will matter.
Melli."

"Yes, mother?" Melli leapt to her feet and bowed her head.

"You will take Ms. Scott and her companions to the front line,
to the war palace at Abhagorm before they return to their own land."

"But, my queen, it's too dangerous. Especially looking as she
does. Her disguise was barely enough for the Gray Road. It won't do
for the city." Melli shook her head. "Please, if you have any belief at
all that Lei is the Raven, you can't ask me to take her there. It's too
dangerous."

"I'm not asking. I am telling. But, you are also quite correct."
Ounathir walked quickly to Lei's side and touched her with two
fingers on each shoulder. "Bring me a guard's cloak!"

Lei felt her damaged plastic armor shifting, shrinking and the
shirt beneath it tear. Great wings, black and broad grew out of her
back, not feathered like a bird's wings but smooth and soft like the
wings of a butterfly. She touched her ears and found them elongated
to points. Lei breathed in and smelled the tangy sweet scent of fresh
pine and cedar and was relieved that it wasn't so strong as to make
her ill.

"This glamour will fall away the moment you set foot in your own world, no sooner or later. None exists who can see through it or smell through it. You will ride to the front lines as my emissary. Talk with my warriors, see my people, and then we'll see if you can still tell me there is no war."

Ounathir turned and walked away, followed by most of her complement of guards.

"I think I pissed her off." Lei stood and tested her leg, pleased to find it capable of taking her full weight again. Two of the remaining guards situated the three-part cloak over her head and wings, fastening the side panels under the base of the wings with ties.

"You goaded her," Melli stared at Lei open mouthed. "You just talked around it until she ordered you to do what you wanted to do in the first place."

"Not quite. She wanted me to see, I just gave her the opening she needed. She couldn't just suggest it herself without an opening any more than it would have been appropriate for me to ask to see," Lei shrugged, absurdly delighted by her beautiful wings. If she'd been able to, she'd have taken a picture. "Come on. Let's go get Blake and go visit this war of yours."

Guards handed them their confiscated weaponry and Drew helped Lei to situate the sword properly again. The ride back to the Sidhe was quick and silent, allowing Lei to stew over all that had occurred. Blake was waiting for them, pacing, just outside the door on the Gray Road where the escorts and beasts still stood, seemingly no worse for wear.

"Well? How'd it go?" He nearly jumped on them the moment the door closed behind them.

"She's a very interesting woman. She almost sacrificed one of her guards to test me." Lei shrugged. "I don't trust her as far as I can throw her. She's conniving."

"Please, Leilani, that's my queen, and my mother, you are speaking of!" Melli looked at her with anger and hurt in her eyes.

"I'm sorry, Melli, but I don't really trust you either. Don't get your panties in a twist though, I don't trust Blake or Drew or really anyone. Let's just go see what she wants me to see and be done with it. I don't feel safe here and I want to go home."

"Fine." Melli walked over to their escorts and talked to them for a moment before mounting her beast.

Blake took Lei with him again. She struggled to situate herself between his wings without getting her own tangled up. Lei enjoyed having them but she was glad they weren't a permanent accessory. Too much of a hassle.

"Why aren't you welcome in the queen's palace?" She kept her voice low, for Blake alone.

"I'd really rather not discuss that here."

"Because you can't ride and talk? Come on, I'm just going to bug you about it until you tell me." She felt Blake's shoulders sag as he sighed.

"Fine. Years ago, I must have been sixteen at the time, Drew sent me to stay with Ounathir, so I could learn from the fairies."

"I thought sorcerers and otherworlders were sworn enemies."

"We have a complicated relationship. For most otherworlders, that's true enough. The elves, the werewolves, the trolls, we have no use for them, but the fairies are a different story. For as long as we have history, sorcerers and fairies have had occasion to work together. For the most part, we don't. An exception was made in my case. Ounathir may not like my mother but she respects her, and when my mother told Drew that I would need to learn the ways of all the otherworlders, she offered to participate in that training. I did learn a lot but it didn't end so well."

"Who'd you sleep with?" Lei laughed, not exactly serious or joking.

"Please let this go."

"Oh my God! You did! You banged a fairy? In her home? I bet it wasn't just any fairy, given the look I got for mentioning your name. Please, please, tell me it wasn't Melli."

"It wasn't Melli. It was her sister."

In any other place, Lei would have laughed joyously. She couldn't seem to muster a real laugh on the Gray Road. "You see? That right there is exactly why I have my rules. I don't need any more enemies than I already have."

Blake muttered something Lei couldn't hear and they lapsed into silence.

The Gray Road was just as bleak and lifeless on the ride back. The same gray color leeched into everything until Lei felt herself turning gray too. As if she would become part of the road if she lingered too long on it. She didn't look too closely at the corpses on the side of the road, though she was certain at least some hadn't been there before, they looked as decayed as the others.

Melli stopped suddenly, her beast rearing up. "We'll stop here."

"What's going on?" Blake slowed, stopping their mount several yards away from Melli and the escorts. Drew stayed close to them.

"The queen wants her to see the war first hand. I have decided it's not the front lines she needs to see." Melli pointed a long finger at Blake. "This time you can come so long as you behave yourself. I promise you, it'll be the first time you've ever wished for your little brother's skills."

Lei held Drew's hand as she jumped down off the saddle and followed Melli into the gray trees, watching as she performed the rites to open another doorway. She stepped through the opening, expecting to feel relief from the gray and finding herself in a broken city instead. Gaping holes in stone walls, smoldering and smoking wood, the attack on the city hadn't been so long before. The cloying scent of charred flesh filled the air.

In the distance, on the edge of a far away mountain, Lei could see a great stone fortress. It was cut into the rocky face of the cliffs, four huge turrets looking out over the land. "Is that the war palace?"

"Yes. That is Abhagorm, the most easily defended place in perhaps all of the hidden lands. We have fought many times to keep it ours but we have yet to lose it."

Melli led them onto a cobbled road, little more than a cracked path between ruined homes and businesses. A crowd gathered in what might have once been a beautiful town square. In the center a gallows stood, the ends of the beams still green and wet with sap. Standing on rickety stools, four very young elves stood, ropes around their necks. The crowd threw rocks and insults, cursing them.

"What the hell is going on?" Lei grabbed Melli's shoulder. "Those are children!"

"No, Leilani. Maybe they would have been children in another time. Those are war criminals. They came to this village, begging for assistance, pretending to be lost and helpless. And they raised the gates for an army of elves. It was a long, bloody fight. Many fairies were slaughtered—men, women, and children all. But you don't need to watch our form of justice. That's not why I brought you here."

Melli continued onward, ignoring questions peppered at her left and right from dirty, tired looking fairies, all wanting to know why the queen wasn't doing more. She led them on a solemn procession through the city, the damage growing less the closer to the center they got, but never was it out of sight. Finally, she approached a large stone building with minimal damage to its walls. She opened the door and ushered Lei, Blake, and Drew inside.

"This is why you are here. You explain to them why you won't help us."

Lei swallowed as she surveyed the room. The dying and wounded filled the room, three rows of cots twenty deep and still others lying on the floor. Healers and medics moved between them quickly. Arrow, ax, sword, and spear wounds. Horrible burns, crushed extremities. Nothing Lei had ever seen came close to the horror before her, not outside of a movie theater anyway. It was the smell that made it real. She'd never smelled anything like it and never wanted to again.

When she took her first step down one of the rows, someone grabbed the end of her cloak. He was a young fairy, barely more than a child himself. A ruined white wing hung down from the edge of the bed, red stains blossomed on the blanket pulled over him, the skin on the lower left part of his face bubbled red where fire had touched him.

"Please." His voice crackled with pain and fear.

Lei bent closer to him, kneeling on the ground beside his cot and took his hand in hers. His flesh was cold against hers and Lei realized he was shivering.

"Please. It hurts." Tears flooded his eyes.

"What's your name?" She squeezed his hand lightly.

"P...Pike." He gritted his teeth and moaned. "Please."

She looked up at Melli who merely shook her head. "Let me try and get you something for the pain. I'll be right back, I swear it."

The fairy coughed and turned his face away.

Lei stood and whispered in Melli's ear, "Isn't there anything you can give him for the pain? Don't you have any kind of pain medication?"

"It's so limited we have to restrict it to those who have a chance of surviving." Melli walked away, further down the row, leaving Lei, Blake and Drew standing there.

"Isn't there something either of you can do?" She turned to them with tears in her eyes. "No one should have to die that way. Not anyone."

"I'm sorry, Lei." Blake pulled her to him and held her for a moment. "If we do anything, they will know we aren't one of them and it will be us out there on those gallows."

Lei rushed to catch up to Melli, desperately trying to block out the fairies she passed, their pain, their wounds, their dying pleas. "How long has this war been going on?"

"Too long, more than twenty years now." Melli stopped walking and spoke quietly. "Longer if you count the skirmishes between pretty much everyone and the trolls. The goblins will work with anyone for the right price. We haven't been at peace, not really, in probably six generations."

For a moment, Lei could say nothing. In many ways, the hidden lands reminded her more of Afghanistan or Chad than of any magic realm. "Tell Ounathir that I'll do it. What I can anyway. I want to go home now, Melli."

The pretty fairy smiled. "You are a bleeding heart after all."

"No." Lei shook her head. "You were smart bringing me here, I'll give you that. I'm no bleeding heart, but there is an innocence that all children ought to have and I'm not seeing it here. That makes me sad."

"So, you want to protect for others what was taken from you, is that it?"

"I had a wonderful childhood. Maybe I'm just human enough to see the senselessness of it. Why are you even fighting with each other?"

Melli shrugged. "I don't know that anyone even knows anymore."

When they passed Pike, he was dead. Lei paused long enough to pull the stained blanket up over his face.

"How very human you are, Leilani." Melli led them back out into the city, what was left of it anyway.

In the square, the crowd had dispersed, all but three young women who were tasked with removing the limp, lifeless bodies from the gallows. Leilani didn't stay to watch. She just kept walking, wishing for once that the fairy in front of her would move faster.

When they finally reached the place where Blake tied off his red ribbons, Leilani almost missed it. The ribbons hung limp, frayed and graying, only a small trace of their color left. Their escorts took the gray beasts and rode quickly away, leaving them alone on the Gray Road to pass back into the outer world.

The moment Lei stepped through the entryway, Queen Ounathir's magic dropped away, stripping her of her wings and the points on her ears. The removal of the magic did not, however, repair the tears in her shirt. Which disappointed her as she'd liked that shirt and she didn't have an endless supply of clothes in her bag.

"Do you think what is happening here has something to do with what's been going on in the hidden lands?" Lei asked Melli as they returned to Drew's Jeep.

"I know it's why I left with my daughter. And many others like me." Melli sighed. "I think there are some in the hidden lands who are desperate now. No one wants to lose this war, to lose face that way, and there is no real edge to be had. We can all be equally evil to one another. The only thing that keeps the balance is the Gray Road. If there was a way to open a path that bypassed the Gray Road, can you imagine what human technology would do to us? We would annihilate each other within months."

"I don't know." Blake opened the door for Lei. "Maybe what's happening here is related to what's happening there, but I think maybe it isn't. Maybe it's something altogether different. Or I just haven't figured out how they tie together just yet."

"And do you have evidence to back up what you are saying?" Melli slid into the Jeep beside Lei as Drew started the car. "I know for certain that families are leaving the hidden lands in droves for the relative safety of the outer world—hunters and Justices not withstanding."

"We do have some evidence that we're dealing with something else. But it may be both." Drew started the drive back to his cabin. "There are activity spikes in places humans have long thought were gateways to the Netherworld. To Hell. You've got upheaval in the hidden lands, distraction in the outer world, but nobody is thinking about the Netherworld, no one is watching them."

"The Netherworld is sealed. That was part of the arrangement too. The river way was sealed, made inaccessible to the other worlds." Melli fidgeted in her seat, her fingers dancing nervously on her seat belt.

"What does that mean?" Lei asked.

"Styx. Rasa. Sanzu. It's had many names, most of which have been forgotten. The Gray Road of fog and mist separates the hidden world from your world. The Black River separates the Netherworld from everything else."

"Who lives there? What kind of creatures are we dealing with?"

Drew pulled to a stop in front of his house. "We don't know much but I'll show you everything we've got once we get inside. Give me a moment to check everything. Stay in the car."

Blake turned to look at Lei with a grin. "This won't take us long. Just stay put. There are enough wards and protections on this car that nothing in our world, or any other, could get in."

After both men left the Jeep, shutting the doors behind them, Lei stared out the window, watching them do their search. "Does it ever get old? Being treated like you're incompetent or stupid just because you don't have a dick?"

"You can't look at it that way. Believe it or not, in their case, it's not a dick that you're missing, it's the magic. If you had any ability with magic, you'd be out there checking the magic traps or whatever too," Melli laughed.

"How long have you known them?" Lei watched them out the window, not quite sure what they were doing.

"I've known Drew a very long time. He and my mother were once friends, though I don't know what happened to change that. She and I helped school them both on our ways, our cultures, taught them how to move on the Gray Road without causing suspicion. I've known Blake pretty much since he was born. They're good people, Leilani, but I think you already know that." She reached back and patted Lei's hand. "I know you and Blake didn't get off to a great start, but that's as much his mother's fault as anyone's. He's worth giving a chance. We all are. I don't know you well, but I like what I've seen so far. Regardless of this Raven thing, I think you'll be a valuable ally for us."

"Which 'us' are you referring to?"

"I could blow smoke up your ass, but I won't. I mean for us fairies. The last few years have had very little good to offer for us and now, there's you. There's a chance for us to maybe have peace again somehow because of you."

"Look, I'm not saying I'm not friendly or whatever, but I'm not your ally. I don't know who is right or wrong in your wars—if anyone is. And I don't care. My concern is here, in this world. If I can help stop your war, hey, that's great, but please don't take my desire to see your children have an actual childhood as anything more than that."

For a moment, Melli looked a little crestfallen. "Believe it or not, I do understand what you're saying. I also know you pride yourself on fairness. Maybe to a fault. You want the whole damned world to be fair and righteous."

"Unfortunately for all of us, I'll never get what I want." Lei watched as Blake came back to the car and breathed a sigh of relief when he opened the door and let her out.

**

Once they were safely ensconced in the house, Lei excused herself to take a shower. The fairies had done a good job patching her up but the slash wound on her arm was going to hurt for a while. She let Blake tend it after she'd pulled on a pair of jeans and a tank top. When they were all cleaned up and comfortable, the four of them settled into the chairs around the kitchen table with a pot of coffee and a very large leather bound book.

Drew pushed the book toward Lei. "There isn't very much in the way of good information on who inhabits the Netherworld. Even in the hidden lands, much of that history has been lost. We know it's where the demons live and, if we fall into the most ancient ways of thinking, we have to believe Death exists there. If angels exist, they would certainly be there as well. We just don't know. There may be Nephilim, Rephaim, dragons, asuras, and who knows what else. Creatures that have fallen from our own myths."

"Where do the vampires fit in? Shouldn't they belong to the Netherworld?" Lei turned the pages of the book delicately, afraid to tear the ancient paper and enthralled with the detailed drawings.

"Perhaps but, they didn't exist when the agreements were laid down so long ago. As such, they have none of the protections of the agreement. They have no safe residence in any world and only our world is cursed with them," Drew stated.

"If the demons belong to the Netherworld, then there has to be a way to open a gate between there and here. Demons are nearly the first lesson I learned from Willy. She said they weren't common but they were easier to deal with than a lot of the monsters I'd come up against."

"She was right, for the most part. The kind of demons that usually get summoned here, they aren't the big bad demons." Blake held out his hand for the book and turned several pages without much care at all, handing it back to Lei open to a page on the leaders of the demons. "You'll never see the ones like this here. They can't be summoned; they have to be let out. Like you can't summon a fairy or an elf. The demons you've seen, that people like us have dealt with, they're more like ghosts. They have very limited real power."

"I don't think I'd like to come up against this one here." Lei stared at the picture for a long moment. The hideous creature's long face was cut with crevices so deep it appeared his flesh was melting. His bones stood out beneath his skin, stretching into broad, leathery wings outstretched behind him.

"That would be Asag. The myth says his very presence will cause fish to be boiled alive in all rivers within sight of him."

"What would happen if the ones who are not conjurable found a way here?"

"I don't know. I can't imagine it would be good. The world was chaos before the agreements. Blood spilled had no value. War was never ending. We were too busy protecting ourselves to be able to think, really think, and create. In the many millennia since the divide, humanity has come a long way. If the Black River is opened, if the Gray Road is opened, I think chaos will return and bring destruction with it." Drew took the book from Lei and stood up, carrying it into another room. He returned with a map in his hand.

Drew spread the map out on the table, using their coffee cups to hold the corners down. It was a map of the world with various locations marked and numbered. The numbers went all the way to 253. "When Blake first came to me and started talking, I honestly didn't believe him. I set out to prove him wrong, to show him he was overreacting to very common activity, instead, I proved he could very well be right. So I went back even further, through news reports, weather activities, and the like. I combed through ten years of archives all over the globe. The first few years, the instances are sporadic and inconclusive at best. Three years ago though, that changed."

Blake took over the conversation. "The places marked on the map are all instances of activity, numbered chronologically. We have new hauntings, possessions, appearances of otherworlders, ritualistic killings, sacrifices, and the like. Initially, these instances were all close to or on top of ley lines. Then they moved on to burial mounds and standing stones. We don't know exactly what was done there, why, or who did it."

"The most recent occurrences are different." Lei stared at the map, digging through her memory for things that would tie together Greece, Rome, Ireland, China, the Netherlands, and Mexico. Then Scotland, North Dakota, England, France, and Germany. "There's not a lot on your map here that's really local. That doesn't really jibe with what I'm seeing myself."

"That's because I think what you're noticing is different. Almost like the creatures prone to other locations are all coming here—whether they are running from something or to something I don't know." Blake took a deep breath. "What they all are is scared. You wanted to question them, I know, but I don't think you'd have gotten anything useful anyway."

"You don't know that." Lei glared at him for a moment. More than once he'd taken her chance to get information from monsters and all because he didn't think they'd be able to give her answers? "Who benefits from all of this? If the road is opened up, if the river is opened, who benefits?"

"No one." Drew answered.

"Bullshit." Lei stood and began to pace through the kitchen. "Someone has to benefit. Why else would anyone be doing this? No. We figure out who benefits and we might figure out who's doing it."

"You make it sound so easy." Sarcasm gave Blake's voice an edge.

Lei stuck her tongue out at him and leaned on the counter. "I'm sorry, Blake, this is bigger than me, than any of us. There are two hundred and fifty-three spots on this map that may hold a clue to who's behind this. You need more than a hunter with a handful of years' experience. You need an army."

"There aren't a lot of options. The Justices may well be working with whoever is doing this, the sorcerers don't work well with anyone outside of their own clans, and the hunters don't trust anyone. Who exactly are we going to get?"

"You and Drew are from two separate family clans, right? And your mother surely has ties to a third. And your bride-to-be is in a fourth, and so on through your family. That's half a dozen or so right there, right?"

"Well, yes, but it's not that simple."

"Make it that simple." Lei cut him off and flipped her braid back behind her. "I know a few hunters who are sort of reasonable. We can't always work solitary, you know. As for the Justices, we don't know anything for sure until we have a chat with that vampire in Pittsburgh. That's where I'll start."

"Absolutely not!" Melli shouted, making Lei jump. She'd nearly forgotten the fairy was there at all. "You aren't going anywhere unprotected. Not until there is peace in the hidden lands."

"You've got to be kidding me! I've done just fine all by myself for years. I'm not helpless so quit treating me like I am!"

"This isn't about you, not really. This isn't about me or this stupid plot to make the humans suffer, or whatever it is. You are the key to bringing peace to my home and until you've been recognized as the Raven by all the otherworlders, I will *not* let you just walk into Death's waiting arms. Period. If I have to tie you up and stick you in a tower in the war palace, that's what I'll do."

"Try it." Lei stood, laying her palms flat on the table and glaring at Melli. "I won't go easy and I won't go willingly."

"I'll keep her with me." Blake put his hand on Melli's shoulder, turning her to face him. "You know I won't let anything happen to her. Besides, I want my mother to meet her, see what she can see."

For a moment, it looked like Melli would argue, would try and take Lei with her, but then the fairy's face softened, a light lit in her too green eyes. "That may be a better plan. Even Queen Ounathir recognizes your mother's ability as a seer and she hates admitting any human has talent. If your mother said Leilani was the Raven, all the nations of the hidden lands would believe."

"You've got to be kidding me! Where I go, what I do, it isn't up to you." She looked at Melli. "You and I have different priorities. My first, my only, duty is to this world and the humans in it."

Blake grinned and Lei wheeled on him.

"You're no better. I don't need a babysitter or a protector. I've been all by myself for the last few years and I'm still here, still in one piece. Apparently, I've been able to manage just fine without either of you!"

"Okay. Settle down." Drew laid a hand on Lei's shoulder and she shrugged it off. "Everyone has a point."

"This is such bullshit." Lei sat back down in her chair and crossed her arms over her chest.

"Melli is only thinking of her people, same as you. You'd want the same thing in her position. But, I agree that's not an option." Drew said before Lei could argue with him. "But if going to see Carie, Blake's mother, will appease Melli, and possibly help us gain support from the other clans, I think that's our best plan. As you said, we're going to need all the help we can get."

"Besides, I left my car in Pittsburgh and I kind of need a ride. I promise I'll try not to protect you from anything if that makes you feel any better." Blake looked at Lei, a laugh on his lips and in his eyes. "Consider it a favor. Will you drive me around until we're ready to take on that nest? I'll help you—not because I don't think you can handle yourself but because sometimes it's nice to have backup."

The two sorcerers waited for Lei and Melli to respond.

"I'm amenable to this plan." Melli nodded, though she didn't look too happy.

"Well that's just wonderful." Lei grumbled. "Fine. I'll take you to your mama. Then, if it pleases everyone, I'm going to go see some vampires about a city and try and figure out what the hell is actually going on. That is non-negotiable. End of discussion. I don't really want to see any of you right now so, I'm going to bed."

She stood and stormed down the hall, the sound of the slamming door reverberating through the whole house.

Chapter Seven

Lei did not sleep, pressing her ear to the door of her room, listening to the others as they argued and bickered amongst each other. No way was she just going to do what she was told like her opinion didn't matter. Blake, Melli, and their heavy-handed tactics could all go hell and stay there. When the voices had died away, long after she heard Blake go into the room across the hall, Lei finished packing up her gear. When she could no longer hear Drew or Melli, she pulled on her coat and checked her weapons one last time.

The narrow window in her room was just big enough for her to squeeze through and didn't appear to have any kind of alarm on it. She hadn't seen any sort of system in the house but it was a sorcerer's house. There was bound to be some kind of alert system, some kind of magic she couldn't see. "A risk I'll have to take," she muttered as she opened it and tossed her bag on the ground beneath it.

Silence permeated the air, not a sound came from the house or the woods surrounding it. It was odd not to hear bugs or scurrying critters, but she couldn't wait any longer. She was not going to capitulate because they said so. They treated her like a child, like someone incapable of making her own decisions.

Carefully, Lei climbed out of the window and dropped down the few feet to the ground. Picking up her bag, she ran as quietly as she could for her car. As she rounded the corner, she cursed aloud. Blake was waiting for her, his bag slung over his shoulder and a grin on his face. "Son of a bitch! I don't need a chaperone!"

"Maybe. Maybe not. I need a ride though, remember? I left my ride in Pittsburgh." He held out his hand for the keys. "I'll take the first shift, since you're itching to get on the road so badly."

"I heard you go into your room."

"And I heard you leave yours." He motioned with his hand again for her keys and she sighed as she handed them over.

"You cheated. You used your stupid time bubble thing. I bet you even got some sleep in, didn't you?"

"No. I didn't need to keep it open that long."

Tossing their gear into the back of the car, Lei slid into the passenger seat and fastened her seatbelt with a frustrated growl. As they pulled out of the driveway, Lei stared out the car window and seethed. She still didn't like the arrangement, and, like a petulant child, she pouted and gave Blake the silent treatment. When Blake tried to speak to her, she reached over and turned the music up.

She didn't need a babysitter. What she needed was to find a good library and spend a few days surrounded by books, or at the very least, a few hours on the computer. Lei needed time to study, to prepare. The nest was growing quickly from what she saw, likely put together by a vampire who'd been around a while, maybe a long while. It would make sense for an older vampire to have something big enough to hold over a Justice's head to ensure the Order had no choice but to follow his plan. The sooner she found the answers, the better, but everyone else had other plans.

Lei slid her gaze towards Blake. He conveniently left out a lot of information. His secrets shone in his eyes, in all the words left unsaid. They weren't driving to Kentucky just to get his mama to talk to some people. He could have done that with a phone call.

Given the time to think, to inspect everything that had happened in the last few days, Lei's unease grew. So many things weren't adding up quite right. Ounathir condemning one of her own to test Lei—and it had been a test everyone knew about but her and Drew. The scrolls, the fairies, the hidden lands, all of it packaged up so neat with a pretty Blake-shaped bow.

What if she'd only come to notice Blake and his shadow magic because he allowed her to? What if he, and the other sorcerers, could really stay hidden from her? How could she know for certain who rode in the car with them even now?

Slyly, Lei turned to inspect the back of the Land Rover. Even with the seats strapped to the sides, with her gear and Blake's bag, there wasn't anyplace a person could sit that Lei couldn't reach. She reached into the back for one of the candy bars she kept stashed in the back pocket of the passenger seat. Carefully, she reached back further, feeling only empty air in the only places large enough for a person to sit. Reassured, she grabbed two Payday bars out of her stash and tossed one on Blake's lap.

"Thanks."

"Whatever. Let me know when you get tired of driving."

"I'm good. I'm used to making this drive by myself. I could probably do it with my eyes shut," Blake laughed as he tore open the wrapper.

"Let's not do that, okay? I happen to like this car all in one piece. If you want to do tricks, we should take you back to your own car."

"That's all right, I'll behave myself. Maybe I'll pick it up when we go back through Pittsburgh. I'm not worried about it. What I left behind is perfectly safe."

"You're very sure of yourself, aren't you?" Lei bit into her candy bar.

"I am. But in this case, it's more about being confident in a safe house that's been used by sorcerers for a very long time."

"So all of you know about it then? Aren't you worried about one of them?"

Blake covered his mouth against a laugh. "They won't mess with me. Most sorcerers are afraid of me. Besides, the clans don't hate each other. It's more a rivalry than an adversarial relationship."

"That seems a little weird." Lei shrugged.

"You need to trust people a little more."

"That never works out well for me."

"That's a shame but it doesn't mean you should shut everyone out either." He smiled at her and the pity in his eyes bothered her.

Lei munched on her candy bar and kept happily quiet. They did trade drivers about half way through the night. With the exception of the occasional eighteen-wheeler, they had the roads to themselves. Traffic got heavier when they approached a city, but not too much. Most cars, and people, were tucked away for the night. They kept the music on, only changing the channel when distance added static, but mostly sticking to rock and roll. Once, Lei switched to CD when the only clear station was in the middle of a fire and brimstone preacher's late night talk show.

Just after three AM, they stopped for gas, coffee, and to stretch a little bit. The gas station was small but clean. The woman behind the counter paid more attention to her tabloids than to them. Lei felt a chill run through her. Something was just a little off. She couldn't quite put her finger on it. The shadows were clear. The air wasn't tinged with the cold that often accompanied spirit activity. She hadn't seen any signs of the usual creatures she came up against.

Coffee in one hand, the other wrapped around her gun, Lei made her way back to the car. Blake stared back at the gas station, grim consternation pressing his lips into a thin line.

"Glad to see I'm not the only one feeling it." Lei looked back towards the door and shuddered.

"I don't like it. I don't know what it is; it's not something I recognize. I don't like things that feel unfamiliar."

"Begs the question, would we feel this way if we didn't see the pattern? Are we reading too much into a stillness in the air? Is this just something we're projecting?"

"Valid point. I'll feel better when we're in Kentucky. If nothing else, Mom will know several ways this could all work out."

Lei slid into the passenger seat and waited for Blake to get in. "So she doesn't actually see the future then?"

"Not so much *the* future as many possible futures. That's the funny thing about the future. One choice you wouldn't otherwise have made without some bit of information from her or something to that effect can change everything. And because people are singularly unpredictable, always doing the illogical, the crazy, the outlandish, the future is never really set in stone. A decision you'd make right now might not be the same one you'd make in five minutes."

"I guess, in a way, that's almost comforting. Maybe we still have some kind of say in the way our lives play out. If I believed everything we do is predicted, everything is already planned, then honestly, what would be the point of any of it?" Lei sipped her coffee. "I'd rather believe the things I do, the choices I make, make some kind of difference."

"I can understand that. If everything is set in stone then you might as well wring your hands and join the 'why me' parade."

"That won't get you anywhere," Lei laughed.

"Nope."

"Why does anyone even go to your mom for answers?"

"People want to know what they're facing. Maybe they want to know they have some kind of power over what happens to them, make the decision to go one way or another. Some of them feel helpless, I guess. I don't think that's something you'd understand."

"Oh no. Helpless I understand completely." She touched her belly; the wicked scars there practically burning beneath her fingers.

"I've been helpless and I didn't like it. I refuse to ever be helpless again."

"No one *likes* being helpless." Blake pulled back onto the highway. "Maybe some people don't believe they can do anything about it. Who knows what you would have done if Willy hadn't been there, hadn't wanted to take you under her wing."

"I know exactly what I would have done. I'd have been a hunter anyway. Maybe I wouldn't have lasted long, but I would have tried. I'd already made up my mind before I tracked her down and begged her."

"You mean it wasn't her idea for you to join up with her?" The car swerved just a hair as he turned to look at her.

"She didn't want to do it. Willy told me to move on, live a normal life like nothing ever happened." She laughed bitterly. "I couldn't have done that."

"I always assumed she pulled you in. Most people who come across their first werewolf or vampire, if they survive it, move heaven and earth in their heads and hearts to forget or find alternative explanations. Why didn't you?"

"I guess I'm not wired that way. I can't just forget something I've seen. I can't unknow it. Plus, some part of me wanted revenge. Even though Willy put down the dog that killed my parents, I wanted to kill the rest of them. I wanted them all to suffer the way they made my parents suffer."

"You've come a long way since then."

"I've learned a lot. One sick pup doesn't mean the whole race is bad. Granted, I think the otherworlders have more than their share of bad apples. That doesn't change the fact that a good number of them just want to live their lives, have families, hold jobs, and be productive members of our screwed up society—even if they can't ever be who they really are. I can respect that, maybe even admire it."

A phone rang, the ring tone long, sharp, and barking. "That would be my mom."

Lei shut her mouth as Blake answered the phone.

"Hey, Mama." Blake's smile fell. Lei couldn't hear what the woman was saying but, according to Blake's expression, it wasn't good. "No. I am not dropping her off. I don't care if Whitney is there, you know as well as I do she's not supposed to marry me."

Lei cringed and sank back in the seat, pressing against the door. She really didn't want to be part of a family's ridiculousness.

"Mama, you know I'm right. She belongs with Marcus. I'm not marrying anyone." Blake shook his head and mouthed a silent apology to Lei. "Okay, Mama, how about this: I'm not marrying anyone anytime soon and certainly not someone you choose for me or someone you trick into the agreement."

Lei cringed again and thought about shoving her fingers in her ears and humming loudly. She felt like she was intruding on something very private.

"Look, we'll be there in a little less than two hours. I'm not coming to screw anything up or break up the family. There are bigger things going on." He paused as his mother said something. "No, Mama, this isn't Lei's idea. I imagine she'd like to be just about anywhere but here, thanks. When you meet her, maybe you'll understand."

Blake hung up on his mother and sighed heavily.

Lei put her hand on his arm. "Sometimes family sucks, but it's always better to have them."

"I know. But I'm about to destroy mine."

"You didn't do shit, Blake. It was her choice and made before you were even conceived. Maybe she did it for a good reason, maybe not so much. It doesn't matter, that is not on you. She shouldn't expect you to live the lie she told. Do you want me to drive for a while?"

"No. I just need to turn up the music for a while. I know better than to let her, or anyone, get under my skin." His knuckles tightened on the wheel, growing stark white.

"Hey, relax. It can't be that bad." Lei put her hand on his arm and pulled away as he shocked her. "What the hell was that?"

"Sorry. Sometimes, I don't know, it just gets the better of me. You might want to watch touching me. I just need to calm down before an actual storm hits."

"Say that again?" Lei stared at him.

"Sometimes, if I'm really upset, lightning hits. It's never actually hit me, but it's come pretty damned close and I'd like not to have to deal with that right now." Blake sighed.

"So, what? You can control the weather?" Lei looked cautiously out her window, inspecting the clouds, reminding herself just how little she knew her new partner.

"Not so much. I haven't exactly figured out how to control it. It just sort of," he paused, as if searching for the right word, "responds to me."

He turned up the radio and Lei stayed quiet, alternately watching the sky and Blake's face. She breathed a little easier when Blake relaxed and his knuckles returned to their natural shade. He was pretty okay at calming himself. Lei supposed he had to be. Odds were it was something he'd always had to be able to do. She felt a new, grudging respect for his mother. Baby throws a tantrum; house gets hit by lightning. What fun his childhood must have been for his parents.

As Blake's mood calmed, so did his speed. Which was a good thing as they were beginning to creep into morning traffic. Most people were just beginning their day rather than ending it. Including the cops getting ready to catch their morning speeders.

Lei watched the highway slide by, watching for signs for Mammoth Cave National Park. Blake's enormous family were sorcerers, but they were also farmers and apparently, purveyors of kitsch. They ran a touristy side of the road kind of shop with crystals, geodes, and a random mishmash of antiques, junk and handmade oddities. Normally, exactly the kind of place Lei could lose herself and have fun in. But, she didn't think anything about this trip was going to be fun.

Glancing in the backseat of her car, Lei figured, if all else failed, she could sleep in the backseat like she sometimes did. Of course, first she'd have to tell Blake that she was not staying with his family. In no uncertain terms. She'd been railroaded enough.

Blake pulled off the highway and made his way through the early morning fog to a long driveway that ran past a long, darkened building Lei assumed was the shop. The house at the end of the drive shined like a lighthouse. Several windows flared yellow light, the rays struggling to push back the shadows and be a welcoming beacon. Except maybe for Lei—she felt a lighthouse warning deep her gut.

Before the car stopped, a slim woman with fiery hair who walked like she owned the earth, the sky, and everything in between, flew out of the house. Lei checked her gun and dagger. The woman looked furious and Lei didn't think her anger was reserved solely for her son.

"She looks scarier than she is, I promise." Blake patted Lei's hand reassuringly.

"I shouldn't even be here." Lei opened her car door and took a deep breath before standing up. The woman stopped mid-stride and stared hard at her. Lei had to force her feet not to step back and shut the car door with a solid metallic thunk.

"Mama," Blake moved quickly to stand beside Lei. "This is Leilani Scott. Lei, this is my mother, Carie Pratt."

The woman approached slowly but not cautiously. Her gray-blue eyes raked over Lei, appraising and judging. "You may call me Carie."

"Mama." Blake's voice held a stern warning. "Behave yourself."

"You shut up, young man. You and I have a great deal to discuss when we are alone. For right now, you will go inside and make some tea for Whitney while I say a few things to this *lovely* girl." The anger permeated Carie's voice.

"I don't think so, Mama." Blake stood tall beside Lei, his feet still as stone. "Whatever your problems are, they're with me and you know it. You've always known it. Stop taking it out on other people."

Lei squeezed his arm gently. "Don't worry about me, Blake. I can hold my own, even if you don't believe me. Go on. I'll be fine."

Blake took his bag and headed for the house, giving his mother one last warning glance.

When Carie turned her attention fully back to Lei, the anger and frustration vanished behind her eyes. It was like looking at a different woman, the lines in her brow smoothed, her body relaxed slightly. Something akin to curiosity edged the soft lines around the woman's eyes and mouth now. "May I touch you?"

"Do you have to?" Lei found it impossible not to step back this time.

"I'm not trying to pry, I promise. I only want to see a little bit. Besides, isn't that the very reason Blake was so insistent on bringing you to me? So I can see for myself if you are what he wants you to be?"

94

"So he says, and Melli too. I'm just not very comfortable with the whole idea."

"I can understand that. You've stepped into a situation you are not prepared for." Carie motioned for Lei to walk with her. "Come on. I'm sure your legs would like a bit of a stretch after so much time in that car of yours. Much better suited to the job than Blake's little Honda, but still, a car."

Lei nodded and walked with her, staying just a little out of reach. "For what its worth, I'm sorry about the timing."

"I don't believe you are, not really. You don't believe our family has any bearing on you so why should you care? Besides, you've already judged me. It only seems fair that I get the chance to do the same, doesn't it?" Carie looked at Lei and the anger returned to her wide green eyes. "When Blake first started asking around about you, I tried to see all the roads you could take, how they intersected with my son. I wasn't sure which Leilani Scott would be standing in front of me. Now I know and I'm not pleased. This path is the path I dreaded most. This *situation*, as you think of it, has made Blake defiant."

"I'll bet you don't like that." Lei's hackles rose, a little ember of her own anger festering inside her. "You know what *I* don't like, Mrs. Pratt? I don't like being used. Not by the fairies, not by Blake, and certainly not by you. I won't let you use me to hurt him. See, you don't scare me. You just don't like losing control."

Carie glared at Lei, looking down her nose, eyes narrowed to furious slits. "You don't know me."

"That's right, I don't. But I know your type. You're a manipulator. Being a seer makes it worse. Everyone does what you say because you're a seer. They believe every word you say because of it. No one doubts you or questions you. You aren't going to like me because I won't do anything but." Lei crossed her arms over her chest, knowing she should shut her mouth and completely unable to do so. "Blake and I had a lot of time to talk on the drive to Wyoming and then here. You're pissed at me because he's not playing along with your plan and you think I had something to do with that. You want to blame it on me because it's easy. You don't want to take responsibility for your own lies. I won't let you put that on me."

"I dislike you a great deal, Ms. Scott." Carie walked around the back of the farmhouse and sat on a low bench. "I liked you much better when Willy refused to teach you and you died before my son ever heard your name. Kneel before me."

Lei refused to kneel for her, for anyone. Instead, she sat cross-legged on the ground at Carie's feet. She sat very still as Carie laid her hands on either side of Lei's face and stared into her eyes. For a moment, it was as if the rest of the world fell away and all that existed for Lei was her own reflection in the seer's eyes. Stripped bare of pretense, of attitude, of bravado, she'd never been so naked before.

"You aren't what he so desperately wants you to be," Carie whispered, the hissing voice full of venom.

"I've already told him that. The fairies too, but I've already promised to pretend to believe for them." Lei tried to lean back, pull out of Carie's grip, but the woman dug her rose colored nails into her flesh.

"You are going to play a large role in the months to come. You are edging closer to some answers that will bring you nothing but pain. If you don't do things just right, your future is full of darkness and fire. Every choice you make, every step, will change the future of this whole world. I may not like you, but I love my son, this Earth the way it is, and we are all depending on something you must do."

"What?" Lei asked, a shudder running through her.

"I don't know yet. There are too many paths to give you a true answer. So many futures and all of them muddied by something I cannot see."

"If the whole world is depending on me, then I'm going to need help. I'm going to need your help, the help of all the sorcerers."

"No." Carie shook her head, her red hair shimmering in the light of the rising sun. "This is my family we're talking about. I can't let them follow you."

"This is a whole lot bigger than just your family, you said so yourself." Lei finally pulled away from Carie's hands.

"No. I won't lose everything." A tear slipped down her pale, freckled cheek.

"And if you don't help me? What do those futures show you? Are they futures you can live with?"

Carie reached out and shoved Lei into the dirt. "You fight dirty, just like Willy. It isn't fair."

"No." Lei sat up, trying to maintain her composure. "It isn't. Not much in life is. Was it fair for my parents to be butchered the way they were? What about Whitney? What happens to her when she's matched up with Blake? How does her life work out? And what about Marcus? What happens when she's paired with the one your two families actually bargained for?"

"You don't know anything about the situation!" Carie turned away, covering her face with her hands.

"I know enough to know you won't answer those questions anyway. Not for me, not for him, maybe not for yourself. You just want so desperately to be right that you can't, or won't see anything that might show your own failures." Lei stood up and brushed the dirt from her back and bottom. "Just tell Blake and the fairies what they need to hear, if it comes to that. I really don't give a shit how this affects you."

Carie looked up at her, cheeks damp with tears but her eyes all too clear. "I had to make the choices I did. Don't you dare judge me. I had no choice. Marcus wouldn't have lived long enough to show his true abilities."

"So you created a child who would deflect it all." Lei put her hands up and stepped back, taking a deep breath to calm herself. "No. Never mind. I've said more than I meant to. I've got no part in this whole melodrama."

Carie laughed. The hollow, ragged sound contained no mirth.

"What Blake chooses to do here and now, it's up to him. I'm not staying."

"Where will you stay?"

Lei knew she wasn't asking out of concern for anyone but herself. "Don't worry about it. It won't be here."

Lei walked away quickly. Once she got her keys, she intended to drive a very long way away. Lei wanted no part of the power struggles within any family, let alone one with enough magic to level an entire city. It'd been a long time since she'd had to deal with family but she remembered how messy and cruel it could be. No one could cut you deeper than family.

"Well? What did she say?" Blake practically pounced on her the moment she reached the door.

"You're going to have to discuss that with her. Right now, I want my keys. You and your family have a lot to discuss and I want no part of it." Lei held out her hand for her keys.

"In a minute, okay?" He took her outstretched hand in his, gripping her tightly. "Please, Lei, just play along. Don't leave yet."

"What the hell?" She didn't get the chance to struggle much as he pulled her through the quaint house and into the kitchen.

A very pretty young woman in a dark blue silk robe sat at the table pouring tea into dainty little cups. Her honey blond hair lay on the fabric, shining almost as much as the silk. She looked up as they walked into the room and the calm happiness in her face faded into fear.

"Hello, Whitney." Blake took a small step back, away from the fragile looking woman, barely older than a girl, with a deer in the headlights expression. "I wasn't aware you were here."

Lei knew he was lying but didn't understand why.

"Blake." She looked to Lei with a forced, too bright smile. "I'm Whitney Hallister."

"Lei."

"Is that short for something?" The girl's hand trembled slightly as she lifted her teacup to her mouth.

"Leilani. My mother was Hawaiian."

"That's a beautiful name. Would you like some tea?"

"Thank you, but no. I'm just leaving." She turned to Blake, challenge in her eyes. "I need my keys back. I'm really tired and want to find a place to sleep that isn't here."

"Oh. Yeah." He dug her keys out of his pocket. "Sorry. Thanks for the ride."

"Thanks for driving it. I'll see you later." Lei looked back to Whitney who stared openly at her, but at least her stare contained no trace of malice. "It was nice to meet you."

"You too?" Confusion filled her young, pale face. "Sleep well."

"Thanks." Lei took her keys and practically fled for her car, nearly slamming into Carie on the way out.

"Will you be coming back here?"

"No. I'm going to find a nice, quiet hotel with blackout drapes and no sorcerers. Then maybe I'll be able to get some rest." Lei forced a smile she didn't feel and got in her car, readjusting her seat and mirrors before turning around and speeding back down the driveway.

It wasn't her finest moment, abandoning Blake to his crazy mother but Lei wanted nothing to do with the drama about to unfold at Casa Pratt.

Chapter Eight

Blake closed his eyes against the sound of Lei's car peeling out of the driveway. Whatever his mother said to her, it hadn't sat well with Lei. He'd talk with both of them later, try and smooth it over.

When he opened his eyes again, he realized Whitney was staring at him. She hadn't changed since the last time he saw her. Her hands still trembled when they stood in the same room. She looked at anything and everything, except at him.

He shook his head and got a glass down out of the cupboard, filling it with water from the tap. He leaned against the counter just as his younger brother came into the room.

"Hey, Blake." Marcus grinned, his dimples deepening in his tanned skin. "Who was that woman you drove up with? Your Prelude finally bite it for good or something? Why didn't she stick around?"

"First, the Prelude is fine and will certainly outlive your shitty ass Omni." Blake smiled back, slapping Marcus on the back and noting how much broader his shoulders had gotten in the nearly six months since he'd seen him last. "As for the woman, Leilani is a hunter and she didn't stay because she needs to sleep. Something I plan to do very soon myself."

"Good morning, Whitney." Red blossomed on Marcus's cheek.

Blake turned away to hide his smile. He watched them together for a moment as Whitney poured tea for Marcus. The two of them made a good pair. Both quiet, shy, and nurturing. Blake was many things, not all of them good, but he wasn't cruel. He wouldn't force a girl who was scared to death of him into a marriage neither of them wanted.

He watched quietly as his family filed into the kitchen. They said their hellos and everyone but Blake took their places around the very large table. Everyone was home. His mother had called them all in one way or another, even if no one realized it. Brothers, sisters, nieces, nephews, Whitney and her father, even him, though he'd taken his own time in coming. Even if she refused to admit it, his mother knew the facade needed to end.

As they settled in, they all watched Blake with a wary eye. He wondered if any of them still believed he was a true Pratt. They all knew he was different. For a long time, maybe they could believe it was simply because he was the seventh of a seventh, but Blake figured most of them already suspected the truth of it.

Whitney's father, Carl, was particularly astute, watching his daughter, Blake, and Marcus. Blake figured he'd have to be blind not to suspect. He looked nothing like a real Pratt. Where they were light-haired, freckle-faced cherubs, Blake was dark, broad, and brooding. If Carl ever met Drew face to face, the truth would be out for sure.

Carie came into the room last. She smiled at them all as if there was nothing unusual about them all being in the same place. When she looked at Blake though, her eyes flashed with fear and anger. A warning to him to keep his mouth shut. He'd seen that look before, a million times. And, so far, he'd always done as she asked. He couldn't do it anymore. He and Whitney both deserved better.

For a few moments, the kitchen filled with conversation and noise. It all seemed so very normal, too much so. Children laughing, parents comparing war stories, all smiles and joy, except for Whitney's father, Carl. He had a stern and sad look to him, like he was about to do something he didn't really want to do.

Blake took a deep breath and stepped toward the table. "There's something I'd like to say."

"Can't it wait until after breakfast?" Carie stared hard at him, trying to read his intent and quite unhappy with what she was seeing.

"I don't think it can. It's waited long enough." He turned to Carl and Whitney. "I'm really sorry, this has nothing to do with how much I value the cooperation between our clans or you and your daughter."

At Blake's words, a look of relief washed over Whitney's face. "We do as well, value that connection, but I don't—" But before she could say more, her father gripped her arm, silencing her with a stern look.

Henry's eyes darted from his frowning wife, to the disgruntled Carl, to his stubborn son, and finally to the gawking faces of his extended family. He stood. "Blake, this is a matter that might best be discussed in private." Henry looked to his children and grandchildren. "Carl, Whitney, Marcus, why don't you join us in the living room for a moment."

"Me?" Marcus looked surprised, blushing as he looked to Whitney. "Are you sure?"

"Come on." Henry gestured to the swinging kitchen door.

More than a little confused himself, Blake brought up the rear of the procession, leaving the breakfast clatter and whispered speculation behind. When he entered the living room, his parents were sitting on one couch, Cal and Whitney on another with Marcus perched on the arm of the sofa beside Carie. Blake took the large armchair between them, trying to build up the courage to say what needed to be said. He'd hidden the truth from his dad for as long as he could remember, always afraid he'd look at Blake one day and see nothing but betrayal.

"I appreciate you're having us, especially on such short notice. From the scene that just played out in the kitchen, I think you all know what we've come here to discuss." Carl looked at his daughter who stared into her lap.

"Before you say anything else, Carl, I wish you'd hear me out." Henry smiled. Carie looked as though she might say something but he put a hand on her arm. "Before we rush into anything that might fray the peace between our clans, there is something you need to know. I know what you've come to say and I agree with you that Blake isn't the right son for your daughter. I believe Marcus would suit her, and you, better. I happen to know my youngest son is quite smitten with her."

"Our contract was for the seventh son, not the eighth. Whitney is young and beautiful. There are other clans with suitable mates for her." Carl's soft hands clenched.

Henry raised an eyebrow and sighed. "What I am about to tell you can't leave this room, for the safety of everyone here. When I offer you Marcus, that is what and who I am offering you. My seventh son."

Blake froze in his seat, staring at Henry Pratt like he'd never seen him before. He started to say something but Henry looked at him and shook his head.

"I guess we were deluding ourselves that we could keep this charade forever. From the day he was born, there have been people who wanted to kill him. Hunters, Justices, otherworlders, even some of the clans. The idea of a seventh son descending from my father scared them all. Dad was a powerful man. I understand why they worried. You see, under that kind of threat, Marcus would never have lived to puberty. We did what we had to do to ensure his safety. Unfortunately, that meant bringing a child into the world to be a shield for him."

Tears tracked down Carie's face, but Blake thought they were more out of relief than guilt. "You've seen what Marcus can do, Carl. The world needs more people like him, maybe now more than ever before. But, he is a healer, not a warrior and the world would not have been kind just because his gifts were of no threat to anyone. I'm not sorry I've deceived everyone all this time. I can't be. They believed my seventh son would be more like my father than me, a warrior. So we gave them what they wanted to believe."

Blake noted every time his Dad used the word "we" and knew it was a lie, that he'd never had a choice in the matter. That he was taking responsibility for his wife's actions and declaring them his own.

Carl looked as relieved as Blake felt. "This is the truth? You aren't just saying this?"

"No." Henry smiled at Blake again. "Drew Stanton is his biological father."

Carl looked at Blake for a moment, inspected his face. "That explains his gifts." He looked back to Carie and Henry. "I assure you, I'm not going to judge you for this. In fact, I am overjoyed by this. I didn't want to sever the bonds this marriage would make between our clans, but I didn't want a life of danger and death for my girl and that's all Blake has to offer. No offense, son."

Blake waved him off as if his words didn't matter but it was difficult not to be offended. "I wanted to tell you sooner, I know Whitney was unhappy about the match, but—"

Henry cut him off. "I needed to make sure you would be willing to hear the truth and believe it. I must ask you to keep this to yourself, if you can. Marcus and Whitney will both be safer that way. If anyone questions you, you can tell them a partial truth. Our children are in love. That's rare to our way of life, and it's a magic all its own."

"Of course. I will try and explain the situation to my wife to some degree and we can continue planning for the union of our children." Carl and Whitney both smiled for the first time that morning.

"While you're here," Blake leaned forward and put his arms on his knees, "there's something I need to discuss with you all."

Everyone looked at him, except for Whitney who kept her eyes down.

"I need to get the leaders of the clans together, all of them. We need to have a meeting. There's something really big coming and I need help."

"*You* need help?" Whitney's shy voice surprised him. "I don't think there's any problem big enough for that."

"I wish that were true. I do. I hate asking for help, but I can't do this on my own. I've already recruited some people, but it's still not enough. Someone is trying to open a door to the Netherworld. At least, that's what we think they're doing." Blake reached into his pocket for the map, spread it out on the coffee table, and started explaining his theories to them.

"None of this matters." Carie pushed the map back at Blake when he was finished. "The leaders won't meet. Certainly not here."

"Maybe not all of them." Carl laid a hand on the map and looked closely at it. "I hate to say this, but I agree with Blake. This is too big for any one person, for any ten. But they'll want neutral ground. I think I can get two or three clans. I'm sure Henry can get a few more. And what does Drew think?"

"He's already gone to talk to his clan. Hopefully one of his kin has connections to others, because none of them will give Drew the time of day any more than they will me. And we already have a place to meet. My friend, Lei, she has a place in Texas."

"I don't think she'd like you volunteering her safe place so readily. She struck me as a very private person, one who doesn't like her space invaded." Carie stood and turned her back on them.

"It's already been done. I just haven't exactly found the right way to tell her yet." He smiled. "I know she'll agree to it if it's small, just the leaders."

Carie's shoulders drooped slightly in defeat. "I'll make what calls I can."

"Thanks, Mama." Blake took the map from Carl and folded it up.

"We're done here." Henry stood up, staring after his wife as she left the room. "Blake, I'd like to talk to you for a minute, then you can go on up to bed and get some sleep. You're exhausted."

Blake stood with some trepidation and followed the man he'd always called Dad out of the living room and onto the porch.

"I hoped I'd never have to do that. Tell anyone." Henry leaned up against the railing.

Blake didn't say anything.

"I know you've spent a good bit of your life worrying about when I'd learn the truth, what it would mean. I've known since you were a kid, Blake. It doesn't change anything. Not one bit. You are every bit as much my son as Marcus is."

"Not really, Dad. This won't be able to be kept quiet now. It won't be long before all the clans know."

"Look, it doesn't matter. I don't care what anyone thinks and you never have before either. Don't you dare start now. You listen to me, what I said back there, that was for Carl and your mother. I know what her reasons were and I know she thinks that's all there is to it. I don't. I think she wants to believe she did it all for Marcus. She has a tendency to forget what she wants to, to edit the past as much as she tries to edit the future. The things Marcus can do? They're great, no question. The world does need more truly great healers. But the world needs her warriors too—those protectors who lay it all on the line every single day to make it safer from the rest of us. There's no one I'd trust with that job more than you. Do you understand me?"

Blake nodded. "We're still good then?"

"No matter what. I know Drew is your father. I came to terms with that a long time ago. But, I'm still your dad. I will always be your dad. Maybe I don't say it often, or enough, but I love you. Now, get to bed before I put you to work in the shop."

"Yes, sir." Blake smiled briefly before disappearing into the house. He took his bag and headed for his bedroom. He figured, correctly, that his mother would be there waiting.

Carie sat on his bed, her face in her hands. When she looked up at him, Blake saw she'd been crying. "All this time and he already knew. How did I not know? How did I not feel it?"

"You were never really good at reading your own futures." Blake shrugged, a little surprised at how little her tears mattered. "What's done is done. What did you see when you looked into Lei's future?"

Carie's face contorted slightly, something that unnerved Blake. "I don't want her around you."

"That's not what I'm asking." Blake took a step closer but he couldn't sit beside her, he was still too angry. "You know what I'm asking, what the fairies will be asking."

"I have no intention of answering either of you." Carie wrung her hands. "You need to walk away from this woman, the moment this meeting is over. You won't need her after that."

"Are you kidding me? You're the one who told me to find her, told me to find a way to make her listen to me. You told me there'd be a moment when I could help her so that it mattered, so she would hear me out and that's exactly what happened."

"I thought she would be the frightened and wounded Leilani. Not what she is. She's a vow away from being a Justice! I didn't know she would be quite so horrible. I don't like her and I don't want her around you. As soon as this meeting is over, I'd prefer to never have to see her again. Do not bring her back to my home. Am I understood, Blake?"

"Oh, I understand. But you need to understand a few things too. I have no intention of deserting her now. If I had my way, she'd stick around for the long haul. At least she's not afraid of me." Blake opened the bedroom door. "I need to get some sleep and you need to get a grip. I'm thirty, not three. Who I spend my time with isn't up to you."

Carie stood, moving past him to stand in the doorway. "She's going to get you killed and she won't even care. You don't mean anything to her."

Blake shut the door in his mother's face and collapsed on the bed.

**

Lei wasn't surprised when she woke to pounding on the door of her motel room. She knew it was Blake before she even got close to the door. She pulled a sweatshirt on before she opened the door. "Evening."

"So, my kid brother is getting married, everything is out in the open—sort of—and it looks like the leaders of the clans are going to agree to a meeting so long as it's on neutral ground." Blake came in, his words streaming at a fast clip as he handed her a large coffee and a paper bag. "Compliments of my middle sister."

"Thank you to your sister." She took the bag, opened it, and breathed in greedily. "Yum. Let me guess, you're thinking Willy's place. Unfortunately, there's not a lot of room there. I'm not even sure it qualifies as a proper house."

"The clans are good travelers. Most have campers or tents. They'll make it work."

"So, what? They're like gypsies or something?" Lei pulled a pastry out of the bag and bit into it.

"Please don't ever call us that, okay? Trust me, it's not worth the aggravation."

"So noted." She sipped her coffee and sat down on the edge of the bed with her Danish.

"Drew is planning to meet us there with anyone he can convince to come. I'll need help explaining this and it's not likely the clans will agree to meet with you."

"Because I'm not one of you or because of Willy?"

"Both." Blake shrugged. "There's a lot of bad blood between the Clans and the Justices. A long history of hurts on both sides. Nothing you or I can say will change their minds."

"And how about your mind? Are you convinced now that I'm just me? Nothing special. None of this Raven bullshit?" She opened the bag again and pulled out a chocolate drizzled croissant.

"Right now, I wouldn't put too much stock in anything my mother says where you're concerned." Blake looked away, a shadow of hurt in his eyes. "I'm assuming she told you that you aren't the Raven."

"I already knew that. It doesn't matter. Even Ounathir doesn't really believe I am, she just thinks she can make a valid enough case to maybe bring about a treaty for a while. That can't be a bad thing."

"I don't think I'm wrong."

"What the hell? You want some kind of apocalypse hanging over us? Are you kidding?"

Blake leaned against the door, looking up at the ceiling. "Maybe I do."

Lei shook her head and took another bite of her pastry. "These are really delicious, by the way."

"Glad you like them. My sister makes them." Blake stood there for a moment, watching her eat with gusto. "So, what's the verdict? Can we meet at Willy's?"

"You've already told them to anyway. Technically, the place is mine now. All legal and everything." Lei shrugged. "So long as they don't mind parking their campers and pitching their tents in an empty pasture with no utilities, I guess that's fine on one condition. When it's all over, you help me with the nest in Pittsburgh. I'm telling you, that nest is part of this, one way or another."

"I don't disagree with you but we've got to run with it while we've got cooperation from the clans. It won't last long. When we're done, I swear, we'll go to Pittsburgh. I'll let Dad know to tell the rest and we can get on the road tonight."

"Yay. Great. More driving." She grumbled into her coffee.

"It's for a good cause, remember that."

"Just go get ready. I'll be there to pick you up in about an hour."

"Awesome." He grinned and quickly let himself out of her motel room.

The moment she realized what she'd done, she cursed at herself. She'd just partnered up again without even stopping to think. He had access to some vehicle of his own here—otherwise how'd he get to the motel—and she just offered to drive with him, like partners. Lei preferred to work alone. She didn't care to be told what to do, or have her safe house offered up for a meeting. It was all happening too fast, too easily. In her experience, nothing came together so easily without something bad happening.

In the back of her mind, she wondered if it could all be a setup. Maybe someone wanted to get the leaders of the sorcerers together to take them out. And everyone would blame it on her if it went south.

Lei finished the pastries Blake had brought and took her time packing and loading the car. She wouldn't have another moment to herself in who knew how long. Once she picked up Blake, she would officially be someone's partner, whether they talked about it or not.

Driving back to Blake's family's home, she kept mulling over the idea of a setup. Lei trusted her instincts and something felt odd about the whole situation. Too many things could go wrong. She couldn't shake the feeling. It irked her that her first gut response was to talk to Blake about it. Lei didn't need to get Blake's opinion on her own instincts, and yet, she really wanted to. As soon as the meeting was over, she had to get away from him. Period. She couldn't afford to depend on anyone. The moment she did, they'd just be ripped away and she'd be alone again anyway.

When she pulled up to Blake's house, she wasn't surprised to see so many people clustered around a small camper, loading it. The guy had an enormous family—which kind of went hand in hand with the whole seventh son bit. There were some girls in there too. Lei's body clenched in commiseration. She'd never given birth, didn't seem likely to ever have the pleasure, but she couldn't imagine doing it nine times. Her craziness aside, Blake's mother looked pretty damned good for it too.

Blake and his father met her as she got out of the car. "Thank you for allowing us to use your property for our meeting."

"Well, Blake had already offered it. It would have been a pretty bitchy thing to do to put the kibosh on it just because it wasn't my idea. Are you following me or do you need directions?"

"Directions will probably be better. We still have several things to do and a few more people to contact." Blake's dad extended his hand to her. "I'm Henry, by the way."

"Nice to meet you, Henry." Lei shook his hand and quickly pulled away.

Henry and Blake laughed. "I can't do the same kind of things my wife can do. Touching me doesn't open up any kind of connection between us."

"Good to know." Lei looked to Blake. "You ready to go or what?"

"Yeah. Give me just a minute." Blake walked away leaving Lei alone with Henry who was staring at her and smiling.

"I understand you and my wife didn't really hit it off yesterday." Henry smiled, the lines beside his blue eyes extending out towards his ashy blond hair.

"That would be an understatement. I haven't had a lot of experience with seers, but I guess your wife isn't quite what I was expecting."

"I imagine she feels the same about you." Henry laughed; it was a deep, rich sound. "She's protective of Blake, much more so than she'd have anyone believe. You might not believe me, given what you likely know of the situation, and don't ever tell any of the kids this, but Blake is her favorite."

Lei almost laughed.

"Carie can't get a good look at your future, or his when you're part of it and that scares her. She's always said our boy has only one weakness."

"Only one?" Lei crossed her arms over her chest.

"His heart." Henry paused for a moment as if waiting for Lei to say something, but she didn't. "Anyway, it was nice meeting you and thanks for letting us use your place."

"Don't mention it." Lei got back in her car and shoved Henry's words far out of her mind. She situated herself in the driver's seat and waited for Blake. She watched him in the mirror as he said something to Henry and moved quickly, with long strides, to the car. He tossed his duffel bag in the back and slid into the passenger seat.

"Ready to go?" She started the car and waited for him to fasten his seat belt.

The drive began in near silence; a low murmur of music accompanied the miles. Lei kept one eye on the road behind them, just to be sure. She didn't see anything, but that didn't reassure her.

"If you keep looking behind us, you're going to miss something in front of us." Blake chided.

"Sorry. I just can't shake the feeling that there's something off. Something isn't right."

"Don't worry so much. My mom says we'll be fine so, it's very unlikely something will happen now. I know it's got to be hard for you to trust us, to trust her. You've got no real experience with sorcerers beyond what Willy taught you and my mother's poor behavior yesterday. I swear to you, Lei, if there were any threat looming, my mom would see it and she *would* tell us. I know you trust your own gut, I don't blame you, and we'll try to prepare for that when we reach Willy's, but you need to trust us, trust me."

"It's going to be hard for me to do that. There was a time, before I knew better, that I could trust anyone, and routinely did. I can't say I'll ever have that kind of blind faith again. Right now, I don't have a whole lot of choices and it irks me. You got in my way over and over, screwed me up and made my job difficult. But, when it mattered, you were right there and willing to help me instead of being your usual assy self."

"Excuse me? I am never assy." He glanced at her, trying to hold in his smile. "Almost never."

"And you also have a selective memory. How about when I had that wraith cornered and you stepped in with your fancy shmancy Latin and sent her away? I wanted to question her. I might even have learned something if you'd just kept out of it."

"You can't just question a wraith. There's no way to make her stay and talk."

"Shows what you know," Lei laughed. "I have a box that will in fact hold a spirit indefinitely, certainly until they're willing to talk to me."

"There's no such thing."

"There is. If you behave yourself, maybe I'll show it to you. In any case, I didn't actually need your assistance on that one, but no, you had to step in and send my prisoner packing. You did it again and again and then asked me to trust you."

"Okay, maybe I overstepped a little."

"Maybe? You absolutely did! You also assume I can't possibly know anything about what I'm doing and that's bull. Maybe I haven't been at this as long as you, but I've had good teachers. I was thrown into the thick of it without anyone to count on. I think I've done pretty damned good considering that A: I'm still alive and B: the only scars *I* have, I got during the attack that killed my parents, before I knew anything."

"Maybe I've just been in bigger fights than you," Blake grumbled as he touched a finger to the scar beneath his eye.

"Doesn't matter. Not really. You owe me more respect. If, and that's still a hell of a big if, I decide to work with you, I'm not working *for* you. I will only do it if we have a partnership, a real one. I won't be treated like anything less than equal. Period. Am I clear?" She pressed her foot down on the gas pedal. "No more of this you making decisions for me bullshit. I deserve better than that."

Beside her, Blake grew very quiet for a few minutes. "I'm sorry. For what it's worth—if it's worth anything—I really am sorry. I haven't worked with anyone in a long time, especially not someone who can actually hold her own. Not since Drew cut me loose about fifteen years ago."

"Fifteen? You aren't that old."

"I've worked alone, more or less, since I turned fifteen. A kid can get places, get information that an adult can't."

"It must have been hard on you."

"I preferred it, to be honest."

Lei flipped the turn signal on. "I'm getting coffee. You want to drive for a while?"

"I can do that. I could probably use a soda or something too."

They stopped long enough to stretch and get something to drink. When they got back on the highway, Blake drove. They talked just to keep the boredom at bay, mostly sticking to safe topics. Not that either one had a lot of time for television or movies or friends.

Though she continued to watch, Lei didn't see anything out of the ordinary through the entire drive to Texas. As they neared her property, she took a little more care in watching the road and the horizon.

From a distance, everything seemed untouched. Lei paid her bills electronically, kept her pantry stocked with non-perishables and canned foods, and her neighbors kept an eye on the place. The ranchers next door were very good people. She remembered the peach pie Margo had brought when Willy died, the lack of pity but depth of understanding in the old woman's eyes.

The house itself wasn't much, a small ranch house with one bedroom, a kitchen, a living room, and a tiny bathroom. It never really felt like home, but it was the safest place Lei knew. Symbols designed to keep bad things out or alert her to the presence of others covered the walls. They were all Willy's doing, but they still worked. One little kanji in the corner of the living room would be getting quite the workout. It would be glowing a mad red for a few days with so many sorcerers in such close proximity.

"We'll set the clans up in the pasture over there." Lei pointed to the grass behind the barn. It was the only area that had both a good, working fence and enough clear space. "I've got to check my perimeters."

"Give me a minute and I'll go with you."

"You don't even trust me to protect my own place?" Her fists clenched in frustration.

"Lei," Blake leaned over the console and took her face in his hands. "It has nothing to do with trust or doubting your ability. I thought maybe I could add a layer of my own to what you've got."

112

"Oh." She pulled away from his touch. "Fine. I'm going to check the house really quickly, then we'll see if the quads are working."

"Quads?"

"I love this car partly because it will go anywhere I need it to, but the perimeter of this property has some pretty rough terrain and I'd really rather not twist an axle or rip out the drive train, okay?" She smiled and got out of the car.

She took her bag with her into the house. Everything was exactly as she'd left it, minus the accumulation of a month's worth of dust anyway. She liked that. It was a comfort knowing that no one had been in her space while she was gone. Lei set her bag on the floor beside her bed and stripped out of her clothes. She pulled clean jeans and a sweatshirt from the dresser and put them on.

After sliding her feet into her work boots, she strapped on her holster, shoved a dagger in her belt and made her way into the kitchen to make coffee. At least her property was only sixty acres, not several hundred like the neighboring ranches. They could do the perimeter check in an hour.

Pulling the bright blue tarps off the quads, they looked good. The tanks were mostly full and only one required a jump to get it running. She let them idle for a few minutes while she waited for Blake to join her. "How long do you think we'll have before the clans start coming?"

"I imagine it'll be about a day or so. It'll give us plenty of time to get things ready."

"Maybe. Now, so long as your spells or whatever will respond to me, since this is my place, you can add whatever you think is best." Lei straddled one quad and motioned for Blake to take the other. "You do know how to ride, right? Or do you need a lesson?"

He grimaced but got on. "It's been a long time but I've ridden one of these before."

"Good. Just don't crash it into the barn, okay?"

Lei laughed and took off with a lurch towards the road and the boundaries of her property. The wind rushing around her, through her hair, felt good. For all too short a moment, she felt free.

As they traveled the narrow, worn path around the property, they checked Lei's wards and added to them with Blake's magic. Alarms for various creatures. Defenses against both sorcerers and

Justices. Things that would keep innocent humans from venturing into things they didn't need to know about.

"You know," Blake stared at a symbol carved into a large tree at the corner of the property, "for someone who is so distrustful of people who can wield magic, you certainly depend on a lot of it."

"There's a difference between carving or painting some symbols and being able to bend time, don't you think? What I use isn't the same thing. Anyone could use these symbols if they wanted or do a simple exorcism if they had the right book. You don't need books or spells, you just think things and make them so."

"I've been known to use a spell or two, but I get what you're saying." He went to work knitting his magic together with her symbols so they worked together, both alarm and protection.

No single piece of property in all of North America was so well defended at that moment. The only point of entry was the gravel driveway and that would be guarded at all times—mostly by Lei and Blake. Sharing that particular responsibility was an easy decision. Lei didn't trust the sorcerers but she didn't really have anyone she could call for help either and she couldn't do everything herself. She would take the day shift and leave the nights to Blake.

By the time they got back to the house, it was late in the afternoon and they were both exhausted. Lei sent Blake into the house to get some rest so he could take over the night shift. He'd offered to do his little time bending trick, but Lei refused. She needed to stay awake for a few more hours if she wanted to have any hope of changing her body clock over without feeling like shit for it.

Lei was standing on her front porch when she spotted someone on horseback headed towards her gate. She didn't need to see the face of the woman, she knew immediately it was Margo, her neighbor. Lei walked down to meet her at the gate, where she was already tying her horse.

"It's been so long!" Margo pulled her into a hug. Lei didn't fight her. Margo was harmless and sweet, if a bit too touchy feely for Lei's taste. In some ways, Margo reminded Lei of her mother. "I saw you pull up and I just knew you wouldn't have anything in that pantry of yours worth eating."

Lei smiled as Margo pulled her backpack off and handed it to her. "You really didn't have to do that, Margo."

"Tosh. Every time I see you, you've gotten even skinnier. You need to stick around for a while sometime and let me fatten you up."

"The way you cook, I wish I could. Unfortunately, that's just not possible right now. Work has been keeping me awfully busy."

"I know, sugar. You're just as bad as dear old Grace ever was."

Lei smiled. Margo had been the only person Willy had allowed to call her Grace. "I know. Would you do me a favor? Do you think you and Dan could go visit Lisa for a few days?" Lisa was their grown daughter who lived about an hour away.

"Well shoot. Are you expecting trouble then? What is it? Vampires, werewolves, ghosties?"

"Excuse me?" Shock nearly had her dropping the backpack.

"Oh now, we're simple folks maybe, but we've seen a thing or two over the years. Of course, Grace did her best to protect us too, even helped teach us what to do if something showed up when she wasn't around."

"You're kidding me." Lei felt a warmth in her heart. Her mentor wasn't such a curmudgeon after all, taking even her neighbors under her wing.

"We don't talk about it much, never have. Honestly, most of us do our best not to think about it."

"Us? Who all is 'us'?" Lei couldn't imagine Willy explaining anything more than absolutely necessary to just anyone.

"Just about every adult in this area really," Margo shrugged and patted her horse.

Lei thought about that a moment. There was a lot the woman hadn't explained, after all. "How did Willy come to live here, Margo?"

"About thirty years or so ago, we were having a bit of a problem. People were dying all over the place and others just weren't themselves anymore. Well, this young woman shows up. Smooth talker Grace was, when she had a mind to be. Turned out, our sleepy little farm town had become a haven for vampires. She cleared out the town and, in exchange, we gifted her the land and house. She always promised she'd leave us another warrior when her time came. And she did."

"I should have known." Lei laughed. "Keep your eyes open for a few days. I'm having some guests, but they shouldn't cause you any problems. I'm hosting a bit of a family reunion you could say."

"Oh dear." Margo looked at Lei's face for a moment. "They ain't the ones you're worried about though. You think something may come along after them, is that it?"

"Maybe. Hopefully not. I'm probably just being paranoid."

"A good dose of paranoia has kept you breathing a time or two, I bet."

Lei nodded. "At least. Still, I'm probably worried about nothing. But, just in case I'm not, I'm going to be setting some traps."

"Well, good luck, dear. You need anything at all, you let me know. Be sure you come by for dinner before you leave again. Let me get a real meal in that belly of yours. I promise I'll make you a peach pie."

"Nothing better than your peach pie. I'll be by, Margo." Lei smiled as Margo got back up on her horse, tipped her hat, and headed back for her own home just up the road.

Lei put two of the sandwiches and one of the sodas in the otherwise empty refrigerator and took a sandwich and a Coke back out onto the porch. Settled in with dinner, she watched the road with a wary eye, looking for the dust cloud that usually preceded any vehicle headed down it.

Chapter Nine

Feeling rested and ready, Lei left her house the next morning to take over for Blake. Two campers and pickup truck sat in the field beside a bright blue tent. She stared at the field for a moment, picking apart the defenses in her head. Even with the protection of Willy's and Blake's wards, there were weaknesses. Too many vulnerabilities. After the rest of the sorcerers arrived, she'd figure something out.

Blake waited for her by the gate, exhaustion lining his face. "You all set for today?"

"I'll be fine." Lei waved her thermos and her book at him. "I'm just going to sit here and enjoy the sunlight while all these crazy people fill up my land."

"I promise, most of us aren't all that crazy."

"Guess it's just you, then." She laughed. "Go on. Get some rest."

"Fine. I'm going to bunk in my parents' camper if you need me. I don't want to put you out any more than I already have."

"Appreciate it. Rest well." Lei watched him go and settled in to watch the gate and the road that led to it.

Several more clan leaders arrived and Lei directed them to the pasture where the others were busy setting up. As she directed a blue truck from Colorado, she noticed Carie walking towards her and tried to ignore the woman. Prepared for the worst, Lei said nothing.

Carie sat down on the dry grass beside Lei's chair, staring at one blade with particular fascination. "I wanted to thank you for letting us use your land."

"Did Blake make you come up here?"

"No. Henry did. He also wants me to apologize for the things I said to you back at the house and I have no intention of doing so." Carie sat up a little straighter but still wouldn't look Lei in the eye.

"I wouldn't have believed you if you had." Lei cracked open the seal on a bottle of water and drank. "I've been around long enough to know how it works. I'm not one of yours, you have no loyalty to me and I don't expect you to. If it comes down to it, you'll sacrifice me to save your own and never think twice."

"I'm so glad you understand. I wish you would explain that to my son—that you are not one of us. You don't even like us."

Lei shook her head. "You might be able to see the future but that doesn't mean you can see into a person, to know them. And you don't know me, Carie. Neither does your son. Not really."

"I know enough. You think you have him wrapped around your little finger, that he'll turn his back on his culture for you."

"Look, lady, even if I did feel that way, which I don't, Blake is your son, not your subject. You don't get to decide his life for him. I'm pretty sure he's had enough of that since he was born."

"No, you look. I've spent my life trying to protect my family. Whatever choices I made were to protect everything that matters. The choices we make in life, they matter. They change the way the future unfolds. How much are you willing to risk? Every choice you make has repercussions and I don't think you're woman enough to do what needs done."

"I guess we'll find out."

"Just remember, you had your chance to walk away and you chose not to." Carie's voice turned shrill and loud.

Lei stood up and walked away from Carie without another word, going to an arriving camper to direct them to the pasture. When she turned around, Carie was gone. She breathed a sigh of relief as she settled back into her chair and opened up her book, flipping the dog-eared pages until she found her current stopping place. It'd been a long time since she'd read *Something Wicked This Way Comes* and it never failed to enthrall her.

Just before eight, Blake appeared with two plates full of food. He handed her one and sat down on the grass beside her, setting his plate on his legs before digging two cans of soda from his jacket pockets.

"I've seen your pantry. I thought you might like something not marketed to little kids."

"Thanks." Lei grinned and picked up her hamburger. "You ready for the night shift?"

"Just about. I imagine it'll be pretty quiet."

"Try not to fall asleep," Lei laughed.

"I doubt that will be a problem. I'll probably have company off and on most of the night. Beyond their curiosity about this meeting, they're finding out about the change in plans with Whitney. Lots of conjecture going on. But, all of my parents seem to want to keep the truth buried. So, I guess I'm still a shield after all."

"I'm sorry, Blake. That can't be easy."

"It's not easy for any of us. I hope you can remember that when you deal with my mother. She's under a lot of stress right now and she doesn't react well to stress. I know she's hard to put up with."

"Don't sweat it." Lei finished eating and sat with him a little longer. She enjoyed having someone to talk to. Maybe she'd have to consider opening her life up, just a little. Not with Blake, but with someone.

"You should go on and get some sleep. You look pretty good when you've actually slept well."

Lei rolled her eyes. "Too bad I can't say the same for you."

Blake helped her to stand, stepping too close and leaning in closer still to whisper in her ear. "If you ever change your mind about that whole 'no touching' thing, all you have to do is say the word."

"You'd better step back before I do break that rule of mine and smack you solidly into last Thursday." She stood her ground. "Besides, you just want me because your mama says you can't have me."

Blake's smile faltered and he finally stepped back. "That was pretty low, Leilani."

"And maybe a little more true than I thought. I was mostly joking about that part." A flash of regret pushed away an apology that fluttered on her tongue. "I'm going to get some sleep. Have a good night."

She slid into bed, but sleep didn't want to come. Her brain filled up with everything that could go wrong. If she was really lucky, the last of the leaders would arrive overnight and the clans could get down to business and leave. It wasn't good for them to be all gathered together. Someone was sure to notice soon. The longer they stayed, the more danger they were all in.

The most vulnerable moments wouldn't be during the meeting itself but when the sorcerers all left her property on the deserted back road highway. It was the most likely point of attack. She'd have to see what could be done to mitigate the risk.

Lei fell into sleep dreaming up ways to get everyone away without getting anyone killed.

***

The next morning, Drew stood with Blake at the gate. Lei adjusted her light day pack on her shoulders. There would be no book today. She planned to close the gate completely, leave the sorcerers inside their safe bubble, and see if she could find a good exit strategy.

Drew eyed her, taking in her camouflaged attire and the pack on her back. "I don't think so, Leilani."

"Tough. My place, my plan. Nobody is stupid enough to attack the meeting directly, but I'm going to take a look around, set a few traps, and see if maybe I can't figure out a way to get everyone on the road safely. The best odds are we'll get hit as they leave."

"Why?" Drew stroked his chin as if in deep thought.

"Because it's exactly what I would do if I were looking to cause as much damage as possible with the least amount of risk to myself. They'll attack when we're distracted, at the moment of the most confusion."

Drew nodded. "I think I might have underestimated you."

"You owe me that beer sometime soon, Drew." Blake grinned like the Cheshire cat.

Lei whirled on him. "Exactly what were you betting on? Whether or not I can do my job? If I'd see the weakest point? What are you? Twelve? You think I'm that fucking stupid? Who's going to double-dog dare me to go out and take a look around for myself? No takers? Well, there aren't any frozen flagpoles around for me to stick my tongue to, so I guess it'll just have to do, right?" She stood with one hand on her hip and the other wagging an accusatory finger at both men. "Why the hell would either of you condescend to work with me if you think I'm so utterly stupid?"

Both men laughed. "Calm down, Lei. It's all in good humor."

"Bullshit. It's not funny, it's offensive."

"She is a firecracker, isn't she, Blake?"

Lei was stunned into silence for a moment at his audacity.

"Look, I'm sorry. I really didn't mean to offend you. I just don't know you yet. I still haven't really seen what you're capable of. Besides, I've got a little back up of my own."

"Who?" She asked Drew.

"You met Melli already. She brought a few fairies with her and a couple of elf friends of mine are keeping guard on the roads from here to the highway and then a few miles in each direction." Drew smiled a little more warmly. "I like that you're taking the initiative. I can respect that."

"Back up or not, no one knows this road, or the surrounding properties like I do. I know where to look and what to look for. I'm still locking you all in and doing what I need to do."

"Suit yourself." Drew continued to smile. "If we're lucky, this will all be over today."

Lei shrugged and readjusted her light pack. "You should get to that meeting of yours. The sooner everyone is safely on their way, the happier this firecracker will be."

"Be careful." Drew walked off towards the gathering of vehicles and tents.

"If you need any help out there, let me know." Blake looked back over his shoulder at the makeshift village. "If I didn't need to be there, I'd go with you."

"Don't you worry about me. You just get all those clan leaders to help watch the possible gates to the Netherworld. That's your only job, pretty boy."

Blake grinned. "So you do think I'm attractive."

"And a brat, too. I'll be back by sundown."

"If you aren't, I'm going to come find you." Blake's eyes lost their sparkle for a moment and he looked like he wanted to say more, but instead turned on his heel and walked after Drew.

Lei rolled her eyes and stepped over the property line, sprinkling a mixture of salt, holy water, the ash of an oak tree, and ground holly berries, sage, and hawthorn across the entrance. She said a few words in a long dead language and trusted her other barriers to reach across the divide and strengthen there. Just because she had no magic of her own didn't mean she couldn't use the magic inherent in the world around her.

For a few moments she stayed on the road, well in view of any of Drew's so-called backups. She didn't necessarily want to drop in unannounced on any of them, plus they needed to see that not everyone involved trusted them. It might keep them on their toes a bit. The fae weren't really who she was concerned about. The Justices had been to Willy's before. There were at least two who knew some of the more roundabout, secret ways to get in and out of the house without having to pass through the barriers. She completely destroyed one tunnel shortly after Willy's death. But she'd left one—her quick exit if she ever needed it. Well, so long as she wasn't trying to escape the Justices anyway.

Lei veered off the road, heading towards Margo and Dan's ranch. They didn't know about the passage, but they never had a problem with Lei exploring a little bit on their land. Plus, she needed to check in with them. Now that everything was in place, she didn't want them to wander too close.

Margo stood on the porch looking in the direction of Lei's. From there, Lei knew she could see the tent city the sorcerers had built. The older woman didn't really look too happy about the situation. "Honey, I think those people are taking advantage of you."

"That's all right, Margo. It's only for tonight, maybe tomorrow, then they'll all be on their way again." Lei sat on Margo's front step. "Sorry to come haunting your porch. I just needed some time away from them. They make an awful lot of noise, you know?"

"I can imagine. But you're not coming by to sit and chat dressed like that," Margo laughed. "Honey, you go on and do whatever it is you need to do. You just make sure you come see me before you run off again."

"I will, Margo. I promise." Lei stood up again and headed through the high grass and low mesquite.

It took her three hours to set the traps. If anyone broke her barrier on the real entrance, she would know it. If anyone went into either of the false entrances, they would be trapped there. She scouted for a while, finding Melli's hiding place and two other fae as well.

Near noon, a motorcycle approached Lei's gate and she took off running. She had her right hand on her gun and her left on her dagger. She recognized the man on the bike and felt no relief. Taj was a Justice she didn't know much about except that he'd worked with Willy for a time.

"What are you doing here?" Lei stepped into view and the Justice turned towards her.

He pulled off his helmet and got off the bike. He was coffee black, tall, muscular, and intimidating but, when he smiled, Lei could almost forget he was a threat. "The Order sent me. You can't gather all this power together without *someone* noticing."

"Really? Seems to me there are other powers gathering that the Justices haven't noticed yet." She thought of Blake's marked maps.

"Not all the Justices. Some of us have even gone to the head of the Order with it, wondering why we're just twiddling our thumbs."

"Then why aren't you doing anything about it?"

"I don't know," he shrugged. "I volunteered for this mission, Ms. Scott. I knew Willy pretty well, considered her my mentor for a time. She would never have brought someone here, let alone give them the place, unless she really trusted them. Unless she had faith in their ability."

"And if she really trusted the Justices, don't you think she would have made me her apprentice officially? Taken me to the Council for testing, had me swear the oaths and perform the rites to be one of you? I think maybe I'm not the only one who sees there is something wrong in your Order."

He didn't make any move toward her, instead lifted his hands to show her that he was unarmed. Lei didn't let that lull her into feeling safe. Every Justice had a few tricks up their sleeves; Taj was no different.

"How did you get all of them," he nodded toward the tent city, "together? They've never done this, not in all the years we've been watching them."

"It's just a wedding. I offered them a safe place to celebrate," she lied smoothly.

"Celebrate?"

"Tying two of their clans together seems cause enough for celebration to me, don't you think?"

"You trust them?"

"I don't trust anyone. Not them. Not you." Lei shrugged. "Just goes with the job, I guess. You'd think we'd all be able to work together, given our common goals, but no. Everyone has to get all territorial and shit. It's ridiculous."

"You know the Order's mission. How can we work with the sorcerers and the otherworlders when it's those freaks we're trying to rid the world of? You aren't seeing the big picture."

"Big picture my ass. Some of the people you kill aren't hurting anyone, in fact, they go out of their way not to. But you don't care. It's your way or no way and screw the Earth if something comes along that's too big for any one of us to handle without help." She took a deep breath to calm herself. "I've said my piece and I'd like you to leave now. I've got this covered. I won't let anyone hurt them while they are under my protection. And that includes the Justices."

"But all the leaders are together! Don't you see how easily we could dismantle their movement right now?" Taj stepped toward her.

"Their movement? They aren't a club or an organization. They're a race of people. You're talking about exterminating people." Lei stepped back. "Not now. Not here. Go about your business somewhere else, Taj, before I lose my patience. I won't put up with any shit today. Got me?"

"You're as bad as they are."

Lei shifted and aimed her gun at him. "I don't care what you think of me. I honestly don't want to hurt you, but I will do what I have to do to keep my promise to the clans back there."

"You wouldn't dare shoot me." His eyes narrowed, focused on the barrel of her gun.

"You don't know me. I'm not Willy. Are you willing to take that chance?" Lei held her ground. "I might not shoot to kill you, but I will wound you badly enough that you'll have no choice but to do as I've asked."

"This isn't over, Ms. Scott. Not by a long shot. When I get back, I won't be alone."

"And I'm warning you, I don't want to see anyone near this property for seventy-two hours. Not a soul. Leave now, Taj, or I will shoot you."

Taj shook his head, his glare trying to set her on fire, but he got back on his motorcycle and sped back the way he'd come.

"Damn." Lei watched him leave, not taking her eyes off him until he disappeared from view. She didn't need seventy-two hours and the Justices wouldn't give them to her anyway. Hopefully, she wouldn't need more than two. Once the meeting was done, she was getting every last sorcerer the hell out of Texas—as quickly and quietly as possible.

Another hour passed quietly. A little too quietly. Lei didn't trust the Justices not to pull something. And she was more than a little concerned that she'd seen no sign of the otherworlders beyond the fairies and elves Drew brought with him. It didn't sit right. Something would come; she had no doubt of that. She only hoped they would be able to handle it.

When she reentered her own gate, Blake was waiting for her and she could see the tent city behind him dismantling. "You and Drew get through to them all?"

"Most of them, not all. Enough. We've divided up the major historical 'gate' points, at least in this country. Two of the clans are going overseas to try and get help there. I think, once the ball gets rolling and things start happening, the rest will jump in." Blake leaned on the fence, looking out into the pasture. "The real question is, how do we get everyone out of here?"

"Quickly and carefully. And soon. I had one run in with a Justice already and I don't think they're going to stay away long."

"Agreed. I've told them to drive up this way as soon as they're packed up. You'll have to drop your little barrier here to let them out."

Lei nodded. She pulled an acetylene torch from her pack and lit it. Holding it to the ground, the flame ignited the oil she'd poured there. Thin veins of orange fire shot into the air between her and Blake and disappeared. "You should be all set now. I'm going to head up the road a bit and provide cover."

"Not alone you're not."

"And who's going to make sure everyone gets moving?"

"Drew can do that." Blake waved his arm and brought Drew running toward them. "If we stand together, Lei, they have a better chance. And so do we."

"Fine. I hope you're ready. There's no telling what we'll come up against."

"Kiss for luck?"

Lei laughed. "I don't think we need such drastic measures yet, okay? But points for trying."

They hurried down the road just past the drive to Margo and Dan's house. Lei hoped the old woman had listened to her and at least was holed up inside where she might be safe.

The first of the cars followed right behind them, fleeing as quickly as they could from the gathering. Lei counted, each car that passed bringing some measure of relief. The moment the fifth car passed out of sight, they heard a large explosion and spotted four distant motorcycles headed their direction.

"Justices coming up quick!" Lei yelled across the road at Drew while she tried to figure out the best way to get rid of them.

Suddenly from the tall grass, three heavily armed fairies sprang, bows pulled taut, sending flaming arrows toward the motorcycles. Two of the arrows missed, but not by much. The third arrow struck the wheel of the third motorcycle, catching the rider off balance and tumbling him to the ground.

Blake whooped like he was having fun and sent a spell flying in the direction of the oncoming Justices. Another car pulled up behind Lei and some sorcerers got out to help. Lei turned to see a large black cloud in the east, moving quickly toward them.

"Get back in the car!" Lei screamed as she raced toward them, trying to put herself between the oncoming thing and the sorcerers.

The cloud shifted as if on the wind and circled them, moving faster than any wind Lei had ever seen with her own eyes. As it neared, the cloud took on a shape—a head and long arms with wispy fingers. Those who fought turned away from each other and towards the oncoming mass. Lei shot at it, Blake and the other sorcerers chanted at it, the Justices flailed their great, magicked swords, and the fairies shot at it with their arrows, both flaming and not. Still the cloud-form came, shrieking like a tornado bending metal.

"Let's keep this son of a bitch busy! Send the cars through— we'll do our best to keep its attention!" Lei yelled to Blake, expecting him to direct traffic. He didn't, but the sorcerers got the idea on their own and began running down the shoulder of the road past them.

The cloud-form swooped down, surrounding Taj, whose screams were just barely audible over the creature's own noise. She rushed toward Taj, grabbing up his fallen sword and hacking at the mass of air and dust, listening to his screams. In her peripheral vision, Lei saw Margo and Dan on their horses, galloping toward them. Lei tried to scream, to warn them away, but it was too late. The thing had her.

Pain like nothing she'd ever felt before, pain that made the werewolf's claws seem dull and harmless, bore into her as the cloud-form surrounded her, formed a piece of itself to a hard, sharp blade that cut and stabbed. Lei lashed out with Taj's sword but every time the blade came down, the form shifted, became like cold vapor once more only to solidify somewhere else. She fell to her knees inside it, weak and losing blood.

***

Blake raced toward the creature that enveloped Leilani. Behind him, he heard the man on horseback speaking in Sumerian. The cloud-form shrieked and reared back, releasing Lei and the black Justice. Lei was bleeding but still whole, the same could not be said for the Justice who was little more than a mass of exposed tissue.

The farmer and his wife continued speaking the words that seemed to keep the beast at bay and even looked to be shrinking it.

Blake swept in and gathered Lei in his arms and started running. "Drew! You've got to help me!"

He nearly fell at his mentor's feet. Lei was pale and losing too much blood, but she was still breathing.

"She needs more than you can do here." Melli appeared at his side, fear in her eyes. "Let me take her. My people might have the best chance of saving her."

"There's not enough time."

"Trust me." Melli dropped her glamour and fluttered her great wings. Margo shrieked to see such splendor. Melli's four soldier friends reached them and did the same. "Take her. We don't have much time."

"I'm going with you." Blake stood as the soldiers took Lei from him.

"No. You'll get in the way." Melli lifted up and flew toward the mesquite, her soldiers behind her. They moved almost too quickly to watch.

"I know where they're going," Drew put his hand on Blake's shoulder. "I'll go. I'll keep an eye on her. You have work here to do."

Blake stared down at his hands and shirt, stained red with her blood and said nothing as Drew ran to Lei's quad and took off after the fairies.

A motorcycle pulled up next to him, a bloodied Justice sitting on it. "What was that thing?"

"I was hoping you'd know." Slowly, Blake stood. "You should probably ask the farmers. They seemed to know how to handle it."

"I did ask them. The old man said Willy gave him a book a long time ago, made him learn to say the words. He doesn't know anything except the one Willy marked as 'For Demons' worked. My name is Ron. I've never seen anything like that before. Whatever that was, it wasn't from us. I hope you believe that. We're not looking to start a war."

Blake laughed bitterly. "Of course you are, you wouldn't have been here otherwise. Now that the leaders are gone, you can afford to be magnanimous. Whatever that was, it was sent here by someone who is going to bring far worse to this world. If I knew who was behind it, they'd be dead right now."

"I've got to report back to my superiors, explain what happened to Taj. For what it's worth, I hope she's all right."

Blake said nothing as the Justices rode slowly away. He looked back towards Lei's home. The sorcerers were all gone except one lone camper—the one belonging to his parents. A whirlwind of emotions spun through him at the thought of his mother and he started running for the house.

She stood at the bottom step as if nothing happened, even having the audacity to smile. Blake clenched his fists and felt the rage bubbling up inside him, sparking in the air. "Nothing bad will happen, you said. We'll all be safe there, you said."

"And we all are. Our people got away just fine. Barely a scratch, if you don't count the Jacobsen's truck anyway. They'll need a new one." She sat down on the porch swing and pulled a stray piece of grass from her skirt.

"You didn't tell me Lei would be in danger, that she might die."

"She isn't one of us, Blake." Carie's voice grew cold and stern. "She is not the Raven you were hoping for. That woman is nothing but trouble."

"Mother, did you see her dying here today?" The air around him grew agitated.

"In several paths, yes she did. She's got more guts than skill." She said it as if it meant nothing.

"You deliberately withheld that information."

"Of course I did. This meeting had to happen, you said so yourself. Because of her, it was able to without fatality."

"There's what's left of a Justice back there that says different. And there's a good chance Lei will join him."

Carie shrugged as if it didn't matter.

"Leave. Now." Blake looked to the clouds gathering above him. "I want you as far from me as you can be. Better move quickly, it looks like it's going to storm."

Carie eyed the sky warily, a smudge of fear darkening her eyes. "You don't mean that. You won't push me out of your life for that…that…nobody!"

"I can't believe you! You don't care about anyone but yourself. God forbid you open your eyes and actually look at the world outside our people. This is on your head and I won't forget it. Not now, not ever!" Blake clenched his fists, trying to calm himself, trying to leash his anger. "I don't want to see you, hear from you, or feel you poking at me for a very long time."

"She's not what you want her to be Blake. I can't change that. I did what was best for us all. You can't let her destroy this family!"

"Leilani did nothing to this family, do you understand me? You've done it all by yourself. I don't care if you *can* see the future, you don't know everything. You don't know me and you sure as hell don't know Leilani."

"Neither do you." Carie backed steadily away from him. "All you know is what you want her to be."

"Wrong, Mom. She's brave, smart, and pretty good on her feet. She's not afraid to stand up to you, to me, to the Justices that scare even you. I don't care if she is or isn't the Raven. Lei's got more honor in her little finger than most people do in their whole soul. I think that's why Willy brought her in and I think that's why you don't like her. You're awfully small in comparison. Sure, you can see things, but what else?"

"How dare you talk to me like this?" Carie stood, anger pouring off her in hot waves.

"How dare I? How dare you! How dare you convince me that this damn meeting wouldn't get anyone hurt."

"It didn't get anyone important hurt." Lightning struck the ground a few feet away from Carie, the scent of ozone filling the air. She didn't wait for the next one to come, turning on her heel and running for the camper where Henry sat waiting, the engine idling.

The moment the camper left Lei's property, the sky opened up and rain pelted him. It washed Lei's blood from his hands, sending tiny red rivers into the thirsty ground. He sat down in the dirt that was slowly becoming mud and let the rain wash his storm away.

Chapter Ten

Blake sat on the sofa in Lei's empty house trying not to give up. He clung to the hope that Lei was still fighting, believed he'd know if she wasn't. Almost twenty-four hours of pacing, worrying, and trying to explain himself to concerned neighbors had gotten him nowhere.

Lei's neighbors didn't trust him and he didn't blame them. Lei didn't trust him either, not really. He promised himself that, if, no *when*, the fairies fixed her up, he would do whatever it took to prove to her that he was worthy of her trust.

He retreated to her home hoping to find some comfort being near her things but there wasn't much of Lei in her own house. Plenty of her mentor, but nothing that spoke to the woman Lei was beyond the light lingering scent of her jasmine soap.

There were no pictures from her life before becoming a hunter, only a handful of worn paperbacks ranging from science fiction to historical romance and a stack of DVDs. The other books that filled the shelves to overflowing were hunters' books, old tattered grimoires and texts, journals full of notes written mostly by Justices. Willy's journals, Willy's mentor Travis's journals, and a new one that was Lei's. He toyed with reading it but it was a line he couldn't bring himself to cross. She wouldn't want him digging through her life. If he crossed that line, it was like admitting Lei wouldn't be back to yell at him.

He opened a can of ravioli and began eating it straight from the can. A shrill whistle filled the little house. Blake scanned the many runes and symbols on the walls and leapt up from the couch when he realized the one that was flickering was designed for fairies. He opened the door before Melli even thought of knocking.

"How is she?" Blake searched the fairy's face, seeing nothing more than fatigue.

"She's alive, but she's not well. She regained consciousness for about half a minute this morning." Melli stepped past Blake into Lei's home and dropped her petite frame onto the worn chintz sofa. "I wish I had better news for you."

"Are you kidding? She's alive! There's still a chance she can pull through right?" Blake sat down beside her.

"Honestly, I'm not sure. I guess I expected her to respond better to our healers. If she does though, there will be peace in the hidden lands." Melli smiled weakly. "All of the leaders have been to see her. Understand I'm getting my information from one of the Queen's guard so I can't promise it's entirely accurate. They have agreed that, if she survives this demon's attack, she must surely be the Raven. I'm inclined to believe it myself. Hell, even my mother said as much and this time she wasn't just hedging her bets!"

"Leilani would tell you that's a fool thing to do. She'd tell you she's no one special."

"Well, we both know she's wrong about that even if she's not the Raven. She tried to save a Justice. No one does that." Melli leaned back and kicked her feet up onto the scarred coffee table.

"Apparently, she does. And now she's paying for it. I just hope it's not with her life. I'm staying here until I know for sure she'll make it but I've got to do my part. I've sent everyone off to some legendary location of a Hell gate, I've got to do the same. Now, I guess I'll have to do it on my own." Blake sighed. "I can't just not go because I'm worried about Lei. I dragged everyone into this."

"Maybe you won't have to do it yourself." A sly look flashed in Melli's green eyes.

"Are *you* going to help me? I've already sent everyone away to do their own part and I need Drew to stay with Lei. I don't want her to be left there alone."

"Well, if she makes it, we should know in a day or two."

Blake stood up. "So what? Those wounds will take months to come back from."

"Good thing she has you then." Melli looked up at him, the gleam in her green eyes grew stronger. "I know you like to keep your hand close to the vest. I know you like to keep some of your abilities hidden but not all of them have gone unnoticed."

"I have no idea what you're talking about." He forced his voice to stay firm and level.

Melli rolled her eyes. "Your little time shift trick. How long can you make it last and can you take multiple people into the shift with you?"

"Look, I think you've got the wrong sorcerer here." Blake looked deep into Melli's eyes, trying to call up some kind of spell that would stop the conversation. "No one should play with time. It wouldn't be safe."

Melli leaned close to Blake, her voice an angry hiss. "You listen to me, Blake Pratt. I know perfectly well what you are capable of and I'm not the only one who is. This idea comes straight from Ounathir so don't you sit there and pretend you have no clue what I'm talking about. We're talking about saving a woman who could bring peace to my home. I won't let your needs get in the way of that. I don't care if it kills you if it saves her."

"It would serve me right. It's my fault she's hurt." Blake looked away and bowed his head. "I supposed I could make it last indefinitely if I had to and, as long as I'm touching the person, I should be able to bring them into the bubble too."

Fear filled him for a moment. That kind of power, that abuse of it, really could kill him. Worse, it could fry his abilities completely and leave him a worthless shell, no more than human.

When he spoke again, his voice trembled. "You believe she's going to pull through or you wouldn't be talking to me about this."

Melli nodded. "Not everyone does. And even if she does, she won't be ready to fight when you need her to be. If my people can get her stable, will you do it? Will you bring me and Drew as well?"

Blake looked at her for a long moment. He'd never heard a fairy beg before, not for anything. Even the one time he'd had to kill one, there had been no begging. "What can you do that Drew or I can't?"

"For all you know about Lei, there's more that you don't." Melli turned her head away from him. "She's a woman, Blake, one with a great amount of pride. She's much more likely to accept help from me than you for some things."

"I guess you have a point there. We'll be eating a lot of cold things and there won't be coffee often. Every second is a minute, every minute an hour. If we make coffee, it'll take the machine several hours in our time to make it. It's not easy to adjust to. Things are very different when you're inside the bubble."

"We'll make it work. It'll be worth it. Unless you want to head off into the apocalypse without back up." Melli stood and walked over to Blake, taking her hands in his. "If we can get her well in a matter of days, for most people anyway, the leaders will see it as a miracle and there will be peace, Lei will be able to help you, *and* you'll have the entirety of the hidden lands to help you fight whatever it turns out to be."

"You need to get your stories straight. First, you're only bringing me information from a guard, then you say Queen Ounathir sent you here, to make this deal with me?" He pulled his hands free and took her face, forcing her to look at him. "Whose idea was this? And don't you dare lie. I'll be able to tell if you do."

She had the decency to look ashamed of herself. "Mine. I'm just trying to do what's best for everyone, don't you see?"

"You don't have the authority to promise me help from anyone." Blake closed his eyes and sighed.

"Maybe not, but you'll see, they will do anything once they've officially decided she's the Raven. There will be peace again if you help me. If she stays there much longer, the leaders will only see a weak, frail girl. The girl sleeping in that bed in the hidden lands couldn't possibly be the Raven. We have to try. Please, Blake."

"How will you get her here?"

"I'll make something up. I'll steal her. I'll figure it out." Melli put her hands over Blake's. "Please. I'll do whatever I have to do, just tell me you'll do this."

"I need a few days to prepare and stock up. We're talking a few months for us and everything has to be pretty well ready to eat. I'll go into town and do it. I'm just telling you it won't be easy." Blake swallowed hard. He'd be weak while they were in the bubble, unable to do much of anything but keep the bubble open.

Melli stepped back. "You won't regret this Blake. We're going to manufacture our very own miracle and you'll get an army and my homeland will get peace. At least for a year or two."

"Do what you have to do. I'll get things ready." Blake escorted her to the door and watched as she fled.

With a sigh, he picked up Lei's keys and locked up her house. At least the Land Rover was big enough that he might be able to stock up enough for a long while. On the upside, nothing would spoil so he could buy plenty of cold cuts, cheese and bread. There wouldn't be much cooking. It'd take hours just to cook up a few steaks—not that it wouldn't be worth it every now and again, just not often.

He took off down the road, headed for the nearest super market.

***

Three days later, in the dark hours of early morning, the little rune whistled again. He'd managed to get the house stocked and a tent set up outside for him and Drew to sleep in. He didn't want to crowd Lei.

Blake met them on the porch and tried to cover his surprise at how terrible Lei looked. Lei's skin was so pale, so stark white, she nearly glowed beneath the thick bandages and heavy cloak.

"I think I have everything you should need." He spoke to Melli so he wouldn't have to look at Lei. "Gauze, witch hazel, tea tree oil, anti-bacterial cream, mint, rosemary, bay. It's all categorized on the table beside the bed. Take a look before we do this. I can make another run out if there is anything I forgot."

Melli took Blake's arm, drawing him away from the door so Drew could take Lei inside. "I'm sure you've done fine. You've probably thought of things I hadn't. I'll double check to make you feel better, but I'd just as soon get started if we can. Every minute we can extend can only be helpful."

"Get her situated in her room. I need to get myself ready. I've never made a bubble this big or for this long before."

"But you *can* do it, right?" Fear edged out the bravado in the fairy's voice.

"In theory, yes. Just…give me a minute, okay?"

"Of course. Whatever you need." Melli bowed her head slightly and went into the house.

Blake sat on the porch and looked up at the sky. So many stars. Out in farm country, so far from the light pollution of the cities, there were thousands more stars visible, an endless canvas of freckles. It was humbling in a way, made a man feel small and insignificant. He breathed in deeply, hoping he could manage to be slightly less insignificant for a little while.

Drew stepped out onto the porch behind him. "How are you holding up?"

"I don't know. If you want the truth, I'm not so good. I don't know that I'll be able to do this." Blake put his head in his hands.

"You don't know because you've never tried. The worst that can happen is that we'll come back to regular time before she's recovered. She's strong. She will recover. We just need to help her along a little bit." He sat down next to Blake. "I don't think this is entirely about Leilani. I think you've had a few days to really brood. You're shook up and I get that, but I think you're shook up over the wrong things. You've always known your mom was a manipulator. Hell, you should be grateful she is, otherwise, you wouldn't be here at all."

"I know that. I do. But still. She should have told me. I should have known she was holding back, wording things just right so I wouldn't question her. So no one would question her. Like she's always done." He tunneled his fingers through his hair and stood, frustration rolling off him. "I dragged Lei into this because of her. I didn't give Lei a choice. It's my fault she's hurt. If she dies, it's on my head."

"No. If she dies, it's on the head of the demon that attacked her and whoever sent it. Leilani knew the dangers. Her eyes were wide open going in and you know it. Hell, she'd probably be pissed to hear you talk about her like this." Drew held up his hands as Blake turned toward him with violence in his eyes. "I'm not saying you don't have a right to your anger, you do. I'm just saying what happens to Lei isn't on you so, knock it off."

"Was it worth it? What was done here, did any of it matter?" Blake shook his head. "What if everything we did was for nothing?"

"How can we know anything yet? The clans are mobilized now. We'll start checking in with them when we come out of the bubble, but they should be getting into place even as we're sitting here. But we have to believe what we did here mattered. If nothing else, the Justices may have had their eyes opened and that can't be a bad thing."

"I don't know about that. They put out an order to actually allow a vampire nest in Pittsburgh to grow. I wouldn't count on the Justices being any help, at least not officially."

"Damn. I didn't think about that."

The door behind them opened and Melli stepped out onto the porch. "We're ready as we're ever going to be, if you are."

"I guess we'll see if I can do this." Blake stood and wiped his sweat-dampened hands on his jeans. "You all need to be touching me when we do this, flesh to flesh."

They walked into the bedroom and circled around Lei's bed. Blake pulled his shirt off to give Drew and Melli enough room to grab a hold of him. Gently, he rolled up the thin fabric of Lei's nightgown and found her shoulders unencumbered by bandages. He laid his hands on her skin and closed his eyes. "Hold on tight."

Drew put both of his hands around Blake's left bicep and Melli, not wanting to take any chances, wrapped her bare arms around his waist.

Slowly, carefully, Blake began his chant. The ancient words filled the room, wrapped them in their embrace and, as he finished, dissipated.

They looked around for a moment, no one moving, only the sound of Lei's breathing filling the room. "Did it work?" Melli asked as she let him go.

"Probably." Blake rolled his aching shoulders. "We'll go watch the clock out in the living room for a minute. If the second hand isn't moving, then we're all in the bubble."

Melli ran for the living room and a moment later she shrieked, "It worked! It worked! I can't believe it!"

"Guess I'm good for something after all." Blake released Lei and sat down in the chair beside the bed. "She doesn't look good, Drew. Has she been awake at all?"

"For a few minutes here and there. Long enough for me to tell her I was taking her home. At least she won't be surprised to be here when she wakes up next. Maybe she'll heal quicker here, in her own space."

"Maybe." He leaned back in the chair, his eyes closing.

"Are you comfortable here or do you want to go lay down on the couch?"

"I'm not moving from this spot for a while. A couple of hours probably."

Blake heard Drew leave the room but nothing after that for a long time.

***

When Blake woke, Lei was staring at him, deep smudges under her eyes told of her pain and exhaustion. "Next time I want my good luck kiss." He moved from the chair to the edge of her bed and took her hand in his, ignoring the deep throbbing in his skull.

"No touching." She tried to pull her hand away but Blake held tight.

"I don't think so. You're just going to have to put up with me being close for a while. We've got to get you better. There are still monsters to fight."

"The war will be over before I'm back on my feet." Her voice was scratchy and low.

"For every minute, an hour, Lei. I think we'll be in plenty of time to help." He smiled at her, reaching out a finger to move a stray strand of hair on her face.

Worry furrowed her brow and he rejoiced in it. If she didn't care, she wouldn't worry.

"Everything will be fine." He brought a cup of water with a straw close to her lips and let her sip. "You need to rest."

Lei shook her head. "I need to ask you something and I need to tell you the absolute truth."

"Of course." So long as it was something he could give her the truth about.

"Why me? What made you decide I was the one you were looking for?"

Startled, Blake nearly let her hand go. It wasn't a question he expected, but it was one he could give her the whole truth about. "I was on a job, working a werewolf pack. I had their head bitch on a leash. So she begs me to let her go, tells me she has information I could use. That her son was killed by a Justice while he was trying to turn someone very important to the kings and queens of the hidden lands. I didn't believe her at first, but she gave me enough details to find you, to research you for myself.

"After that, I went to my mother. She sent me to you, told me how to approach you. It's my fault for trusting her."

Lei shook her head, grimacing at the pain. "All of the leaders came to see me when I was recovering. They thought I was more dead than I was, that I couldn't hear them or that I wouldn't remember. One stood over me and told his friend that he'd once ordered me brought into the fold, turned into a werewolf like them so they could control me, just in case. I think they've killed or turned a lot of women born in Hawaii during the '91 eclipse. Even if I don't believe all that crap, they do."

"I wish that surprised me. There's a good reason people like you exist, working on keeping the otherworlders out of this world. Doesn't matter. Your tenacity will surprise the hell out of them."

"Maybe. Maybe not." Lei's eyes closed and Blake squeezed her hand. "Sorry. You could have handed them any one of the women from there, from then, and you'd be getting the same reaction. They all want peace; they just need an excuse. I'm handy."

"Except maybe for the wolves."

"Even them for long enough to rebuild." She closed her eyes tight. "I hurt Blake, like death was inside me. Like there's nothing left of me in here."

"I know different. Me, Drew, and Melli, we're going to fix you right up and then we're going to show these bastards what we can do. I don't give a shit about the scrolls at this point. You and I, we can do this regardless."

"As long as we're on the same page." Lei's eyes closed, pain furrowing her brow and reducing her to whimpers.

"We'll talk more when you're feeling better." Blake pulled the blanket up to her chin and pressed his lips to her forehead. "Just taking your temperature. A thermometer won't work in the time bubble."

She didn't even try to push him away or scold him. Blake watched her for a moment, rubbing his aching neck, before leaving the bedroom.

***

Day by day, within the bubble, Lei grew stronger. Melli tended to her wounds, helped her with things she wouldn't allow Blake or Drew to do. But, as Lei grew stronger, Blake grew weaker. The magic spent keeping the bubble going drained him. He fought it hard, not letting anyone see, but he slept more than he should have needed to, eating mostly protein to try and combat the terrible loss of energy.

Inside the tent he'd set up, Blake surrounded himself with things meant to energize him and soothe the sharp pounding in his head that refused to go away. Almost two days had passed in the real world, where time was moving. Inside, it had been nearly four months. Lei's wounds were nothing more than scars; her strength had returned.

Drew unzipped the flap of the tent and scowled at Blake. "How bad is it? And don't lie to me, son."

Blake started to say something, started to get up off the air mattress he'd set up, and couldn't do either.

"Drop the bubble now. Before it kills you, damn it!" Drew grabbed Blake and pulled him up over his shoulder in fireman's carry. "You're an idiot, boy. You should never have let yourself get so weak."

Blake grunted, or tried to, and his stomach clenched and rolled.

"What the hell?" Lei rushed towards them as Drew brought Blake into the house. "Put him in my bed."

Drew laid him down as gently as he could and Lei sat down beside him. "What did you do?"

Blake reached up and brushed his fingers over one of the scars on her shoulder.

"You drop the bubble right now, do you hear me? It's killing you!" She took his hand in hers.

The fear in her eyes was quite real, tears gathering in their corners. Elated, Blake whispered the words that would release them all and sunk into unconsciousness.

***

The scents of coffee and cooking beef filled the little house as Lei worked on dinner. She glanced back toward her bedroom where Blake was still sleeping. She wouldn't be in her kitchen at all if not for him. Stabbing a fork into one of the steaks, she flipped it and smiled as it sizzled in the pan.

Suddenly, she felt eyes on her. Melli was in the hidden lands, attending a peace party and Drew was working on his car out front. She turned slowly to see Blake standing in the doorway to her bedroom. He looked better than he had, but not quite himself yet. "How are you feeling?"

"Like I've slept for days."

"You have." She wiped her hands on the towel slung over her shoulder and stepped towards him. Lei felt his forehead with the inside of her wrist and was relieved to find his fever gone.

"How many days?"

"Two. I guess you slept a whole day for each one you had the bubble open. You shouldn't have done that. You could have killed yourself."

Blake smiled and put his arm around her, pulling her close. "Had to. Couldn't let it be my fault."

Lei wriggled and pushed but Blake held tight. "So it's okay for it to be my fault that you go and kill yourself? That's just stupid."

"Fighting won't change anything. Not on this and not on us. I won't hurt you, but I'll challenge you. This spark, I know you feel it, same as me. So, when you're ready, you just let me know. I'm not going anywhere."

"Just because I've become accustomed to your obnoxious presence in my life doesn't mean this is anything more than a business relationship." She looked away. "I'm not worried about you hurting me. Everyone I've ever really loved is dead. It nearly destroyed me. I can't put myself in that position again."

He let her go. "That's a very lonely existence, Lei."

"Being alone doesn't make one lonely. I have no heart to give you; it's dead. I can be your friend. I can work with you. Please, don't ask me for more." She stepped away, back to the stove to check the steaks. "Sit down. These are almost ready. Hopefully, you'll be ready to work in another day or two cause we've got a lot to do."

He said nothing more to her as he shuffled over to the table and dropped his large frame into one of her sturdy but small chairs. The dark smudges under his eyes were still there but much lighter than they were. A little bit of gray had crept into his beard and at his temples, making him look a bit older than his thirty years.

"I went back to the hidden lands while you were sleeping." Lei stirred a little more butter into the mashed potatoes. "They had a ridiculous ceremony that no one but the leaders could attend anyway, since I'm human and everything."

"So, the war is over there?"

"All official like and everything. Melli is there now, at a celebration of some kind with her kid. She'll be back before we're ready to go."

Lei set the table for three, not expecting Melli to arrive back in time, and went out on the porch. Drew stood beside his car, drinking a beer, and talking to Dan. There'd been a lot of explaining to do when they came by to check on Lei and found her nearly healed.

"Hey, Dan." Lei waved. "You interested in some dinner? There's extra."

"No thank you, Lei. But I appreciate it. Just came by to deliver some of Margo's famous peach pie." He held up a covered tin and waggled his eyebrows. "Mighty kind of you to ask though."

"Tell Margo thanks for me. I love her pie. Whenever you boys are done talking cars, dinner's on the table, Drew."

"Thanks." He nodded at her.

"You might want to know, Blake is up."

Drew turned to her with wide eyes. "You could have led with that, you know."

"Could have." Lei grinned and walked back into the house.

Blake sat pretty much where she'd left him, though he'd gotten up to get a cup of coffee. Lei busied herself putting the steaks on plates with mashed potatoes and some easy-mix biscuits. She wasn't the best cook but it would be good enough.

Drew set the pie down on the table and knelt beside Blake, asking him questions, taking his temperature, reading his chi, or whatever it was sorcerers did when they were worried and fussing over a child. Lei remembered when her mom and dad had done the same and a throbbing ache filled her chest.

She sat down to eat, watching them and missing that connection. She'd made the mistake of allowing Willy to step into a sort of grandmother role instead of keeping her at arm's length as just her mentor. Of course, when Granny comes in guns blazing and saves you from the real life big bad wolf, it's hard not to feel some kind of connection.

Lost in memories and overwhelming sadness, she didn't taste the food she moved mechanically from her plate to her mouth. Once, she caught Blake looking at her the way he did, with desire and understanding both, and she lost her appetite completely. Had the demon killed her, Blake would honestly miss her, mourn her. Wouldn't she if something happened to him? Hadn't he already slipped around most of her defenses anyway? At this point, her rules were a bit moot.

Lei excused herself from the table and retreated to her bedroom. She undressed and stood in front of the mirror on the door. The new scars were haphazard on her flesh, not like the scars left by the werewolf's nasty claws. Eventually, they would all blend together in the patchwork pattern that her skin was becoming. Disgusted, she pulled her nightshirt on. If she got desperate, she could always use them to scare Blake off once and for all.

She crawled into her bed, breathing in the scent of him. Closing her eyes, she found she wasn't tired. She didn't want to be around anyone else either though, so she stayed in her bed and grabbed a book off the nightstand.

Chapter Eleven

The darkness unnerved Blake, sent an unfamiliar spike of fear through his spine. Lei jogged too far ahead of him, the thin beam of her flashlight bobbing against the craggy rock and occasional multi-limbed saguaro cacti. He tried to catch up, but his feet slid on loose rock, his hands failed to find purchase. His voice gave out as he tried to call her name. Instead, he slid, rock tearing at his clothes, chewing up his skin. When he found his balance, he looked up just in time to see Lei walk into and through a solid cliff wall.

Blake woke, heart pounding in his chest, a panicked scream lingering, unreleased in his throat. For a moment, the dream clung to him. One moment he was somewhere dark, cold, and powerful, the next he was sprawled haphazardly over the air mattress. He didn't remember going to bed or falling asleep. He only remembered the fear in that bleak place.

Though he was his mother's son, it was very rare for her gift to spill over to him, but he knew that dream had been no dream. He knew that truth all the way to his marrow.

Shaken, he rubbed his face and sat up. The throbbing in his skull had lessened. Sort of. He could work through it, had to. Frustrated and annoyed with himself, Blake stumbled into the kitchen, following the scent of coffee. Drew sat at the kitchen table, flipping through one of Willy's journals. Outside, darkness crept up over the horizon.

"You look like hell." Drew looked up, concern furrowing his brow. "Are you all right?"

"Not really. I'll tell you what, if I was going to get some of my mother's abilities, it should have damn well come with an interpretation manual. How do I know if I'm seeing the future or seeing an allegory?"

Drew laughed, not unkindly. "Them's the breaks kid. Next time you see her, maybe you can talk her into writing one just for you."

"At this point, I very much doubt she'd do it." He poured coffee into a thick handled mug and sat down at the table. "We didn't really part on good terms."

"I know it, Son. But just you watch, things have a way of righting themselves." Drew patted Blake's arm and nodded. "You'll see."

A moment later, Lei came in. "I see you're awake again. How are you feeling?"

Blake paused to look at her for a moment, debating on whether or not to tell her. "Better enough, thanks. I think we're okay to get started, if you're feeling up to it."

"Well then, I guess I should let Melli know we're all going to be headed for Pittsburgh, after all."

"Pittsburgh?" Blake asked. He noticed Drew didn't seem surprised by that information at all.

"We're going to go hit that nest." She poured herself a cup of coffee and sat down with them. "We're going to find out why the head of the Order of Justices has declared that nest, that head vampire off limits. Given the timing, I don't buy that it's coincidence, do you?"

"No. But I have a feeling this is the second time you've had this conversation." Blake looked pointedly to Drew who pretended not to notice.

"I wasn't sure you'd be feeling up to it." Lei shrugged and sipped her coffee. "Because of you, I'm on my feet again. Maybe feeling better than I have in a while. I haven't had down time like this since…well, in a long time. But, playtime is over for me. I've got work to do. I won't ask you to join me if you don't think you're up for it."

"I can be a hunter even without my magic. If I can't use it, well, so what? You're not getting rid of me that easily. I believe I've made that clear." His voice left no room for argument.

"So long as you're sure," Lei nodded and shrugged. "Sit down, rest some more. We'll take care of all the preparation."

"We'll take two cars. That way we can divide the city up between us." Drew closed the book and turned his attention to them. "Melli and I will take my car. You and Blake take yours. We stand a better shot of getting in there quickly and finding it this way."

Blake nodded. "Makes sense. Do you think we should use the safe house there as headquarters or set up someplace else?"

"Given our company, someplace else would be better." Drew's eyes darkened. "As much as you and I have come to trust them, you have to remember, for the clans, we're still working with the enemy."

"We'll find a place on the way." Lei jumped in before Blake could argue. "There are some areas of the city that haven't been so well maintained—abandoned houses where we run a low risk of anyone realizing, or caring, that someone is squatting in them. Places where people don't call the cops. I'll start getting things set up if someone else will cook."

Drew laughed. "I'll take care of it."

While Drew worked on feeding them, Lei and Blake pulled out the most useful books from the shelves and stacked them in the front seat for a little research on the go. They searched through Lei's weapons for the standard vampire tools and things that could potentially be used against demons—just in case.

Even that much exertion drained Blake. Exhaustion filled every bone, every molecule of himself. He'd never been so quick to tire before. He couldn't let the others see just how bad he was. He would push through. He'd plaster a smile on his face and cover the pain, the tiredness, the weakness, until he dropped if need be.

They found scarce information on demons in the books they collected, certainly nothing designed specifically for them. Apart from the few exorcisms scattered throughout books and journals, they were flying blind. Lei copied the one Dan used against the thing that nearly killed her. They found a box full of ancient religious relics on a shelf in the barn. They had some holy water, and the incantations and blessings required to make more if they needed to, though the Catholic holy water seemed to work better than blessed water or Amrita.

They packed the back of both cars with guns, blades, and stakes, putting them under false floors. Lei added high-powered binoculars, listening devices, night vision goggles, and communication equipment.

Melli arrived from the hidden lands in the middle of the night elated and nearly floating. She hugged Lei tight, thanking her over and over again. Blake saw the discomfort on Lei's face as plain as anything but the fairy was either oblivious to it or didn't care. Either way, it was a little funny. A little shred of hope ignited inside himself that he could still find humor in things.

Just before they bedded down for the night, they prepared two coolers with the last of the cold cuts, fruit, and some soda and water. Lei tossed granola and candy bars in plastic bags and tucked them behind the passenger seat for relatively easy access.

***

They woke early, just as the shadows of dusk crept along the very bottom of the horizon. After a quick breakfast using the last of the eggs and milk, the four of them loaded into the cars and headed out toward Pittsburgh.

During the drive, Lei and Blake talked more about the case, but also about themselves. Lei was hesitant to talk about her life before the werewolf attack that changed her life, mostly because it saddened her to remember how innocent and naive she had once been. Her childhood had been much happier than Blake's. For her, Christmas had always been about Santa, presents, and charity. For Blake, it had been more about Black Pete and protecting their home from the darker side of the holiday that most people didn't really believe in. Birthdays had been much the same. Lei had dolls, parties, wishes, and cake. Blake had weapons, talismans, and real magic.

"I don't think I could raise a child in this life, knowing everything they would miss out on." Lei sighed. "How could I bring a child into the world knowing they would never know the kind of peace and happiness I knew?"

"There's nothing that says you need to raise them with nothing but this life. My experience wasn't normal even for sorcerers. You have to remember, I wasn't so much a child as a project. Manufactured. The way things were done with me wasn't necessarily how they were done with my siblings. Yes, they know the dangers, the signs to watch for. They know the truth about the boogie man and the monsters under the bed. But they have fun. They do all the things most typical kids get to do. They play. They have tea parties and clubhouses. So long as they could control their magic, they went to public schools. One of my older brothers played football. Normal is relative."

"Be that as it may, I just don't think I could do it." Lei shrugged. "When I was a little girl, I always figured I'd grow up to have it all—the house, picket fence, a couple of kids, and my very own Prince Charming. But, that's not going to happen."

"You never know." Blake's face smiled, but it didn't reach his eyes or his voice.

Lei felt as though she'd somehow failed a test and had no chance to for extra credit. She couldn't just snap her fingers and feel differently. She would never have children.

Conversation quieted for a while as Lei used her phone to search for a good place for them to set up. "I think I may have something. There's a church, not too far from downtown Pittsburgh, but not quite in it either. It's scheduled for demolition in two months but there haven't been any write-ups or news stories. If we're caught squatting, we can always say we're protesters."

"A church might be a really good place, actually. Maybe it being sacred ground will deter a demon."

"Maybe, maybe not. Depends on the church and the faith. Let me see what I can find out." Lei tapped on her phone a little more, flipping from link to link. "Evangelical Protestant? From what I can see, there's some basis for belief in demons there so we might find some wards or other protection."

"Unlikely unless the church is really old, like two hundred years old."

"No such luck, only just over a hundred years. But, it doesn't really matter. It's a place to go that we should be able to stay in unnoticed, so long as we're careful anyway." Lei called and relayed the plan to Drew along with the address.

Lei knew she'd chosen well when they neared the section of Pittsburgh where the church was settled. Even occupied homes were sprayed with graffiti and had several boarded up windows. It was the kind of place where people kept to themselves. If you don't see anything, you can't testify and aren't at risk. Just the kind of neighborhood they needed to hole up in.

The church wasn't grand or even very pretty. Its red brick was faded, the mortar in dire need of repointing. Dirt and grime caked the thick Plexiglas that covered what were probably beautiful stained glass windows. The Plexiglas was peppered with chips and dings but no breakage. The awning over the red double doors was busted, buckled on the left side and hanging down too far on the right. Plywood covered all of the regular windows.

"Looks like someone cared enough to keep it safe from vandals and squatters." Blake eyed the large, overgrown yard in the back that hid much of the building from view. "Someone who might care enough to check on it."

"We won't be here that long. If we're good, no one will even notice we're there." Lei pointed to a small access drive cordoned off by a chain. "I'll take care of that long enough to get us in, then repair it."

Reaching under her seat, Lei grabbed the heavy-duty bolt cutters and a replacement link and hopped out of the car. This was not the first locked chain she'd come across, nor would it be her last. She should have been a Boy Scout, always prepared. Laughing to herself, she cut the chain and moved it aside long enough for both cars to enter the overgrown but small parking lot behind the church. She rewound the chain and replaced the cut link with one that was designed to open.

Blake was picking the lock on the back door when Lei reached them. Drew and Blake had parked nearly inside the enormous mounds of honeysuckle. It wasn't likely anyone would notice the cars unless they were really looking for them.

Inside was much better than they'd hoped for. It was dirty but the kind of dirty that came from years of disuse and neglect. A clean dirty, in a way. She turned on the tap in the small kitchen, hoping for water and got nothing. So much for comfort. The main sanctuary still had its pews and the pews still held Bibles and hymnals. A great wooden altar carved with some kind of scripture sat at the head of the church. Lei couldn't read it though as it was in German.

"This seems like a good enough place to set up." Drew looked around and nodded. "I'll try and find the belfry and make sure the bell can't ring. Just in case something decides to follow us back here. No sense in alerting the community."

"Good. We'll split up and figure out the layout, make sure we aren't going to be surprised by any other residents."

"In a place like this, how has this building not been used by vandals or teenagers looking for a quiet spot?" Blake ran his finger through the dust on the pulpit.

"I know the answer to that," Melli said as she spun in small circles, arms open wide. Above her the cracked plaster was falling apart, revealing the beams beneath it. "There are very old markings on those beams. I think if we'd come here looking to cause harm to the place, we wouldn't have been able to get in."

"Guess this place was built by someone who knew the truth, a hunter maybe." Lei looked at the beams, committing the shapes of the marks to her memory, and taking a few pictures with her camera for good measure. "That works in our favor. Maybe not with the vampires, but with the other big bads out there."

The four of them parted ways to check out the rest of the building, mostly to make sure there were no other residents but also to find the most defensible room to set up in—the one least likely to draw unnecessary attention to their movements. Preferably one without windows. Even through a boarded up window, light could still escape. Especially if someone with magic was looking.

By dawn, they were unloaded and settled into a meeting room in the basement. Lei and Blake brought in a table they'd found in storage and chairs that looked like they could still hold weight. They laid their sleeping bags along the wall behind the door. It was like camping, without the stars and with no fire to scare off the rats.

***

Just after dark, armed for vampires, the four of them split into pairs to search the city. Lei wished Cam had told her where to start. He knew—had to know—exactly where the nest was based. While he seemed honest about what was going on, he'd been evasive too. She wanted to believe that he needed her help, wanted to think the best of him, but it was hard to do. She hadn't seen any sign of the Justice or his people anywhere yet and that had to count for something.

Blake and Lei headed for one of the college campuses. The bars and nightclubs there would be prime hunting ground, depending on the kind of vampire who was at the head of the nest. Melli and Drew focused on the bars with older, more established clientele. A young vampire would want to surround himself with people he thought were beautiful enough, worthy enough. A young vampire still considered it a game, a gift. An older vampire, though, they'd be looking for people in power—people with connections to protect them and feed them.

The first bar was a total waste of time, except to rule it out as any kind of hunting ground. The bartender there was a werewolf who had no patience for any otherworlders. Not that he had any love of hunters or sorcerers either, but Lei's name had spread far enough in the community that the poor dog would have begged if she'd asked him to. Lei didn't like that one bit. She felt she was lying to them all and it didn't sit well with her. But, she reminded herself, it was for peace, for the children. Small price to pay for something so monumental.

The second, third, and fourth bars weren't much better. Lei was on the verge of giving up, at least around the campus, but Blake pushed to keep going even though she saw the ragged edge of exhaustion all over him. After all, it was still early by vampire time. Not quite one in the morning.

So, they walked through the city, looking to all the world like any other couple. Any other couple out hunting monsters anyway.

Blake and Lei were standing by a light post, feigning interesting conversation and looking for signs when they saw a young, beautiful woman pass them. She was wringing her hands, looking over her shoulder, and moving a little too quickly. Almost impossibly fast.

After exchanging a look, Blake and Lei started following her. They kept a good distance from her, ducking into shadows when she looked back. Her blond hair streamed out behind her as she picked up her pace and Lei and Blake had to run to keep her in their sights.

Lei grabbed Blake's hand and pulled him into the shadows. "They're baiting us. Unless the head of this nest is completely inept, we're being led somewhere. I don't like being led around."

"I don't disagree." He leaned close to her ear. "Last time, they were on to you pretty quickly. Maybe they are again."

"Changes things a little. We could go walk into their setup. See what happens."

"Not without backup." Blake pulled out his phone and texted Melli.

"I'm not arguing." Lei smiled and searched her large purse, making sure her most useful tools were closest to the surface. She had her vamplight, an industrial flashlight modified with the same full spectrum bulbs used for reptiles, and not the cheap ones either. A polished silver stake, six stakes whittled from oak, and a squirt gun filled with holy water.

Blake looked up from his phone. "They'll be coming. Melli from above, Drew is already walking toward us. We'll meet in the middle if they don't stop us first."

"Good." She shifted and arranged her purse so her hand was inside it. "You think this vampire is cocky enough to be stupid? He's got a free ride from the Justices. Maybe he thinks they'll protect him from me. Us."

"I remind you. We don't know that they won't." Blake stepped out of the shadows first and into the light of the streetlights.

All around them, the late night city traffic moved. Lei knew Blake had put them under some kind of spell when the thugs crowded around one stoop didn't so much as look in their direction. The pretty blond who'd been in such a hurry before stood against the wall beside a dark alley. When she smiled at them, she bared her fangs, four long, curved needles beside her two front teeth and wicked sharp bottom teeth, to keep the prey in place.

"Yep. He's that stupid," Lei muttered under her breath.

"Don't underestimate him just yet." Blake took the first step toward the woman with Lei right behind him.

The woman laughed and retreated into the darkness, waving at them, taunting them.

"You're going to have to cover me." Blake winked at Lei and started muttering in another language as they walked to the mouth of the alley. He clapped his hands and a great light shot up from them.

In the alley, fifty voices cried out at once in great pain, their illuminated flesh burning as Lei painted them with her full spectrum light. The once beautiful woman clawed at her smoldering face, shrieking. Blake plunged a stake into her heart and moved on to the next ugly, toothy critter. Lei used the light with one hand and her silver stake with the other, plunging it in and pulling it out as they put the wounded out of their misery.

Those not touched by Lei's light fled, shrank into the shadows of the night. For every vampire they killed, at least two got away. Fleeing to safety, likely returning to their master to tell the story of the hunter and the sorcerer who were working together. Lei hid her smile as she cut off the head of a particularly pretty young man. Definitely a young vampire, surrounding himself with an army of pretty children.

Leaving the mess behind for the sun to clean up, Blake and Lei walked toward the diner they'd been in before. It was a good place to wait for sunrise. They wouldn't return to the church until the sun crested the horizon. Blake leaned heavily on her shoulder; he shouldn't have used so much magic so soon. He hadn't been himself since she woke up. Blake was there, with her, but somehow, less solid.

Melli arrived at the diner about half an hour after them and sat down across from them. "Drew should be here any minute. I passed him about three blocks from here."

Lei just stared at her. "Did you find anything?"

"Oh yes, your dumbass plan worked just fine," she smiled through her sarcasm. "They're apparently living in a pretty swanky building. There are humans there too, but most of the top half of the building is full of vampires, from what I could smell anyway."

"What's the security like?" Blake asked.

"You'll have to ask Drew. I was in the air, didn't look around much on the ground level." She paused in her telling and ordered coffee and pancakes.

By the time Melli was done ordering, Drew walked in. "I'll have whatever she's having." He told the waitress as he slid in beside Melli.

They waited until the waitress was gone before picking up their conversation. "What's the security like?" Blake asked again.

"It won't be easy, but it won't be the most difficult we've seen either." Drew pulled a pen out of his pocket, flipped the paper place mat over and began to draw. "The two men at the door during the night are vampires, so the ones on during the day are probably friendlies to them too. Maybe werewolves or some other disguised otherworlders. No way to know until we get there, really. The fire escape can't be pulled down to ground level and it didn't look too sturdy anyhow."

He laid the quick drawing of the building in the center of the table. "There are low windows here, here, and here. They look to be utility rooms. At least one was the laundry room. I'd wager to say there are probably guards at the elevators too. Likely on each floor that houses sleeping and vulnerable suckers."

"Can't Blake just do his time stopping thing and go in and get him?" Melli asked.

"No," Lei and Drew answered together.

"The last time he used that ability," Drew continued, "it took too great a toll on him. If he uses it again so soon, he could completely burn out."

"It could kill him," Lei inserted when it looked like Melli was going to argue the point.

The fairy held up her hands in defeat. "Fine. But a ground assault isn't going to work and if we're talking about going in during the day, I can't be seen flying around the top of this building."

"Right on both counts." Blake agreed and looked closer at the building. "What are the buildings on either side like?"

"Unfortunately, it stands all by itself. And it looks like recent construction so we're looking at something that may have been designed specifically for these bastards." Drew tapped on the table with his thumb. "I don't think one of the standard ploys will work, not when they know we're in town and not under the orders of the Justices. Besides, they'd smell Melli a mile away."

"If this is a recent build, they'll have vaults." Lei pulled the sketch to her. "There's no good way in, not if we plan on getting back out. We'll have to do this another way. We bring him out to us."

"They know we're here now. There's no way he'll leave the safety of that place until he thinks we're gone or dealt with."

"I disagree. This vampire is fairly new, young, I think. None of the vampires back in that alley were very old. They were beautiful people not useful people. I don't think he knows all the rules just yet and I think he's cocky enough to believe he's smarter than us. Besides, I've got an ace up my sleeve." A Cheshire cat grin spread over Lei's face.

Chapter Twelve

Lei and Blake traveled the short distance through the city as quickly as traffic would allow. "Are you ready to tell me the truth yet? We all know you're not at full capacity here. I need to know just how bad it is."

"I'll be fine," Blake assured her. "I just need to avoid using the magic for a while, even if we're in a tight spot."

"Will you ever get it back?"

"It's not like it leaves me," Blake laughed. "It's like any other muscle and right now, it's sore and bitching at me so I need to stay off it. I just need rest."

"It's hard to get enough rest when you aren't sleeping well."

"I promise, I'll be fine. Eventually."

His explanation didn't exactly appease Lei but she chose to let it go, for the time being anyway. As she pulled into the Station Square parking lot, she rolled down the window to take a ticket from the machine. It was a beautiful evening. Unless one knew the kind of monsters that lurked in the dark. Lei parked and walked with Blake to the main entrance to wait.

At precisely ten o'clock, a sleek silver sedan slid to the curb and a muscular woman in a chauffeur's hat got out of the driver's side and walked around to the passenger side, opening the door with all the flair of a bored librarian.

"I was very surprised to hear from you, Leilani." A deep voice came from inside the car, slipping out through the shadows collected there. "From your choice of companion, I am assuming this is a business discussion, yes?"

"That would be a safe assumption, Yemi." Lei moved toward the car and waited expectantly.

A very tall, broad shouldered man stepped out of the car, his skin nearly the color of the shadows he stepped from. He wore clean blue jeans and soft red silk shirt. He smiled with a closed mouth but his fangs made distinct bulges in his lips. She trusted him enough not to step back when he brought his mouth close and kissed her lightly on the lips.

"Still so determined not to show your fear. You can't help being afraid of me. It's instinctual, even if you know I would never really hurt you." He laughed brightly and held his hand out to Blake. "I can only assume you had no idea who Lei called for help."

Blake paused for a moment before taking Yemi's hand in his. Lei saw the hesitation, the immediate distrust in his eyes, part of which was likely directed at her now. "Another very good assumption."

"Our little Leilani here does play things close to the vest, doesn't she?" He laughed again and tucked Lei under his arm as he led them down the sidewalk. "Since the two of you are so heavily armed, I believe we'll conduct this business in a restaurant. There is a very good one not far from here."

"Fair enough." Lei walked beside Yemi, almost regretting her hatchling plan. Guilt nagged at the edges of her thoughts. She should have warned Blake. She should have trusted him enough to let him in on her plan. He'd be pissed at her now and rightly so. Being wrong sucked.

Blake did not look pleased as the host sat them at a secluded table in a restaurant that had once been a train station. In fact, he glared at her over the top of the menu. Lei shrugged. She had a plan, a damned good one. Later, she'd apologize to him for not trusting him. For once, she was the asshole in their relationship.

Yemi ordered raw oysters and very rare filet mignon. Lei ogled the menu and the prices for a moment before deciding not to give a damn and ordering the crab legs and a shrimp cocktail in lieu of a salad. Blake stuck to red meat but ordered it medium.

When the waitress left, Lei took a sip of her water and looked at two people whom for a great many reasons, she shouldn't trust but whom she total faith in. "We need your help, Yemi. There's a nest here in Pittsburgh that is not just growing but being fostered by the Justices."

Yemi nearly jumped out of his seat. "The Justices? You've got to be kidding me. I've had run-ins with a Justice or two who very clearly believed none like me should be allowed to live. There is no way they are purposely allowing a nest to grow."

"That's one of the things that bothers me about this particular nest. They've built themselves a pretty fancy center of operations. From what I can tell, this is a fairly new vampire. He is surrounding himself with youth and beauty and that tells me he's still pretty new at this. I figure he made some kind of deal with the head of the Order and, with everything else going on, we need to know what that deal is. Why has the Order told one of their most just Justices to leave him be?"

"What is it exactly you called me here to do, Lei?"

"His nest is too well guarded. We need you to go in. He's new. He's probably never had much guidance. He may look at you and see the perfect mentor material. At least, if you don't tell him how you've managed to stay alive and hidden." She looked over at Blake who studied them both. "Yemi doesn't harm people. He's a good vampire."

"Then how do you survive? Is that even possible?" Blake leaned forward anxious to hear.

"It wasn't always." Yemi smiled and sat back. "I own a series of blood banks. Basically, I pay people for the blood that keeps me and my family healthy and happy. It is a small price to pay for being left alone by most hunters. We still have to hide from the Justices. They have no...gray...we'll say."

They paused their conversation as the uniformed waitress brought them their appetizers and made sure there was nothing more she could do for them.

"Why do you think this vampire will confide anything in me?" Yemi ate his oysters with far more grace than Lei expected.

"I don't. What I expect is that he will trust you enough to leave his vault and take a drive with you. Get him out of that building. I don't honestly care how you do it." She took a bite of her shrimp and enjoyed it, and the quiet, for a moment. "I'm not going to kill him unless he gives me no choice, Yemi. I promise you that. I'm going to make him a deal. He gives me the information I need and he and his people get to go with you and set up somewhere far away from this city. All they have to do is stop hunting, stop turning innocent people into monsters."

"You can't do that!" Blake leapt up out of his chair and pointed at her. "You can't give these murderers that kind of leniency!"

"Now, sit down. You're making a scene." Lei's whisper was more of a hiss. "Why not? If it gets the information we need *and* gets them to stop hurting civilians, why can't I?"

Blake scowled but sat. "And if he doesn't agree to this deal?"

Lei looked to Yemi who sighed. "The deal is perfectly suitable and more than fair. A better deal than he would get with anyone else.

If he refuses, you and she may do as you must and I will not lift a finger to stop you. Nor will my family hold it against you."

The waitress arrived with their entrees and for a few minutes, the only sounds at the tables were appreciative murmurs, the scraping of silver on china, and the clink of ice against crystal.

"I have to ask this, Yemi." Blake wiped his mouth with his napkin and leaned away from his empty plate. "Why are you helping us?"

"Last year, Leilani saved my daughter. I owe her my very life, if she asked it of me." He smiled, his teeth too sharp, too white against his ebony skin.

"No offense, but can't you just turn another one?"

Lei laughed quietly. "Not exactly. He doesn't mean his daughter in the vampire sense. In the vampire sense, they are siblings. They share a sire."

"I came from Africa on a slave ship when I was a very young man." Yemi's eyes grew distant as he spoke, as he remembered. "For a time, it was as happy a life as a slave can expect. I had a wife and a daughter. I worked well for my master, who was a kinder one than most. When he died, his wife sold mine. I never learned what happened to her. My daughter was all I had. When she got sick, so very sick, I went looking for a cure, any cure."

For a moment, Yemi was silent. Regret and sorrow passed over his face. "I found a cure for one disease by giving us both another. Had I understood, I wouldn't have done it. But, I didn't and I have no wish to die. We lived like savages for many, many years. Now, we don't need to. Now we can be like the humans we were. I have already done a great deal to ensure my daughter's safety and happiness. One little vampire is a small price to pay to have her home safely."

"Once you get him out, we will meet you back here, or close to here, and then we'll take him from there. I'll make sure he knows how to contact you once I get the information we need." Lei reached into her pocket to get her wallet.

"No, Leilani." Yemi laid his hand on her arm. "No using your fake cards here. It will be far simpler if I just get this tab."

"Suit yourself," Lei shrugged.

"I usually do." Yemi smiled again, not shy about his teeth now.

Blake paced in the shadows near Lei's car, parked in the far corner of the lot. "What if he can't get the leader to go with him?"

"Quit worrying. He will. Yemi has a way with people. He can be very formidable and intimidating when he needs to be or fatherly and kind when he doesn't."

Blake sat down on the curb in front of the car beside Lei, rubbing his temples. "Where do you draw your line? I've seen you fight, even nearly torture some kinds of otherworlders. I've seen you risk your life for a *Justice* who probably would just as soon killed you as look at you. And now this? He's a vampire, for goodness sake!"

"My *line* as you put it isn't a hard one. I learned my lesson years ago and I'm still paying my penance for it." She sighed heavily and looked away from him, out towards the river, watching a late night dinner cruise sailing by. "Early in my training, just after Willy got too sick to go out with me on jobs, there was this man. It was in a little town in Wyoming and the local papers were full of stories and theories about a killer in the mountains. Everything there pointed to some kind of creature but it was a tossup between a werewolf, a Sasquatch, and a wendigo. At least that's how I read it, Willy too for that matter when I talked it through with her later."

"What happened?" Blake asked when Lei lapsed into silence.

"I went into the mountains with a park ranger named Nate. We were both looking for the same thing, though he thought it was an animal. We'd hiked all day up into the mountains and were setting up camp. It'd been a long day and we'd found next to nothing. All of a sudden, there's this howl and I took off running towards it. Nate was right with me but he was armed for bear. He was convinced that was all we were looking for. I don't know what I was expecting. No. I do. I was expecting a werewolf and that's what I got.

"The wolf was fighting this large man, fighting hard. I'd heard snarls like that before and I know how strong they are. How vicious they can be. I did what I had to do. I shot the dog. As Willy would have said, I put him down. Then, the big man, he turns to me with this horrible grin and takes off into the woods. Of course, I chased him. I'd had the dangers of wolf bites drilled into my training since day one, obviously."

Lei rubbed her eyes hard and her voice got very quiet. "I caught up with him at this little campsite but I was already too late. He had a woman in his arms. She was mid-transformation, between human and wolf. She was screaming for her mate to save her, two kids lay dying on the ground. I was seconds from being able to save her. I'd stood on the wrong side of the line and protected a very human serial killer over a werewolf that was just trying to protect his family."

"It was a mistake anyone could have made." Blake put his hand on her shoulder, pulled her against him.

"It opened my eyes. I made a vow to myself that night that I would never find myself on the wrong side of the line again. That what people were didn't matter so much as who they were. I guess it was the first time I ever really thought of these things that I hunted as being people, as having families. I had my family ripped from me in the cruelest way possible. How many otherworlders now hate all hunters because of one job I did?"

"Don't do that to yourself. You can't always tell good from evil. You can't expect yourself to always know."

"That's right. Now, I do my best to give them a chance to answer a few questions, unless I am seriously outnumbered or in real danger anyway. I want to die with a clean conscience, not as a martyr." Lei looked up at Blake. "Yemi does his best to be a good person. To live a good life and not hurt anyone. Do I think he regrets being what he is? He probably does. Do I think he regrets doing what he's done? I know it. But would he go back and change it? I don't think so. Not if it meant losing his daughter."

"So if we were to come across a case that was human on human violence, you'd still do the job?"

"If it didn't look like the cops had it under control, I probably would."

"All you need is a utility belt and a side kick."

"Who says you aren't my side kick? Now, shut up. Here comes Yemi." Lei stood up and opened the back door of her car. "You want to drive or guard?"

"I'm not completely up to a real fight yet. I should probably drive." Blake's shoulders hunched slightly.

"You said yourself, it'll get better soon." She rubbed his back for a moment.

Yemi's car stopped beside theirs and the back door opened, the sleek car exhaling Yemi's tall form like smoke. "I don't know how much information you'll get from this child. He wishes to be called Karma."

"Are you kidding me?" Lei almost laughed. "Can there be such a thing as a hippy vampire?"

"Apparently." Yemi sneered with disgust. "I know you wish to foist him on my shoulders and for a time, I will take him under my wing, but I am rather hoping he proves to be uncooperative. I don't know that I will be able to tolerate his incessant yammering."

Yemi's chauffeur opened the trunk and picked up a very large lead box as if it weighed nothing and slid it into Lei's back seat. "You may keep the box. I would suggest getting your sorcerer here to magic it into whatever hovel you've settled into."

"Thank you, Yemi. I wouldn't have asked if it wasn't important." Lei took both his hands in hers.

"I understand, little Leilani. I do. That is why I dropped everything and came. You could have called me in to help with those new wounds that have you weakened so I can only assume this is even more important than your life."

"If I ever have any desire to be a vampire, I promise, you're the first one I'll tell." Lei smiled. "Besides, I wasn't actually conscious enough to call anyone for help. Hell, the fairies had to patch me up. Them and I think a couple of elves."

Yemi arched a brow. "You have always kept strange company, but really. Fairies? They've at least managed to keep you alive, but you still aren't quite yourself. If I'm not mistaken, your choice of partner is not at his best either."

"It cost him a lot to save me." Lei's shoulders rose and fell slightly with her smile. "But, alive is a hell of a lot better than not, no offense."

"None taken. I don't disagree with you." He laughed and reached close to kiss her on the cheek. "Next time though, please call me first, if you can. My ways might be old and touched with a little bit of hoodoo, but they work better than fairy dust and elf poultices."

Lei and Blake got into the car, her in the back set beside the box and Blake driving. It was still dark when they arrived at the church. Drew and Melli used their magic to work the box out of the car and into the windowless room in the basement.

"It's awfully small for an adult." Melli looked at the box, careful not to touch it.

The box was three feet by four feet of smooth metal with a lead shell. Lei crouched beside her, touching the first of seven sliding bolts that held it closed. "You'd be surprised how small a body folds up. For Yemi to stick him in this, Karma must have really annoyed the shit out of him. I know you don't know him but he is the most patient person I've ever met. Even without the vampire hypnoshit, he could probably charm anyone to do anything. This is incredibly extreme for him."

"Hopefully he didn't outright kill him." Blake started undoing the locks. "Get ready. This sucker is going to be pissed off."

As they opened the box, Lei restrained the giggle that bubbled up inside her. The small man in the box was about as frightening as a sloth with horn rimmed glasses. "I take it you would be Karma."

The young man nodded, his gray eyes pleading with her as he looked back and forth between her and the plethora of weapons aimed at him. "Please. Please don't hurt me." His voice was very quiet and full of fear.

"How the hell are you not dead?" Lei stepped back to allow him room to get out of the box.

Karma wasn't very tall, only about three inches taller than Lei and about as skinny as a fence post. "What do you want from me? Where is Mr. Yemi?"

Lei raised an eyebrow. "Mr. Yemi went home. I'll let you know where to find him when we are done here. After you give me the information you need to give me."

Karma shook his head, his unruly dirty blond hair swaying into and then out of his very alert eyes. "I don't know anything."

"Right. Because it's just every day that a freaky little punk gets to build his own nest at the behest of the damned Justices." Lei leaned against the table. "I'm betting those Justices got rid of your sire and every vampire in the area who could take your place. They let you build up your army of beauties and didn't so much as teach you the rules of the game."

"I don't know anything. I swear it."

Karma didn't look at her, not once. He looked everywhere else. Likely searching for a way out of the room but Drew and his shiny silver stakes blocked the only door. "Maybe you don't even know what you know. Sit down." Lei kicked a chair toward him.

He sat and clasped his hands in his lap to keep his fingers still. Lei watched as Blake secured him to the chair with industrial zip ties and a length of silver chain. The zip ties wouldn't do much except give them an extra moment if things got out of hand. An extra moment with a super fast vampire could mean all the difference.

"There's a lot I think you know and there's more I don't think you understand." Lei took another chair, spun it backwards and straddled it, laying her hands on the back and putting her chin on her crossed wrists. "There are many ways to hurt a vampire that don't require killing him. Did you know that?"

Karma shook his head.

"You should know that I know all of them. I studied at the side of a master. You've only seen the happy, cooperative side of the Justices, I'll bet. Let me tell you, they've been hunting, torturing, and killing vampire scum like you for centuries and I know all the tricks. While my friends here are excellent at killing little shits like you, I'm better at hurting them. I don't think you're as stupid or as afraid as you're pretending to be right now. I think you think I'll take pity on you, pathetic little toothy worm that you are. You don't know me from Eve so you don't know that's a foolish and stupid tactic. I don't have patience for play-acting so let's respect each other enough to be ourselves."

Karma's demeanor changed immediately. He sat up straighter, he shook his hair out of his face. The panicky young man disappeared and a very astute and controlled man took his place. "I've heard of you. In fact, it was a Justice who warned me about you. You are even smarter than they gave you credit for, using another vampire to lure me out."

"I have a lot of tricks up my sleeves that no Justice alive knows. I'm not looking to kill you. In fact, if you agree to my terms, you can live a very long life."

"But it won't be much fun will it? No hunting, no turning, no companionship." He crossed his legs and picked a bit of invisible lint from his charcoal slacks. "What is life without fun?"

"A hell of a lot better than dead." Lei stood up and walked away from, purposely turning her back on him when she went to get the bag she'd packed especially for this moment. She hefted its weight and brought it back to the table, slowly opening it and pulling out each instrument one by one. She didn't like to torture anyone, but it was a skill that had come in handy more than once.

"I imagine you haven't been a vampire long, a couple of months at most. Most of things I have in my handy dandy little bag here, you've never seen, let alone know what they can do."

"You seem to think you know a lot about me." His voice was more sure, stronger, than it had been, but Lei heard the fear in it too.

"I don't need to know about you specifically. I know enough about your kind to fill volumes and I was trained very well by a woman who had a special dislike for wanna-be fang-worshippers like you. Maybe even especially like you. Drawn to the idea of vampirism, the power, having all that beauty at your fingertips. A few of the right words, the right suggestions and any beautiful woman will spread her legs. Well, any beautiful woman with less than half a brain anyway."

She felt him then, trying to push a suggestion into her mind.

Lei laughed and picked up a long delicate stiletto. "Steel not silver," she said as she jammed it deep into his thigh, "I really don't want to kill you."

He screamed and strained against the silver chain but it held fast.

Lei bent very close to him. "I don't want to kill you but I will hurt you until you are begging me to. Try to touch my mind again and you'll find I will be less careful about where I aim this."

She pulled the blade from his flesh, stolen blood welling up and dripping onto the floor.

"Tell me what I want to know and you can live the life Yemi has offered you. I won't hurt you anymore." She flashed a small, ancient device in front of his face, not relishing the fear that danced there.

"You'll just kill me anyway." Karma tried to press himself backward in the chair, as far from the barbed blood spike as he could.

"I haven't harmed Yemi at all, have I? And I've known him for two years. I even saved his life." Lei put her hand on Karma's knee. "The Justices promised you safety but for how long? When they get what they want, who do you think they'll go after first? I'd lay good money on you. Working with you goes against everything in their rule book, Karma. I'm willing to bet they think they have a good reason to open up Hell, but they're wrong." She watched Karma closely, looking for reactions and was rewarded when his eyes grew larger at her mention of Hell.

"If you know so much, what do you need me for?"

"I know what they're doing, yes. Anyone with an eye for current events, history, and a map can see that. The why is what's important. The why or the who and I figure you know one if not both of those things. Hence, our little meeting tonight. I don't want to kill you, Karma. It's not something I enjoy doing, but I *will* do it if I have no choice. I will kill you and I will unleash death upon your pretty, pretty minions. Tell me what I want, do what I'm asking you to do, and you are all free to go. So long as you leave Pittsburgh immediately. Within twenty four hours of your release."

"If I tell you anything, he'll kill us all anyway." Karma turned his head away.

"They've tried killing Yemi before too. They've tried and they've failed every time because he is smarter then they are. You go to him and he can teach you how to survive. For as long as I live, if you harm no humans, you will give me no cause to harm you. If all I wanted was to kill you, I'd have just blown up your precious little vault in the middle of the day. You are young still, Karma. You could have a life that spans centuries if not millennia, if you are smart about it."

"How can I believe you? You tell me I shouldn't believe the ones who've given me everything."

"Have they? Makes it that much easier to clean up after themselves when you're no longer useful, doesn't it? If they gave it to you, they can take it away. I'm not giving you anything, really, just a chance to attempt to retain some shred of the humanity you once had."

"Like that ever did shit for me." Karma hung his head and took a few deep breaths. "You'll let me take my people with me?"

"You'll have twenty-four hours to get everyone out. We are going to destroy the building. It's as much for your protection as ours. If you get out carefully and quietly, the Justices will believe you died in the explosion. They'll have no reason to look for you."

He thought for a moment. Lei could almost see the thoughts churning in his head as he weighed his options.

"Fine. I'll tell you what I know. It isn't much, I swear."

The whole room seemed to breathe at last, Lei's relief the most palpable as she returned her tools to her bag. "Thank you, Karma. I really didn't want to have to start taking pieces of you."

Karma didn't reply to that, but he began his tale instead. "Two years ago, I was a nothing, a nobody. A dorky little computer science major. I applied for, and got, a job to help cover my expenses. College isn't cheap, especially when you don't get piles of scholarship money. It was easy stuff, just a low level maintenance gig, and the hours were perfect. I kept all my classes first thing in the morning, worked the night shift, and slept during the day. Anyhow, one night I'm there when the big bosses came in. I didn't think anything of it. Just went about my business until I heard a woman scream. Of course I went running, thinking I could be some, I don't know, hero I guess."

Karma looked up, his eyes finding Lei's. "I never saw it coming. One minute I'm trying to help a woman, the next, I'm getting chewed on. I woke up feeling like death, not realizing I was dying. Called in sick to class. That night, my boss came to visit me, explained things. Said I was too useful to kill and he kept me around like his own personal IT guy. So I was there, in his office, when he was. He treated me like a fucking dog. I didn't have a whole lot of choice but to put up with it, at least that's what I figured. So I did the job, kept my head down, fed on the boss's leftovers. Slept in the vault at the office. One night, I'm working on the boss's computer system. He'd gotten pissed at it and smashed it so I had to replace it. So I'm in the office and this guy comes in. He's armed to the teeth and crazy looking. Tells the boss he wants to speak in private. Well, my boss looks at me and laughs. Calls me his pup, says I'm not worth worrying about, since I never leave the building."

"What did this man look like?" Lei asked him.

"He was a big guy but not enormous. I guess he was older than me, had some gray in his hair. No beard, crazy eyes. He called himself Cam. Said he was there representing someone else but didn't say who. Said he was looking to make a deal, a big one. The kind of deal that could bring vampires into the light, so to speak. That we wouldn't have to hide. That we could raise humans like cattle. So long as we did what they needed us to do."

"Which was what?"

"You have to understand, I had no idea what they were talking about at the time. I still half don't. But the Cam guy wanted to talk to someone on a road."

"Did he by chance call it the Gray Road?" Blake took a step closer and nearly lowered his crossbow, but he caught himself and returned his aim appropriately.

"Sounds right. Anyway, a couple of days go by and my boss tells me we're going on a little trip and I'm not to say a word, just pretend I'm following along and that I understand everything. He made me change into this ridiculous outfit too. I felt like I was going to crash some kind of goth medieval LARP event. So we go to this place, like no place I've ever seen—not dead, really, just not living either. We go to this kind of bar."

"Can you think of anything you saw on the way there, in the not dead place?" Lei glanced up at Melli to make sure the fairy was paying attention.

"Just a lot of gray and trees and ugly looking dead things. The place we went though, it wasn't anything like anyplace I've ever been before. The people there, they looked like people but they didn't smell like people and they were all talking in this language I couldn't understand. So my boss, Mr. Whittaker—"

"Whittaker? Jules Whittaker?" Lei's eyebrows arched in surprise.

"Yeah, my boss. I catch on that he's introducing me and I play along. A little while later, and a whole lot of yammering about stuff I really couldn't understand. But this other guy walks in. He's really pale, like what I expected vampires to be I guess, and his hair was like snow. But the freaky thing was more the ears, they were kind of pointed up. He had a real soft, musical voice. I have no clue what the hell he said and, really, after a while, I just quit paying attention. And then the pale dude takes this crazy long sword and chops off Mr. Whittaker's head. Bam!"

"They killed Jules Whittaker?" Drew's voice gave away his stunned surprise.

"Why do you say that like it means something?"

"Whittaker is one big bad vampire. Or he was. He wasn't the oldest of them, but he was damned sure up there. The best we figure is he may have be one, maybe two levels removed from the first vampire." Drew spoke quickly but didn't once look like he was about to let down his guard.

"Wow. Wonder what the hell he was doing in Pittsburgh. It's not like it's New York or DC or somewhere important." Karma shrugged. "So everyone else, they're looking at me and what the hell can I do but play along, pretend I understand what the hell just happened. So that Cam guy starts offering me the sun and the moon to just keep my mouth shut."

"Wonder why they didn't kill you too." Lei eyed him with deep suspicion. Too many things weren't quite adding up in Karma's telling.

"Guess I knew too much."

"Bullshit. You're a liar. And not even a good one." Lei turned back to her bag and started unzipping it again.

She heard the chair break behind her. Before she could spin around, stake in hand, Blake, Drew, and Melli had all released their weapons into him. A stake to the heart from Blake's crossbow, one in the shoulder from Melli, and Drew's stake buried in his forehead.

"Damn it!" Lei tucked her stake back into her pocket. "Tomorrow we blow up that beauty of a building. Let them think we buy it, at least a little."

"No way anyone killed Whittaker if they were looking to make a deal." Blake stood over Karma's body and hacked his head off with a long, thick knife.

"Nope. And Cam is likely a set up too. He's the one who clued us in. Plus, he's an ass and a bigot. Maybe the most racist person I've met." She did not remind Blake that Cam might have come in second to Carie. "There is no way he was working with any of the otherworlders. He'd like to see them all dead and the hidden lands cleaned out entirely."

"You seem awful sure of that." Drew helped Blake fold Karma's body up and put it back in the box.

"If you met Cam when he didn't want a favor and lived, you'd understand why. I may need to tell him, to warn him that he's being set up."

"So we're really no closer to finding out anything, are we?" Blake asked.

"Not exactly. I'm pretty certain he wasn't lying about everything. Whittaker being involved makes perfect sense, so does his alliance with the werewolves and at least one elf. If they're serious about opening up the Netherworld, they'll need someone who knows how to do it and Whittaker is old enough and powerful enough to fit that bill. But, no, we don't know for sure." Lei stretched and yawned. "Let's get that box in the sunlight and open it up. We'll sleep for a little bit and take out the building on our way out of town."

"Why bother with it now?" Melli stepped out of the way as Drew maneuvered the box out of the door.

"It'll keep whoever is setting this up thinking we bought it. At least for a little while, maybe." Drew answered for Lei as he disappeared into the hallway.

Chapter Thirteen

The highway stretched out before them in the dark, the occasional pair of headlights or lonely lamppost dotting the way like distant stars. Lei drove with purpose, her foot heavy on the gas pedal, the speakers pumping out hard rock while Blake slept. And slept some more. It seemed to be the only thing he was capable of now.

He slept in the church while she and Drew set the explosives that imploded the vampires' building. He slept so much they all worried over him as they'd stuck around, volunteering to help dig through the rubble. It took two days to reach the vaults, all but one of them broken. Drew had opened the intact vault himself, letting the sun do his work for him as the three vampires inside collapsed into ash before any of the other volunteers got a good look at what was inside.

Lei had wandered the streets of Pittsburgh on her own, looking for Cam. She had to warn him. He had to know that his own people were setting him up. She found no sign of him or his people and that didn't bode well at all. If he'd been called in, he was in more trouble than he knew.

Blake wasn't in any shape to travel the Gray Road, so Drew and Melli were on their way back to Drew's place and then to the hidden lands to search for answers there. She and Blake were headed for only slightly less dangerous waters.

When the laws in Connecticut got too stringent for them, the Order of the Justices moved their headquarters to the Black Hills, building between ranchers and heavily armed survivalists. The Justices were well armed, well trained, and ruthless. Only a fool would try and knock on their door and expect a warm welcome. But, Lei knew more about the place, and the people, than most. Willy wrote extensively about her time there in her journals and Lei would use every bit of information she could against them.

They kept the building well defended. The Justices were both smart and arrogant. Walking up to their front door wasn't an option, but Lei had to get in. Someone in the compound knew what was going on. Maybe only one or two, but they knew. From what Blake told her, the Justices who'd been in Texas had been just as surprised by the attack as anyone else. The one who'd spoken to Blake after even made it seem like he might do some looking into it on his own. If the cards fell right, she might even be in time to save Cam's sorry ass.

"Fat lot of good that will do." She muttered to herself as she drove, fingers tapping on the steering wheel in time with the music. The idiot vampire, Karma, had lied about a lot, but he'd gotten enough truth mixed in with it for his lies to reveal a lot more than he'd probably wanted. That Whittaker had a contact on the Gray Road who could and would open the door for him. That vampires were accepted in at least one of the roadside taverns that led into the hidden lands. And he'd known about the Hell Gates. Factored in with the protection of the Justices, it didn't make for a good equation for them or any human, really.

She needed one or two Justices willing to stand up for the charter, for the organization they'd sworn oaths to. If Taj hadn't been decimated by the mist creature, maybe she could have reasoned with him. Maybe that's why the thing went for him first, before the other two Justices. Maybe it was targeted like a missile. Might as well take out the biggest threats to the safety of the triggerman as possible. It was a disturbing train of thought.

For the first time, Lei was glad Willy was gone. It would have broken her heart to see the organization she'd devoted her life to take such a huge step in the wrong direction. Of course, with everything laid out, she may have known, may have seen the signs long ago.

She glanced over at Blake, troubled sleep creased his brow, his eyes danced through dreams. He wasn't himself. He wasn't physically weak, but the toll using his gift had taken was huge. And all for her. It was the guilt that would break her. Which was why she never should have agreed to work with him in the first place. Now, it was too late. If something happened to him, she would mourn him as deeply as she had Willy, as she had her parents.

Fighting through exhaustion, Lei never once woke him to take the wheel. Instead, she pushed through until nearly dawn. Just outside Sioux Falls, she pulled off the highway and went looking for a motel. Blake woke when she pulled into the parking lot and started to protest. She ignored him and went inside to get a room.

Blake got into the room under his own steam, but not much farther. He collapsed, face first, on the bed without even taking off his boots. Lei just couldn't leave him like that. Carefully, she stripped off his leather jacket and rolled him over onto his back. Her deft fingers made quick work of his boots, placing them quietly on the floor at the foot of the bed.

She got ready for bed, slid into the far bed and closed her eyes. Sleep had no intention of settling in on her; instead, her mind raced, paused to ponder, and picked up the chase again. Turning on the television for a little background noise, she watched Blake sleep. He'd been sleeping far too much. He needed something more than she could do for him. He needed a real healer. Like his brother.

She flung herself out of bed and began searching for his phone. She found it in the inside pocket of his jacket and began searching through the programmed contacts. When she reached Marcus's number, she paused. There was a good chance he wouldn't help. Blake and his family hadn't parted ways on the best of terms and there was no telling what their mother had told them.

Lei looked at Blake, saw the pain and the age in his face, and dialed the number anyway.

"Blake?" Marcus answered, his voice thick with sleep and surprise. "Are you all right?"

"No. He's not all right. He needs your help. If you can help him." She touched Blake's cheek with her fingers, slightly relieved not to find him too warm. "If you will help him."

"Where are you?"

She heard the rustle of movement and assumed he was dressing. "Can we trust you, Marcus? If I tell you where we are?"

"Look, I don't know much about what happened in Texas. I haven't gotten much out of anyone. I know my parents aren't speaking to each other and every sorcerer I know is watching weather reports and packed to fight at a moment's notice. They're keeping me in the dark. I see no reason not to do the same to them."

"Are you in Kentucky?"

"I won't be for long."

"Head for St. Louis. Call me when you cross into the state and I'll give you the next step." Lei didn't wait for any further discussion, just hung up. She wanted him to prepare for everything. That way, if she didn't explain it right, he'd still be ready.

Sitting down on the bed, she watched Blake for a little longer before finally plunging into sleep herself.

When Blake began to stir, Lei was already awake, watching him in the dim light that still trickled in past the heavy curtains. He moved slowly, fingers massaging his temples, near where the gray was beginning to take over.

"It's getting worse, isn't it?" Lei asked, watching him jump at the sound of her voice.

"I don't know what you're talking about. I'm perfectly fine." His voice was rougher, edged with pain he struggled to hide.

"Of course you are. That's why you've been asleep for the last sixteen hours." Lei sat up, pulling the light quilt tight around herself. "Don't be angry with me."

"Why would I be?" He turned to look at her. "What did you do?"

"The only thing I could. We're not going anywhere for a while. Marcus is on his way here."

Blake reached for his jacket, missing it completely on his first attempt but retrieving it on his second. He dug for his phone but Lei had it in her hand. "You shouldn't have done that. Our mother will never let him come."

"He's already on his way. He'll call when he gets to St. Louis." She got out of the bed, quilt still wrapped around her and went for her bag. "Lay back down. I'll go get us something to eat. You're not doing anything until your healer brother takes a look at you."

"This is ridiculous. We're wasting time!" Blake stumbled toward the bathroom. "Just let me get a shower and I'll be fine."

"You can't even walk in a straight line." Lei dropped the quilt and pulled her jeans on. "If you keep pushing, I'll just leave you here and go on without you. And don't for a minute think I wouldn't."

"That's right. No attachments in our line of work." His voice turned hard and bitter.

"If you were feeling like yourself, you'd have had a much better line than that." Lei pushed her feet into her boots and tied the laces.

"I'm fine, Leilani, just sick and tired of lines, of fighting with you, of listening to your bullshit excuses." Blake slammed the bathroom door behind him.

With a sigh, Lei let herself out of the room, his phone and hers both tucked into her pockets, along with the car keys. She didn't want to go far so she walked across the road to a combination gas station-convenience store. A few sandwiches, chips, and some sodas in a bag, and two coffees in hand, she made her way back to the room. There was a little juggling as she put the key in the door and opened it.

She set everything up on the tiny little table in the room. The shower was running still. Lei knocked lightly on the door. "Blake? I'm back."

Her only answer was the sound of the shower running.

"Blake?" She knocked louder, gut tightening as no response came. "I'm coming in, Blake!"

He was unconscious in the tub, warm water pelting his body. Lei grabbed him by the shoulders and shook him. "Blake! Come on, don't you give up! Wake up, damn you!"

She shut off the water and grabbed a towel, rubbing him dry and trying to warm him up. He didn't respond to her touch, to her voice. Lei leaned in close, pressed her lips to his temple. "Don't you leave me now." Her whisper echoed against the tile.

Lei left him there and hurried back into the bedroom, ripping the comforter off her bed and grabbing Blake's phone off the table. She wrapped him as best she could, tucking the fabric under him. Dialing the phone, she paced the small length of the bathroom.

"How far away are you?" She started talking the moment Marcus picked up the phone. "He's unconscious and unresponsive. Tell me what to do."

"First, calm down." Marcus's voice was calm and firm. "You can't help him at all if you freak out right now. Where is he? What happened?"

"I went out to get breakfast and he headed for the shower. I wasn't gone long. He was pissed because I'd called you for help. I came back and he was just passed out in the tub. I turned off the water, dried him off and covered him with a blanket. I'm not strong enough to pull him onto the bed. He doesn't have a fever. He doesn't feel cold. Tell me what to do. Should I call for an ambulance?"

"Don't bother. They can't help him. Give me a second to pull over. You're going to give me the address of the motel and take a deep breath. It sounds like you've done what you can. Just sit with him, talk to him, make sure he keeps breathing. That's all you can do until I get there. You said you went to get something to eat. Go get it and take it with you into the bathroom."

Lei rattled off the address as she walked back into the bedroom to get her coffee. She ignored the sandwiches. Her stomach rebelled at the thought of eating anything. Marcus kept her talking. She told him what happened in Texas, though she didn't know exactly what happened between Blake and Carie. She explained how Blake had been acting, how he'd risked himself to save her.

"The delayed reaction is common, Lei, especially if he used any sort of magic afterwards. Drew and Blake both should have known better. He should have called me in from the start."

"This is all my fault." She sat on the edge of the tub, coffee in one hand, phone pressed between her ear and shoulder as she stroked Blake's head. "I'm so sorry, Blake."

"Stop it," Marcus nearly yelled at her. "This is *not* your fault. You didn't know what would happen. He knew the risks and accepted them but the game isn't over yet. He's not dead and he's not going to be if I have anything to say about it. I owe my brother a lot and I'm not going to let him die. I'm going to get off the phone and I'm going to push. Hopefully, there won't be much in the way of traffic or cops. If I have smooth sailing, I'll be there in about two hours. Maybe a little bit more. Try and keep calm. Call me if anything changes."

She put the phone down on the counter and tried to collect herself. Marcus sounded very sure of himself. She hoped he was half as good as Blake said he was. Lei sat beside Blake, speaking of nothing, mostly just to fill the time and keep her nerves level. Blake was sleeping too peacefully, too quietly. Not even a hint of his usual snore.

When Blake's phone rang, Lei practically jumped out of her skin, slipping on the tile floor in her haste to answer it. "Hello?"

"What room are you in?" Marcus's voice brought too much relief.

Lei told him, then made her way to the door to let him in, trying not to think about how much she didn't want to lose Blake. It wasn't fair how he'd weaseled his way into her life. Now she was exactly where she had never wanted to be again—about to lose someone important.

She peered through the peephole and opened the door for the young man who looked a little ragged around the edges. He had a large bag with him but hadn't brought anyone else. "Marcus?"

"You must be Leilani. I'm sorry we're meeting like this."

"Me too." She stepped aside to let him in the room and closed the door behind him.

"I'll need your help to get him to the bed." Marcus set his bag on the floor carefully as if afraid to break something. "After that, I think you should go take a walk, find a movie theater. Anything."

"Hell no. I'm not going anywhere. I want to help." Lei made her way into the bathroom, trying to figure out the best way to help Marcus get Blake out of the tub and into the bed.

"My experience is that loved ones shouldn't be in the room for what I'm going to need to do." He took hold of Blake's arm and bent down, pulling Blake into a fireman's carry. "When I get him out of the tub, take his legs. Take some of his weight."

Lei struggled to take as much weight from Marcus as she could as they moved awkwardly out of the bathroom and toward the bed. With as much care as possible, they laid him on the bed and covered him with blankets.

"I appreciate your wanting to spare me all kinds of weirdness, but he's my partner not my lover." She resisted the urge to push a stray lock of hair out of Blake's face. "Anything you need me to do, I can do it. Let me stay, Marcus. I have to help."

"No. I'm sorry, Leilani. I wouldn't let him help if I were here for you, either. Whatever lies you tell yourself are your business. If you help me and this doesn't work, you will spend the rest of your life blaming yourself."

"The same goes if I'm not helping, damn it. If I walk out of here and you find you can do nothing for him, I will always wonder if it would have been different if I'd stayed. Either way, I'm screwed. I'd rather hurt knowing I did everything I could than hurt wondering what else I could have done. Can you understand that? Please? I'll beg if I have to."

Marcus stared at her for a long moment and turned away to his bag. "Fine. First thing I need you to do is go across the street and get a couple of cups of coffee. I'll get set up while you're doing that. Just remember, you asked for this."

"Thank you," Lei nodded, biting down against the tears that threatened to come to the surface and left the room.

She ran across the street and into the convenience store. As she poured the coffee into to-go cups, she craned her neck to see out the window, to watch Marcus's car and make sure it didn't move. When she had to turn away from the windows to pay, a cold fear trickled down her spine that she'd turn back around and they'd both be gone.

Lei hurried back to the room and locked the door behind her. Marcus had laid a line of raw gemstones in varying colors on Blake's naked body. Oils, quartz crystals, herbs, and three amber-colored bottles lay spread out on the tiny nightstand. Three handmade cones of incense burned in a shallow pot filled with salt, the too-sweet smoke rising up and spreading around them. Marcus held a bundle of smoldering sage and waved it over Blake, bathing him in pale smoke.

Saying nothing, Lei set Marcus's cup of coffee on the table and watched as he cleansed the room. Whatever she'd been expecting from a great healer, she didn't think it was this. The old ways had their purpose, but a few ancient and not-so-ancient pagan tricks didn't seem like it would be enough to pull Blake back. It was going to take everything she had not to call for a different kind of help. She'd give Marcus a day, no more, and then she was going to call a hospital. Then Yemi. Not to turn Blake—she'd never do that to him—but maybe a little hoodoo wouldn't hurt.

Marcus laid the sage down in another dish of rock salt and picked up the first amber bottle, extracting the small dropper. "Hold his mouth open."

Lei did as he asked without question, counting each of the ten drops as they struck Blake's pale tongue. She stepped away as Marcus began rubbing oil on Blake's scalp in small circles.

"I want you to sit beside him. Take his hand in yours. Picture in your mind a great white light encompassing him. Close your eyes, Lei. Picture first the white, let it fill him, chase out all the shadows inside him. Hold that thought for as long as you can."

Again, she did as she was told. She peeked twice to see what Marcus was doing as the scent of tea tree oil and bay leaves burned her nose.

"I'm sorry, I know it doesn't smell so great." He smiled sweetly when he caught her peeking the second time. "This isn't what you were expecting, but I promise, I know what I'm doing. Now, fill your head with the future, Lei. See him standing beside you, working with you on a new case. See it and believe it will come to pass."

She tried, cursing as every image she tried to create seemed false. And then there was one that did not. It felt right, though it made her blush. She couldn't see a new case in her head, but she could see him—them—together in the dark. Skin to skin, heat to heat, the rise and fall of the most ancient of dances.

Suddenly, heat flooded the room. Lei opened her eyes and nearly screamed. She held her breath as she watched blue and white flames dancing from Marcus's hands to Blake's bare chest, rainbows refracting through the crystals and onto the walls. Completely entranced, she watched the delicate flames pass through Blake's skin and return to Marcus, like a needle with no thread. Each time the flame returned it was as red as blood.

Beneath Marcus's hands, Blake twitched and moaned. The slight sound sent a thrill through Lei. To her, it sounded like hope.

With a deft hand, Marcus poured the entire contents of another amber bottle down Blake's throat, massaging the liquid down. Lei watched, astonished, as the rough golden topaz on Blake's belly began to glow. Every vein in his body showed against his skin—as if Blake's skin had paled or his blood darkened to trace its map through him. Marcus picked up a long needle and pricked the bottoms of Blake's feet like fruit being readied for preserving. He rubbed a pasty clay from a wide mouthed jar over the wounds and wrapped them in lengths of undyed cloth.

"Now, we wait. It will take a while." Marcus bowed his head and began packing up his equipment. "You did better than I thought you would. If this works, if he gets better now, you should know that he'll likely remember everything that you projected onto him."

Lei blushed again and shook her head. "I never know what to expect from you people. Even my own thoughts aren't safe inside my head."

"Not when you're projecting. I'm sorry I didn't warn you." He screwed lids on jars, wrapped the crystals in velvet pouches, and tucked everything back into his bag. Except the salt. That he threw in the trash with the ashes of the incense and smudge stick. "I'm going to clean up and then I'm going to need to sleep."

"Are you hungry? I still have those sandwiches." She glanced at the bag still on the table.

"I'll eat but only if you do. You aren't well enough yourself to be forgetting to eat. The fairies did a good job with your wounds. I can't see much residue left at all. Though I suppose that's to be expected when your body has actually had months to heal."

"Months Blake is paying for now, right?"

"No, Lei, that's not what I meant." Marcus took a step toward her. "I hope you will come to see that I am nothing like my mother. I don't blame you for this and I can tell you Blake doesn't either. He'd make the same choice every time. Please quit trying to pay penance for a choice that did not belong to you. The two of you are more alike than either of you will ever admit."

Lei looked away, busying herself with covering Blake with the blankets, making sure he was warm enough in the cool motel room. By the time Marcus exited the bathroom, Lei had the sandwiches, chips, and sodas sitting out on the little table.

"Thanks." He sat down across from her. "When I'm done eating, I'll go get a room of my own so you can get some sleep too."

"I'd rather you didn't. Just in case something happens, I'd rather you were here. I'll sleep on the floor or next to Blake or something. I just…just in case."

Marcus must have heard the desperation in her voice. "All right. We should know in a few hours if what I've done is enough anyway."

"What exactly did you do?" Lei asked as she opened her soda.

"Well, you have to understand, being a sorcerer is not without its risks. Especially with the kind of magic Blake can use. Effectively, he had magic poisoning. I know that sounds weird. It kind of is weird. It's like alcohol poisoning. He used too much magic in too short of a time frame and all the backwash didn't have a chance to dissipate, to return to its natural, inert state."

"So, no regular hospital would have been able to help him?"

"No. You did exactly the right thing. It would have been better if I'd been called in just after he released the spell that caused this, but I think I was in time."

"Can magic poisoning kill him?"

"Yes." Marcus looked over at his brother for a moment. "If it's not treated properly, by someone who knows what they're doing, it absolutely can."

"Did you take it from him? Will you be all right?"

"I didn't take it. My crystals did. They'll be worthless now—to me anyway. They'll make pretty jewelry or something. What's been locked inside them can't get out or I would destroy them."

They ate their dinner in relative silence and Marcus crawled into Lei's bed, falling into sleep practically before his head his the pillow. Lei made sure he was covered and went into the bathroom to change.

She slid into bed beside Blake and watched him sleep for a little while before exhaustion finally won out.

***

His lips were firm and warm on hers, his hands pulling her closer. Lei didn't resist, melting into his kiss, relishing the warmth that spread through her body.

"What happened to your rule?"

Lei opened her eyes, realizing that it was not a dream at all. She threw her arms around his neck and pulled him closer. "You broke it."

"You broke it first." He pulled away and smiled. "What did you do?"

"I called your brother. And don't you dare start yelling at me, he told me himself it was exactly the right thing to do. You had some kind of magic poisoning."

"I've had it before. Just never that bad." Blake turned his head and saw Marcus asleep in the other bed. "Okay. I won't yell at you. But only if you promise me one thing."

"I can't promise anything until I know what I'm promising."

"All I want is to pick this up, exactly here, when he's safely headed back home." Blake wrapped his arms around Lei and lay back down.

She didn't push him away, instead she snuggled closer, laying her head on his chest and listening to the powerful rhythm of his heart. "I can promise that."

He kissed the top of her head and held her close until they both found sleep again.

Chapter Fourteen

"Next time, Brother, you make sure you call me. This could all have been handled and done in a matter of an evening but no, my big bad brother has to prove he doesn't need anyone." Marcus finished loading his things in his car and checked Blake over one last time.

"Look, I appreciate your help, I do, but you know Mom is going to throw a fit when you get home. I didn't want to put you in that position." Blake scratched a little at his rough beard. "Plus, I didn't think it would get that bad. I've come through a poisoning before without anyone's help."

Marcus put his hand on Blake's shoulder, squeezing slightly. "You don't get it, do you? You shouldn't have to do it alone. You've saved my life a thousand times over. The least I can do is be around to help when you need it. And don't worry too much about Mom. I'm still the baby, I can get away with anything."

"I doubt it will be so easy this time, Marcus. Lei shouldn't have called you." He could already see Carie's reaction, the screaming and wailing, the forbidding any further contact with Blake.

"If she hadn't, you might have died."

"And I might have just slipped into a coma for a day or two and woken up just fine."

"If you call losing all your magic fine, sure." Marcus shook his head. "You are a stubborn bastard, Blake. Can't you just say 'thank you' and let me worry about the rest?"

Blake laughed. "All right then. Thank you."

Marcus pulled Blake into a brotherly hug and whispered in his ear, "Be gentle with her, Blake. There's a lot more to Lei's wounds than you know. She's fragile under that shell of hers."

"I know it. But I have to try and make her see that we can work. I'll regret it forever if I don't." Blake's smile grew bigger as he watched Lei cross the parking lot carrying bags. "And here she comes now."

Lei's damp hair hung loose over her shoulders like wet silk. The way her jeans fit, hugging her narrow hips, the way her over-sized shirt slipped down her shoulder, showing the sensitive skin at her neck, it fuzzed Blake's brain. And he didn't figure she even knew how much he wanted to bury his face where her neck met her collarbone and just breathe in her scent.

"I know you've got a long drive ahead of you so I brought you some lunch to take on the road." She held out one of her bags to Marcus.

"You didn't have to do that." He smiled and took the bag. "Thanks."

"It was the least I could do. Drive safe." She smiled back and bowed her head slightly before retreating into the motel room with the other bag.

"Make sure you call and check in sometimes, okay?" Marcus opened his car door and paused for a moment. "For the record, if we're keeping one, I hope it works out with you two. I truly do."

"You're just saying that so you don't feel guilty for marrying Whitney." Blake grinned. "Please, you're doing me a huge favor. This, whatever it is, will play out the way it's supposed to, one way or another."

Blake watched Marcus pull away, standing in the doorway until he couldn't see the little blue car anymore. When he closed the door behind him, Lei had set out their meal on the tiny table. He saw the nerves dancing in her trembling fingers.

"I've seen you in a lot of moods. Nervous isn't one of them." Blake sat down across from her. "What's wrong?"

"Nothing. Everything. I don't know." She took a sip of her soda, her eyes looking down at the table and not at him.

"Are you afraid of me now?" A hollow ache began in Blake's chest as he stared at Lei. She shook her head but said nothing. "Leilani, it's not like you to sit there and say nothing. Whatever this is, whatever is bothering you, I can't help you if I don't know what it is."

When she looked up, tears glistened in her eyes. "It doesn't matter. No matter how I feel, how you think you feel, this won't last."

"How I *think* I feel?" Blake stood up and moved to her side, turning her chair to face him.

"It's easy to be sure in the dark, where we can be blind to some things if we want to be." She stared down at her hands in her lap.

"There's nothing about you I'd want to be blind to, Lei." He knelt before her and took her hands in his.

"You say that now because you don't know. You can't know."

Before she could pull away from him, Blake gathered her up in his arms and held her. He kissed the top of her head. "Then tell me. There's nothing you can say that will make me walk out that door. Do you understand?"

"You're not listening." She pushed away from him and stood up, turning her back on him. "It's too late to step back but I promise I'll try not to hate you when you leave."

"What are you talking about?"

With her back still to him, Lei pulled her shirt off over her head and reached around to unhook her bra, letting them both fall to the floor. Slowly, she turned around. Pain ripped through Blake. Her flesh was almost more scar than skin, a patchwork of raised ribbons, old and new, but the worst of them were claw marks, deep stripes across her abdomen. The new scars were more like stab wounds, peppering the already marked flesh with angry lines, puncturing her breasts so very close to her heart.

"Oh my God." His whisper filled the room.

"I warned you." She lifted her arms to cover herself.

Blake rushed to her, putting his hand under her chin and forcing her to look at him. "You thought a few little scars would scare me off?"

"Little? I think that poisoning affected your eyesight." She closed her eyes, turned her head away. "It's not just the scars, they're bad enough, but—"

He pulled her to him, pressed his lips to hers. Gently, he teased her mouth open with his tongue, desperate to taste her but patient. There was more at stake for him than one night. Leilani pressed against him, deepening the kiss, pulling him in. The fear was still there, in her eyes, in her trembling hands. She wrapped her arms around his neck as he lifted her and carried her to the bed they'd shared.

She reached to turn out the light and he grabbed her wrist, pinning it gently to the bed. "If you don't trust me, we shouldn't be doing this. We can stop."

Lei shook her head.

Blake kissed her again, releasing her wrist so he could run his fingers through her hair, over her face, down the taut, tense skin of her body. She smelled faintly of jasmine, soft and feminine. His heart thundered against his chest as she pulled his shirt off, pressing his flesh to hers.

Working his way down her body, he kissed each of her scars in turn, leaving none untouched. Blake pulled her jeans away and threw them on the floor, for a moment, he looked at her, wished that she could see herself the way he saw her. He laid his hand over the worst scar, the first scar, lining his fingers up with the claws and shuddered. It had been a big werewolf that had almost killed her.

This time, when his lips touched hers, there was no hesitation. She opened for him and drew him in. She gasped and her eyes fluttered as his fingers danced lower, teasing her. The last of her fear vanished as she pulled him closer, her nimble fingers pulling at his jeans. Blake backed away for a moment to remove the last barrier between them.

They moved together in a slow tangle of flesh, driving each other to the edge and over it. Whispers of pleasure passed between them, evolving into ragged breaths and thundering hearts twined together until they became as one. They crested the wave together and fell over the edge.

For a long time, they lay there in quiet, holding each other close. Lei finally broke the silence. "We should get moving."

"We should." Blake rose up on his arm and captured her mouth with his.

"What happens now?" Lei pulled the quilt tight around her and watched as Blake dressed.

"I guess we head for the Justices and see if we can't get their help." He shrugged into his shirt.

"That's not what I mean."

Blake looked at her for a long moment, surprised at how fragile she looked, how lost. "I know what I want. The real question is, Leilani, what do you want?"

"I…I guess I don't know." She reached for her clothes and pulled her shirt on over her head before coming out from under the quilt.

"Why are you still hiding from me, Lei?" Blake took two steps and gathered her into his arms again. "I know you don't believe me yet, but I swear I'll find a way to make you. Yes, you have scars. So fucking what? It doesn't change anything."

She stepped away from him. "I get that you believe that, but maybe you won't always feel the same way."

"Don't get ahead of yourself, or us. Let's just take this one day at a time. I'm not going anywhere. When you figure out what you want, we'll go from there." Blake laid his forehead on hers. "For now, we'll deal with the Justices and the gates and maybe enjoy the time we do have together. Everything else kind of has to wait anyway."

"All right." She let out a shaky breath as she composed herself. "If we hurry and pack, we should be able to get to Rapid City. That will bring us close enough but still be in a big enough place that maybe we'll go unnoticed."

Blake leaned in close and kissed her. "This wasn't a one-night anything, Leilani. Just so you understand."

Lei nodded and hurried to pack up their things.

**

The motel in Rapid City was nice, nothing special, and close to the traffic of the casino. They unloaded only what they needed and grabbed a few breakfast sandwiches from a drive-thru.

"The Justices are situated not far from here. The place looks more formidable than it is." Lei sketched the general outline of the property from memory. "That's not to say there aren't protective measures in place. I'm sure the guards will be armed for pretty much anything. Willy didn't think they took their safety seriously enough. It was one of the reasons she tried to avoid going to headquarters as much as possible."

"Are we going in?" Blake peered at the sketch as he ate.

"I don't think that's the best idea, even knowing the couple of weak spots that Willy found. There's no way to be sure they haven't shored them up now. Especially when they must know Willy told me everything. No, I think we wait and catch someone going in or out. All we need is to see if the Justices who were sent to the attack in Texas have been able to talk some kind of sense into the leadership."

Blake shook his head. "If you're right and there's at least one high-ranking Justice helping to open the gates, I doubt a couple of rank and file guys are going to convince that person to change his or her mind and come back to the side of humanity."

"We don't need them to. We just need a couple of Justices to decide that the leadership is being stupid. It's a damn shame Taj was the one who was killed. I think he'd have helped us, once he understood. All we need are a couple who believe more in their oaths than their leadership. For all their training, these men and women are still human, still reasonable."

"Maybe that's why the demon went after Taj. Maybe it was a kind of cover up. Maybe they're slowly removing any Justice who they know can think for himself."

"I had the same thought. Hopefully, we'll be able to get some backup before they finish the job." Lei scratched her head. "We'll settle in, get some rest and stake out the place. See if we can catch anyone outside their compound. Maybe we'll find help, maybe we'll find trouble."

"Is it worth the risk? Really?" Blake finished eating and gathered up his trash.

"I think so. If we find trouble, we head for the gate we're supposed to be watching. We'll head straight for Arizona. If we find help, maybe we get someone inside keeping an eye on things or better, some additional manpower at the gate. The Justices have dealt with demons a lot more than the rest of us. Imagine the tools at their disposal. Willy had some useful stuff, but in that compound are texts after texts on dealing with the more shadowy side of our business. So, for me, yeah. I'd say it's worth the risk."

"All right." He untied his boots and set them aside. "We'll go out there and see what we can see."

Lei nodded as she finished eating. She no longer knew what to expect from him. Wasn't sleeping with the man supposed to change things between them, change how he treated her? So far she hadn't seen it. He was still Blake. Still obnoxious and arrogant. Still wonderful to look at. Her whole body felt electric in his presence but she had no idea what she was supposed to do.

"Quit it." Blake laughed. "You're over thinking things. You've practically got steam coming out of your ears. Come on, let's get some sleep."

Lei said nothing, but threw away her trash and stripped down to her t-shirt. As she climbed into bed beside Blake, he pulled her close to him. It was a little too easy to curl up against him, her head on his chest, as if they'd been together for years. Sleep came a little too quickly, too easily. Her last thought before sleep pulled her under completely was that something was bound to go wrong now. She wasn't allowed to have anything good.

***

The cold night air bit at his face and hands as they climbed the rocks. Lei was ahead of him, bound to him by a length of climbing rope. The moonlight played over the reflective strips on her black pack. In the distance lightning flashed, but it did not come from the sky—it came from the ground. Energy charged the air, spoke to Blake in a taunting whisper. In the darkness, swirling electricity popped blue and white as it appeared for a moment and then vanished only to reappear even closer.

Distracted by the approaching light show, Blake took another step and his foot slipped. He cried out as he fell, his leg folding in the wrong direction, sending a sharp, stabbing pain through his entire body. In moments, Lei was beside him, holding his hand.

"It's not broken." Blake assured her even though he wasn't completely sure of it. His toes moved on command, his leg responded to his requests with both movement and pain. "I just need to sit here for a minute."

Lei pulled her pack off and began rummaging through it until she came up with the extra tent stakes. Using the cord from her survival bracelet, she fashioned a crude brace for his leg to help take the weight. "It won't do much, but maybe it will help."

"Thank you." He grabbed her hand and squeezed it. "It's fine. I've been worse off than this. We should get going."

Lei helped him to stand and stayed with Blake as they climbed back up to the place where he'd fallen. Slowly, she took the lead again, creeping farther and farther away as the electricity got closer. Fear gripped him as the bursts began appearing in the rocks around them.

He slipped again, managing to catch himself before he slid back down the steep embankment. The electricity exploded right in front of him. He stared into it for a long moment, seeing stars through it that did not belong to the Earth's sky. It vanished as quickly as it had come.

Blake looked up the incline at Lei just as another vortex popped up.

"I've got him!" She cried as she started forward, into the vortex.

"Lei! Don't!" Blake pulled hard on the cord that bound them, trying to pull her back but she was already gone and the cord hung limp in his hand.

"Blake!" Lei's voice brought him back to the moment as she shook him. "Are you all right?"

He nodded and pulled her to him, clinging desperately.

"What the hell was that?"

"A dream." He whispered in her hair. "One I'm going to make damn sure doesn't happen."

Lei sat up some to look at him. "What does that mean? I didn't think you could see the future."

"I'm not sure that's what it is. Not really." He sighed. "It's never the same twice."

"You've had this dream before? It must have been pretty bad for it to have you this shaken up." She pressed her lips to his. "Don't worry, I won't let anything happen to you."

Blake laughed. "You think I'd be this worried over myself? Man, you've got a lot left to learn about me."

"Tell me about it. If I know what you've seen, I'll know better what not to do, won't I?" She smiled at him and settled in to listen as he told her about the dream he'd had not once but three times now.

When he finished explaining it, Lei mulled over the facts for a few minutes. The terrain he described fit pretty well with where they would be heading when they were done with the Justices. Lei had been there once before on what turned out to be a wild goose chase after a bigfoot-type creature called a Mogollon Monster. The Superstition Mountains, tucked away in Arizona, were ripe with ancient legends of tunnels and portals and vortexes. She hadn't found anything but very large and ugly bugs.

"Answer me this, did you get assigned this gate or did you choose it?"

For a moment he looked away. "I did the assigning. That gate is the one I'm supposed to be at. I had the dream the first time before the clans met. Originally, it was only me in danger. Something changed after you got hurt. By the time you appeared in the dreams, the assignments had already been handed out. I couldn't change it."

"Look, Blake, we have to go there, it's the job, but I promise you I'll be as careful as I can. You need to be too. In every one of your dreams that included both of us you've injured your leg. So let's make a deal." She put her hands on either side of his face and leaned in close. "You will watch your step and I won't get ahead of you. We'll stay together."

"You make it sound so easy." He pulled her toward him for a kiss, still trembling. "Let's go catch ourselves a Justice."

***

Armed with a thermos of coffee and a pair of night vision goggles, Lei and Blake hiked into the woods near the Order's compound. They huddled in the dark watching the Justices' headquarters. There were lights on in various windows of the large stone building but it was quiet. At first, the only movement was the standard patrol along the border, each of them armed with rifles that Lei didn't think looked exactly legal, but what did she know. Somewhere near midnight, they spotted something else.

One by one, a small group of Justices crept out of the main house and gathered in the shadows near the boundary where Willy's notes said there was a tall, electrified fence. There were four of them but they were too far away to see much detail.

Slowly and silently, Blake and Lei made their way through the trees, inching closer to the group who had their heads together as if discussing something very important. Their body language spoke volumes. They certainly weren't agreeing with one another. When they got close enough to see them better, Blake pressed his lips to Lei's ear. "The short one doing the talking, he was in Texas. Said his name was Ron. He seemed genuinely surprised by a lot of things."

Lei nodded and turned her head to reply. "Are you okay to do magic now? Can you still shadow up?"

Blake nodded and did so.

"If it starts to go funky, pull me in." She leaned into the shadows and kissed him, missing her mark slightly, pressing her lips to his rough cheek.

Quickly, making enough noise to get the attention of the Justices, but not enough to call up the patrol, Lei made her way to the fence.

"My name is Leilani Scott." She spoke clearly, just loud enough for the four of them to hear her.

"That's not possible," the Justice Blake had pointed out spoke as he peered into the night.

Lei stepped out from behind a low shrub so they could see her. "The fairies and the sorcerers saved my life. I wish they could have saved Taj too."

"Like hell," one of the other Justices muttered and Ron elbowed him.

"She tried to save him, Evan, and it nearly killed her too. If it hadn't been for that old lady on horseback, we'd all be dead."

"I was there too." The tallest of them had the quietest voice. "She really did, Evan. I thought for sure you were dead, ma'am."

"If you're calling me ma'am, you haven't been a Justice long." Lei shook her head. "That makes two of you that have some idea what we're all up against. We can't do this alone."

"Why are you talking to us?" the doubter, Evan, asked.

"Like a hunter can just walk up to the front gates. Besides, you've got a problem in your own house, boys. Someone in the Order is helping these demons. They made a deal with Jules Whittaker."

"No way. No way anyone here makes a deal with that shit-bag vamp." Evan spat on the ground.

"Then why did the Order tell Cam he couldn't flush out the nest in Pittsburgh? Though, to hear the vampires tell it, he's the one who made the deal."

"Your vamp is a liar." The fourth member of the group finally spoke. "That's bullshit."

"Hello again, Cam." Lei set her shoulders. "I did what you wanted and your name came up before I took out the baby vampire holed up in Whittaker's vault. Fortunately for you, you are one of the biggest bigots I've ever met in my life. You'd die before you'd make a deal with a vampire. Let alone one of the old ones. Plus, you put me on the scent yourself."

"What are you doing here?" Cam took a step towards the fence, looking like he was ready to call an alarm.

"Something big and horrible is coming and I need your help. Watch your leaders. Question them about what happened in

Pittsburgh and at my place in Texas. Are the higher ups even letting you look into it? What are they saying now?"

"To leave it alone. All of it." There was silence for a moment before Cam turned on his heels and walked away.

"I should go before he reaches the compound." Lei began to step back into the shadows when Ron's voice stopped her.

"Tell me what I can do?"

"Be ready. When I come back here, I'll be coming in to remove whoever is spearheading this. When I do, just have my back," she shrugged.

"That's not enough. I can do more than that." Ron stepped closer to the fence. "Something isn't right here at the compound. We can all sense it. But you want us to wait until you get back? I can't do that. You're not a Justice, I don't expect you to understand, but our vows mean something to those of us who take them. We don't say we'll serve and protect humans so long as our leaders say so. We have sworn to protect humanity from the otherworlders at all costs. To me, if that means working with a few of them for a short time then so be it."

"Where are you going from here?" The tall one asked.

"Arizona." Lei didn't give them any further information, just in case she was wrong about these three.

"I know one of the Justices there pretty well." Evan stepped toward the fence, dropping his voice to a whisper. "We'll be in Apache Junction in three days. If you decide you're going to trust us, if you decide you need help with what's coming, we'll be waiting."

"That was a quick decision." Lei stepped back, suspicious. "You didn't even discuss it."

"What happened in Texas is all we've been discussing for the last two weeks. Just not where anyone can hear us. It's been declared an off limits subject." He shook his head. "We've been looking for something real we can do to help. Going to Arizona to help you would be better than sitting here watching our order fall apart."

"That is exactly what most Justices are already doing, isn't it? You'll forgive me if I'm a little paranoid at the moment. Who's to say one of you isn't working with the leaders? How do I know you won't rat out me and anyone looking to stop what's going on?"

"What *is* going on?" Ron asked.

"I don't have all the answers but I do know someone has been opening up gates between this world and another, Hell maybe. At least, if you follow the mythology. Someone working with Whittaker and at least one person from the hidden lands who may or may not be an elf." Telling them so much information was a calculated risk. They needed all the help they could get. And she and Blake would know soon enough if any of the three Justices were working with the leaders. If they were, they'd be waiting for her in Arizona and then at least she'd know who they were up against.

"Why would anyone want to do that?"

"That's the big question, isn't it?" Lei took another step back to where Blake was waiting. "Apache Junction it is. We'll see what we see there. Keep your heads down. Don't let them see your doubts or you might not get off the grounds."

Blake's arms came around her, wrapping her in shadow and they walked slowly into the woods toward the small back road where they'd left the car.

Chapter Fifteen

Lei checked herself in the mirror one more time. Being pale and blonde wasn't something she'd ever really imagined for herself. Even in school, she'd never had the desire to look like her cheerleader friends. The reflection she saw looked nothing like the woman she knew herself to be but more like the girls she'd laughed and giggled with before the attack. She shuddered. Looking at Blake and his long red hair and too narrow face was just as weird. "You're absolutely certain this is going to work?"

"I wouldn't do it if I wasn't." He smiled as he pulled on his shirt.

"And it's not going to hurt you to do it?" She fiddled with the ends of her hair, disliking the color.

"There's no harm to this magic, not really. Marcus really did remove all the poison. I might not be back up to my full strength just yet, but I'm well on my way. I promise." He kissed the top of her head. "You don't like being a blonde? I thought all women wanted to be blonde at least once in their life."

"Not me. But then, it does look right with this face."

"I prefer your true face." He held her chin in his hands and looked into her eyes. "We're only doing this for a little while."

"I know but I don't have to like it. No matter how cool it is that you can do it." She smiled at him. "All right. Let's go track down some Justices and see what's what."

She picked up her purse and tried to wear it like a regular girl, not one who wanted to make sure she had easy access to her gun. The tank top she wore was too tight to cover a holster and it was too damn hot to wear a coat. Not that she even owned a gun the Justices hadn't seen before.

Blake took her hand and led her out into the Arizona afternoon. They made their way down the street to the bar they'd seen Ron go into earlier. His arrival in Apache Junction didn't mean much. They needed more information before deciding whether or not to trust them. It was just as likely he was sent to hinder them as it was he'd come to help.

The bar itself was nothing special. Styled to feel like it might have been during its heyday, the bar stank of beer and stale smoke. Ron sat at a table not too far from the bar with two other men. One of them they recognized as Evan. The other they didn't know. Blake and Lei sat at the bar, their backs to the Justices but listening closely.

"You're sure she'll be here?" The unknown Justice asked.

"She's not stupid enough to come in here and make a scene, Gabe. We've given her every reason not to trust us. You don't trust her."

"Shut up. You've put me in a bad enough position as it is."

Lei shifted slightly, angling herself to get a better look at Gabe. His face was turned away but what she saw of his skin was deeply tanned and lined with age. His thick braid fell between thin shoulders, a steel rope of hair.

She heard Blake order beers for both of them but was too intent on the Justices to pay much attention to the bartender.

"What do we do, Gabe?"

"We can't do anything. We took an oath to the Order."

"We took an oath to humanity too." Evan set his drink down hard. "Something is rotten in the Order and if we do nothing, we're as bad as them."

"But you said she's working with the sorcerers?" Gabe shook his head. "We can't trust them. What if they use our moment of weakness to kill as many of us as they can?"

"Oh, like we tried to do to them?" Ron stood up and stomped over to the bar for a moment, ordering another round for his table and laying cash on the bar. He glanced up at Lei for a moment and smiled.

Lei smiled back before giggling as if Blake said something funny and leaned in for a kiss, hoping they'd see nothing more than a pretty couple of kids. "I think Ron and Evan actually want to help. Not so sure about this Gabe fellow yet. But none of them seems to be working with the leadership."

"We'll give them time to think about it while we get our gear together. We'll come back in tomorrow night and see where we stand." Blake laid down a tip for the bartender and took Lei's hand in his and walked with her out into the town.

They got in the car and headed for the large camping outlet they'd seen on their way in from Phoenix. Lei had a nearly empty card with a $5000 limit in her pocket. It would be useless after the first or second use, but they only needed one stop. Hopefully. She hated it. Lei didn't enjoy stepping over, around, or through the laws.

But sometimes there wasn't a choice. There were things they needed and the woman whose identity she was using for this was dead with no family, so she wasn't putting some innocent woman out.

Lei zipped through the store, grabbing a large external frame pack designed specifically for a woman's body. She felt Blake watching her even as he picked out his own gear. She knew he saw everything she picked up. That he understood she wasn't just planning for a few days in the desert but also just in case his dream wasn't so much a dream and she disappeared. She wanted to make sure she could survive long enough to be rescued.

The two of them made quite a dent on the limit of her card. She was as ready as she could be. If something happened and they did get separated, if she did pass through a vortex, she felt certain she'd at least stand a chance of surviving until Blake could find a way to bring her home. It surprised her to find she truly trusted him to be able to do so. It had been years since she'd trusted anyone like that.

Blake bought less, would pack lighter, but he hadn't vanished through a stone wall. It seemed neither of them wanted to talk about it. The possibility that his dream was an actual vision of what might be hung between them, colored everything they said and did.

That night, they brought everything into the motel room and packed, unpacked, and repacked their packs, looking for the best way to distribute the weight. He didn't argue when she insisted on carrying a bivy sack or too much water. Lei took that as a good sign, that he agreed it was better to be prepared, just in case. And when they returned to the motel room after it was over, they would laugh together over how silly it was to take enough for at least a week for just a single overnight.

When Lei tested her pack, pulling it up on her shoulders and adjusting all the straps designed to try and distribute the weight a little better, she groaned. It was damn heavy. She wouldn't be able to move fast. She took the pack back off and reached for the straps that held the upper portion closed.

"Lei." Blake's voice filled the darkened room. "We've packed enough for one night. Come to bed. We need to rest. And I need to hold you for a while."

She closed her eyes for a moment before she stepped away from the pack and walked across the small room to the sink. As she filled the plastic cup with water from the tap, Blake came up behind her.

194

She set the cup down as he turned her, crushing her to him. His lips bruised hers, his tongue demanding, his hands roaming her body, tangling in her hair.

He picked her up and Lei wrapped her legs tight around his waist. Carrying her to the bed, his kiss deepened. Pawing, tearing at clothes, they stripped, breaking contact only briefly as they gasped for air. Outside it started to rain. They rode the storm, thunder shaking the windows as Blake lost control and pulled Lei under with him.

As they fell into exhausted sleep at last, Blake held her as if he were afraid she'd vanish while he was sleeping.

***

When they woke, it was near noon. They left the room without the glamours and headed for the bar where they'd seen the Justices the day before. Ron and Evan sat waiting for them at a table, large mugs of coffee and sandwiches in front of them.

Ron stood up. "I didn't think you'd come. I mean, I didn't figure you'd actually meet with us."

"I wasn't sure we would myself." Lei offered him a small, reassuring smile as she took the seat across from him. "If we can't trust you, we've already lost. Those mountains are too big to cover by ourselves and I don't think we have time to wait for backup."

"That's a very good point." Gabe came into the bar through the kitchen doors and looked Lei and Blake over. "I am Gabriel. This is my territory so I hope you don't mind these young ones bringing me in."

For the first time, Lei got a good look at his face. His brown skin was sun worn and lined with deep creases. His high cheekbones, ebony eyes, and the steel silver of his hair marked him as Indian, possibly Apache but Lei wasn't going to ask. "If you're willing to help us, you are more than welcome."

Gabe moved an empty chair and sat at the head of the table. "You're not what was I was expecting." He took Lei's hand in his and looked at it for a long time. "I suppose I was assuming you were a white girl. I've never met woman hunter who wasn't."

"I'm half. My mother was Hawaiian, my father was not." She pulled her hand free.

"A pity. I was hoping maybe you had some Indian in you."

"My father claimed to have Cherokee blood in his line, if that makes you feel better. Though I'm not sure why it matters."

"The Superstition Mountains have a long history with the Indian." He sighed. "No matter. The boys here have explained the situation as they see it. I am willing to hear you out before I decide."

"That's fair." Blake nodded and began explaining all they had learned from the beginning. Gabriel stopped him once or twice to ask questions but mostly let him tell it uninterrupted. He listened with an intensity that unnerved Lei, his dark eyes focused on Blake's face as if he could see the words leaving his mouth.

When Blake finished, silence spread over the table. Gabriel was considering their plan quite seriously. Lei fidgeted in her chair. There wasn't time for this. They should already be heading for the mountains. If they were going to stand any kind of chance of stopping Whittaker from opening up the gate within, they needed to find the damn gate, not sit in a bar waiting for an old man to decide if he was going to allow them or not.

"Miss Scott, you must have patience if you want to be able to find this gate. Running out into the desert haphazardly will do nothing but get you lost." Gabe spoke as if he'd read her thoughts. "We need a plan of attack."

"If this is their next gate, Whittaker is already here, holed up in a cave that gets no light. If we find the cave, we'll find the gate. He won't be far from it." Lei chewed her bottom lip as she thought. "He's one of the old ones, Gabriel, he knows all the tricks."

"I imagine Willy would say different." Gabe smiled at her, showing his aged yellowed teeth. "I knew Willy quite well. We're of an age, you know. I was shocked when she refused a direct order from the Heads. I knew she was sick but I also knew she wasn't sick enough that she couldn't travel. At least she hadn't been then. I went to see her during your training. You were off on your first mission at the time. She told me how you came to be her student. And why she wouldn't take you to the Order."

"Then you know more than I do. She wouldn't even tell me at the end when she barely knew what she was saying through the pain."

"You didn't need to know then." Gabriel smiled again at her and winked. "She said the Order would baby you too much, not give you a chance to really learn what you could and should do. That the Order would suck the humanity right out of you. The attack that killed your parents almost did that anyway and she worried for a time that you'd be like her, unable to get it back."

Lei stared at him for a moment. She would never understand Willy or whatever happened to her to change her views on everything so completely. Lei had read all of Willy's journals, heard countless stories from the otherworlders. She'd been a heartless Justice, cruel and vindictive, for decades. Something changed just before she met Lei. Maybe it was the cancer, but maybe not. Willy kept her isolated but maybe it hadn't been a final act of cruelty after all.

"Do you know what changed for her? How she went from being consumed by the annihilation of the otherworlders to trying to make sure I didn't take that same path? I've met a lot of people who knew her and the woman they knew and the woman I knew were so very different."

"I don't know everything. I do know that she met someone who changed her mind. It was maybe a year before she took you under her wing. She never spoke of it. Never explained it."

"She never really explained anything about herself."

"Willy was a good teacher though. She taught you what to do, so do it." Gabe's smile disappeared, his face taking on a stern, very professorial expression.

"Point taken. You know this place better than any of us. Where would you go, if you couldn't let the sun touch you? We'll start there."

Gabriel looked at the other Justices. "Do you have your gear ready?"

Both gave crisp answers of "Yes, sir."

"My boys have brought their sniper rifles with night scopes. I have headsets for all of us. You can follow me out toward the mountains. I know where I would go if I were a vampire. Hopefully we can pick up a trail there."

"If we don't, we'll go on to the next most logical spot, just like Willy would do." Lei nodded. "So, you have no problem going against the Order on this?"

"Willy was a very good friend, once upon a time. In the end, she didn't trust the Order as far as she could throw them. I took this territory mostly because none of the Heads ever come down here. You haven't told me anything I hadn't already suspected." Gabriel stood. "I'll meet you out front in ten minutes. Is that enough time?"

"Just." Blake answered for them as he stood.

Outside, Blake took her hand in his and they walked back towards the motel. "This could totally backfire on us."

"Yep." Lei agreed as she slid her key in the door and opened it wide. "I believe him though. Gabe, I mean."

"For what it's worth, I do too."

They took their gear out to the car and loaded it in the back. As Lei got in the driver's seat, she reached under the dash and pulled out a set of keys. "I know we're not talking about it but just in case we *do* get separated, put these in your pocket."

"We're not going to get separated." But he took the keys anyway and shoved them in his pocket.

Gabe was waiting for them when they pulled in front of the bar. He held two headsets in his hands. "We should maintain contact at all times. They're all set for you. All you have to do is wear them."

"Thanks." Lei took them from him and handed one to Blake. "Lead the way."

Gabe grinned and tipped his cowboy hat as he turned to get into his beat up pickup truck. The other Justices were already sitting on the bench seat inside, waiting for their mentor, their gear piled in the bed.

The drive was a long one, starting out on nicely paved roads with beautiful scenery that no one had the time or inclination to appreciate. As Lei drove, staying close to Gabe's truck, Blake watched the horizon for places where the shadows gathered deep, where the sun might never break through at all. There were a few places to pull off the main road, mostly trail heads where a car arriving in the dark would surely be noticed and noted. Not likely for one so careful as Whittaker.

"There's a lot of open space out here and no real way of knowing who is where. This may be a bit of a wild goose chase, but I know a couple of caves that might fit your parameters." Gabe's voice came over the headsets very clearly. "We'll check there first."

Lei followed him as he pulled off the main road and started down what looked more like a path than any kind of road, overgrown and pitted, clouds of dust rising up behind them. The road wound around the backside of a low hill. As they rounded the hill, out of sight of the main road, they found a car.

"That's from the Order." Ron said, a little more loudly than he needed to.

"Are you sure?" Blake asked.

"I work in our garage sometimes. I know our cars. That one is usually reserved for when one of the three Heads of the Order needs to go somewhere."

"If they're parked here, they didn't go in here." Lei said, more to Gabe than anyone.

"Agreed. We'll go a little further on. Pull up here so I can turn around."

The cars got turned around and headed back down the main road until it branched off, the smaller road heading out into the wilderness. They passed that road and went further, driving until Lei was just about ready to go back to the car they'd found to wait and follow.

"We're getting pretty close to the foothills now." Gabe's voice broke a little over the headphones as they bounced through the desert. "We'll park up here and work our way towards the caves. It's got to be in this set of caves, otherwise that car would be too far away to do them any good."

"Sounds good." Blake responded and glanced over at Lei. "Here goes nothing."

"Yep." She pulled into the shadow of the hills behind Gabe and parked. They all got out of their vehicles and grabbed their packs, looking to all the world like nothing more than a group of campers out for some fun in the great outdoors.

"You're packed awfully heavy for what shouldn't be a very long trip." Gabe looked at their packs. "What do you know that you aren't telling us?"

"It's probably nothing." Blake adjusted his pack, fastening the straps around his waist. "I've had dreams lately but Lei and I were alone in all of them. It's possible everything has already changed just because of your presence."

"What did you see?"

"He saw me walk through a rock face." Lei answered for him as they began walking in the direction of the closed road and the mountains beyond it.

"Around here, that's actually a possibility. At least, that's how the legends go." Gabe took a pace that put him beside her. "I wish you'd said something about this before. I'd have made sure you had some kind of guide."

Lei laughed. "We probably don't have time for any of that shit. The only reason I'm sure we haven't missed the gate opening is that nothing strange has happened around here. If Ron is right and that car belongs to a Justice, we're pushing the limits of our time already. We've just got to do what we've got to do. Whatever happens, happens."

"You're much too calm for a woman whose lover saw her walk into the Netherworld. You'd be wise not to be quite so glib."

"Not glib, just a realist. We have to stop Whittaker. If we're in the right place and the other sorcerers aren't, no matter what happens, we have to do what we have to do. We're probably not at the big one anyway, there's thirty or forty gates being watched by sorcerers now. They could be working at any or all of them even as we speak."

"You don't fool me. Your man strikes me as the kind of man who always takes the hardest road for himself." Gabe looked at her and paused. "You don't think there's anything that can be done to change what he's seen, do you?"

"I think we've changed all we can change and he's still having those dreams. I'm not going to back away from the job because I'm scared. Whatever has to happen to put an end to this, I'll have to do." Lei shrugged and kept moving, picking up her pace a little to catch up to Blake.

They hiked for about ten minutes before they came to a path in the dust, footprints from more than one person. They all got down and inspected the ground around the path. Evan found a trace, a few sets of footprints heading out toward the east. The trace was a little more evident as they traveled the same direction.

"It's likely they traveled at night. This is an awfully sloppy trail." Gabe carefully stepped around the tracks, following but not disturbing them.

"Could it be a trap?" Ron asked.

"At this point it doesn't matter if it is. If it's a trap, at least we know we're in the right place." Lei shrugged and kept moving.

As they rose up on the crest of the hill, Lei stayed low, peering over the edge to get the lay of the land. Nothing stood out to her except another hill leading closer to the mountain. "Here's what we're going to do. Blake here is going to do a glamour on us and he and I will hike right past that cave, see what we can see. We'll make enough noise and keep any eyes on us so you three can get up above the cave. When the shit hits the fan, I don't want them to be able to retreat into it."

"Good thinking." Gabe agreed and watched with amusement as Blake performed the glamour and turned them back into the young, nature-loving couple they'd been in the bar. "I wondered why you didn't seem too put out by my presence."

"Sorry, guys. We can't afford to outright trust anybody."

Blake and Lei set out over the hill, talking and pointing things out to each other like real tourists. They laughed and stomped over the rough terrain, making as much noise as they could without being suspicious. Without getting too close to the mouth of the cave, Lei saw prints in the dirt leading into it but not back out. She tried to count how many different ones but she was too far away to see that kind of detail.

"We're in position." Gabe whispered in their ears through the headsets.

Lei and Blake changed nothing about their movements, didn't hurry or suddenly start being quiet. But they made their way out of the clearing in front of the cave and up over the next rocky hill. Once out of view of the cave, they circled back, climbing the rocky incline to rejoin the others above the cave and settled in for a long evening of waiting.

Chapter Sixteen

The five of them stayed quiet as the day wound down, careful to keep hidden in the low shrubs and small outcroppings of rock. More than once Lei wondered if they had the wrong place but she wasn't giving up until after the sun set. Whittaker couldn't show himself before then regardless.

Just before dusk, when the sun hung low on the horizon, deepening the shadows and blessing the sky with a last touch of warmth, she heard people approaching from all directions. Noise from the direction of the cars, noise from the direction Lei and Blake pretended to travel in, and noise coming from the direction directly across from the cave. She stayed very still, wishing for even deeper shadows as there would likely be someone coming in from behind them too. It was a careful and well thought out plan of arrival to make sure there were no bystanders.

Lei froze in the cover of overgrown sage as two sets of footsteps approached from behind her. She quieted her breathing as they came so close they could have stepped on her.

"I smell humans." A gruff voice was a little louder than it probably meant to be.

"Shut up, Trin. We're meeting with humans. The idiot Justices are probably already here. Plus there's the girl. You're going to smell humans. The real question is do you smell the vampire yet?" The second voice was very pretty, musical. Something about it struck a chord of memory but Lei couldn't risk shifting to look at the speakers.

"Whittaker is already here. From the strength of his scent, he's been here for a few days."

"If things go bad, run as fast as you can. Meet me back at Black's Tavern." The melodic voice drifted further away, Lei strained to hear what they were saying.

"You're the one who brought him in. If things go bad, this is on your head. We didn't need the bloodsucker to meet with the Generals."

"It's not the Generals we're after, fool. I can't open the door. It has to be someone from the Netherworld. The rules are the same there as in the hidden lands. Belonging to either is a gift that comes with power. If I could do it myself, don't you think I would have? When Malphas is free, we won't need Whittaker anymore. You can do whatever you wish, after the ceremony." The voice laughed and finally slipped beyond where Lei could hear him.

She thought for a long moment about the name he'd used. Malphas. She'd heard it before, she just couldn't remember where.

Down below, voices gathered among the shadows as night became complete and she felt comfortable enough to creep out from her sage and peer over the edge. Gabe and Blake joined her. Ron and Evan stayed tucked away in their hides, armed with M110 semi-automatic sniper rifles.

The small congregation lit a fire and set up torches as their unexpected witnesses watched from forty feet up. Gabe pointed out Michael Walker, one of the three heads of the Order. Lei put a face to the voice she'd heard a short time before, an elf named Eminithous. The werewolf who stood beside him like a guard was likely the same one who'd accompanied him to the meeting, Trin. Ron's voice came through the headsets, pointing out Geoff Gibbons, another head of the Order, as he emerged from the cave below them. There were others that no one recognized. There were thirteen gathered around the fire.

"Eminithous was one of the people who saved me after the attack in Texas." Lei kept her voice as low as she could and still have the headset pick it up. "He helped put me back together, but the whole time he was asking questions. He wanted to know what I knew about the thing that attacked me, where I thought it came from. He was testing me, feeling out our information. He asked me about the Danann scrolls, if I believed in the prophecy of the Raven, if I knew what any of it really meant. I told him the truth. I didn't care, really, but assumed the prophecy referenced the Celtic war-goddess, Badb. Her symbol is the raven. Now I'm not so sure."

"Why?" Blake asked.

"Gabe, how much do you know about demons?"

"More than I want, probably less than we need right now."

"Have any of you ever heard the name Malphas?" She asked, still staring down into the clearing, making sure no one down there reacted to her words.

"He's mentioned in the Lesser Key of Solomon the King." Evan's voice sounded soft, almost embarrassed. "He appears first in the shape of a crow."

"Maybe that has more to do with why the werewolves hunted girls born the same day as me. Maybe they made a different assumption." Lei thought about it for a moment and did not like the thoughts in her own head.

"Maybe you should go back, get out of here." Gabe laid a hand on her shoulder. "Maybe this really is an elaborate ruse to get you here, nearly unprotected."

Conversation below them stopped as Whittaker stepped out of the cave.

"Too late."

Lei slipped her night vision goggles from the side pocket of her pack and pulled them on.

"Welcome, friends." Whittaker's snake-oil voice carried well on the night air when he meant it to. "Tonight, we bring an old ally back from his prison. Tonight, we bring this world back into the dark and remind the humans what they really are."

The group gathered around something Lei couldn't see. The torches interfered too much with the night vision gear, so she flipped them up onto her forehead. At the edge of their circle, tiny red lights danced like fireflies spit from the fires of Hell itself.

Whittaker opened his arms wide and looked to the sky. "Tonight, all the gates will open and into this world will come an army that has been locked away far too long. Their punishment is long over, decreed by a jealous Father. Tonight, we change the world!"

He and the others began chanting in a language none of the witnesses recognized. In the distance, lightning flashed from a cloudless sky.

***

Blake watched everything from his gathered shadows, debating on whether or not to attempt to get closer to the circle. To the west, light gathered and pooled where there shouldn't have been light. The swirling blue and white sent a sharp spike of fear through his gut. His first instinct was to gather Lei up and flee, but he knew she wouldn't let him. Wouldn't even let him bind her to him, not that it would do any good.

"Look." Gabe's voice filled their headsets. "That's a woman down there. I'm going down, getting closer."

"No." Lei hissed back. "They'll kill you."

"They're going to sacrifice that woman. I'm going to give you a distraction so you can save her. That's my job. Don't you worry about me. The job is what it is, right, Lei? Circle around while you have the chance. Make sure you get every last one of them. Every damned one." Gabe took off his headset and tucked it into the front of his shirt.

Blake heard the slight rustling of Gabe's clothes, his breathing. He hadn't turned it off; he was going to let them hear everything.

Lei shifted to start down the hill, pausing to kiss him briefly, touching her fingers gently to his cheek. Just as Lei disappeared from sight, Blake spotted a single headlight in the distance, headed their direction in the dark. He hoped it was backup and not someone coming late to the party. Blake caught up to Lei and pulled her tight into his shadows, using more magic to quiet their steps to even the most sensitive of ears. They made their way down the hill slowly but steadily.

Gabe moved silently in the night, moving away from the group, giving Lei and Blake time to get into position. Blake held tight to Lei, trying to watch both the group and the swirling pools of light that popped up closer and closer. Sweat beaded on his brow, fear trickling through his system.

Gabe made enough noise so everyone heard him coming. The circle had a moment to pull themselves together before Gabe came into view. If he hadn't watched them begin the act, he might have fallen for it. The Justices took aggressive stances toward the others who seemed more than happy to play along. Blake didn't like how smooth the transition played out.

"Looks like I got here just in time." Gabe stepped into the flickering torchlight with a gun in each hand. "You should have called me in, Sirs. This is *my* territory."

"There wasn't time." Michael turned toward Gabe.

To Blake it looked as though the Head Justice said something to Gabe, but he couldn't be sure, nothing came across over the headset. He only knew that Gabe's guns both fired as Geoff, the other Head of the Order, shot Gabe in the back. Michael fell to the ground, blood pouring from his eye as he lay dying. From the rocks, the sniper fire started—silver bullets flying down and picking off werewolves, the other Justice, and a few more.

Panic set in among the group as Whittaker took a silver bullet to the left side. It wasn't a direct heart shot and wouldn't kill him but it would slow him down. He grabbed the woman who had to be unconscious since she wasn't screaming. He ran toward where Blake and Lei hid, cloaked in Blake's shadows. Trin and Eminithous followed close on his heels, dodging to avoid the sniper fire that picked off their comrades.

Blake readied his gun, waiting as long as he could before taking the wolf down with a shot to the heart and revealing their position. Whittaker's eyes grew wide with shock and surprise as he shifted the woman so she covered his heart better. Eminithous broke away, running to the right as Whittaker bolted to the left.

"Let the elf go." Blake took Lei's hand and they started after Whittaker and the woman. "We know where to find him later."

***

Lei led with her gun drawn, moving as quickly as her pack allowed. Knowing Blake was right beside her was some comfort, but she had a pretty good idea where this chase would end. Nothing to do but do it. Kill the bastard, free the girl, and pray she didn't get sucked into one of the bouncing light pools. No problem.

Whittaker stumbled on the rocks, shifting the woman up over his shoulder as he moved. Lei wondered if the woman was already dead. She hadn't moved once. But if she were already dead, Whittaker would have left her, not taken her with him.

"Get up ahead of him if you can." Lei whispered to Blake.

"I don't want to split up." His voice held a trace of fear but Lei couldn't acknowledge it. If she did, she would have to admit to the fear that coursed through her own veins.

"If we're going to save the woman, we have to do this. You can move faster than I can. Hurry."

She kept moving, straining against the weight of her pack but not losing any ground between herself and Whittaker. Blake moved faster, probably using a touch of magic to do it. He stopped and Whittaker was forced to make a choice.

Whittaker turned on his heel, woman still in hand, and ran toward Lei. She pulled a stake from her pocket and prepared to take him out.

"This is just the beginning." Whittaker laughed and threw the woman down, her limp body rolling down the steep embankment.

Without a word between them, Blake leapt to catch the woman. Lei charged Whittaker who turned just as a portal opened and stepped through it.

She heard Blake scream her name, but it was already too late. The moving light swallowed her and she was no longer standing on solid ground but sinking in stinking muck.

Chapter Seventeen

The muck turned out to be a riverbank. Lei watched as Whittaker sliced through the water nearly fifty yards away and raised her gun. Or she would have if it hadn't fallen into dust in her fingers along with her watch. She didn't want to think about the phone in her pocket. She peered into the water and screamed to find, not her reflection staring back, but the face of a long dead man whose beard rose and fell with the water.

Leaping out of the water, she pulled off her pack and sat down for a moment beside the wide, black river. She watched Whittaker pull himself out of the water on the other shore. There was no way she could swim it with her pack and, since she didn't have any clue how to open a portal home, she was going to need everything in her pack.

Lei thought for a moment, calmed her shaking nerves and trembling hands, and went through her inventory in her head. She had enough water for two, maybe three days, enough food for the same.

She argued with herself. Stay where she was and pray for rescue or chase down the bastard and find her own way out. She knew Blake would do all he could to get to her. But, she had a debt to pay to Whittaker. Plus, she'd be a sitting duck waiting on the riverbank.

She took a deep breath and looked around. On the banks of the river there were tall, pale trees, only about as broad as her forearm. She unzipped her pack and dug down for her hatchet. It took too much time to chop down a few of the shorter trees and lash them together with the cording from her bracelet, but it would get her gear across the river. She would swim and pull the raft behind her. Anger and hatred consumed her heart. Whittaker would regret every life he'd ever taken, every family he'd destroyed, and every thought he'd ever given to opening the gates. She'd make sure of it.

***

Blake stared at the place where Lei had been standing, shock freezing him in place. It hadn't mattered. Nothing they'd done mattered. He couldn't save her. Maybe he was never meant to save her. Sometimes, no matter how badly he wanted something, Fate just had to prove that her will was stronger than his. And Lei was paying the price now.

He scanned the night, but the energy that had drawn the portals was gone. All that remained were bodies, blood, and an unconscious sacrifice. They succeeded in only one thing. The gate was still solidly closed. Whatever good that did them.

He checked the woman and found she was alive but unconscious. Carefully, he lifted her up and carried her back to the clearing. The sound of a motorcycle's engine broke the silence. The light from the headlight shone over the gore in the clearing. Blake stood there, still holding the woman, not really caring who was driving up. Good, bad, it didn't really matter to him. It wasn't Leilani.

"What the hell happened here?" The man on the motorcycle took off his helmet and surveyed the horror around him.

"You missed the party, Cam. Were you invited or crashing?" Slowly, Blake laid the woman down on the ground and prepared for an attack. As much as death might appeal to him, he couldn't get Lei back if he died.

"Damn it, I came to help Leilani." Cam shoved gloved fingers through his dark hair and cursed. "I asked for her help and she came through. I came to hold up my end of our deal. I'll ask again. What the hell happened here?"

Blake didn't pay him any attention. "Look around. We've got a couple of dead werewolves, a few kicked up vampires, and a handful of dead Justices. Some of those Justices were helping Lei and I stop the gate from being opened. Some were helping Whittaker to open it. Leilani is gone, through the portal with Whittaker. You can either help me clean this up or you can fight me. I don't much care. I'm kind of itching to put a beating on someone anyway."

A groan from one of the bodies stopped them both from saying anything further. Cam and Blake both ran toward the sound and found Gabe, bleeding badly from his shoulder and gut, weak but not dead. "We didn't think you'd come."

"I followed Michael's trail from headquarters and it led me here. I knew something wasn't right when he left the compound. I'm just sorry I didn't get here sooner. I was looking for you. It took nearly all day before I could find someone who'd seen which direction you headed." Cam stripped Gabe's shirt off to get a better look at his wounds. "Anyone have a first aid kit?"

"Yeah. I have the little one. Lei has the big one with her. Thank god for small favors I guess."

Cam looked around slowly. "Where is she?"

Blake slipped his pack off his shoulders and opened the top compartment where he'd stowed the first aid kit. "Through the looking glass. Whatever they were doing here, it nearly had the gate open. There were small portals popping up. I'm honestly not sure where they led but Lei followed Whittaker through one."

"No shit?" Cam opened up the kit and began searching for what he needed. "That little wannabe had the balls to follow one of the big vampires into a place no one knows anything about?"

"Bet you she's better at the job than you are and she doesn't even get paid for it." Blake's eyes narrowed, his hands clenched to fists at his side.

"Boys. There's no time for this." Gabe winced as Cam cleaned the bullet wound and prepared to stitch it up. "Damn it, that hurts. Blake, start cleaning up. By dawn, we need to make sure there's no sign of this mess. Then we'll see if I can't help you get your woman back."

"What?" Blake leaned down closer to Gabe, interrupting Cam mid stitch. "You have a way to cross over?"

"Not me. But I know someone who can. I may know several someones but only one is close enough to help. Get this place cleaned up. You two take care of the mess. I'll check on the woman." Gabe struggled to sit up and Cam pushed him back down waving the still threaded needle. "Fine. Just finish it up quick."

***

Lei leaned against a gnarled tree, pulling her foot free of the thick mud. She'd thought the collapsible hiking poles might come in handy when she'd bought them; it never occurred to her they might save her life. Or at least keep her from getting pulled down into the bog with all the other dead things she felt at her feet.

The scent of decay and stagnant water filled the mist that settled in the bog. Every so often, the water shifted, rippling with the movements of some unseen creature just beneath the murky surface.

Lei closed her eyes against the panic. There wasn't time for fear. She couldn't afford to feel sorry for herself. She could freak out all she wanted when she was safe and warm in her own realm. Until then, she could not allow herself to remember what fear was.

"Giving up so soon?" Whittaker's sharp voice echoed through the mist, coming at her from every direction at once. "This place, it's not meant for those like you. Those with beating hearts are not welcome in the land of the dead. In time, your heart will come to realize that truth and stop all on its own."

"Not going to take that honor for yourself? I would think lunch would be a little hard to come by for you here." Lei pushed away from the tree and stabbed at the thick water with her poles, testing the bottom before moving her feet. As she walked, she swung the poles, deflecting any creature that might see her legs as dinner.

"Not so much as you'd think. I can survive on the blood of the creatures here though I very much don't enjoy it. As for you, I have bigger plans than lunch." Whittaker laughed and the sound retreated.

She paused for a moment but could hear no movement at all. She cursed and screamed. Maybe Gabe was right and it had all been a trap and she'd just gone and walked right into it. For what? Vengeance? Justice? She cursed her own idiocy and arrogance.

There was nothing she could do but move forward. The list of her disadvantages in this situation was long and daunting. It was, in fact, the story of her whole damned adulthood. From the moment she graduated from high school, hell, from the moment the werewolf picked her house, she'd been the underdog and it had served her well thus far. Perhaps it would again. Everyone underestimated a good underdog.

Strands of colorless moss hung down from the smooth-barked trees, running ghostly fingers over Lei's head as she trudged on, following Whittaker's trail of broken branches and disturbed mud. It had been hours since she'd last heard him. More than an hour since the sun came up. She hoped the rules for vampires were the same here as they had been in the real world, but she couldn't count on it. He'd opened the portal; he was from this land. A little niggle of doubt whispered in her mind. Vampires weren't supposed to belong to the Netherlands but Whittaker must. Was he not truly a vampire? Was he something else entirely?

Exhaustion dragged at her heels, tried to pull her deeper into the murk and mist. There was no solid ground to be found for a campsite. But there were trees. Lei rubbed the trunk of one, cursing its smoothness. There was, however, more than one way to climb a tree. Reaching into one of the side pouches, she grabbed a length of rope and a carabiner. Attaching the rope to the heaviest thing she could pull out of the pack without making a mess, she took aim and threw it up over the lowest, thickest branch. The first few times, the rope and the rolled up sleeping pad came tumbling back down. Just as she was about to give up, it finally tumbled over the branch and came back to her.

She tied one end of the rope through the frame of her pack, hoisted it up about two feet from the surface of the bog and tied the other end of the rope to the tree. She cut a section off the end of the rope just long enough to make a harness out of and fashioned it the way the guy at the camping store had explained. She unzipped the side of her pack and stuck her hand inside, feeling around until she found both her foot spikes and a protein bar. Having eaten the protein bar, she took a little sip from her water reservoir and fastened the spikes to her boots with the heavy leather buckles.

Grabbing hold of the rope that held her pack, she stepped one foot on the side of the tree. The spikes sunk into the flesh of the tree a little too easily. The sap that poured from the bark didn't look like any sap she'd ever seen before. It poured like blood and, unless she was completely mistaken, the tree shuddered with every step she took. Pulling the bulk of her weight on the swaying rope, she used her feet mostly for stability.

"I'm really sorry, Mr. Tree. I hope you understand that I have to do this. I'm really tired and I need to rest. I don't mean to hurt you." She talked mostly just to hear her own voice but she didn't know the rules of this place. She'd never been in the Netherworld, and hadn't ever thought to ask the demons she'd faced about the place. There was a real possibility that this bleeding tree had once been a person. Whatever they did that was horrible enough to make them live out their eternity in this fashion, she didn't like knowing she was adding to their punishment.

By the time she reached the cradle of the wide branch she'd put the rope over, her arms ached, her legs screamed from the strain. Lei took a few moments to rest, her back against the tree, before she pulled up the pack. Fortunately, it was easier than she'd been expecting. Forty pounds was a lot easier to lift than her own hundred and some. Lashing herself to the tree so she wouldn't fall out, Lei finally gave in to her exhaustion.

***

Dawn broke over the Superstition Mountains in shades of gold and pink with just the promise of blue. The bodies were buried and concealed with a little help from Blake's weakened magic. The woman was finally coming out of her drugged stupor, frightened but grateful to them for saving her and mostly unharmed, though she'd never be the same. Blake drove Lei's Land Rover, following Gabe, Ron, and Cam back to Apache Junction. They'd lost Evan to a werewolf but the Justice hadn't gone down without a fight.

Once they arrived in town, Gabe and Ron took the woman, whose name was Marla, over to Gabe's for questioning. They needed to know everything she knew about what happened and why. Blake went back to the room he'd shared with Lei long enough to take a shower. He used her soap, breathing in her scent and praying he'd see her again.

When he got out of the shower, his phone was ringing. Thinking it was Gabe telling him to hurry up, he answered without looking at the screen. "You ready?"

"It's already happened then?" His mother's voice stabbed him as surely as a blade.

"I told you not to contact me." Blake nearly hung up on her, but he couldn't do it. "Did you know this would happen?"

"*You* knew it would happen. I tried to show you." For a moment, her voice softened. "I never wanted this path for you."

"You think it would have been better for her to die in Texas." He sat down on the bed, defeated. "I tried everything I could to make sure it didn't happen."

"Some moments of our fates are not as malleable as others. I called to tell you that your sister, Rachel, is dead. She and three others were killed at the gate in Virginia. We fared better in Washington and Ohio. They aren't done. Not now. They'll try again in Arizona. Drew thinks that's where the one who is orchestrating all of this will come through. I wanted you to know that we are on our way. All of us."

"Oh God. I'm so sorry, Mama. I really am." Blake closed his eyes. In his head he could see his older sister's smile, the faces of her two children.

"I know."

"What about Marcus, is he okay?" He thought of the brother who had saved him.

"He's hurting right now, but he's fine. Learned an important lesson. Even he can't heal the dead." Her voice broke.

"Mama, listen. See if anyone knows anything about Malphas. The demon that wants to come through here, that's his name." Blake had no words for the loss he felt too keenly. He'd never fit in with his family, but he loved them all. Each and every crazy, obnoxious, ridiculous one of them.

"Last night, even with the help of all the clans and the fairies, we were still spread too thin. Nearly every gate had some activity, but it seems like most of it was a distraction to keep us spread out and weak. We were too late to save all of the sacrifices but we rescued some. We also exorcised several demons who'd taken up residence in Justices, of all people. We likely missed enough for them to regroup and try this again. Be ready. We'll be there soon." Carie hung up on him without another word.

Blake sat for a moment with his head in his hands, elbows on his knees. Had anything they'd done mattered in the slightest? Rachel was dead, Lei was lost, and the elf and the vampire had gotten away.

A knock on the door made Blake jump. He threw open the door and let Gabe in. "Are you ready to go?"

Gabe nodded. "You need to take something of hers. Something personal, if possible. My friends, they're going to want to know the kind of person they're looking for."

Blake looked around the room but there wasn't much of Lei there. He took the keys and went out to the car, looking for the right kind of thing. He didn't figure a gun or a knife would be what they'd need. He opened up the glove box and found nothing. He searched under the seats, behind the seats, in the cargo space. Sitting in the front seat, Blake almost gave up. Lei just didn't seem the type to hold on to anything. Desperate, he pulled down the sun visor and two photographs fell from their place there.

The first photo was about as old as Lei herself. It had been taken in the hospital where she'd been born—a military man and his beautiful Hawaiian bride holding a tiny little newborn between them. Their eyes were so full of love and awe, of hope and promise. The second photo was much newer, the same three people about eighteen years later. Lei looked a lot like her mother, beautiful and small. They were so happy, untouched yet by the shadowy world Lei'd come to exist in.

He tucked the pictures in his pocket, locked up the car, and climbed into Gabe's truck. "Do these friends of yours know we're coming?"

"Yes." The old Indian started his truck and headed out of town. "I didn't tell them much about the situation, just that I need their help."

"Once they know, do you think they'll still help us?"

"I know they will." Gabe nodded. "They may not know all the things people like you and I know, but they know enough to understand why it is important to find your girl."

"You're making it sound like something horrible will happen if we don't. Like this is more than just helping an ally." A cold chill raced through Blake's blood.

"There's a lot about the Netherworld that we don't understand. There are many things that could happen, very few of them good. If a demon kills her there, her spirit will be trapped where she died and her body will be his to use to cross over without a gate. There are other possibilities too, none of them any better." Gabe pressed his foot down on the gas, speeding down the highway.

"She's strong. She'll survive long enough for us to get her out. She has to." Blake pounded a fist against the dash. "I won't lose her now."

"Whatever happens, you need to keep believing that strongly," Gabe nodded.

"What did you learn from the girl? Anything that might help us?"

"Honestly, she didn't know much. Someone grabbed her off the street when she went for her morning run. They kept her sedated."

Blake cursed. "I was hoping for more than that."

"So were we," Gabe shrugged. "Ron is taking her home. Maybe he'll get something more out of her on the drive back to Seattle. She was too scared to give us much anyway."

Chapter Eighteen

Lei stumbled over a thick root, catching herself on a low hanging branch and trying not to cringe as the bark sloughed away beneath her fingers, opening the red flesh of the tree to bleed. Everything seemed to bleed here. She touched a finger to her brow, where a long thorn had gouged her and found her own bleeding had not stopped.

She muttered to herself as she made her way through the bog, munching on an MRE applesauce packet and trying to relocate Whittaker's trail. She'd lost it, but she wasn't giving up. Instead, she searched and bargained with God to help her get out of the mess she was in and please not see fit to turn her into a bleeding tree when her time came.

The hours passed slowly as she trudged. Somewhere above the tangled canopy of the bleeding trees, a moon traveled the sky, its faint light reaching cold fingers through the dark leaves to touch her. Lei ached in places that had never ached before. Her body craved water, but she was rationing it severely. There was no way to know how long she'd be lost.

A sly, creeping voice in her head told her to lay down her pack and sleep. That everything would be all right, if only she could sleep. All of this was just a dream begging her to wake. But her heart proved true, pushing her onward when the rest of her longed to give up.

"That's the only thing to do. Move forward." She talked to herself partly to be certain she still had a voice at all. "If, no when, I get out of this place, I'm going to make myself a t-shirt. 'I survived Hell and couldn't even find a lousy t-shirt.'"

"You're not in Hell."

The deep voice startled Lei and she would have fallen face first into the thick, gripping mud, if a hand hadn't come out of the cover of trees to catch her. The hand was incredibly large. It covered Lei's chest with room to spare. She tried to scramble free, but the hand held fast.

"I won't hurt you." The rustle of leaves accompanied the voice.

A face appeared above Lei and she swallowed her scream. The man had to be at least twelve feet tall with wavy black hair and a dark complexion. His beard was short and glossy and his smile kind and crooked.

"Who are you?" She struggled to maintain her composure even as she looked for a way out of his reach.

"I am Suriel, descended of the Nephilim." He moved his hand slightly as if to prove he was no threat. "If you let me help you, we can be out of the bogs before the sun rises."

"And how do I know you won't just scoop me up and eat me?" Lei eyed the hand warily.

"You look like you might give me indigestion." He laughed, loud and deep and trees nearest to him shuddered. "You're in danger here, miss. Those whose hearts still beat are forbidden for a reason. This place will keep you and keep your soul, make you part of the landscape."

Lei looked up at the bleeding trees and shuddered. "I chased a vampire, or what I thought was a vampire, through a doorway. I had no idea where I would end up. It was as much a surprise as anything when I was standing at the river."

"Maybe I should leave you to your own devices then. If you want to be turned, that's no business of mine."

"No, Suriel. I'm here to kill him before he lets someone named Malphas out into the real world."

Suriel bent near to her, his face filling her vision, his eyes like blue topaz in the rough, blue freckled with brown and gray. "What do you know of this Malphas?"

"Not much. I know he's a demon who sometimes appears as a crow and that Whittaker wants to use him for something. I can't figure that part out yet."

"Well, little girl, we should move quickly. We need to get somewhere safe, out of this bog, where you can tell me your story."

"My name is Lei and I can talk while I walk."

"Would you let me carry your things? Your bag looks heavy."

Lei shook her head. "I'm sorry. I think I'd rather keep my things with me. For all I know, you're just as bad as Whittaker."

"Oh no. When my ancestors walked the face of the earth, they were great heroes. Their fathers were angels, their mothers human."

"So the Nephilim are what, giants from heaven?" She stumbled again and did not struggle when Suriel put his hands around her waist and lifted her like a child, putting her on his shoulders as a father would his daughter. "Thanks."

"I can move faster with you there." And he did, each stride covered more ground than six of Lei's. "The Nephilim are the children of the fallen. Which sounds much worse than it is. Not all of the fallen are bad, just the ones who went on to make a name for themselves. Just like with humans, you can't judge us all by the actions of one or two."

"That's good to know." She held on tight as Suriel jumped over a creature with wide, gnashing jaws and a scaled, prehensile tail that whipped and searched for his legs. "Is there any good in this place? Is this how it is to die? To become one of these monsters or run from them?"

"No. If you had entered this divided kingdom in a different place, you might not want to leave it at all. Though, if this is your idea of fun, you might get very bored and choose to haunt these lands instead. Others have and do." When Suriel shrugged, Lei rose with his shoulders and grabbed hold of his ears. "Ow!"

"Sorry. I thought I was going to fall."

"No chance of that little Lei." He laughed and his whole body shook. "Tell me why you are here to kill this vampire. I may not be able to help you get back where you belong but maybe I can help you with that."

Lei told him her story, from the beginning, as much to pass the time as to fill Suriel in. If he wanted to know why she was hunting Whittaker, why she'd made the decision to follow him, knowing it was a damned fool stupid thing to do, he had to know everything. Why she felt it was something she was supposed to do. Why it seemed everything in her life prepared her for this one choice. Blake or no Blake. She had to do it.

"It's likely your vampire would have shown up at whatever gate you were assigned to."

"That's impossible. No one knew where we were going but us."

"Just in your telling, you've listed many people who knew— sorcerers, fairies, some of the Order. I think you may underestimate this vampire."

Suriel brought them out of the dark forest and onto a large, open prairie. Here they could see for miles upon miles in every direction but for the one they came from. A small ribbon of green ran through it some yards ahead. Lei leaned down some. "Is that water up ahead?"

"Probably. I can't promise it is good water but it might not kill you." He changed direction slightly toward the ribbon. "The waters of the bog are poison."

"I figured. If I can maintain my rationing, I've got water enough for three or four more days, but I need to see if I can get more. I'd really like not to die here."

"I think that's wise." Suriel adjusted their course and took her to the river.

They stopped beside the small trickle of water, maybe three inches deep and a foot across. Lei took off her pack and dug through it for her purification and filtration kit. She filled up her two empty bottles and dropped two small tablets in each one, placing them on the most level surface she could find. She sat down, leaning against her pack. "This is going to take some time. That has to sit for 30 minutes before I add the next tablet and then it'll be another 30 minutes before I can use the UV-C pen."

She reached into the kit for the pen and it wasn't there. "Or not. Guess that turned to dust when I got here too."

"Will those pills make the water okay for you?" Suriel eyed the bottles with wary unease.

"I guess we'll find out. Do you think we'll be safe here for a while?"

"Yes. If you wish to sleep, I will keep watch." Suriel sat down beside her, throwing his shadow over her.

"Aren't you tired?" She looked up at him, feeling very much like a child.

"I'll be due for a nap in a week or so." He smiled, but it didn't seem as frightening now. "I *am* part angel, Lei. It does have its benefits."

Lei nodded and set about setting up her little camp. After she put together her bivy tent and laid her sleeping bag down inside it, she did a little work to camouflage its bright orange color. There was no sense in drawing attention to herself. Before she lay down, she added the neutralizer tablets to her water bottles.

"I've been thinking about how you got here and why." Suriel watched her as she got comfortable in her sleeping bag through the open flap. "These Justices you spoke of, it's likely that, when this began, they didn't realize they were dealing with demons. Would they, in their fight against those from the hidden lands, try to call on the angels for help?"

"I don't know. It's possible. If one of the Heads was more religious than usual maybe. Why?"

"Demons are very tricky. They listen to things the angels ignore. Most angels pay no attention to your world at all. They have enough to do in their own place. It's possible the Justices connected with a demon. Once the demon took control, it would have been too late for the Justice. Possession is everything here. If a demon has your body or your soul, they have complete control. You said they were trying to free a demon named Malphas."

"That's what the elf said. Maybe Whittaker had other plans and didn't tell him."

"Malphas is a king here, the leader of many generals. He is one you cannot summon but must set free. He has no need of a body to possess. As they failed in opening the gate, it is possible your vampire came here hoping you would follow. He needs living blood to open a gate for more than just himself. You have likely done exactly what he wanted you to."

"Then we'll have to get to him, and kill him, before he kills me."

"Rest for a while, Lei. We'll find this vampire of yours tonight." Suriel nodded as if he knew all the fates of the world.

With Suriel sitting beside her, she felt safe as she drifted to sleep. The faith she had in him was almost instinctual. With him, she felt protected, even comforted. With him, she still felt hope burning inside her. His presence counteracted the soul crushing apathy that begged her to give up, to lie down and die. Plus, he was probably right. The Justices had been played by demons. It was far more comforting to believe that than to believe one could have fallen so far from the tenants of the Order as to call up a demon on purpose.

**

Gabe drove them to the edge of town, past faded buildings and tourist traps and pulled his truck up in front of a small ranch style house with sun-bleached vinyl siding that might once have been a cheerful yellow but was now a sour butter color. Gabe led Blake into

the tiny house already too full of people. Each of them looked at
Gabe like he'd betrayed them in some way, which didn't bode well
for Blake or for Lei.

At the head of the room, nearly swallowed by a threadbare
recliner, an ancient man sat staring at Blake. His face was a
landscape of age, deeply lined copper skin, silver hair in a braid that
hung over his shoulder. His dark eyes flashed with life and wisdom.

"This is the young man I told you about, Blake Pratt. It's his
woman who stepped through the portal." Gabe bowed his head and
turned to Blake. "This is John Whitefeather. If there is anyone alive
today that can find her, it's him."

"I appreciate your agreeing to meet with me." Blake bowed his
head low, as Gabe had done.

The silence drew out. Blake could feel their eyes on him,
inspecting him, and he raised his head. He wanted them to know
who he was, why he needed them. Slowly, he pulled the pictures out
of his pocket and held them out to John Whitefeather. His hands
trembled slightly as he waited for the man to take them.

"I could sit here and tell you what a great person she is, how
brave and smart and worth saving and it would all be true, but that's
not all of who she is. She's flawed, irrevocably human, and she's
made mistakes that she has spent years trying to atone for. Most
importantly, to me, I love her. I couldn't stop her from going through
that portal to chase after a monster who'd like to see the whole world
burn. If you show me how to follow her, tell me what to do, I'll go
myself. I'll do whatever it takes to bring her back."

He laid the pictures on Whitefeather's knee, silently pleading to
the stone-faced man. The silence continued. Unnerving, aggravating,
infuriating silence. Blake tried to keep his nerves under control as he
stilled himself beneath their judging gaze. He failed. Thunder rolled
in the distance and he clenched his fists, his short nails digging into
his palms.

At last John Whitefeather spoke, his voice clear and smooth.
"Gabriel, you didn't tell me you were bringing a storm talker here."

Gabe shook his head. "I didn't know."

"You don't know this man at all then. Do you know this
woman?" Whitefeather looked at Gabe, his dark eyes pinning him.

"I admit, I know very little of Leilani Scott." Gabe sat down on
the floor, cross-legged. "She struck me as very bright, dedicated to

what she sees as her job. More, she was right about the Justices. I had to kill one of my own, knowing that, if he didn't die, he would continue trying to bring about the end of the world. I knew her teacher, loved her like a sister, and mourned her passing. Leilani reminds me some of her, though they share no blood."

"Gabriel," Whitefeather's voice got very quiet, "this world is not a thing you can end. We will someday go into the next world and hope we thrive so well there as we have here. The world is not a place, or, not just a place. It is a many-faceted jewel, a many-petaled flower. Change is inevitable. It is not always bad."

"It would be in this case. If the demons come into this world, it won't just be a simple change, it will be the end of everything good."

Whitefeather turned to Blake. "Storm Talker, what else can you do?"

"Nothing that will get me to Lei. I can bend time, dress myself in shadow, and bring light to the dark, all of which are useless now." He pointed to the pictures on the old Indian's lap. "Please. Please help me. Help her."

He took the pictures from Blake and traced a weathered finger over Lei's smile. Warmth and compassion touched his own smile. "I had a great love once. I remember how that earliest time feels, when one cannot bear to think of life without the other. I also know that it fades. Once the love is gone, the pain does pass."

"And if Malphas takes control of her there?" Blake looked into John's eyes, his face stern and cold. "This isn't just about my love for her. If it was, I could accept your refusal."

Whitefeather raised an eyebrow. "No decision has been made yet, young man. What you are asking me to do isn't without risk and the choice is not mine alone to make. Gabriel will take you away now. We will send word of our decision."

"How is it even a question? How can you just sit there...?"

Whitefeather held up a hand to silence him even as Gabe grabbed Blake's arm and pulled him hard. "These things can't be rushed, Storm Talker. Go. You will have to give me the trust you guard so well. Know that we will do what is right."

Gabe practically dragged Blake out of the house. None of the other men spoke to them but, as they left, the sounds of heated discussion filled the air.

"We've done everything we can do here. Come on, I'll buy you a drink and you can show me all your tricks." Gabe opened the passenger door and shoved Blake into the cab. "Don't worry so much. He liked you a lot, Storm Talker."

Chapter Nineteen

Leilani took a risk and tasted the water she'd tried to purify and immediately vomited it back up. She was rapidly running out of water and trying not to drink anything at all, just sucking on electrolyte gummy blocks, applesauce, and peanut butter packets from her last MREs. Hope of her own survival was dwindling but she was damned well going to find—and kill—Whittaker before she died. She wished she'd packed nothing but water. Everything else was just weight now.

"I am sorry, Leilani." Suriel picked her up again and carried her. "This place isn't meant for the living. Only the dead can thrive here. You rest. I'll do the walking for us both. If this vampire is anywhere, he is near the cliffs."

Suriel pointed ahead of them to the distant black ridge rising up from the plains to a height Lei didn't even want to think about.

"Why do you think he's there?"

"That is the home of the first vampire. She began her existence, as most here do, as a mortal human. In life she was a slave and sold her soul for her freedom, only to find she'd traded one kind of shackles for another. After her death, she was reborn here as a demon. Alda was determined not to be bound to this place, to the pain that infests every inch of this world.

"She plied her trade, bargaining for souls for her master until she met a woman with no soul. That happens sometimes, a body will come into the human world with no soul. When the soulless die, they simply end. They don't go on to the place of everlasting joy, or the place of eternal pain, or into the wall, or anywhere at all. She took the woman's body for her own and liked it. Alda did not want to lose the body she'd come to love, but it was aging. She desired immortality. To do that, she had to kill the body here, in this place of pain. But to do so, she had to create a portal—something that should have been impossible.

"Alda performed a very old ritual, no one knows where or how she got it. With the shedding of innocent blood, she somehow opened a gate between the human world and the Netherlands and brought her chosen body here. Then she killed the body on the banks of the river, making it immortal. The need for blood and hatred of light were unintended—but for Alda, acceptable—consequences. Taking possession of the transformed body, she became a living dead thing. Here, she does not need blood but to thrive in the world, she must take life to live. She went back into the human world, closing the gate she'd opened and went on to build an empire. The vampire you chase was her acolyte. Once human, now demon, he worshipped her and when the chance arose, she gave him the gift she'd stolen for herself—another soulless body to take as his own. They are the parents of all vampires everywhere."

A great chill passed through Lei. The hope of her being able to get out alive dwindled lower. "If I die here, can one of them take my body and make it live forever?"

"Yes." Suriel nodded. "But I won't let them. If you do die here, I will burn your body to ash and take charge of your soul."

"Promise me." She laid her head on his and closed her eyes. No tears came but a sob wracked her body.

"I promise, little Lei." The giant picked up his pace until he was nearly running. "There are clouds over the plains and if it starts raining, there's no telling what it will do to you."

Lei didn't say anything but tightened her grip on him and prayed that he could outrun the rain. Sorrow filled her, pushing everything else out, leaving no room for any thought of rescue.

***

The alcohol wasn't helping take the edge off. In his younger days, alcohol had soothed many pains and wrongs. Not so much anymore. Blake eyed the shots Gabe kept pouring for him. "I appreciate what you're trying to do, but I don't think you'd really like to see me completely wasted."

Gabe raised his eyebrows and looked hard at him. "Oh, I think I might. What I'd like to do is get you absolutely plastered and take you out where you can't hurt anyone and see what you can really do. I don't think even you know what your real potential is. I bet, if you were really pushed, you could do some incredible things. I also think Whitefeather likes you. It's not everyone he gives a name to, Storm Talker."

"There's a vast difference between liking someone and respecting their abilities." Blake leaned back from the bar. "You really want to know what I can do? Why?"

"Would you believe me if I said professional curiosity?" Gabe smiled.

"No. You'd like me to forget that you are a Justice. Like your friend Cam over there who looks like he'd really like to see me dead. There's a long history between my people and yours and none of it is pleasant." Blake picked up the whiskey and toasted Gabe. "Let me give you a small list. It's not everything and it's not even the best stuff but it'll give you some idea. Yes, I can call up thunder and lightning. I can also hide myself in shadow, change my appearance to pretty much whoever I want to be whenever I want, and, if I need to, I can make some people think what I want them to think."

Gabe shook his head and laughed. "That I'd like to see."

"You don't believe me?" Blake smiled and looked over at Cam who was still brooding. He knew it was a horrible idea but he didn't care and that wasn't just the whiskey swirling in his blood. "All right then. Just remember later, this was your idea. Make sure you tell him that when it matters."

He concentrated on Cam and was surprised how susceptible the man was to suggestion. A new song came on the jukebox, a good-old-boy kind of country tune. Cam was already singing it in his head. Too easy. Suddenly, Cam's voice joined the singer and got louder. He even looked to be enjoying himself for the first time since Blake met him. The other scattered patrons stared and laughed as Cam climbed up on the table and, still singing, began to strip out of his clothes.

"Enough." Gabe laid his hand on Blake's arm before Cam managed to finish unbuttoning his pants.

Blake let Cam's mind go and felt no mirth as the man stumbled off the table and collected his clothes. "You asked."

Cam pulled his shirt back on and strode across the room, fury in his eyes, fists clenched. Blake saw the hit coming but did nothing to stop it. He'd crossed the line and the Justice deserved at least one good solid hit. "Get out of my fucking head!"

Blake held up his hands and shook his head at the bartender.

"Cam." Gabe laid a hand on Cam's shoulder. "I'm sorry. I goaded him into it. That's my fault."

"And no excuse!" Cam glared at Blake. "You should have used that on Lei! Then we wouldn't be in this position, would we?"

"Wait," Gabe spoke before Blake had the chance, "could you have stopped Lei from taking that step?"

"Yes." Blake picked up another shot and threw it back.

"Why the hell didn't you?"

"For the same reason I didn't force Whitefeather to help me." He closed his eyes as his heart screamed at him. "I can't lose their trust that way. Lei would have hated me. It would have broken everything good between us. And Whitefeather, once he crossed over and was free of me, would just have come home. It's one thing to push a guy to do something he's always wanted to do, it's something else entirely to make decisions for someone about things that matter. Besides, Cam will never really trust me anyway. I'm not human enough for him."

The door of the bar opened and all three men turned, hands near their weapons. Gabe sat up straighter, anxiety rolling off him in waves, when a young man with long black hair strode in and headed for them. He wore jeans and a t-shirt emblazoned with the picture of some rock band or another.

"Chris." Gabe stood and shook the man's hand. "I take it a decision has been made."

Chris nodded as he studied Blake. "Whitefeather called you Storm Talker. Said I should talk to you alone for a minute."

"No problem." Blake stood up and followed the man to a table tucked in an empty corner of the bar.

"I've never seen the old men argue like they did tonight." Chris held up his hands before Blake could say anything. "I'm not saying that's a bad thing. It just means that we all care very much about what happens to Whitefeather. People like him don't come along very often, in any race. But the decision has been made by people with more influence than me. We'll meet you at dusk the day after tomorrow at the place where she went through."

"But she could be dead by then! We need to go now." Blake pounded his fist on the table.

"If he goes through now, unprepared, we don't stand any chance of getting her back and it could kill him." Chris stood up. "For what it's worth, there are a number of our elders who'd like to see

Whitefeather turn you down completely, so just be glad he's going at all. He's very important to us and this journey could be his last."

When Chris left, Gabe and Cam sat down across from Blake and he told them the plan.

"Look, I don't like you and I certainly don't trust you, but I wouldn't want to be in your shoes right now so, we'll chalk it up to your being stupid and hurting right now so we can work together." Cam's voice betrayed little of his emotions as he opened the door for a truce.

"I imagine you'll find a very creative and painful way to pay me back." Blake shook his head.

"Someday I probably will, but I'm willing to let it go for now so, be grateful. I'm going to go back out to the site, take a look around during the day, maybe go into that cave you said Whittaker was staying in. Maybe I can find out something."

"I'll go with you." Gabe laid some money on the table, enough to cover all three of their tabs. "Go get some sleep, Blake. We're going to do everything we can, but Whitefeather is the only man I know who can do this. Well, no, but he's the only one I trust to do it. I wish I could promise you he'd be in time."

"I think I'd know if she wasn't alive. Maybe I have to believe that. Just come and get me when it's time. We'll take Lei's Land Rover out there. If she's hurt, I can load her in the back where she'll be more protected than in your truck."

"It's just one more day, Blake." Gabe patted his shoulder as if they were old friends. "Do yourself a favor and sleep through it."

"Right." Blake stood and knew sleep wouldn't be any kinder to him than waking.

***

Lei ate stew out of a pouch and a few more electrolyte gummies. She was a few sips from being completely out of water, but the moisture in the MRE foods was helping. Sort of. She was running out of time.

The sun was setting and that meant Whittaker would soon be on the move. Suriel showed no sign of slowing. Lei knew she'd never have stood a chance at surviving long enough to reach Whittaker without Suriel. She owed him more than she could ever repay, even if she had no chance of making it home. She looked around, taking stock of where they were.

The bog and the river were so far behind them, she could no longer see their darkness on the horizon. The cliffs however, were much closer. The sheer black walls of rock shot up miles from the earth to the sky. There were steps carved into the rock but they only reached up about a quarter of the way. There, jutting out of the rock, on a narrow ledge, was a small castle of sorts. Diminutive compared to the wall, but likely as vast as any great castle once standing at its door.

"Let me guess, that's where Alda lives?" Lei asked.

"Yes. We won't be going there." Suriel shuddered beneath her. "She cannot be killed here."

"But she can be killed?" Lei asked as if it actually mattered.

"If she ever chooses to return to your world, yes, she can. She hasn't left her home here in many, many centuries." He paused to look up at the rock wall.

"Maybe she can't. Maybe she's dead."

"Look closer at the castle. Really focus on it. Distance, like time, is a funny thing here, Lei. Perception can be tricky—things that look close are far and things that are far can be so close they seem like you could reach out and touch them. It is not like your realm here, there are rules that can be bent, even broken, if you try."

"Is this why you didn't need Whittaker's trail?"

"Yes. I have been watching him and he has been watching us."

Lei looked up at the castle, focusing on the gray stone against the black rock. It was as if her eyes became binoculars, pulling the castle close enough to see the lines of the mortar, the glazing on the windowpanes—and the beautiful woman who waved at her from behind one. "Holy shit! She can see me the same way, can't she?"

"Yes. Don't worry. Alda has no interest in you."

Lei waved back before she looked away. "If she was so determined not to be trapped here, why doesn't she leave this place?"

"Only Alda knows that and I don't think we'll be asking her today. Are you absolutely certain you want to kill this vampire? You wouldn't rather let me take you over the wall into the land of joy? I can't promise you'll survive here much longer. At least, if I take you over the wall, you will not suffer."

"I'm not done here, Suriel. Whittaker is going to end here if it ends me too."

"I wish you'd change your mind." He took her from his shoulders and set her on the ground before him. "If you die on this side of the wall, you will be trapped here forever. There will be no hope, no love, no joy. Only pain and emptiness."

"As long as they can't use my body, I'll take the risk." Lei patted his hand. "I appreciate your concern, Suriel, but this is what I have to do. What I know in my heart I'm supposed to do. I know that sounds silly."

"No. I understand." Suriel smiled.

"Nephilim!" A familiar voice boomed across the empty prairie and Lei spun, trying to find him. "You have something that belongs to me!"

"Her heart still beats. She does not belong to any of this land!" Suriel's voice bellowed, louder and stronger than Lei had heard it before.

She looked at him, really looked at Suriel for the first time. He was truly a giant, a formidable one. He wore simple clothes, an undyed shirt and pants that fell loose on him. He carried no weapons, no supplies—he didn't need them. His feet were bare and unprotected save a layer of dirt. At once, she knew the truth of him to her very marrow. This was no Nephilim, descended of angels. Suriel was a true Angel.

Suddenly, Whittaker dropped down from the sky. Lei took a step back. She'd never known a vampire who could fly. He'd had to come from somewhere, but where? Whittaker held a long sword in one hand and a spear in the other. "I led her here! She came of her own free will. She belongs to Malphas now!"

"Leilani followed you, yes, but she did not come of her own choosing. Ignorance is not choice. She would have followed you anywhere. She has no clue where she is, what this place is. The laws are clear, Hadrian. The innocent here are mine."

"How dare you speak my true name? You think you can change anything, Nephilim? You have no power here. You can't have her! Not now. Her purpose was foretold to us all before the division of the world." Whittaker charged at Suriel.

While the two tangled, the spear piercing Suriel's fleshy side, Whittaker's femur snapping, Lei dropped her pack and reached into her jacket for the long, silver stake she'd made sure to bring, just for this moment.

She tried to jump into the fray, but Suriel knocked her gently back with his wide hip. Whittaker's sword plunged deep into Suriel's chest and the giant roared. Lei screamed as she plunged the stake into the old vampire's back, piercing through his heart and out through his chest.

Whittaker turned to her, laughing as black blood dripped from his wound, from his mouth. "You can't kill me here, you fool. You think you know so much, but you know nothing!"

"Tell me then," Lei goaded as smoke rose from the wound.

"Like my mistress, I am demon born, not bitten. This is my homeland, where I am strongest." Whittaker pushed the tip of the stake until it slid out of his back. Even as she watched, the wound knitted itself back together.

She tried to swallow but she couldn't seem to produce any saliva.

"You and your idiot companions ruined our best plan, but we are not without a backup. You are here, after all."

Lei tried not to look behind Whittaker as Suriel got to his feet. "Why do you even want to set Malphas free in the first place? If Hell extends to Earth, eventually, there will be no humans left for you to feed on."

"Humans are cattle, Lei, little insignificant beasts. My children and I will raise them, breed them, milk them, and slaughter them as you do cows. The world should never have belonged to you."

"No," Suriel spoke, standing up. His wounds hadn't healed but there was no blood. What dripped from his flesh was pale, like dandelion sap. "The world was always meant to be theirs. You are an abomination, not created but changed. You have been many things, Hadrian: a human, a demon, and now this. This shell of a thing that hasn't the power to survive without the deaths of others. Lei isn't the only one who thinks she knows everything," Suriel spoke and his skin seemed to glow in the darkness that surrounded them. "She can't kill you here, but I can."

"Impossible!" Whittaker spun, turning his back on Lei.

Suriel grabbed Whittaker by the throat and held him up in the air, bringing the vampire's eyes level with his own. "When in the darkness shines a beacon of innocence, a mission shall be given to the last of the fallen. To finally have purpose after so many centuries of being lost. I will not fail."

The night exploded with light. Lei turned away, shielding her eyes. Whittaker's scream was blessedly short lived but the silence that followed it was deafening.

"Who are you really, Suriel?" Lei turned toward him and wasn't surprised to find nothing more than a pile of ash at Suriel's feet.

"It doesn't matter and you wouldn't believe me." He looked as though he would say more but stopped and stared into the darkness. "We need to go now."

Suriel lifted her easily back onto his shoulder and began to run.

"What's going on?"

"Malphas is coming."

***

Blake heard the hiss and pop that preceded the opening of a gate and stood up. Lei walked through it, toward him, unaided. Whitefeather stood behind her, head bowed and silent. He didn't see any sign of dehydration or battle. How had she come out of Hell without a scratch? Confused, he tried to read her. She smiled, but it was not Lei's smile.

He stepped toward her with open arms and she pressed against him. "I'm so sorry, Leilani." He whispered in her hair as he pulled the knife out of his sleeve and plunged it into her back.

"Fool! You can't kill me now." Leilani, who was no longer Leilani but something wearing her skin, stepped back and laughed, reached around behind her, tilting her arm at an impossible angle to pull his blade out. "Nothing in the whole of your pathetic little world can kill me now."

Blake fell to his knees before her, disjointed images of the future flooding him. Cities on fire, mountains of corpses being ravaged by demons and beasts alike, buildings toppling, the screams of ten thousand children filling his head. He screamed, clutching his ears, trying to drown out the sound of millions being slaughtered, tortured, dying. Above it all, Lei's victorious laugh ran him through as surely as his own knife pierced his heart.

Blake woke thrashing, the image of Lei's inhuman smile etched forever in his mind. Sweat poured from him, drenching his sheets and the shirt he clenched tight in his fist. The shirt Lei most often wore to bed. It must have been tucked under a pillow, maybe even by Lei, so he'd have something of hers if something went horribly wrong.

He sat up, wondering what Whitefeather would say of his dream if he knew Blake's dreams were sometimes more than just dreams. Would he still try to find her? Should they? For a moment, he thought about calling his mother, but he already knew what she'd say. For whatever reason, she wanted Leilani out of his life. No way would she help him get her back. He needed to talk to Whitefeather.

***

Lei watched behind them as Suriel ran back toward the great river she'd paddled across chasing Whittaker. Dozens of figures chased them, gaining on them. Their screams made Lei's blood run cold.

Suriel simply couldn't run fast enough. Nothing could have. With the river still a smudge on the horizon, Leilani and Suriel were overtaken.

They were hideous, disfigured creatures. Perhaps their shape had once been human, but they weren't now. Their faces contorted into violent Daliesque masks. They stabbed Suriel with crude swords and spears as they pulled Lei screaming from his back.

Several demons held Suriel back, binding him with great chains, gagging him with strips of grimy cloth, blindfolding him. He fought against his bindings, stronger than any of the demons seemed prepared for as they struggled with him.

"You've been summoned," The monster that had a hold of her growled in her ear and licked the side of her face. "We've promised to take you to Malphas alive, we didn't promise you'd be unharmed."

One of the demons cut Leilani's pack from her back and left it on the ground. They bound her in heavy chains smaller than those they'd used on Suriel and poured putrid water down her throat. She tried to spit it all out, but they kept pouring it into her.

"Can't have you dying on us. Not yet anyway." The demon who appeared to be in charge strapped a leather collar around her throat and took hold of the leash. "Come on."

"No." Lei fell to her knees on the ground. "I'm not going anywhere."

"Vepar! The lash!" He grabbed her jacket and just to show her a taste of his strength, he pulled the Gortex apart as if it were paper, the lycra of her shirt and the cotton of her tank fell apart like damp tissue paper in his fingers, leaving her back completely exposed.

At the leader's command, another pulled a great whip from his belt and cracked it in the air as the other demons shrieked with delight. As every stroke came down, the crowd around her cheered and crowed. Suriel's voice bolstered her; even muffled by the gag, she could feel his strength in her. The leather sliced open her skin but worse was the incantation Vepar spoke after each lashing that brought infection to a raging boil in her blood, on her skin. She screamed as the whip came down over three already infected wounds.

"Enough!" The head demon pulled on her leash. "Get up and walk."

Lei struggled to stand and with her hands bound behind her, she fell flat on her face, getting a mouthful of sandy soil.

The demon crouched beside her, his face inches from hers, his breath rank. "You have spirit, but that is easily broken. If Malphas didn't need you alive, I would take great pleasure in killing you. As it is, you will be begging for death before we reach our king."

"Malphas is your king? What about Lucifer? Isn't he king?" Surprise and pain loosened her lips and Lei spoke with a hoarse, croaking voice.

The demons all laughed. "What they believe in the living world and the truth of our world are vastly different. The fallen holy boys aren't welcome here. Only us—the pure, the loyal. You know nothing here, woman."

She heard how he said woman. How it felt like he just noticed her gender and cold fear flooded Lei. She tried to swallow but her mouth was dry. Looking into his eyes she saw the flicker of lust as he stared at her. Lei fought against the pain and stood.

"That's a good girl." He laughed and pulled hard on her chain, forcing her to move forward.

Lei struggled against her fear, against the overwhelming hopelessness. She wasn't dead yet. They'd taken her pack but not her jacket or her belt. She could still get to her knife if she worked at it. It wasn't much but, with Suriel bound, it was all she had. A small smile crept over her face, the skin of her lips cracking where the liquid they'd poured down her throat had touched them.

"Bring the Nephilim! Malphas may reward us extra for him!"

Lei struggled to keep her face from revealing anything. They didn't know what Suriel really was. Maybe if he had enough time, he'd heal enough to get them out of the mess she'd gotten them into. He had to. The whole of the world depended on him now. Everything good that ever existed—would ever exist—hung in the balance.

Chapter Twenty

Blake paced near the spot where Lei disappeared. Gabe and Cam sat on rocks nearby, not saying a word. Cam was still out of joint about the incident at the bar, offended that some filthy sorcerer could take control of him so easily. It was the only bright spot in Blake's life and he was grabbing onto it, trying to keep the humor of the moment fresh enough to hold his fear at bay.

He watched the road, wondering if Whitefeather had changed his mind, if maybe the other elders convinced him it was a horrible idea. Fresh pain flooded him when he thought that maybe those other men might be right. Every minute that passed pressed down on his shoulders, squeezed his heart. Lei was dying, he could feel it. They were already almost too late. Something horrible was happening to her and there wasn't a damned thing he could do.

The sound of a truck approaching brought Gabe and Cam to their feet as well. No one moved as three young Indians hopped out of the back of the truck and went to the passenger door to help Whitefeather out. They walked with him, one on either side to lend support, the third behind him, just in case.

The man looked old. More frail and weak than Blake thought he was. How could this man be strong enough to help? Hope dwindled to nothing inside him. "I wasn't sure you'd really come, Mr. Whitefeather."

"I wasn't sure I would either." Whitefeather looked at Blake with a clarity and a sharpness that surprised him. "There are things you need to say to me, Storm Talker."

Blake nodded. "I'd rather speak with you alone, if I can."

Whitefeather nodded at the young men walking with him and they stepped back as Blake took the place of the one on the right.

"You've seen something you don't wish for everyone to know, young shaman."

"I'm no shaman. Just a man with a little magic in his blood."

Whitefeather shrugged. "No difference. Tell me, what did you see?"

"Hell on earth. When you find her, if she's not dying, don't bring her back with you." Blake closed his eyes, cursing the words he'd spoken, wishing he'd never had the vision.

"This woman of yours, do you believe she has fight? Enough fight to keep herself alive?"

"I wouldn't ask you to find her if I didn't. She's still alive but she's dying. Right now, she's dying." He closed his eyes against the haunting image of the smile that did not belong to Lei. "I saw something in my dream. You brought her home, but it wasn't her. It was her body, whole and unhurt, but there was nothing left of Lei inside that shell. Something rode her through the portal. And if you bring that through, it will be the end of this world."

"Not the end, just a change." Whitefeather patted Blake's arm. "Did you know the word 'apocalypse' means simply that: change?"

"You aren't listening to me! It will mean the end of everything good, everything we fight for, have fought for."

"I am listening, Storm Talker. I do hear you. I know you think I'm too old, too weak, for this. In the land of the dead, I am as my spirit—as strong and as pure as the soul inside this ancient body. I will fight for her soul. I will bring her soul back or I will come back alone. I promise you this." He stepped away from Blake, far more steady on his feet than Blake had expected. "It is time to begin."

The young Indians, their skin painted black and decorated with red and blue patterns Blake had never seen before set to work building a great fire, adding bundles of sage to the kindling. Around the fire, they laid two piles of hoops wrapped in bright, colorful ribbons.

The driver of the truck and one of the young men, Chris, brought two drums and a beautiful flute over to the rocks near the fire. The driver and Gabe sat down with the drums, Chris with the flute. As the night filled with music, the two young men Blake didn't know and Whitefeather began to dance. He moved with a grace that shocked Blake, like he hadn't struggled against arthritis just to walk.

The dance became frantic as the boys used the hoops to mimic shapes: Eagle, Rabbit, the very world itself. Suddenly, the fire blazed blue for a moment, drawing Blake's eyes to its too bright center. When the light faded away, Whitefeather was gone. The drums kept beating, the flute kept singing, the boys kept dancing, so Blake did nothing but watch. And pray to every deity he'd ever heard of for Lei to hold on, just a little longer.

***

Lei's legs shook, threatening to give out completely with the next step. They had been walking for what felt like hours without slowing. She fell to her knees and bowed. "Please. Please. I need to rest."

The demons looked at her and laughed. "You can rest when you're dead."

"I'll be dead before you get me to your master if you don't let me rest." The words scraped her raw throat like sandpaper but she spoke as clearly as she could.

"Fine." The head demon, the one the others called Botis, sat down beside her, leering openly. He reached over to her, grabbing the scraps of fabric that clung to her chest with sweat. He smiled, showing his sharp, predatory teeth. "Give her water."

Lei shook her head and pressed her lips closed as the demons gathered around her, holding her, groping her. One held her face in his hands, forcing her mouth open as another poured the stinking fluid into her mouth, pouring until it overflowed and coursed down her body. Each drop that touched her skin burned as if it were acid.

When they released her, she fell on her side, retching and heaving, cursing as none of the poison came back up though it held her guts in a vice grip. Lei opened her eyes, staring at the ugly feet surrounding her and then past them. To one side was the great wall that divided the Netherlands in two, joy from pain. Behind them was nothing more than a vast emptiness, but ahead of them, far in the distance, a great red structure rose up nearly half the height of the black cliff beside it. It didn't look like any castle or fortress Lei had ever seen but she was certain that was their destination.

Using the same trick Suriel had taught her, she brought the palace into focus. The walls were red, undulating red and black. Smoke seeped out of the cracks and she could smell the scent of burning flesh. As she watched, the wall shifted and a face emerged—a charred, human face with its eyes gone and blackened teeth exposed. People. The palace was made of burning people writhing together in a dance of pain that never broke the plane of the wall. Whatever she had to do, whatever it took, she had to slow the demons down. She knew through to her bones that she couldn't let them take her there.

Lei flung herself back on the ground and began twitching. The demons crowded around her, trying to hold her down, their claws opening great gashes in her arms and legs, slicing through what was left of her clothes, her skin. The blood made her slippery. She rolled and convulsed, trying to make it look as real as she could. She hoped none of them had ever seen a living human in the throws of a real seizure as she had no clue what she was doing.

"Pick her up!" Botis ordered and several of his minions fought over who should have the honor.

As Vepar, the one with the whip, won the honor and scooped her up into his strong, grimy arms, a thundering whoop filled the air. As one, the demons looked to the wall that split the Netherlands in two as a thousand painted horses came pouring over the top, riding down the slick surface as if it were flat as the plains. Warriors in white paint on frothing horses charged down and into their midst, howling and screaming. White feathers braided into the tails and manes of the horses blazed like white fire.

A piercing shriek split the air, silencing the warriors on both sides. A great shadow rose in the east from the red castle. The demons cheered as if they'd already won, chanting the name Malphas even as the Indians resumed the battle, cutting through their ranks with tomahawks and war clubs.

One of the warriors, his chest partially covered by an aged bone chest plate, looked into Lei's eyes and smiled. For a moment, Lei believed she would see home again with her own eyes. She struggled against Vepar's grip, trying to break free.

Behind her, several warriors worked to free Suriel from his bindings only to be pulled away and torn apart by demons. The demons seemed to be multiplying, more coming to join in the fray with glee and blood lust in their cries. For every warrior that rode over the mountain, ten demons swarmed the gory plain and they just kept coming. As if there were an endless supply of them.

The shadow from the east was nearly upon them when a warrior with cloth-wrapped braids and a maniacal grin took Vepar's head clean from his body with a great knapped stone ax. Leilani fell to the ground on top of the demon's twitching body. Slowly, she pushed herself forward, unable to use the hands tied behind her back. Suddenly, she was yanked up off the ground.

A great beast, even larger than Suriel, pulled her up to his face. It had a sharp beak for a mouth and tiny black eyes that burned.

"Mine." Its voice was a crow's call, shrill and harsh. It cawed again. "Broken!"

With his free hand, Malphas grabbed Botis up out of the reach of the Indians and shook him. "She is tainted! What did you do to her?"

"Nothing. She was thirsty, we gave her water." Botis shuddered, his voice pitching with fear.

"Fool! You failed me. Our water is poison to her!" Malphas shook the demon until his bones snapped and his head lolled to the side. He tossed Botis away like a broken toy and strode across the battlefield, knocking aside demons and Indians crushing both beneath his great feet.

When he reached Suriel, he pulled a great knife free of its sheath and sliced deep into the Nephilim's side. He pushed Lei's face to the wound. "Drink it!"

"No." Lei turned her head away, pressing her lips together as firmly as she could.

Malphas dropped his knife and grabbed hold of her face, squeezing until she had no choice but to open her mouth or have her jaw crushed. Warriors sliced and hacked at Malphas, leaping onto him, but he shrugged them off like bugs and pressed Lei's open mouth to Suriel's side. The white sap filled her mouth. She tried to spit it out, to keep from swallowing it, but, in the end, she had no choice.

"Don't fight him, Lei. It will save you." Suriel's voice filled her head.

She looked up to find him smiling at her, the same sleepy, contented smile of nursing mothers. "Let me save you so you can save yourself."

As Suriel's blood filled her belly and spread into her body, the change was immediate. Her thirst died, her wounds healed, the dead and cracked skin sloughed off like a lizard's shed, replaced by new skin, a paler shade than she had been. Even her scars were lighter, somehow less then they'd been.

"Why heal me if you're just going to kill me?" She asked as Malphas released her face.

"Why would I kill you when I have waited millennia for you? I have no desire to kill you. Yours is a body I do not want to wear. If I only wanted a body to wear, I would have ignored the prophecy and had Hadrian bring me a male." His squawking voice shook with laughter. "Where is that bastard?"

"Dead." Lei stared at him, trying to keep from trembling in his hard grip.

"Impossible!" He snarled, staring at her with cold, black eyes.

"I watched him turn to dust. Your vampire friend can't help you now."

"You have destroyed my chance to go through the gate myself!"

"I feel really bad for you. Really." She managed a bit of sarcasm even as her heart split in two—one part breaking at the loss of her life, her love and the other rejoicing, knowing Malphas had no way to cross into world without the vampire.

Malphas sighed. "Fortunately, there is another way. You see, Alda would never let me keep you here. Even if your spirit warriors hadn't arrived, she would rescue you, help you get home. So I will let you be rescued, dear Raven, but you will take my spawn with you when you return. He will take what should always have been mine. Rather than be my queen, ruling over all the worlds at my side, you will take my son into the world."

Lei looked at him for a moment, understanding the demon's plan at last and began to laugh. "You picked the wrong woman to be a mother."

"I only need your womb."

"That's my point. I don't have one." Lei laughed again, her whole body shaking with it. Her absolute relief made it possible to laugh, her fear tinged it with hysteria. "Your werewolf friend marked me, but he did it wrong. The claws went too deep, opened me up too much, ruined things for both of us I guess. A few months after the attack, I hemorrhaged and they had no choice but to take it out. I had a hysterectomy—no womb left in this little body. Sorry."

"No! You lie!" Malphas looked into her eyes, the din of the battle that raged around them lost in the intensity of the moment. Lei saw the truth sink in, saw the beast realize she was telling the truth and braced herself.

Malphas screamed in anger, his caw shaking the ground. He stabbed his claws into her belly, into the place where her womb should have been, ripping her open. Shaking her violently, he threw her to the side. Her back twisted and the sickening snap shot through her like fire. As Malphas turned away from his failure, the warrior who'd smiled leapt down from his horse and scooped her up in his arms. He laid her across the back of his horse.

"We can take you up over the great wall where you will have peace or we can risk your soul to get you home. If you die on the way, you will be trapped here, in this place of pain."

Lei tried to answer but her body betrayed her, would not answer her commands. Her voice was dead. She wanted to scream, to point towards the river she had crossed. She looked toward the place where the black river cut through everything and begged the warrior to hear her.

"I understand. Don't die now, little one. You've come so far, you can't give up here. Keep fighting." He spoke to her as they rode away from the fray, toward the river. "Stay with me, Leilani Scott. Be strong. For Blake."

She fought hard to keep her eyes open, not to succumb to the waves of blackness that threatened to consume her. The warrior who saved her didn't ride alone. They were flanked by two others who looked familiar, like she'd seen them somewhere but the pain that fogged her head wouldn't let her remember. One wore a great headdress that flowed over his back, the feathers notched and cut. The other wore no feathers but his hair was cut at his shoulders and he wore a dour expression. Mercilessly, they bludgeoned any demon stupid enough to get close.

She turned her head slightly to look back. Pulling the battle close in her sights, she watched as Suriel pulled himself to his feet. He held one arm tight to his side where Malphas had cut him. The other arm was reaching out for Malphas. His smile was both beautiful and terrible. She hoped the Angel could kill the demon as easily as he'd killed the vampire.

The horses strained against the speed as they raced through the bog where she'd met Suriel. Water splashed and creatures scurried out from under the thundering hooves. Lei stopped feeling pain, floating in a gray fog. No pain. No fear. No hope. She fought to keep her eyes open as they emerged from the bog and onto the banks of the great black river. They stopped.

"Thank you, friends. I will see you again sooner than I would like on the other side of the wall." The silver haired warrior picked her up and carried her across. Either the water wasn't as deep as it had been or the man was running on top of it. The moment they

reached the beach, a great white light filled the world and the
darkness pulled her under at last.

***

Blake watched the dancers, watched them rise and fall as if they
fought a great battle and played all the parts. He knew what he was
seeing but still didn't understand it. Whitefeather had been gone for
hours. Blake had expected him to come right back. It couldn't be
good, that he was gone for so long.

The crack of a branch made Blake jump up. He turned to see
who was coming and his heart sank. Marcus stood there, a large bag
slung over his shoulder. Carie, Henry, Melli, and Drew stood just
behind him. "I thought you might need me."

Blake stumbled forward and pulled Marcus into a brotherly hug.
"How did you get here?"

"Melli brought us on the Gray Road. Mom said we had to come,
to help you through your loss."

"We don't know that she's dead. Whitefeather has been gone a
long time."

Carie stepped forward, her lips pressed together in a thin line. "I
need to speak with you, Blake."

"You know something?" Blake looked at her, all anger forgotten
for the moment. "What did you see? What do you know? Is there
any chance for her?"

"I'm sorry." Carie looked away. "I know you think you love this
woman."

"Think? I don't think, I know. You don't get to pick and choose
anything for me anymore! Even now, you just can't see what you're
doing. This has nothing to do with you. You are not the center of
anyone's life but your own." Blake turned his back on her and
stalked back to the fire. He stopped as the music stopped, as the
dancers froze. The fire blazed up into the night, reaching toward the
heavens.

When the fire died down, Whitefeather stood there with Lei in
his arms.

Blake ran towards them but fell to his knees a foot away, when
he saw her. She was pale and rivers of blood flowed from her

stomach. Her back was twisted unnaturally, her feet dangled at wrong angles.

Marcus pushed past him and helped Whitefeather lay her down on her side. He bent to her chest for a moment and looked up at Blake, trying to smile. "She's still alive. Don't you dare give up on her."

Drew pulled Blake to his feet. "He's right. She didn't give up on you, you can't give up on her."

"How can she survive this? Look at her, Drew." His voice broke as he watched them straighten her back, saw how limp she was. Tears poured down his face. Looking at her, there was no way she could survive.

Whitefeather stepped away from Lei as Marcus set up his stones and herbs. He moved to stand beside Blake. "Your woman is amazing. She did all she could. She fought to the end. She could never have given Malphas what he wanted and he cut her open for it. At least she's going to die here and not there. She will go to the place of joy rather than be bound to that of darkness and sorrow. She is beyond my abilities and, I believe, those of your brother-friend. I am truly sorry. I can't tell you how much."

Blake watched as Marcus worked, drawing on all his ability to fill her with light, to draw out the pain and the injury and push them into the stones scattered on her chest. A tear slipped down Marcus's cheek as he stepped back. "I'm so sorry. There's nothing I can do now."

"No! She can't be dead! I won't allow it!" Blake broke free of Drew and Whitefeather's grasp and ran to her, scooping her up in his arms and holding her close. Willing her to open her eyes.

"Run!" Carie screamed and scattered the onlookers.

Lightning exploded through the night, hot white fingers from the sky, from the ground, from Blake himself, pouring into Lei. Marcus took a step toward them but Carie grabbed his arm, holding him back.

"No. You will not risk yourself for her. I'll be damned if I lose two of my sons to her!"

"Let me go, Mom." Disgust showed clearly on Marcus's face as he pulled his arm free. Marcus stepped closer. The white light flashed around him until it encompassed him too. Whitefeather, Gabe, the young Indians, Melli, and Drew joined them.

"You're wrong, Carie. I don't say it often. I don't stop you when you contrive and manipulate. Maybe I should." Henry laid a hand on his wife's shoulder. "I love you, probably more than you'll ever truly know, but sometimes, I don't like you very much. If you can't understand why we all need to help, you'll lose your whole family. Not just the boys. Me too. And the other kids? What will they think about this when they find out? It's up to you, but maybe it's time for your actions to have consequences."

Carie stood, shocked into silence as Henry joined the circle, the white light growing bigger and brighter around them all. She turned to Cam. "Call the ambulances. We're going to need a lot of them." Carie stepped into the circle of light.

For a moment, Cam was frozen in his spot, watching with horror and hope in his eyes.

***

Blake woke in a hospital bed. Gabe sat in the chair beside his bed, reading a book. "Lei?"

Gabe looked up and smiled. "Still alive, thanks to you. She's in a coma. Her body is pretty beat up but the doctors think she could make a full recovery. If she wakes up."

"The others? Marcus, Whitefeather?" Blake struggled to sit up, but he was too weak yet.

Gabe moved to sit on the edge of the bed and pressed the button to raise him to sitting. He put a cup with a straw to Blake's lips. "Everyone seems to be okay. Your mother was the first to wake and you're the last. Cam called for ambulances. Fortunately, some fairy showed up to get Melli before help arrived. We scared that boy pretty good."

"I bet." Blake took another sip before Gabe set the cup down. "What happened?"

"I guess when the light show ended, we all fell down. Cam thought we were all dead but everyone was breathing and had good heartbeats." Gabe shrugged and toyed with the end of his steel and silver braid. "That was an amazing thing. I'll never forget it. Guess Whitefeather didn't name you Storm Talker for nothing."

Blake smiled because he couldn't laugh. "I need to see her."

"You need to rest. As soon as you're able, I'll take you to her. Whitefeather is sitting with her now. I'll go check on her and come back. There's nothing you can do for her until you're back on your feet."

"Yes there is. But you have to promise three things. First, you don't tell Cam. Second, you don't kill him. And third, you get me a phone."

"What are you talking about?" Gabe's eyes narrowed.

"You worked with me to save a lot of people. You set aside the rules of the Order for that. I'm asking you to do it again. There's a vampire who can help her. He won't turn her. She'd kill him. But he can help her if you will just forget what he is."

"Why would he?"

"He owes her his life. He respects her. Because he's a good guy, if you ignore the fangs." Blake closed his eyes. "I can't even believe I'm asking you any of this but Lei needs all the help she can get and I'd sooner play nice with Yemi than see her die."

"Oh my God, you're serious." Gabe rubbed his temples. "The two of you just enjoy making my life difficult. I'll do it, but only for her. There's an awful lot of people in this world who have no clue they owe their survival to her at this moment. But, this is a one time thing."

Blake nodded. Now he just needed to figure out where to find Yemi's phone number. It would have been in Lei's phone but that was long gone. "Actually, I need one other thing. There's a book, back at our motel room—it's pretty beat up. It's brown leather and hand written. There might be two of them. She's got to have his number in one of them."

"I'll send one of the boys to look for them. Now, please rest until we get you those things, okay?"

Blake slept for a while; he wasn't exactly sure how long. When he woke, he was alone in the room but there were two leather-bound journals and his cell phone on the little table beside his bed. It took him twenty minutes to find Yemi's number. Drumming his fingers on his leg, he counted the rings. Fifteen of them before a young woman answered.

"Hello?"

"My name is Blake Pratt, I'm calling to speak to Yemi. Tell him Leilani Scott has been hurt and I need his help."

He heard a small gasp from the woman. "Lei is hurt? Where are you? How bad is it?"

"We're in Phoenix and it's pretty bad. It's also a very long story that I'd really like to tell Yemi first, if I can."

"Of course. I'm sorry. It's just that Lei saved me. She's my friend. I'll go get my dad."

Blake listened to silence as he waited for Yemi to pick up the phone.

"How badly is she hurt?" Yemi didn't bother with pleasantries.

"If we don't do something quickly, she's going to die. We've done all we can and it's still not enough. I'm calling you from my own hospital bed as it is."

"Start from the beginning, tell me everything. Don't leave anything out. I need to know how to prepare to help her."

As quickly as he could, he told Yemi everything that had happened from the time he left them with Karma to when he woke up in the hospital. He included what he'd learned from Whitefeather about what happened in the Netherlands, though there was a lot of time that was unaccounted for in which he had no idea what happened to Lei.

When Blake was finished, Yemi sighed. "I don't know how she's still alive after all that. I'll be there as soon as I can. I have some things to prepare. I'll be flying down as soon as it's safe for me to do so. Expect me when it gets dark tomorrow night. I'm really hoping you have enough magic to keep people away from her room for a while. What I plan to do, it isn't pretty."

"No problem. Drew and I will take care of everything. Text me when you are on your way and I'll make sure everything is in place."

As soon as the doctors allowed Blake to get out of bed and walk around, he shambled and shuffled toward Lei's room, ignoring the whispers from the hospital staff. They didn't believe the story Cam and Carie concocted for them but neither could they find any other explanation. At least not one their very human hearts could accept.

Eleven people struck by lightning at the same time, the same place, each with the same wounds, though Lei's was by far the worst and Blake's a close second. None of the others had wounds that required surgery.

Outside Lei's door, Drew and Henry paced. When they saw him, they both smiled. "It's good to see you back on your feet." Henry pulled Blake into a quick hug. "Your mother…"

"I know she's gone. I can't focus on her right now, Dad, I just don't have it in me."

"I know. When things settle out, when Lei is on the mend, please remember that your mother didn't walk away. She could have but she didn't. In the end, she chose to help."

"I appreciate what you're trying to do, but right now, I need to focus on Lei."

"There hasn't been any change yet." Drew informed him. "The doctors really don't know what more they can do. She's breathing on her own, her brain shows excellent signs of activity."

"But she's still unconscious."

"Yeah." He nodded sadly.

***

When everything around her went from darkness to light, Lei was certain she was dead. The fact that wherever she was looked nothing like the parts of the Netherlands she'd seen didn't mean a thing. The emptiness felt wrong though. No plants, no rocks, no sky, just a vast white blank.

"You aren't dead yet, little one."

"Suriel!" She raced toward him and flung her arms around him. "I thought for sure you were dead!"

"It would take a lot more than Malphas to kill me. It's you I'm worried about. You should be dead right now. Even with my blood in your system, you should be dead now."

Lei looked around at the whiteness. "Where are we then?"

"The best word I have is limbo. At least the best word that translates right. It's a nowhere place. Not many souls ever see this place. Either they are alive or they are dead, it's not right to be neither one but here you are."

"If there's a way to get me home, Blake will find it." Her voice held more conviction than she felt.

"I'm so glad to hear you say that. If you believe it to be so, it may well be true. But, while you are here, there are a few things you should know."

Suriel sat cross-legged on the nothing and motioned for Lei to do the same.

"Is something wrong?"

"I don't know. You ingested my blood. You also got some inside your open wounds."

"I think it would have been harder not to get your blood on my wounds given that I was pretty much all wound at the point."

"Yes but I think it may have changed a few things. Beyond healing you, I mean."

"How so?"

"I should not have been able to find you here, Lei. But, I knew exactly where you were. Maybe I'll always know where you are, I don't know. If you are now part of my family, of my blood, you must be very careful never to let anyone know."

"Do you mean I'm part angel now?"

"Possibly. If you are, you belong to the Netherlands now as much as you do the human realm. If you wanted to, I'm pretty sure you could open a gate all by yourself."

"Shit."

"Yes. There is only one man you can trust with this. When you heal, you need to go see John Whitefeather—the man who rescued you. He will help you learn what you can and can't do and how to do it."

"He's not just a human is he? Not even a sorcerer."

"No," Suriel smiled. "There are others like him in your realm, humans that have angels for ancestors, but he is the closest to you and will be the most willing to help. Promise me you won't tell your love yet, Lei. It's important. I know you love and trust him. You're not wrong to. But, until we know for sure if this is temporary or permanent, until we know how much of you is different, you must keep it to yourself."

"I hate keeping things from him."

"I know. I'm not asking you to lie forever, just until we have more answers. If anyone knew what might be possible, you would be in great danger." Suriel looked around them. "Something is happening."

Lei turned her head slightly and noted that the whiteness was a little less white, fading on the edges.

"Someone out there is fighting hard for you, little one." He bent and kissed her head. "I hope they win."

***

The doctors moved Lei into a private room. They called her a miracle as she was healing at an astonishing rate. Half the people who touched her were still getting shocked, so most of the staff left her general care to the crazy people who called themselves her family. And though she would argue, Blake knew that's what they were now, a family.

Blake slowly paced the corridor outside Lei's room. He and Drew were tasked with keeping all hospital staff and visitors away. Very far away. Inside the room, Yemi and his daughter danced and chanted in a language Blake didn't understand. It was very primal. Whitefeather was in there with them, his voice and language mixing with theirs in a strange but beautiful harmony.

"Do you have any idea what's going on in there?" Marcus joined him in pacing.

"Not exactly but we've tried everything else. I'm willing to try anything and everything at this point. If you were me, if it were Whitney in there, wouldn't you?"

Marcus pursed his lips and nodded. "Yeah, I would."

"What the hell is going on here?"

Blake spun in shock to see Cam standing in the hall with flowers in his hand.

"What?"

"There's a vampire in there." Cam whispered to Blake, shock and panic evident in his voice. "He is aware that she kills vampires on a regular basis, doesn't he? Why aren't you doing anything? What is he doing in there?"

"Calm down. It's okay. That's just Yemi and his daughter, they're old friends of Leilani's. He helped us out with your little infestation problem as a matter of fact. He's no more threat to her than she is to him. He doesn't kill, maim, or turn anyone. He knows she's a hunter and loves her anyway, and she him." Blake leaned against the wall for support and smiled. "What are you doing here, Cam? I figured you'd have run as far as your motorcycle would take you."

"I almost did." Cam's voice was very quiet, almost too quiet to hear. "You people scare the hell out of me, I can't deny that. But, you all almost died to save her. I don't know anyone who would do the same for me."

"Then you're hanging around with the wrong people." Blake took a step towards Lei's room and stumbled.

"You're not all put back together yourself are you?" Cam stepped forward and put Blake's arm over his shoulder. "When I joined the Justices, I thought I was getting a brotherhood, a family. That's not what they are. They pretend to be. Maybe they were once, but not now. I want to find that for myself."

"I'd say you're headed in the right direction already." Blake smiled a little bigger.

"I just wanted to come, to see how she is. I need to apologize. I've said some terrible things to her." Cam paused again as he led him to a chair and helped him to sit down. "Done some terrible things for that matter."

"You're welcome to stay until she wakes up, so long as you promise not to sing." Blake smiled and even Cam laughed.

"Just don't do it again. Next time, I might do more than deck you."

"Don't give me a reason to. Now that the stick has been removed from your ass, I think we'll be just fine."

Yemi emerged from the room, his skin damp with scented oils and something that might have been some kind of animal blood. "We've done all we can. I can't stay here, especially with so many Justices milling about."

"I understand. I'll keep you up to date on her condition. When she's better, I know she'll want to see you."

"And I'd like to see her for myself again. Take care of yourself too, Blake. I appreciate you calling me. A lot of men wouldn't do that." Yemi took Blake's hand in his. "I know that what I am repels you, that it goes against everything you have ever been taught to trust me at all, let alone with something so important. If you need anything from me, all you have to do is ask."

"Thanks."

Blake watched as Yemi pulled on his long black trench coat and joined his daughter who waited for him with the large carpetbag they'd used to bring everything into the hospital.

After the vampires were gone, Blake made his way into her room and sat down in a chair while Marcus set to work with his crystals. Again. The nursing staff wasn't even fazed by that anymore.

"Blake?"

A soft familiar voice called his name a few times but Blake wasn't quite ready to be awake and it wasn't Lei's voice.

"I didn't come all this way for you to sleep through my visit. I'm here on official business as a matter of fact." Melli perched on the edge of Leilani's bed and took her hand. "You're looking pretty good there for a sleeping woman."

"I'll be happier when she's awake." Blake rubbed his eyes and looked at the fairy. She looked pretty good herself, all things considered but he knew that most of that was the glamour. It was rougher around the edges than usual, not as complete if a man knew what signs to look for. "How are you?"

"Better than either of you." She pointed to a cup on the rolling table. "I brought you coffee, hopefully it'll be better than the swill you get here."

"Appreciate it." He reached for it and breathed in the steam. Definitely an improvement over the hospital's coffee. "Thank you for helping. You could have just went home."

"And you could give me more credit." She sighed. "I know when this started I didn't give a shit what happened to you or her so long as my people got some long deserved peace. I told you both that often enough. It turns out I was lying to myself. Apparently, I care a lot about what happens to you both. Technically, I am on official business though. My mother wanted an update. She has a job offer for the both of you."

"I don't want to hear a thing about that right now."

"I would think you would want to be thinking of the future at exactly this moment."

"I am. It involves a beach and a tropical drink complete with umbrella. Somewhere far away from monsters and magic where Lei and I can rest and just be us for a while." Blake sipped the coffee. "This really is good, thanks."

Melli smiled. "If you don't mind, I'm going to stick around for a couple of days. Maybe a little more fairy magic, on top of everything else will help."

"We'll take all the help we can get." Blake leaned back in the chair, watching closely as Melli applied some kind of oil to Lei's face and neck. What Melli brought wasn't all that different from Yemi's hoodoo except that it smelled much worse.

***

The group took shifts sitting in Lei's room so she wouldn't wake alone. Three days passed. Blake was officially released from the hospital's care. Whitefeather's last wound from the battle finally healed. Lei's body was nearly completely healed, the doctors had no explanation for that and no one was about to enlighten them. But she hadn't woken yet. Her sleep seemed peaceful, untroubled and Blake wondered if she had indeed been left in the land of the dead after all.

Blake refused to leave her side. The others brought him food and company in fits and starts, but his parents and Cam had all gone back to their respective homes.

He had his chair pulled up as close to the bed as he could get it and held her hand in his. She looked so tiny, so fragile in that stark white bed. All he wanted to do was hold her and tell her everything was going to be all right. That she was going to wake up and be fine. But he wasn't sure he fully believed that himself anymore.

Blake laid his head on her chest, listening to her heart beat just to remind himself that it still did. "Someday, we're going to tell this story and they'll never believe it. They'll think we're old jokers just putting them on about saving the world. But we'll know what you did."

"Not done yet." Her voice rasped and made Blake jump.

Tears filled his eyes as he bent to kiss her. "Don't you ever scare me like that again. I thought I'd lost you."

He held on to her for a few moments before pressing the call button and yelling to the staff that she was awake. They needed to check her out, but not more than he needed to hold her, to know that she was not just alive but awake.

The room filled with doctors and nurses who sent Blake to wait in the hallway. He was still standing there when Melli, Whitefeather, Gabe, and Marcus came back from lunch and joined him in rejoicing.

After the initial celebration, Lei stared at them for a moment. "I should be dead. How am I not dead?"

"Everyone in the desert who could, we took a part of your injuries. Split between us all, it wasn't so bad. We might all need to see chiropractors for a while." Blake shrugged and sat on the edge of her bed just to be closer to her.

Lei touched her belly gingerly and moved her hand up her body until her fingers touched, then grasped the small leather bag over her heart. Wide eyed, she looked at Blake. "How the hell did you get Yemi to come? Did you make sure he got home okay? There are Justices here!"

"Don't worry. I made a deal with Gabe and Cam." Blake took her hand away from the bag of herbs and bones. "It was a one-time thing and everyone knows it. Drew and I hid the room so he could do his hoodoo shit. I don't get it, but I didn't want to turn my back on anything that might help and, since you're awake and talking, I wouldn't change a thing."

Lei looked up at Whitefeather. "How are you here? You were there, in that place. You saved me. You and your whole tribe or whatever. You must be John Whitefeather."

"I am." His eyes were full of questions but he didn't give any of them a voice. "The 'tribe' as you call them, the great warriors who fought with me, they come from all tribes, from all times. They are the ancestors of my spirit. They rode with me from the other side of the great wall to find you. It would have been very bad if Malphas had gotten his way. You had us very worried, Ms. Scott. I am glad to see you well again."

"I think it'll be a while before I'm actually well but, because of you, I have a chance now." She smiled at him.

"Lei." Gabe pulled a chair to the side of the bed across from where Blake was sitting. "I have to ask you something. I need to know how Whittaker opened the portals. Can all the vampires do that?"

Lei shook her head. "I don't think so. He wasn't bitten and turned like most vampires. And his name wasn't Whittaker, it was Hadrian. He was almost as old as the first vampire, Alda. They were both demon born, not human. They belong to the Netherworld. I don't know how many vampires there are like that, but we won't be seeing Whittaker again. Suriel killed him."

"Who is Suriel?" Gabe asked.

"An Angel." Lei and Whitefeather said as one.

"More specifically," Whitefeather continued, "he's an Arch-Angel. One who had something of a falling out with his brothers."

"Will he be all right?" She thought of the last time she'd seen him, in her place of limbo. If that had been real at all. He hadn't looked as big or as bright there as he had in the Netherlands.

"I don't know." Whitefeather pursed his lips together. "I hope so. I hope what he did for you is penance enough to return to his own home now. My understanding is that he was the last of the fallen."

"He said something about that when he was fighting with Whittaker, or Hadrian, whatever. He said something about being given a purpose."

Whitefeather bent near to her, so only she could hear him. "This is important. I need you to answer honestly. I saw the demon press you to Suriel's side. Did you ingest any of his blood?"

"I had no choice. I couldn't breathe and Suriel told me to."

"When you are well again, when your mission here is finished, I'd like you to come see me. Gabe will tell you how to find me. There is much we have to discuss, you and I. And I see in your eyes that you already know what I'm going to tell you. Be that as it may, you'll need guidance. Find me when you are ready." He pressed his ancient lips to her forehead. "Rest little one. I believe everything will be well now."

She watched him leave.

"I think I should be going as well." Gabe smiled at her and stepped closer. "Willy would be so damned proud of you right now, Lei. You do us all proud. If you ever need anything, call me and I'll do whatever I can."

"Thanks, Gabe. That goes both ways, okay? I'll be getting in touch to see Mr. Whitefeather soon."

Gabe nodded, and held out his hand to Blake. "Take care of her."

"I plan to."

"We're going to let the two of you catch up." Melli swished to Lei's side, kissed her check, and whispered in her ear. "I'm so glad you're awake. And that doesn't come with any conditions for once."

"Come on, Melli." Marcus grabbed her arm. "It's a relief to see you awake, Lei. Now, we're going to go do something that isn't get in between the two of you. We'll be back in a little bit."

When they were alone again, Lei scooted over to one side of the bed and motioned for Blake to lie down with her. "I think I want to sleep for a month when they let me out of here. Think maybe you'll come home with me?"

"You aren't getting rid of me now, Lei. Face it, you're stuck with me."

They shifted and squirmed for a moment, getting comfortable on the narrow hospital bed as they lay wrapped in each other's arms. Lei felt Blake drop into sleep and sighed, grateful to be home. Home wasn't a place she ever thought she'd see again. In another time and place, with any other people, she would have been. Somehow, she'd gone from a woman with no one and nothing to lose to having a family again. It was kind of nice. She fell asleep with a smile on her lips and warmth in her heart.

Chapter Twenty-One

Two Months Later

The Gray Road stretched out around them as far as they could see. Lei reached out and took Blake's hand in hers. "I still feel ridiculous in this stupid getup."

"I know. At least now, it's an official stupid getup." He laughed and pointed to the sigil on her breast. "You might want to hide that before we go into Black's."

"Probably." She turned to look at Blake and rearranged his black cloak over the green insignia that proclaimed him a Peace Keeper of the hidden lands, same as her. He did the same for her. "Hopefully he doesn't realize how many of the cards of his house have fallen."

"He's got to know. Maybe he doesn't think you know who he is, but he's got to know how badly he failed. Cam said the exorcisms are going pretty well. It may take years to get all the demons who were let free, but we *will* get them all. He also said Gabe refused an offer to take over as one of the Heads of the Order."

"I figured he would. He might stay a Justice in title but I don't think he'll ever trust the Order again." Lei shrugged. "Did Cam say what he's decided for himself? Is he going to stick with the Order?"

"Next time he calls, why don't you answer the phone and talk to him yourself?" Blake laughed as they continued down the road. "He's going to give it a go. I think he wants to see if he can make the Order be what he believes it should be."

Lei shook her head. "That won't last. The politics will creep back in once the dust settles. I hope you told him he's always welcome at our place."

"I did." Blake smiled. He knew she didn't realize it, but she'd made the transition now. It wasn't Willy's place anymore. It was hers. Theirs.

A family of fairies hurried past them, laughing nervously amongst each other. The road had changed. It was still gray and lifeless but it wasn't as dangerous now that the wars were over. There were still the occasional bandits on the road but they were few and far between. It would take time before the road became a place of commerce again but the signs were there. New buildings were cropping up along the length of the road that connected to the hidden lands. There would not be any stops on the other side of the road. Neither world was ready for that.

When Black's Tavern came into view, they paused. "Ready?" Blake asked.

"As I'm going to be." Lei nodded and put her hand on the hilt of the sword Queen Ounathir presented to her at the secret ceremony the leaders of all the nations had held for them, to give them the authority to police the hidden lands as well as the outer lands.

Together they walked into the tavern. The bartender was a gruff werewolf who sniffed at them and growled. "You aren't allowed here."

Lei watched as a figure in a blue cloak slipped out the door. When he was gone, she pulled back her cloak to show the sigil and pointed to it. "This says otherwise, doesn't it?"

The wolf in man's skin stared at them both for a minute before returning to his taps with a shrug.

"We're looking for someone." Lei leaned over the bar. "I'm pretty sure he was just here. An elf named Eminithous. You tell me where he'd go from here, where we can find him, and we'll leave you out of everything. Even though we know you allowed his meetings to happen here, that maybe you were even part of the plot he was cooking up to tear down the walls between the worlds."

The man's eyes grew wide, his features shimmering back and forth between wolf and man for a moment as he tried to contain his fear and anger. A long moment of silence ensued before he cleared his throat. "He went down the road to a bunkhouse called May's Inn. Likely packing up to disappear. He's been waiting here for a long time for someone. Comes in every day, gets a drink and waits."

Lei nodded and they left the building. The hidden lands were beautiful and the people just beginning to recover from the horrors of the great war that had almost destroyed them. There were still signs of the destruction, buildings showing the black scars of fire, the holes from thrown rocks. But there were signs of hope too, fresh paint, fresh flowers, a new park in a lot emptied by violence.

May's Inn looked freshly painted and the window boxes exploded with color as their flowers bloomed joyously. Lei stood on the front stoop and waited a moment until she was certain Blake had reached the back door. A string of bells rang as she stepped through the door.

"Can I help you?" A young and beautiful elf girl stood up behind an unfinished counter. "You'll have to forgive the dust. We're still rebuilding."

"I'm not staying. I'm looking for someone who just came in. Eminithous. An elf who's got some years on you. Pretty face but cold eyes." She smiled at the girl. "If you've got other guests here right now, it might be wise to keep them in their rooms or get them out."

"The one you want, he's—"

The sound of breaking glass interrupted her as Eminithous jumped out of his window and landed on the newly planted grass of the front yard.

Lei nodded to the girl and ran out the front door. "Eminithous!"

The elf looked at her for a moment and ran. Lei chased after him, trying to keep him in her sights even as she looked for Blake. Eminithous was fast and sly, leaping over a low fence and through another yard. Lei kept to the road and watched him as he stumbled over a bush. She was nearly on top of him, his cloak slipping through her fingers.

She cried out in frustration just as Blake came from a side street and took Eminithous down with a flying tackle. Lei smiled. Even if he never attempted his time-shift again, he was no less brilliant for the loss of it.

"You can't do this! You have no authority here!" Eminithous struggled, but Blake had him pinned.

Lei pushed her cloak back from where it had fallen so he could see the sigil. "Funny, that's what the dog back there at the tavern said too. The new Council says we do. It is now our duty to find and punish those from the hidden lands who cross too many lines. I think you've obliterated enough of them to qualify, don't you?"

Fury turned his pretty face ugly. "You bitch! You've got them all snowed but I know the truth! You're no Raven. You aren't who they think you are."

"I agree." She smiled as confusion contorted his features even more. "Hell, most of the Council probably agrees too. The thing is, it doesn't matter if I am or not. Your leaders needed a reason to quit fighting and play nice. I'm a convenient excuse and I'm fine with that. Plus, it gives me the freedom to do my job right. You can't just flee to the hidden lands now, I have authority here too. Throughout all of the hidden lands."

Blake pulled Eminithous up on his knees and started dragging him through the little town towards the square. Lei didn't like doing her job in public, where everyone could see, but that was their custom. Blake said nothing as he tied the elf to the stone block put there especially for the most severe of punishments.

Lei took her sword from its hilt and positioned herself properly. "Eminithous, for crimes against the hidden lands, the Netherlands, and the rest of Earth, you have been sentenced to death by the Council of Seven."

"No! You can't do this! I'll tell you everything! I'll give you names!" His shrill screams drew a larger crowd. The hushed tones of the onlookers grew louder and more boisterous by the moment, like they had a reason to call for his head.

She shuddered in disgust. These people didn't even know why the elf was bound to the stone; they just came to watch his blood spill. She tried to remind herself that it hadn't really been so long since humans did the same. Hell, in some parts of the world, it was likely still done. That didn't make it right, but she couldn't charge them with enjoying watching someone die.

Lei leaned close to him for a moment and whispered in his pointed ear. "Our people have already hunted down and exorcised most of the demons you freed and we'll get the rest before long, mark my words. Whittaker, or should I say, Hadrian, is dead. A pile of ash in the middle of the Netherlands."

"Trin is dead, his master, Gerwald, has been removed from his place on the Council of Seven for the other werewolves to do with as they see fit. Gee, I don't think we need names from you after all, Eminithous."

She stepped back and lifted her sword high, bringing it down as hard as she could, wanting the kill to be as clean as possible.

Eminithous's long blond hair painted the cobblestones red where it rolled and the crowd dispersed as quickly as they'd gathered. At least they didn't linger over it. Maybe they'd one day stop coming to the courtyard to watch at all. Two young men raced forward with a wheelbarrow and with a low bow for both Lei and

Blake, set to work cleaning up the mess. Soon, it would be as if nothing happened on that stone at all.

Blake pulled Lei close and kissed the top of her head. "Is it done now?"

"Done enough." She sighed and leaned against him. "Let's go home. I want a nice hot shower before Dan and Margo come for dinner."

"Maybe we'll get really lucky and Margo will bring us a peach pie." Blake grinned and made Lei laugh. Together, they walked back towards the tavern and the Gray Road.

ABOUT THE AUTHOR

Born in Denver, Colorado, Sarah Wagner got her first taste of people-watching from inside the seventy-five gallon tank that served as her playpen in her parents' tropical fish store. She liked it so much, she continued to people watch whenever she could and it has led to some very interesting characters.

She got her first taste of science fiction early, thanks to her devoted Trekkie of a mom. Science fiction was her gateway genre, leading to fantasy, horror, and superheroes. She hopes to be able to pass this deep love along to her children.

Sarah spends her time torn between the worlds in her head and this one. Her husband and two sons do a wonderful job keeping her relatively grounded in this one. She writes in a little corner where clutter breeds and dust bunnies find refuge.

In what free time she can eke out, she loves to read and drink coffee. She also runs an autism support group. You can find Sarah's short stories in a wide variety of publications including the Sha'Daa anthologies, Ruins Metropolis, and her collection, Hardwired Humanity. You can find Sarah online at www.sarahewagner.com, queenofmygeekdom.wordpress.com or follow her on Twitter @Shade53.

Did you enjoy this book? Drop us a line and say so! We love to hear from readers, and so do our authors. To connect, visit www.boroughspublishinggroup.com online, send comments directly to info@boroughspublishinggroup.com, or friend us on Facebook and Twitter. And be sure to check back regularly for contests and new releases in your favorite subgenres of romance!

Are you an aspiring writer? Check out www.boroughspublishinggroup.com/submit and see if we can help you make your dreams come true.